THREAT LEVEL ONE

Threat Level One
By
Paul Anthony

The Right of Paul Anthony to be identified as the author of this work has been asserted by him in accordance with the Copyright, Designs and Patents Act of 1988

~

The characters in this book are fictitious. Any resemblance to actual persons living or dead is purely coincidental.
This is a work of fiction driven by imagination.

~ ~ ~

First Published 2015
Copyright © Paul Anthony
Cover Image © Margaret Scougal
All Rights Reserved.

Published by
Paul Anthony Associates UK
http://paulanthonys.blogspot.co.uk/2011/12/the-paul-anthony-book-shop.html

By The Same Author

~

In Crime Thrillers…

~ ~ ~

The Fragile Peace
Bushfire
The Legacy of the Ninth
The Conchenta Conundrum
Moonlight Shadows
Behead the Serpent
Bell, Book and Candle
Breakwater
Threat Level One

~

In Poetry…

~ ~ ~

Sunset

~

In Non-Fiction…

~ ~ ~

Authorship Demystified
Scougal

~

In Children's Stories…
(with Meg Johnston)

~ ~ ~

Monsters, Gnomes and Fairies
(In My Garden)

~

In Anthology

~ ~ ~

Coptales
Uncuffed
Scribble with Chocolate

✽

Margaret - Thank you, for never doubting me.
To Paul, Barrie and Vikki - You only get one chance at life.
Live it well, live it in peace, and
Live it with love for one another.

To my special friends - Thank you, you are special.

…… Paul Anthony

~

With many thanks to
Pauline Livingstone and Margaret Scougal
for editing and advising on my work.

~

This is the story of the National Threat Level.
The men and women who make it,
and those who break it

~

Author's Note

~

In medieval times, when a country or monarchy was at the greatest threat from its enemies, a King or Queen would grant someone the honorary title of Knight for service to that Monarch or country. This was usually granted following a courageous military action by the leader of an army or a brave individual encounter with the enemy. A Knighthood was considered a class of lower nobility and gradually became associated with ideals of chivalry and a code of conduct for a truly Christian warrior. Consequently, the landed gentry trusted their Knights who were skilled in battle.

In the twenty-first century warriors are still found in our military, police and intelligence services where modern warfare is much more complex than ever before. The title of Knight, however, remains and is purely honorific. It is usually bestowed by a monarch, as in the British honours system, often for non-military service to the country. The female equivalent is Dame. The prevailing concept of a Knight endures as an elite warrior sworn to uphold the values of faith, loyalty, courage, and honour that anchor a peaceful democracy. A nation under threat might expect people, such as this, to stand up and fight when threatened by its enemies

But will such people oppose the enemy in the way their forebears did - without question, deprived of funding, starved of meaningful government patronage, and devoid of the co-operation, sponsorship and support of the community in which they live?

Accordingly, the destruction of a peaceful democracy will not come from those who attack it by the path of evil. Peace will be destroyed by those who only sit and watch, fail to uncover wickedness, neglect their warriors, abandon their comrades, and lack the courage to stand up and crusade against the wrongdoers - as a Knight might do…

Paul Anthony

~

The Metropolitan Police Anti-Terrorist Hotline
0800 789321

~

Crimestoppers
0800 555111

~

Don't let them get away with it…

~

NATIONAL SECURITY

~

The Threat

~

Threat Level Five - Low:
… An attack is unlikely… Response = Normal: Routine protective security measures appropriate to the business concerned.

Threat Level Four - Moderate:
… An attack is possible, but not likely… Response = Normal: Routine protective security measures appropriate to the business concerned.

Threat Level Three - Substantial:
… An attack is a strong possibility… Response = Heightened: Additional and sustainable protective security measures reflecting the broad nature of the threat combined with specific business and geographical vulnerabilities and judgements on acceptable risk.

Level Two - Severe:
… An attack is highly likely… Response = Heightened: Additional and sustainable protective security measures reflecting the broad nature of the threat combined with specific business and geographical vulnerabilities and judgements on acceptable risk.

Level One - Critical:
… An attack is expected imminently… Response = Exceptional: Maximum protective security measures to meet specific threats and to minimise vulnerability and risk. Critical may also be used if a nuclear attack is expected.

~

DATELINE: Now
Threat Level… THREE…SUBSTANTIAL

~

Chapter One
~

Tikrit,
Iraq,
Twilight.

The sound of deafening gunfire rang in Jack Dooley's ears. Fear of capture, serious injury or death, penetrated his mind. A divine right to live the way he had been brought up burnt into his soul and drove him to survive. Yet around him missiles exploded with a ferocity that galvanised his body when they burst into tumbling clouds of death and destruction. Rocket propelled grenades found their target and blew into a dozen pieces of white hot steel maiming and killing. Machine gun bullets lethally pierced the air. A knife swirled. A dagger plunged. A sword took a life. And another young warrior fell to the ground never to rise again; never to feel the heat of the desert sun touch their skin, never again to caress a loved one.

It mattered not which side they were on or which uniform they wore. Some were women, some were men, and too many were children never truly taught the difference between war and peace, or right and wrong. A limb broke, a vessel bled, an organ failed.

Life was precious, lived for a lifetime that was all too short. A treasured 'once only' moment that can never be repeated.

Mighty walls of an ancient city crumbled during the onslaught, flattened, and then sunk into the desert sands when the evil hordes advanced. No trumpets echoed from without. There was no marching army chanting noisily for the walls to fall.

This wasn't Jericho.

This is *Tikrīt:* the birthplace of Saddam Hussein, a city 87 miles northwest of Baghdad and 140 miles southeast of *Mosul* on the River Tigris. Numbering 260,000, the population of Tikrit were devastated by a war brought about religion, greed, and power.

Those who wanted peace needed someone to stand and fight their corner. They needed crusaders, not Knights of yesteryear with their shields and banners flying above them. Not sword swirling, lance-bearing men on horseback wearing chainmail armour charging wildly into the fray. Not superheroes direct from a Hollywood movie. No, they needed men like Jack Dooley.

Master Sergeant Jack Dooley wanted prisoners. That was his brief following the Iraqi government declaration of a 'magnificent victory' over Islamic State militants in the city of Tikrit. The United States-Iranian backed Shia militia and elements of Iraq's government forces were still fighting to clear the last remaining Islamic State warriors holding out in Tikrit. It had been a month-long battle given fresh impetus only when a US-led coalition began air strikes in the region. Now the enemy was on the run and Jack and his men, from Coalition Special

Forces, were keen to push the militants as far as possible into the desert and away from Tikrit. A victory here would see the Shia militia turn its attention to Mosul – Iraq's second city – in an attempt to drive the predominant Sunni forces of Islamic State from the country.

The region, as far as Jack was concerned, was a cauldron of hate, violence, and depravity the like of which had not been seen since the Third Reich and the Second World War. Jack borrowed a term from German jurisprudence to describe to his friends back home Iraq, Syria and various parts of the Middle East. He argued a 'Rechtsstaat' was needed: a state based on the rule of law where people of both genders share legally based civil liberties and constitutional rights that enable them to use a properly established legal system via the courts. Yet the desert was a thousand miles from any form of western liberal democracy that Jack's friends had experienced. The desert here was hell on earth!

Scanning the ground below Jack clung by an umbilical cord to the framework of an AH-60 Blackhawk helicopter. The attack aircraft was fitted with a variety of 7.62mm mini-guns, 70mm impact-detonating rocket pods, a couple of .50 calibre machine guns, and four Hellfire air-to-ground missiles. On its own merit the helicopter was awesome but when in the hands of Coalition Special Forces it was quite simply formidable.

The aircraft was part of the illustrious 160th Special Operations Aviation Regiment, also known as 'The Nightstalkers'.

It was twilight and the master sergeant had his orders.

Flying low and fast the co-pilot shouted, 'Jack, we got a loner on the road out of Tikrit towards Mosul. It's a pick up and they're making a run for it.'

The helicopter swooped down and Jack glimpsed a view of a Nissan travelling flat out towards Mosul with two males on board. Even from above he could clearly make out two men dressed in black combat fatigues. The rear of the pick-up carried a heavy machine gun mounting which was unmanned.

'I got them,' bellowed Jack. 'Let's take them out.'

Banking hard to his right the Blackhawk pilot kept pace with the Nissan and gradually drew nearer.

Jack readied the weaponry, turned to his men, and ordered, 'I want them alive. Take the front of the vehicle out.'

The Nissan weaved from left to right when the helicopter pitched forward. The down draught from its rotor blades caused a mini-desert storm as the helicopter closed with the Nissan.

Suddenly, the front passenger of the Nissan leaned out of a window and let loose with a salvo of gunfire from a machine gun. Firing wildly, his shots were wide of the target but they surely scared the hell out of the helicopter pilot who immediately pulled left and gained height to avoid being hit.

'Steady, boy,' shouted Jack. 'Are you trying to bail me out?'

'Hang on tight, Jack,' yelled the pilot.

Two seconds later gunfire from below stopped when the Nissan slewed from left to right trying to out-manoeuvre Jack's helicopter. Without warning, the Nissan went off-road in an attempt to throw off its pursuers.

Jack and his men steadied themselves in the belly of the helicopter. Carefully, Jack shouldered a rocket propelled grenade launcher. He aimed it at the front of the Nissan, pulled the trigger, and waited for an impact.

There was an explosion of sand and rubble when the ground immediately in front of the Nissan erupted and lifted the vehicle into the air. Crashing down onto the desert the windscreen splintered and then detached itself from the body before smashing to pieces. The Nissan then rolled over onto its roof, skidded to a shuddering halt, and caught fire when its petrol tank exploded.

'Gotcha!' spat Jack triumphantly. 'Pilot, take us down if you can.'

Gaining height, the helicopter banked in a tight circle, and overflew the wreck allowing Jack to inspect the debris.

'No sign of life,' reported Jack. 'Drop me here, guys. Joe, Charlie, on my back. Keep your eyes peeled.'

Desert sand swirled in retaliation when the Blackhawk helicopter moved in to land. Eventually the pilot held his craft about five feet above the ground.

Three soldiers leapt from the helicopter, primed their weapons, and quickly closed with the wrecked Nissan.

Lying slumped over the steering wheel, the Nissan driver appeared to be dead. His eyes were closed, mouth agape, and blood oozed from his forehead and chest. He was completely motionless when Joe nudged the driver's body with the muzzle of his weapon and watched it slither into the passenger seat.

There was no sign of the passenger.

'I'm out of here,' shouted the pilot. 'Radio for extraction when you're ready but make it quick. I don't want to give the enemy an easy duck shoot, boys.'

The Blackhawk took off in a swirl of sand which gathered in anger around the troops.

'Easy, boys; we're one down and one loose. Look out,' ordered Jack as he circumnavigated the burning wreck followed closely by his colleagues.

Crawling in the desert!

The passenger was crawling away from the Nissan clutching his leg and in obvious agony when Jack Dooley suddenly appeared in front of him.

With a pained expression on his face, the injured man looked up morosely at the master sergeant.

'A live one,' announced the sergeant glaring down at the injured warrior, 'Just what I wanted.'

'He needs a medic,' suggested Joe.

'My orders are to take prisoners, private,' announced Jack. 'We need immediate intelligence on movements and numbers.'

Turning the victim over onto the flat of his back, Jack saw blood oozing from the man's chest, and spoke in Farsi. 'You can live or die in the next five minutes, Mohammad. What you gonna tell me? How many are you? Where's your headquarters? I want to know where you've been ordered to regroup.'

The warrior grimaced but offered no reply.

'I ain't got no time for bullshit, Mo. Are you gonna talk to me or am I walking away? The choice is yours and the clock is ticking,' bullied Jack.'

'You can't do that,' reacted Joe. 'He's dying.'

'And so are our troops and those who would drive this scum from the face of the earth!' scowled Jack. 'It's a war we're fighting, Joe, not a baseball match at the Yankee's stadium. Don't know about you but I'm not living my life stuck on first base. He'll talk or die. I don't much care which.'

'He's on his way out unless I stiff him with a needle and pressurise those wounds,' declared Joe.

'Allahu Akbar!' whispered the victim painfully.

'Well, Mo! Maybe Allah is the best God around and maybe he ain't,' responded Jack directly into the face of the injured man.

'Right now I'm the only man who can stop you bleeding to death and give you back your life. Not Allah and not your mate over there because he's already lining up all the vacant virgins in paradise. Oh I know you'd surely like to go to paradise, Mo, but I reckon you'd rather live it out here a little more because neither you nor I have ever met someone who came back to tell us how good it was. Now ain't that a fact, Mo.'

'Allah is all around,' hissed the injured warrior.

'But I don't see him, Mo, and neither do you.'

The warrior, flat on his back, helpless, exhaled and tried and failed to spit into Jack's face.

'My man's standing here with a needle in one hand and plasma in the other,' divulged Jack. 'Either will save you. Now here's the deal, Mo. You tell me where you're regrouping and you'll get you the medic, a hospital, and a new life. Otherwise I'm walking away and you're gonna die with your boots on here in the dirt. Now what you gonna tell me, boy.'

The victim tried to crawl away, tried to deny the master sergeant's drawl penetrating his ears, and then laughed at his inability to move. Seriously injured the warrior murmured, 'We will win, Yankee infidel! Allah will show the way.'

Joe bent down by the victim and made ready with a pain-killing injection and bandages.

'Wait one,' ordered Jack. He rested his hand on Joe's bandage cautioning his colleague from applying first aid. Then he asked, 'How you gonna win, Mo? Are you hearing me? There ain't no Allah here, Mo. Sure, there's just the three of us and you and no damn sign of your God, my God or anyone else's God.'

A tear escaped the corner of an Arab eye and he winced in pain. The warrior clung to life pleading, 'You will help me?'

'I need something, Mo, and that's a fact,' demanded Jack kneeling by the Islamic State warrior. 'And I need it now if you want to live.'

'Salman…' murmured the warrior.

'Who?' badgered Jack.

'What did he say?' asked Joe.

'You got a tab for the boy, Charlie?' asked Jack.

'Yeah, sure,' replied Charlie shouldering his weapon and lighting a cigarette. Charlie dragged on the tobacco and then handed it to Jack who placed the end of the cigarette in the warrior's mouth.

The Arab inhaled his cigarette, forced a troubled cough, and continued to bleed.

'Is it worth it, my friend?' posed Jack. 'All the fighting, killing, bombing – what's it all for, Mo?'

The warrior did not reply as blood seeped from his upper thigh and spoiled the desert sands.

'Why do you destroy the lands of your birth? Why do you murder and maim those of your faith because someone made a decision that split the Muslim world fourteen hundred years ago? Why do you fight for a global caliphate? Does it matter that much, Mo?'

The warrior inhaled again, closed his eyes with the buzz of tobacco rattling his brain, and tried to shake his head.

'It's not worth it, my friend. Life is for living and loving not killing like you guys do.'

Another puff of cigarette smoke escaped the warrior's mouth.

'Who is Salman?' probed Jack.

'I will live, yes?'

Jack nodded and Joe moved closer to the victim with a bandage and pressure pad.

'Only if you tell me about Salman,' threatened Jack.

'Salman will kill your leaders… He's already on his way.'

The Arab's voice trailed into a defiant chuckle as he closed his eyes.

Bending closer, Jack nodded to Joe to begin applying pressure to stop the bleeding, and pressed again, 'Salman, where's Salman headed, Mo?'

'Salman will kill the western infidel leaders,' grimaced the warrior. 'Ibrahim has sent him to kill them with Allah's blessings. *Allahu Akbar.*'

'Say again, I can't hear you, Mo. Who is Salman?'

The warrior's head dropped back; his eyes opened wide, and he spat out, 'Salman – The man from Tikrit.'

Jack Dooley had been around the block a few times in various wars here and there. He was one tough cookie but now he'd got a titbit. It was a mere morsel of intelligence. He knew the circumstances were not class room approved and the authenticity of the material was questionable, but he was done and life at the sharpest end of the stick wasn't something he ever brooded over.

'The man from Tikrit, you say,' remarked Jack. 'What about him, Mo?'

A body shuddered and life ceased. The warrior died on the desert that was his battlefield with his eyes wide open and three Special Forces soldiers standing over him. The Nissan was still burning when the Blackhawk helicopter grounded, collected the trio, and took off into the darkening skies.

Minutes later, with the Blackhawk a distant dot in the sky above, the driver of the Nissan felt for his mobile phone. He'd watched the soldiers, overheard the conversation, and swore deeply at his friend since departed. Slowly, painfully, he punched the digits of his phone, waited for an answer and said, 'It's Wazir. We didn't make it. We're done for.'

Close to death, Wazir tried to pull himself from the Nissan but gave up and continued, 'Not going to make it. You should know that Omar told them – He told them about Salman – The man from Tikrit.'

The phone fell into the driver's well of the Nissan when Wazir finally died. Devoted to the end, Wazir died knowing his colleague, Omar, had betrayed them.

It had been a long day, thought Jack as he yawned and pulled himself closer to his desk. He poured another black coffee, checked the time, and took another drink. Caffeine late at night, he pondered, something to kill the stress burning in my body, or just a black ugly potion to prevent me sleeping properly?
Sleep, he questioned? Who sleeps out here?
Taking a pencil he began to draft his report thinking to himself - is it really worth it? When this arrives on someone's desk how important will it be in the scheme of things? Will they file and forget or will they actually read the content and try to work out if it's relevant in the war that we fight. What other threats are on the horizon? What's important? What's crucial? And what the hell is a waste of time?
Am I wasting my time? Or is this worthwhile?
To hell, he thought, send it anyway.
He laid down his pencil, read the report back to himself, and powered up his computer.
Jack knew it was just a titbit – a morsel – a thin reed in a haystack of daily intelligence that would be used to define the threat from Islamic State to the western world.
He did not know if the comment made by the dead warrior had been truthful or just propaganda designed to muddy the waters of the war being fought. It might even have been a throw away last ditch remark from a dying man determined to be a problem all the way to the bitter end. Jack didn't really know for sure.
Familiar with the work of the intelligence community, from quick-witted streetwise intelligence gathering to complex intelligence analysis, Jack knew it wasn't the only threat to be analysed that day, and it wasn't the only way intelligence was

gathered. There was 'C.A.S.T' to consider, but would this irrelevant piece of tittle-tattle ever seep into C.A.S.T?

Jack Dooley had seen too much in the war zone to play by the rules. He'd been to places and seen things that friends back home and the politicians who sent him could never imagine. It was a different world to a television news report watched on a sofa with a glass of wine, or a 'YouTube' download sighted on a computer screen whilst drinking a cold beer with your friends, and a million miles away from a twenty second radio report whilst driving to work in the office.

And it was a universe away from a like, share, and two sentence comment on social media.

That night Master Sergeant Jack Dooley made an entry in a computerised intelligence log and submitted his report in the normal manner. The encrypted report read as follows:-

Source reports SALMAN… no further details, believed member of ISLAMIC STATE, has left TIKRIT, IRAQ having been 'sent' by Ibrahim, no further details (but may be identical with Ibrahim Hasan al Din) to ASSASSINATE LEADERS IN THE WEST…..

Provenance: Prisoner intelligence interview.
Source: Not proven now deceased.
Attribution: Not known.
Time of Origin: 1940 hours this date….
Ends….
Sender: Dooley, Jack - Master Sergeant. Operation Nightstalker
Transmit… 2305 hrs…

Master Sergeant Jack Dooley continued his crusade, pressed the transmit button, and watched his message begin its journey into cyberspace.

*

Chapter Two
~

Carlisle, Cumbria.
Recently.
Threat Level Three - Substantial

Flashing headlights and pulsating blue lamps heralded the first signs of a royal convoy when a posse of police motor cycle outriders led the way into the historic quarter of England's most northerly city. Gently easing his 750cc BMW motorbike into second gear, police motor cyclist Martin Duffy reduced speed as he led the entourage into Castle Street. A liveried police car followed at a leisurely pace ahead of the royal car. Behind the royal car a dark blue Jaguar occupied a position whereby its occupants could provide an immediate armed response if necessary. Another police vehicle followed on to form the tail end of the convoy, but it was the royal car the crowd were desperate to see.

The gracious Prince was first in line to the throne of the British Monarchy. Smiling from the plush interior of a Rolls Royce Phantom V1 he waved regally to the anxious throng. His wife, the Princess, sat next to him in the rear passenger seat. She too gestured and beamed charmingly from her side of the car.

They travelled in a unique vehicle. Its size dominated the carriageway and, since it was a State vehicle, it wasn't fitted with any registration plates. The underbelly and windows were toughened to withstand an attack from explosives as well as bullets. More significantly the passengers were of some importance to the British people. The Prince is not just a national figure. Upon ascension to the throne he will become King - the British Monarch - and, as such, is destined to be Commander-in-Chief of the British Armed Forces; Constitutional Monarch of the United Kingdom, and Head of a Commonwealth that relishes their shared monarchy throughout fifteen Commonwealth Realms. The Princess, of course, will one day be his Queen. The British Monarchy is undoubtedly a global institution.

Steadying his motorbike Martin Duffy throttled down to walking speed. Not this time, he thought. I know every manhole cover on this road and I'm not wobbling off like once before. No, I'll stay upright if it kills me and woe betide anyone who steps in front of my bike.

One of a number of police officers in the UK charged with keeping the royals safe, Martin was determined to master the ability of riding a bike at a couple of miles an hour whilst on protective ceremonial duties. The job of looking after the royals fell to the Royalty Protection Specialist Operations Unit of the Metropolitan Police: SO14. This elite group is divided into three sections. The first: Personal and Close Protection, effectively provides bodyguards for the Royal Family, both at home and on overseas trips. The second: Residential Protection, guards the royal homes in London, Windsor and Scotland. But Martin was a member of the third section: The Special Escort Group, which provides protection to the Royal Family when they are on the move. Wherever they are the team is usually supported by 'protection trained' officers from a local constabulary.

Martin led the royal convoy gradually down the street with Carlisle Castle to its rear. Tullie House Museum and Carlisle Cathedral stood to the offside of the vehicle whilst a selection of cafes, department stores and local businesses inhabited the nearside.

But waving Union Jacks and cheering people temporarily hid such sights since both pavements were filled with excited people trying to catch a view of the royal couple. Flags waved, children cheered, cameras flashed, and adults jostled behind barriers to get a good view. Ahead, in the pedestrian area, a line of nervous dignitaries and selected local VIP's stood outside the entrance to the Crown and Mitre Hotel, close to a bandstand, waiting to be introduced to royalty. Some for the first time, others as a matter of routine relevant to the status afforded them by the nation.

A uniformed policeman tried to look serious whilst listening to his cackling radio and a smiling policewoman sneaked a glimpse over her shoulder at the approaching convoy as it gradually neared a pedestrian area. A photographer snapped away capturing images for a local newspaper and a television crew panned the faces of the crowd. There was more cheering, applauding and flag waving when the royal car finally arrived at its destination and a regimental band struck the first chord of its welcoming piece.

A plain clothes detective radioed, 'All units, we have an arrival.'

It had been three years since a member of the royal family last visited the city but today the prince and princess were here to open a charity shop associated with the Prince's Charitable Foundation: an organisation known to raise the sum of one hundred million pounds a year for worthy causes.

Inside the royal car the driver declared, 'Here we are, sir,' as he brought the vehicle to a sedate standstill.

The Principal Personal Protection officer opened his nearside door. His foot touched the tarmac at the same time the car came to a standstill and he immediately stepped gingerly to the rear passenger door. Permitting his fingers to curl around the handle, he nodded to the occupants inside, pulled open the door and declared, 'It's a tad breezy.' Then he retreated and allowed the prince to step out of the vehicle.

Simultaneously, a plain clothes member of the protection team from the Jaguar reached the offside door and opened it for the princess.

Moments later, the royal couple were on the footpath shaking hands with civic dignitaries gathered to welcome them, and, of course, the manageress of a charity shop was there too.

The party paused. Cameras clicked, school children cheered, adults applauded, and a television crew worked the line of faces as a police helicopter flew overhead and a young girl curtsied before handing the smiling princess a posy of flowers. The area was a mass of royal fans waving colourful union flags.

A middle aged man, Francis Littleton, wasn't just waving his union flag – he was wearing it - and it fitted him admirably. His entire suit was a red, white and blue representation of the union flag. He even sported a union flag tie over his pristine white shirt.

Standing out amongst the crowd, Francis stepped forward. Somewhat plump with a rugged facial appearance, he was visibly exited.

Francis waved and shouted enthusiastically, 'Hello! Welcome to Carlisle,' before reaching out across a pedestrian security barrier to try and shake hands.

A police constable stood close by but merely observed proceedings.

Francis reached further across the barrier but this time his arm was fully outstretched when he bellowed loudly, 'Hello! Welcome to Carlisle.'

Turning her head the princess acknowledged his presence with a slight smile but resisted the offer to shake his hand.

Agitated, Francis scowled at his rebuff and pushed the barrier as his weight moved forward.

The policeman moved closer.

Francis tried again and stretched right across the barrier in an attempt to touch the princess on her arm.

Taking a pace forward the policeman held him firmly back with a hand on his chest politely demanding, 'Behind the barrier please, sir.'

Compliant, Francis said, 'I wish I were you.'

'I beg your pardon,' replied the policeman.

'Oh nothing,' frowned Francis coyly. 'You are my hero. You look after them, and you are so lucky to be with them every day.'

Twisting his face in a puzzled manner the policeman declared, 'I'm just doing my job. This is my patch, sir. Now I'm sorry I needed to ask you to step back but that's the way it is.'

Introverted and alone, a timid Francis Littleton gradually melted into the crowd as he studied a policeman who guarded the royals and prevented him from getting closer. Envious of the policeman's task, Francis felt slightly resentful at being prohibited from the close proximity of the royal couple. Almost serenely he withdrew into the heart of the crowd. But his eyes remained on the royal couple and watched every move they made. As luck would have it, his were not the only eyes at work that day.

A youth wearing a dark hoodie, denim jeans and trainers, skirted the rear of the crowd occasionally rising onto his toes to get a better view. Yet his eyes darted everywhere looking for an opportunity to enrich his pockets. Unshaven, his denim jeans boasted a few tears at the knee that suggested either a rough lifestyle or a flavour of contemporary fashion. Bored with proceedings the scruffy adolescent courted more lucrative ideas when the momentum of the crowd swayed as it followed the direction of the royals.

Placing her shopping bag on the pavement a young woman, in her mid-twenties, lifted a small boy onto her shoulders so that the child could appreciate what was going on.

'Can you see them now, son?' she shouted.

'Yes, Mum,' he replied but his answer was almost incoherent when Carlisle's popular mayor was introduced to the royal couple amidst a cacophony of cheering and clapping.

Carlisle and the county of Cumbria could be proud of its turnout since the assembled crowd ran into thousands. Amongst the multicultural swarm of royal enthusiasts, Declan O'Malley cautiously scanned the scene. Wearing a dark green anorak and a scarf knotted loosely at his neck, he remained tight lipped but his eyes were working overtime. Resembling a travelling gypsy, to some degree, he studied how many uniformed police were in the immediate area. Then he spotted plain clothes detectives mingling with the public before gazing on the bare rooftops above trying to find a would-be sniper's position. Declan stepped back into a shop doorway when he caught sight of a policeman in black fatigues watching the crowd through binoculars from the topmost building in the area.

Close by, Dina Al-Hakim also stood alone in the crowd. She carried no flag, held no smile, and voiced no approval of proceedings. Dina wore a hijab: a dark grey headscarf that covered her hair and shoulders but not her face. She also wore a dark chequered jacket and trousers and carried a small rucksack on her back. Dina took a pace back onto a step for a better view. Pretty yet quite petite, she tried not to draw attention to herself.

At the Crown and Mitre hotel introductions were complete. The party moved on when their host gestured towards a charity shop and ushered them inside to meet the staff.

Three hundred yards away, behind a more solid barrier, a group of half a dozen men and women noisily chanted, 'Argentina... Argentina...'

Local media swung their cameras towards the demonstration. Unexpectedly, protesters had commandeered part of the day's events to vent their fury at Britain's occupation of their beloved islands – The Malvinas - or as Britain preferred to call the disputed lands: the Falkland Isles. A small contingent of Argentinians waved the blue and white flag of their country apparently oblivious to a small group of slightly older men wearing England football shirts. Gradually, as the royal party moved indoors, cheers changed to jeers in this area of the crowd where there was more interest in waving an Argentinian flag than a royal visit.

One of the men, Alejandro, an Argentinian by birth, began shaking his clenched fist in the air.

A pot-bellied Englishman countered loudly with, 'Eng-er-land and lunged forward snarling towards Alejandro and his colleagues.

The Argentinians retreated a yard or two when the English bellowed, 'Ar-gee bar-gee... Ar-gee bar-gee...'

Half a dozen uniformed police quickly moved in to separate the opposing factions.

Unfortunately it did not stop the more vociferous wearing English shirts from shouting, 'Go home ya bums, go home ya bums. Go home ya bums, go home.'

A stand-off developed with a line of blue and white shirts and line of red and white shirts separated by a thin blue line of police uniforms.

'This reminds me of a school teacher trying to separate a gang of stupid kids,' mouthed one policemen. 'So damn childish!'

'Well, that's what they do,' replied another.

Flags waved from side to side. Insults were traded, and the local police superintendent suddenly felt sick in his stomach at the dawning realisation that he had failed to pick up on a minor demonstration right in the middle of a royal visit.

'Ar-gee bar-gee… Ar-gee bar-gee…' filled the air countered only by the contemptuous opposition ranting 'Argentina…Argentina…' and a plethora of competing flags waving threateningly at each other.

The superintendent swallowed his pride and radioed for assistance. 'I need twenty officers with riot gear at my location now.'

'You have over one hundred officers deployed to the royal visit,' replied the event commander. 'Redeploy as required.'

'You don't understand,' argued the superintendent. 'A contingent of Argentinians is here and there is a confrontation with our local football hooligans.'

'Argentinians?' queried the commander. 'I didn't know we had any. Have they been bussed in from Newcastle or somewhere like that?'

'I've no idea but they're here now and I'm right in the middle of them. Listen…' The superintendent held his radio up and captured another bout of chanting.

'Understood,' replied the commander. 'There are no reserves – Redeploy your staff.'

Frustrated, the superintendent holstered his radio and signalled one of his sergeants to move his section from one area of crowd control to the demonstration.

As the police reassigned their officers an empty beer bottle sailed across the lines and crashed into Argentinian ranks. The vessel smashed into a dozen pieces and littered the ground. In response, an Argentinian flag was lowered when one of the protestors thrust it forward like a lance trying to pierce a line of football hooligans.

Elsewhere in the vicinity, Billy Boyd and his wife, Meg, along with their two children, were there to enjoy the royal visit. Boyd was taking photographs of the twins against the background of the royal car when Meg asked, 'Did you get them? Did you get the prince and princess, Billy?'

'Yes, but I don't think they were smiling into the lenses and straight at me,' replied Boyd. 'They wouldn't sit still for me.'

'Why not? Don't they know who you are?' joked the wide-eyed honey blonde Meg.

'It's this new-fangled camera you got me for my birthday,' replied Boyd. 'It's got more switches and gizmos on it than soft mick. I knew I should have brought the old one today.'

'Persevere, Billy,' ordered Meg. 'You'll manage it eventually but I can't understand why the royal couple didn't pose for you properly. After all they must surely know who you are.'

'Ha-ha,' chuckled Boyd. 'Very funny but if the prince and princess really knew me they also know this is my weekend off.'

'And that's long overdue,' remarked Meg. 'Just don't go getting any ideas about switching teams and working with the Royalty Squad when you get back to work.'

'Of course not,' laughed Boyd. 'What do I know about princes, princesses and royalty? Looking after the royal family is not my idea of policing, Meg. There's no investigation and too much pomp and circumstance for me. Too many suits, false smiles and trumped up busybodies wasting public money.'

'You mean the prince and princess?' suggested Meg.

'No, I mean the local yokels standing in line as if they were some kind of monkey shoot at a fair ground,' replied Boyd.

A hundred yards away, chanting and jeering increased when about a dozen police officers filed into the area between the two opposing factions. Preparing to advance, they shouldered their batons in a threatening manner and began to push them away.

'No!' declared Meg emphatically when she realised what was happening. 'No, don't you dare get involved. Leave it to the locals, Billy.'

'Don't worry,' replied Boyd. 'They are much more capable dealing with such things than I am.'

Boyd pointed his camera again and began to take more photographs of Izzy and James saying, 'Come on you two. Let's have a nice smile please.'

Suddenly a scream rent the air when a young woman realised a hooded youth with torn jeans had grabbed her purse from the top of her shopping bag. She turned and yelled, 'Thief! He's got my purse.'

Clutching his loot, the thief ran off at full speed passing Declan in his green anorak, a lady of Middle-Eastern extraction called Dina, and a dedicated royal follower by the name of Francis.

Barging his way through the crowd, the hooded youth made his getaway downhill into Scotch Street.

Boyd heard the scream, caught the confusion, and began to run after the teenager.

Meg shouted, 'Billy! It's your day off, for God's sake. Leave it to somebody else... Billy!'

To no avail, Boyd gave chase with his camera hanging loosely from a thin cord around his neck. Tall and athletic, Boyd shouted, 'Sorry, but I can't stand by, watch it happen, and do nothing.'

The youth barged his way through the throng with Boyd hot on his heels. Part way down Scotch Street the youth spun into the Lanes shopping complex and sprinted through the paved area.

Accelerating, the broad shouldered Boyd finally rugby tackled the thief in the middle of the Lanes close to a statue of a man sat playing a fiddle.

A voice on a police radio barked, 'Disturbance in the Lanes at the Jimmy Dyer statue.'

They rolled over each seeking to overpower the other. A knee collided with a groin and a fist smacked hard into flesh. An elbow retaliated and dug into an opponent's ribs. Blood spurted from a nose and a nail scratched skin as two warriors battled for supremacy. A camera flayed through the air and collided with a chin, then an eye, before finally wrapping itself uncomfortably around Boyd's neck. As fit as he was for a man of his years, Boyd couldn't smother the youthful vigour of the teenager. Eventually, Boyd lost his grip and the youth scrambled to his feet, reached inside his clothing, and pulled out a knife.

There was a flash of metal and a gasp from Boyd when he realised the culprit was armed with a six inch blade. The youth lunged. Boyd withdrew. The youth lunged again and Boyd dodged the knife as the pair pranced around the bronze statue of an itinerant fiddler called Jimmy Dyer.

Lunging, slashing and stabbing, the villain tried frantically to outwit Boyd and make his escape. Thrusting the knife towards Boyd's head, the young thug pierced the air as Boyd ducked and dived constantly trying to grab his opponent's arm. There was a sickening rip when the blade tore into Boyd's jacket and slashed the lining.

Angry now, Boyd reached across the fiddler's statue and grabbed hold of the youth. With a heave Boyd dragged his adversary head first into the bronzed body of Jimmy Dyer. A purse fell from the thief's clothing. A knife tangled with the fiddler's bow and clattered on the ground but the youth continued to struggle and snatched at a cord hanging around Boyd's neck.

Boyd's camera exploded on the pavement at the precise time his fist slammed into the thug's face. Blood surged from the thief's nose when he fell backwards.

On top of him in a trice, Boyd barked, 'You're nicked, pal!' before producing his warrant card and identifying himself with the cry, 'Police! You're under arrest!'

Boots slapping on concrete awakened the duo to the arrival of uniformed police.

'Well I never, Boyd!' boomed a voice.

'Alastair!' responded Boyd instantly recognising the local inspector. 'Where've you been hiding all these years? Never mind, it's good to see you and in the nick of time too!'

'Moonlighting are we, chief inspector?'

'Yes, sorry! I always do this on my weekend off. I couldn't help but get involved, Alastair. He was right in front of me when he stole some woman's purse.'

The police inspector stooped to retrieve the purse as more officers attended and surrounded Boyd and his prisoner.

'Thank you,' replied the inspector speaking to his police colleagues. 'Well, ladies and gentlemen, meet Detective Chief Inspector William Miller Boyd of the Special Crime Unit. Cumbria's very own export to the Metropolitan Police and the nation's Counter Terrorist Command, and, if memory serves me well, this is where it all started for you, chief inspector. You were a young bobby on the beat here weren't you?'

'Yes,' countered Boyd. 'This is where I earned my spurs.'

A police van pulled up in Lowther Street and the driver opened the rear doors. Two uniformed officers took the thief into custody as Boyd knelt to retrieve what was left of his damaged camera.

'We'll catch up later, chief inspector,' decided Alastair. 'I need to keep the area secure. Okay everyone, back to your original positions.'

Nodding his understanding of affairs, Boyd threw a broken camera into a nearby litter bin before making his way back to Meg and their children. Walking towards his family, Boyd thought, how can I explain a broken camera. I'll be in trouble again that's for sure.

The royals were back on the street. Union flags fluttered in the breeze. More cheers greeted the prince and princess when they left the charity shop and made for the royal car. Looking up, the princess heard more chanting from the freedom seeking Argentinians as 'Argentina…' and 'Eng-er-land…' vied for attention. A middle-eastern lady wearing a hijab stepped closer; a chap in a dark green anorak reconnoitred the area again, and a middle-aged man wearing a union flag suit tried to reach out and touch the princess once more.

Martin Duffy sat astride his motor cycle and watched proceedings. He knew it wouldn't be long now as he reached for his gauntlets. Oh how, I wish I was a detective, thought Martin. It has to be so much more interesting than riding a motor bike in front of a car. Mind you, the alternative might be escorting an abnormal load at ten miles an hour down a country road for the next eight hours! Although I'll be on the television news tonight and my family will think I'm wonderful because I was with the royal family. Little do they know, I'm bored out of my brain, I want to be a detective.

A police radio suggested a departure was imminent.

Police motorcyclist Martin Duffy gave the signal and his outriders kick-started their machines. A Jaguar's engine fired and manoeuvred into position. A pair of binoculars on a roof top panned and zoomed. A detective advanced the royal couple and mentally assured himself the way was clear and safe for his charge. Protection officers unobtrusively formed a human cage around the pair. There was a final handshake, a wave, a smile for the audience, and an acknowledgement for the waiting Press.

33

A car door opened. The couple entered. They were on the move again.

About a hundred yards away, the departure was like a signal to the demonstrators as they continued to hijack media coverage at local and national level. A woman screamed and the mob surged to one side when a mass brawl erupted and uniformed police quickly moved in to quell the disturbance. A dozen batons came into play before a shower of incapacitating spray rained down on the perpetrators of the unruly gathering.

'Bit of a commotion over there, sir,' reported the chauffeur of the royal car as he pointed to a posse of uniform policeman at the top of Scotch Street.

'Yes,' replied the protection officer. 'I reckon they're spraying the crowd. Drive on please. We are witnessing how not to provide security at a royal visit. It's a farce. Take us out of here, Jim. This is getting a touch dangerous and any confidence I have in the local yokels is waning fast.'

An overweight violent man in an England shirt was wrestled to the ground. He kicked and spat and hurled abuse from an unwritten dictionary. Then a dose of spray from a distance of about four feet – straight into the eyes – put him temporarily out of commission. But there's always one who defies the science of spraying a mixture of incapacitation. Handcuffs were applied and he squealed his dislike when they were twisted awkwardly to bring him under control. A boot struck out and caught a policewoman in the face. Falling backwards out of the game, she smashed against a wall and slumped to the ground. Determined he wasn't going quietly the prisoner head-butted one of his captors before another dose of spray finally subdued him. Scuffles increased as police took the unruly down and fought to bring the violence under control

A medic attended the policewoman and then saw the unconscious Alejandro also lying on the ground. Mayhem ruled when the England shirts surged towards the Argentinians once more. The day of royal celebration had turned into a shambles.

'Squeeze the accelerator, Jim,' declared the protection officer. 'Get us out of here slowly but quickly. I don't want to be caught up in this little lot.'

'As you say,' replied the driver pressing the accelerator.

The Rolls Royce picked up speed.

Martin Duffy on the lead motor bike heard the Royal car throb, glanced over his shoulder, and twisted the throttle a notch. It was just enough to leave the fracas behind with the prince tilting his head slightly to watch proceedings at the scene of the arrest. The Press crowded the vehicle anxious to capture an image of the royal car in the foreground of a battling mob.

A siren sounded briefly when a police van arrived and more officers waded into the affray.

A few minutes later, it was virtually all over. The flags were down and the cheering had ceased for the day. A blood-stained pavement was free from protestors when the last of the protagonists had either been thrown into the back of a police van or left the area of their own accord. Only the remnants of royal exhaust fumes clung in the area as the crowd receded.

Francis Littleton stayed on. Hovering by the bandstand he reflected on the final moments of a less than secure royal visit as the musicians packed their instruments and chatted excitedly about the events of the day. This would make the national news, they discussed. But for all the wrong reasons, it was said. Francis had never witnessed a royal event that had simultaneously incorporated a political demonstration and a criminal act. The day, for Francis, had been just another short engagement with members of the royal family. It was his love; his passion, his raison d'être. Later in the week, he reminded himself, there would be another place where he would go to wave his flag; to reach out, to gain a smile, to take home a souvenir of the day. Such experiences were within his soul - to touch and be touched by royal patronage.

When the streets had cleared and the hubbub died down, Francis eyed a petal lying on a paved area in front of the bandstand.

Furtively, he looked both ways to make sure no-one was watching. When he was satisfied that he was free from scrutiny Francis bent down and picked up the fragile lilac petal. It was from the posy presented to the princess and it had obviously blown to the ground in the breeze. Pleased with his day's plunder, Francis placed the petal inside his suit pocket close to his heart. Walking away from the area Francis patted the outside of his suit jacket where an interior pocket protected his treasure trove from those who might steal it from him. Buttoning his suit tight he strolled towards a car park lost in his own private thoughts.

I've followed her everywhere, he thought, and the prince come to think of it. If the truth be known I've followed them all over the country.

Forlorn, a tear formed in the corner of his grey sullen eyes. Sadly, the lonely Francis Littleton mouthed a hesitant goodbye to a passer-by as the crowds dispersed and normality returned to the streets of Carlisle.

Gathering her hijab to deny a cold breeze biting at her face Dina brushed past an Irishman wearing a green anorak and a sad looking man with grey sullen eyes and a flower hidden inside an anorak pocket. Dina Al-Hakim was gone from the city centre; scornful of Carlisle's imposing cathedral and floral area, and full of hatred for the royal infidels and those around her.

Nearby, walking down a lane towards the market, Declan stepped into a bar and rubbed his hands together announcing, 'Cold, it is. Yes, cold so it is.'

'You'll be having the usual to keep you warm then, Declan?' queried Matt Hobbs, the licensee.

'Aye, a Guinness and a wee glass of whiskey, if you please, and it'll be a Jameson, so it will,' replied Declan. Removing his scarf and opening the front of his anorak, he relaxed.

Filling a glass from the Jameson whisky optic, Matt placed the drink on the bar and said, 'No disrespect, Mister Lynch, but did you get caught up in all the fighting on your way here or what?'

'What do you mean by that?' asked the Irishman. 'I'm no fighting man. I'm a man of peace, so I am.'

The licensee finished pulling the Guinness, placed it on the bar in front of Declan, and suggested, 'I'm surprised a man like you would want to see a royal visit, Declan. That's all.'

'What do you mean a man like me?' explored Declan.

'You're a Dubliner, Declan. You'll be a man for the tricolour and a Free State if I'm not mistaken. Correct me if I'm wrong but that's a Dublin accent you have isn't it?'

'Aye,' nodded Declan. 'That it is.'

'What do you know of Dublin?' queried Declan.

'Oh just a weekend there with the darts team - On tour, they called it.'

Declan nodded and took a drink.

'Did you know that couple might be King and Queen of England one day?' explained Matt.

Declan nodded and spurted, 'Is that a fact now? Oh and yes, I did caught up in the crowd on my way to the bookies and an afternoon bet. I think you've got me mixed up with someone else. I've no interest in Irish politics and I've no problem with English royalty. You know what they say don't you?'

'What's that, Declan?' queried Matt.

'God save the Queen!' offered Declan smiling.

The licensee chuckled and raised his glass saying, 'I'll drink to that, Declan. God save the Queen!'

'Aye,' murmured Declan. He downed his Jameson in one sudden gulp. Careful not to spill the black stout, Declan carried his Guinness to a table near the window. Setting his sights on the scene outside Declan saw a union flag fluttering from above the entrance to the Crown and Mitre hotel. He lifted the glass to his lips and made sure he was out of earshot when he quietly muttered to himself, 'No surrender, my friend, or as they say back home *'aon ghéillead'*. One day there will be no monarchy. There will be only a republic for the likes of me but not for you.'

Taking another drink, Declan wiped his lips with the back of his hand, and murmured, 'Then we will be free from the bastard Brits and their kings and queens or I'll not be Declan O'Malley - a volunteer for the 'RA.'

Declan O'Malley a.k.a. Lynch pulled a smart phone from his pocket, trawled through a list of contacts, and found the number of his co-conspirator, Seamus Logan. He studied the number and then considered a telephone mounted to a wall in the pub.

Which was more secure, he thought.

'Use your phone, landlord?' he shouted.

'Aye, help yourself, Mister Lynch,' came the reply.

Declan made a call.

When the royal flight took off from Carlisle airport later that day the slightly overweight Francis Littleton slid awkwardly into his Peugeot. Reluctantly, he fired the engine and negotiated the country lanes towards Carlisle. Collecting a newspaper on his way he eventually closed the door of his flat in Warwick Road, on the edge of the city, and settled down for the evening. He hung up his suit and settled comfortably into a pair of casual trousers and cotton shirt. Sitting by a dressing table he studied the contents of his collection. It was his life's work.

Upon a mirror many photographs of various members of the royal family were arranged in random order. Kissing the tips of his fingers Francis then placed them on an image of the monarch before moving them to the princesses.

Behind the mirror, on a wall, a mass of photographs from around the United Kingdom and across the globe, had been gathered together to make a huge but impressive collage. Each photograph displayed an image of a member of the royal family at an event of some kind.

Smiling at the photographs as if they portrayed his own family, Francis gently touched them and then moved on before removing a pair of scissors from a drawer. He spread out his evening newspaper, cut away the latest images of a prince and princess, and stuck them loosely to a wall using a smidgen of adhesive.

Standing back, Francis grinned broadly when he realised he appeared in one of the images. His head and shoulders could be seen in the background of one of the royal photographs. The top half of his union flag suit was there for all to see. Was he waving to the royal couple or was he reaching out to try and touch the princess? He neither knew nor cared as long as he was in the photograph.

Finally, Francis opened his wardrobe and carefully removed the petal of a flower from his suit pocket. Gently, he licked it slightly, and stuck it in the centre of the mirror to be surrounded by images of royalty. Francis Littleton's day was complete.

In an apartment close to the River Caldew, Dina Al-Hakim sat in an armchair casually looking out of her window. A follower of the Prophet Muhammad, she watched the Caldew rushing towards the Solway Firth in all its majestic power as it rolled towards the sea and the mighty oceans. Dina knew all about power. As a devout Muslim she needed no lessons in the Quran for she had been able to recite the word of God since her childhood. She fervently believed that the Prophet Muhammad - *Abū al-Qāsim Muḥammad* - was a messenger of God. Muhammad was all powerful in her eyes.

Opening the Quran at verse 4:69 Dina read aloud what she considered to be the word of God as dictated to Muhammad by God. The words resonated in her mind, motivated her, and empowered her very being.

'All who obey Allah and the messenger are in the company of those on whom is the Grace of Allah - of the prophets (who teach), the sincere (lovers of Truth), the witnesses (who testify), and the Righteous (who do good) - Ah! What a beautiful fellowship is Islam!'

Dina knew in her heart that Muhammad was the last prophet sent by God and the most important of all the prophets ever sent by God to mankind. She flicked through the pages of her Quran reminding herself that Muhammad was more commanding than any prophet mentioned in the Hebrew Bible. Muhammad's potent mix of power and inspiration exceeded that of Abraham, Daniel, David, and Ezekiel. They were more influential than Elijah, Isaiah, Jacob, Joseph and Moses. She truly believed that Jesus was merely a second class substitute when compared with Muhammad.

Dina was decided when she read from the pages of her book. She needed no training from Islamic State, Al Qaeda or any other extremist Islamic organisation to help her form those intentions settling in her brain. A Sunni Muslim since her birth in Syria, she recognised liberal Muslims, Shias, Sufis and other sects as heretics that had attacked Sunni mosques and gatherings back in her homeland many years ago. It was here on the outskirts of the city of Ar Raqqah - an Islamic State stronghold - on the northern banks of the Euphrates River close to the Iraqi border that Dina had fostered her hatred of the Shias. Now, as an independent adult, she still hated the Shias more than the Americans, the British, and the so-called civilised western world. These countries were not civilised in her eyes. Such nations were occupied in the main by Kefirs – disbelievers. Her upbringing was such that there was no place for disbelievers in this world or the next. More importantly, it was what her sister had told her before she had left England and answered the call.

Singular in her intentions and motives, Dina turned from the window and her narrow view of the world. She knew it was time for *Salāt*. It was time to pray. Snapping shut the Quran she placed it on a table. Then she stepped towards a mirror on the wall and looked into it. Oh how pretty she looked. Her olive skin complimented her gorgeous brown eyes. Petite, yet subtly sturdy, Dina cut a fine figure. Yet she did not scrutinise the image reflecting from the glass. The mirror had been placed in its position specifically because it was in the same place as the *Qibla*: the direction that should be faced when praying during *Salāt*. The mirror was merely an indication to her that this was the direction of the Kaaba in Mecca: the place where Muhammad was born in Saudi Arabia.

Drawing her hijab closer across her head and neck, Dina committed herself to the daily routine of prayer. Soon, she thought, soon. One day soon there will be a calling within me and it will be time for the death of the infidels and their leaders.

Faraway, south of mainland China; south of Taiwan, east of Vietnam and Cambodia, west of the Philippines, east of the Malay Peninsula and Sumatra; up to the Strait of Malacca in the west, and north of the Bangka–Belitung Islands and Borneo is the archipelago known as the South China Sea Islands.

There was a dull uninspiring building on one of the islands. Paint flaked from its exterior walls and gathered in an unwelcome pile on the ground beneath. Boarded windows behind iron bars and a specially prepared silver metallic lining, plus a flat roof sewn with radio antennae and microwave aerials, were the only clues that the building had a secret to hide.

Inside, row upon row of men and women sat at their desks resting their fingers on the black and white keyboards of their motherboards. They wore casual clothing. There wasn't a uniform to be seen.

Computer screens changed from black to a dull grey. A cursor came to life and pulsated on the screen waiting excitedly for an electronic instruction. Browsers came out of hibernation as the gathering gradually accessed the internet.

The assembled computer operators had no intention of sharing holiday photographs on Facebook or tweeting random quotes on Twitter. There were no images of an English breakfast or a child at play waiting to be uploaded to a chosen digital platform. They planned more than an entry of Twitter's one hundred and forty characteristics in the space provided. Patiently they waited for their leader, Zhan Wen, who was checking her wristwatch.

Gorgeous was the only word to describe the woman who drove and inspired the line-up before her. With long black hair and a shapely figure, the tall leader wore a light blue linen trouser suit that smoothed her bodyline all the way to a mandarin collar at her neck. She paced between the rows waiting for the appointed time. Finally, she clapped her hands as she strolled through the ranks of her cyber troops.

Zhan Wen smiled, held the audience's attention, and gave instructions to commence operations in the Mandarin language.

'Today we shall survey the website of Barclay's Bank. Barclays is a British multinational banking and financial services company with headquarters in London. It is a universal bank with operations in retail, wholesale and investment banking, as well as wealth management, mortgage lending and providing credit cards. We shall investigate and analyse the site to see how vulnerable it is. I want you to look for ways we can communicate with those who run the bank's website.'

'In the usual way?' asked someone in the second row.

'Yes,' replied Zhan. 'Please use your cyber identities to message the bank via Facebook, Twitter and other social media platforms. Ask them about account procedures and any queries that you might have about making investments with them or applying for a credit card.'

The scratch of a pencil followed a rustle of paper when operators reacted to Zhan's words.

'Make a note of their email addresses and look for potential vulnerabilities on their site,' she continued. 'Can you tell if they have discovered your false identity? Do they reply to you? Are they naive? Fill in the form on your desk. We will look at the results later.'

A hand shot into the air and an operator asked, 'Do we send the virus today?'

Smiling an acknowledgement, Zhan Wen replied, 'No! On another day we will deliver malware and viruses to the site via the communication channels open to us. They may be Facebook or Twitter and almost certainly will be email addresses. Once we have found and proved a vulnerable area from the notes you make we will attempt to gain access to the site. Once we're in we will exploit it for our benefit and those who are our paymasters today.'

'Thanks, I just wanted to be sure,' came the reply.

'Total success will see us switching to full encryption before moving money around the system and transferring it to designated accounts. These will be given to you in due course,' explained Zhan Wen. 'However, if the website withstands our probing we may be instructed to close it down with a distributed denial of service whereby the volume of traffic breaks the website system. We have a botnet at our disposal when the time is right, and encryption facilities.'

'Remind me what a botnet is?' asked an operator.

'A botnet is a collection of Internet-connected programs communicating with other similar programs in order to perform tasks,' revealed Zhan Wen. 'This can be as mundane as keeping control of a Chat channel, or it could be used to send spam email or participate in distributed denial-of-service attacks. It mirrors and multiplies everything we do. It controls the environment to the detriment of the website owner is one way of explaining it.'

'Thank you!'

'Is everyone ready?' asked Zhan Wen.

Hushed cursors, willing conspirators in the day's proceedings, moved soundlessly forward on the screens as a multitude of fingers unobtrusively tapped their keyboards and negotiated towards the target website.

Strolling through the ranks of chairs and desks before reaching a suite of onsite servers that fed a score of global networks with their evil feed, Zhan Wen turned and looked towards an area screened off from the rest of her operators. Behind the screen stood the paymaster who was the last link in a long chain of individuals that had hired her illegal enterprise to hack into Barclays. Zhan Wen knew he was the moneyman. She knew nothing of her client. The paymaster was merely the end of a very lengthy chain.

Zhan Wen smiled at their accomplishments to date, wondered about the complexity of a global criminal enterprise, and praised the quiet wisdom of modern warfare.

Behind the screen an Indonesian tongue was detectable in the voice of a man who spoke briefly when he said, 'Excellent! Proceed as instructed.'

The cyberattack began.

Simultaneously, on the other side of the globe, a lesson was being brought to a close.

In a disused quarry near the border of Northern Ireland with the Republic of Ireland Seamus Logan stood in the middle of a crowd of younger men. He was the owner of the quarry and the surrounding land, which he farmed on a regular basis. The menfolk gathered in Seamus's company were mainly aged between their mid-twenties and early thirties. Patiently, they listened to a man lecturing them whilst keenly watching him at work. He was an expert in many fields and they knew him only as 'the Teacher'.

'There are many ways to achieve an objective,' explained the Teacher. 'Some of our so-called leaders thought it could be achieved by the ballot box but there were those among us who thought that process was too slow to reach the final destination and a more direct approach needed to be taken. Then a peace was made. Personally, I think the leadership sold us down the river and looked after themselves first. They've no time for us now. They tell us to enjoy the victory they gave us but the reality is they just need us to be quiet and not cause them any problems while they line their pockets.'

Seamus murmured approval whilst two others present, Donal and Callum Finnerty, both exchanged nods of approval.

'It might be about whether or not you prefer the bullet or the bomb,' revealed the expert as his nimble fingers did their work. 'But we need the Republic to be an island totally free of the Brits and as long as they've got some kind of control over the six counties then that isn't going to happen.'

'You're right there,' voiced Seamus.

The Teacher continued, 'Today I'll show you what only the basics can do but eventually we will move on to much more sophisticated methods using mobile phones, timers, various electronic devices, and different types of explosives.'

Perhaps in his mid-fifties the Teacher's ruddy complexion carried a square chin above a solid frame. Upright in his bearing, he oozed confidence and leadership as he held the attention of his class. A mop of greying hair sprouted from his skull in an uncontrolled manner and finally ran down his neck into a fine grey pony tail that did little to enhance his pretence at a youthful appearance. Yet beneath his apparent cool exterior his heart pounded at a pace too fast for his age and physique.

A bead of sweat formed on the Teacher's forehead and slowly trickled towards an eyelid. The back of his hand quickly wiped the perspiration and he began to fix the wires to the device. Moments later, he felt his pulse increase even more when he tightened the wires for the final time.

'You can be a sniper or a close quarter killer or you can just blast away with a shotgun or machine gun,' he declared. 'We all know what we are about and what the options are. Soon I'm told, very soon, there will be a call to arms. Maybe they'll choose to do it this way this time.'

The Teacher's thin fingers turned a switch. He lifted the plunger and then pressed it down. A spark of electricity jolted a detonator.

Suddenly a car deep in the quarry exploded into a thousand pieces. The sheer noise and ferocity of the blast took the group by surprise. Sure, they'd been waiting for a big bang but were stunned to see a vehicle engine flying through the air fifty feet above them.

'What a sight,' exclaimed Seamus as half a ton of metal spread like dust to the four winds.

Callum ducked in surprise. Donal forced a laugh but the point had been made. Explosives in an expert's hands could do wonders, and cause death, destruction, and mayhem to the unprepared.

When the dust had settled they walked into the middle of the quarry to inspect what was left of a mangled wreck.

'That concludes today's lessons and demonstration,' revealed the Teacher eventually. 'Same time tomorrow please and don't be late. Now I suggest you leave separately but quickly and take the usual security precautions to make sure you're not compromised. Give yourselves plenty of time to get here tomorrow and make doubly sure no-one is following you. We'll be checking out our most advanced sniper rifle for an hour or so. It's just another way we can win our independence and absorb the six counties and I want you all to be able to use the killing machine before tomorrow's session is over.'

There was a shaking of hands and a nodding of acquiescence before the assembly began to break up.

As the group dispersed Callum remarked, 'Donal, make sure you go straight home. Don't you go chasing that fancy woman of yours?'

'I've no idea what you mean, Callum,' replied Donal nervously. 'I've no fancy woman that I know of.'

Donal brushed past Callum Finnerty and deliberately avoided eye contact with others in the party.

As Donal walked away Seamus sidled up to Callum and enquired, 'What was all that about, Callum?'

'Nothing, Seamus, nothing at all.'

'What have you heard, Callum?

'Nothing, sure nothing at all, Seamus,' replied Callum.

'Best be sure on that, Callum. Now I'll ask you again and for the last time. What have you heard about Donal?'

'Just that he's got a fancy woman that's all.'

'And he's married to my sister, Callum. Did you forget that?'

'Sorry, Seamus,' offered Callum. 'Sure, I didn't know that.'

Seamus nodded to all present before quietly strolling from the quarry wondering whether there was any truth in Callum's accusation. As he made for his home close by a ringtone alerted him. He checked its screen to see a picture of his cousin Declan O'Malley staring back at him.

Seamus declined the call but the signal had been received. He would ring Declan from a landline at the agreed time. Security was paramount to their conversations. A landline was much safer.

Ten minutes later, and some miles from the quarry, Donal stopped at a phone box in the countryside. He dialled a number and waited for a reply. Holding the phone to his ear he quickly checked both ways whilst waiting for a reply to his call. He was safe. There wasn't a person or car in sight.

When his call was answered Donal said, 'It's the Quarryman. I'd like to place an order for two dozen pink roses. I'd like them to be ready as soon as possible.'

Donal listened for a few moments and then offered, 'I'll pick them up at the market the day after tomorrow. The roses must be ready then. They're for a family gathering on the mainland and they can't be cancelled. It's urgent that the florist attends to the matter personally.'

Donal checked the countryside again and then returned to the telephone conversation with 'Aye, the florist herself.'

Ending the call, Donal replaced the receiver and returned to his car. Fifteen minutes later he pulled into the driveway of his home in the Republic.

An MI5 officer in the Operation Centre deep in London replaced the telephone, checked the notes he had made, and turned to another telephone. He made a call.

In a lush apartment close to Pimlico Antonia Harston-Browne popped a cork from a bottle of Bollinger's champagne and poured two glasses. She handed one of the crystal flutes to Phillip and then answered her ringing telephone.

Antonia listened, nodded, and replied, 'Thank you, all received.' Turning to Phillip, her companion, she volunteered, 'Ireland! Would you believe I need to go the Emerald Isle?'

'Interesting,' suggested Phillip. 'And perhaps unexpected dare I say?'

'Perhaps, perhaps not,' responded Antonia. 'When will Ireland ever sleep peacefully?'

Tall and slim, Antonia was renowned amongst her male counterparts for her shapely legs and long red hair which flowed down her back covering her shoulder blades. With an hour-glass figure, she was always immaculate on or off duty. Her friends and close confidants called her Toni. She was one of those individuals who just didn't age but thrived on adventure and tension. Every inch a lady, she was articulate, sophisticated, cultured, educated well above the national standard, and of upper middle class bearing. Indeed, Antonia Harston-Browne carried a highly polished professional demeanour wherever she went enjoying two honours degrees and playing a merciless game of squash. At the quintessential exclusive country club she was in her element with the so-called 'county set'. Whilst in the oak-panelled corridors of Whitehall and the highfalutin financial offices of the City, she could wheel and deal with the sharpest of kids on the block. In the City, she wined and dined at expensive restaurants and wore long, flowing gowns that vitalised her sophisticated charms and discarded the facade of her other life. She was privileged, virtually blue-blooded, the daughter of parents since departed: parents who had left her a financial legacy that revealed her to be of comfortable private means. In the city, in the country club, she had no enemies, save those who bitched at her pretentiousness. Moreover, Antonia had connections in every corner of society that one might imagine: the good, the bad, and the ugly. As a senior Intelligence Officer employed by MI5, the Security Service, she was a leading member of the controversial Special Crime Unit. And Phillip, her guest, was the Director General of the nation's Security Service.

'More champagne, Phillip?' she asked.

'Perhaps, perhaps not,' replied Phillip with a grin.

At home in Cumbria Boyd had settled down with a bottle of wine and a Walt Disney video featuring a handsome prince dressed in blue and a beautiful princess dressed in pink. The family were truly frozen to the screen when the phone rang.

Parting company for a moment with Meg and the twins, Izzy and James, he answered the phone ringing in the hallway.

'It's me,' said Antonia. 'The Quarryman rang.'

'I thought you saw him last month?' queried Boyd who then added. 'There was nothing to report of specific interest other than the usual chit chat.'

'He wants flowers urgently and it can't be cancelled,' declared Antonia. 'I thought you'd like to know as soon as possible.'

'Yes, of course, thanks. Where is the delivery?' probed Boyd.

'On the mainland!'

'You're joking!'

'I wish I was,' revealed Antonia. 'We've always known the Irish situation wasn't completely closed – there's too many inside factions vying for a place at the top table - but this is sooner than any of us imagined, I suspect.'

'Yes, I agree,' admitted Boyd. 'Not necessarily a shock but a little earlier than anticipated shall we say. It was always a fragile peace, a little rocky here and there.'

'Exactly!' agreed Antonia

'I take it you've made arrangements, Toni?'

'Yes, I have a flight booked and security arranged at the other end. My office is aware of the movement as is the DG. I thought you would want to know. If the information is true then we'll need to be on the ball ready for the balloon going up.'

'Yes, let's hope it's just a balloon and nothing more,' suggested Boyd. 'Keep in touch and best regards to Phillip.'

'Phillip?' snapped Antonia. 'How did you know Phillip was with me?'

'Pretty obvious really, Toni,' chided Boyd. 'And remember, I have eyes and ears everywhere.'

'Goodness, should I check the room out for hidden microphones?' giggled Antonia.

Phillip shook his head, laughed, and raised a glass to her when Antonia replied, 'You can't be trusted, Billy Boyd. I'll take more care in future.'

'Oh, by the way, Toni,' advised Boyd. 'Take care out there. Don't forget the drill.'

'I won't,' replied Antonia partly closing the conversation as she took the cordless phone for a stroll. When she was out of Phillip's earshot, Antonia said, 'I need to talk to you about Phillip when you've time.'

'Why, what's the problem?' probed Boyd.

'Oh I don't think there's a problem really,' volunteered Antonia. 'There's something I'd like to discuss with you that's all.'

'Another woman?' suggested Boyd in a low pitched voice.

'No, I don't think so. Phillip is no womaniser. It's something to do with the office. That's all I know at the moment.'

'Okay,' declared Boyd. 'I'm always available for you, Toni. Have a safe journey.'

'I will,' replied Antonia. 'Love to Meg, Izzy and James from both of us. When will you be in the office?'

'Tomorrow lunch time on the presumption the train to Euston doesn't let me down,' replied Boyd.

'Good luck! It's all change as from tomorrow I believe,' suggested Antonia.

'Yes, Toni,' confirmed Boyd. 'A new boss to contend with, it won't be a problem.'

'Let's hope not,' said Antonia. 'That should be you walking into the superintendent's office, Billy. I still can't think why they picked someone else instead of you.'

'It's water under the bridge,' replied Boyd. 'Don't worry about it, Toni. I'm hardly destitute because I didn't get the superintendent's job.'

'Okay,' accepted Antonia. 'Goodnight, Billy.'

Out in the Baltic Sea Captain Richard Maynard poured over his maps as his cruiser ploughed north through the brine. His eyes studied the charts and then he walked over to a radar screen to check the position of other vessels in the area.

'Lieutenant,' gestured the Royal Navy captain. 'Double check my bearings please.'

Lieutenant Ken Jones duly obliged and then observed the radar screen.

'Surely not, sir,' remarked Jones. 'I mean… They wouldn't, would they?'

'It appears they would,' suggested Maynard. 'Wireless make to Admiralty the following message… Bears in the water… 100 miles north… Altering course to North by north east… and send.'

'Roger,' replied the wireless operator tapping the message into his encrypted system.

'Have they come to watch, Ken?' remarked Captain Maynard. 'Or have they come to threaten us?'

Captain Andrei Voronin drew the zip of his anorak closer to his chin in an attempt to stay warm. Ahead of him the might of the sea crashed over the bow of his cruiser and splayed across the deck in awesome splendour. It was a hell of a day for the captain and his fleet. The weather was terrible; the storm ravaging.

Reflecting on the Russian Federation Navy's presence in the Baltic Sea Andrei Voronin recalled previous historical periods as he proudly mastered his vessel. The Baltic Fleet had been part of the navy of Imperial Russia and later the Union of Soviet Socialist Republics (the Soviet Union). The Fleet gained the 'Twice Red Banner' label during the Soviet period when it received two awards of the Order of the Red Banner. Headquartered in Kaliningrad, the fleet is normally based in Baltiysk whilst there is another base at Kronshtadt, in the Gulf of Finland. Czar Peter the Great had formed the fleet in 1703. It is now the oldest Russian Navy organisation and is a force to be reckoned with; admired by some, loathed by others, and feared by all.

Captain Voronin knew the fleet's history and the Baltic Sea well. He checked his bearings and ordered a change of direction. Leading the main part of the fleet to his rear, he plotted a course south-easterly. Familiar with his orders he knew what was ahead of him and what was expected of him. Captain Andrei Voronin was leading the Baltic Sea Fleet directly into the path of Captain Maynard's NATO force on routine exercise.

Alone in his thoughts Andrei considered his orders and the things that might happen in the days ahead. He was cold as was the war his father and grandfather had fought in their own particular ways. Rummaging inside his anorak, Andrei withdrew a pewter flask and downed a slug of vodka.

I am a threat, thought Andrei. A crease of a thin grin crept across his face as he savoured the proposition. If it is anything like my country the British will have lots of threats from different people about different things. The threat is merely a catalogue of wicked desires originating in the minds of those who would run things their own way.

Threats, threats and more threats, he chuckled. How to decipher them all and make sense of which is relevant today and which might be relevant tomorrow, he thought. Not my problem, he decided. For it is the work of others to do and for others to have sleepless nights over.

Andrei yawned, took another slug of vodka, and stowed his flask.

Out in the desert, Salman walked alone on a road from Tikrit towards the Syrian border. Exhausted, he plotted a westerly direction and carried a rifle slung across his back and a dagger in his belt. Wearing the black combat fatigues of Islamic State he was battle weary, hungry, and thirsty. Yet he knew what he must do and where he must go.

Ahead lay warmth, food, refreshment and nourishment – a place to regroup, rest, plan the next move, and soldier on.

Tired, unshaven, scruffy, the warrior of Muhammad drank the last of his water, heard an aircraft overhead, and stepped from the tarmac onto the desert sands.

Moments later, his stomach hugged earth as he made for a wadi, fell into the gulley, and crawled into a rocky recess to shelter from the aircraft, the cold of the night, and to grab some sleep.

Damn you, Ibrahim, he thought. Damn you for not providing food and water. But then how were you to know this would happen?

The enemy aircraft flew low, perhaps searching, perhaps merely looking for a mobile target. Salman did not know. As the aircraft banked to its left and then climbed Salman formed the shape of a gun in his right hand and pointed it at the aircraft.

'Boom!' he voiced and then blew the end of his fingers as if they were a six gun.

Turning onto his side, Salman hugged his rifle tight to his skin and tried to sleep.

His walk would be long, dangerous, and rewarding but Salman's journey had begun.

*

Chapter Three

~

The Mountainous Region, Islamic State
The Following Day.
Threat Level Three - Substantial

Deep unobtrusive caves sheltered the warriors of Muhammad from the freezing cold of a desert night and fierce sandstorms that whipped across the desolate plains and into their heartland. Yet these rugged inventions of nature also protected them from enemy drones and surveillance satellites. The caves gave them freedom and space in which to plan and shape their path of evil. It was these caves in which their leaders lived and where, in the name of their God, they plotted their media campaign of hatred and intimidation. It was the hub of operations.

Three bearded men dutifully emerged from one of the caves into the sunlight. They assumed an air of supreme confidence when they stepped forward to present themselves before a video camera, mounted on a tripod, which was under the control of a man who looked to be much older and in his early sixties. His name was Ibrahim Hasan al Din and he was one of their leaders.

Lengthy facial hair failed to hide the obvious youthfulness of the trio since they were all aged somewhere between twenty and twenty five years. It was perhaps difficult to tell until one of them spoke imperfect English in a voice that signalled youth rather than age. Dressed in black fatigues the trio were each armed with an assault rifle. One of the men also held a very large curved sword that measured over three feet in length. With pistols hanging loosely from leather holsters on their belts they immediately presented an evil portrait for the camera.

The thinly built grey–haired Ibrahim Hasan al Din operated the video camera. His frail looks deceived his true persona for he was the infamous leader of the group. Extremists the world over worshipped every move he made whilst his enemies dreaded his sinister evil plots.

Ibrahim nodded to the trio and began filming. Behind him, a further small handful of elders gathered to watch proceedings. They were all armed with various rifles and small arms. One cradled a rocket launcher. Yet it was a strange atmosphere. It was as if the schoolchildren were about to present an end of term concert to teachers and parents alike.

One of the players clapped his hands smartly and turned to the entrance of the cave to welcome two young females who were also dressed in black garb. Whilst the girls each carried the black flag of Islamic State, they also dragged a man in chains to the centre of proceedings.

Thin, dirty, dishevelled, manacled, the man was quite obviously petrified when he was dumped nonchalantly before the camera for all to see. Those who had contrived at making the emaciated subject appear to be a pathetic wreck of a human being had succeeded.

The victim rolled over trying to find enough momentum to gain an upright position. Struggling to his knees with some difficulty the prisoner began pleading for his life in a French-Canadian accent as saliva dripped from the corner of his lips and bruising on his face became apparent. Ignoring him, the two girls took positions behind their trio of bearded colleagues to hold the black Islamic flags up high for attention. Quite intentionally, they had calculated the whole scene purely for media impact.

The camera rolled in complete silence, which was broken only by one of the bearded youths who looked into the lenses and spoke directly to his audience.

'It is time for our brothers and sisters in the west to move to another stage. Now is the time to rise up and fight. The infidels must feel our wrath, and taste the cold tongue of Allah and his revenge. The spies of the west come to our lands in many ways. They are undone. Such men are betrayed by Allah who sees and knows all things. They are not welcome. They are but infidels who deserve no tolerance of any kind. This is how we dispose of the enemies of Allah.'

Another of the young gang stepped forward, withdrew his pistol, and shot the blubbering petrified man in the head from less than an arm's length.

The man's skull exploded in a mix of blood, bone and gore. He fell to the ground and twitched violently as life ebbed from his soul. Blood spilled onto desert sand that had witnessed so much evil in the past. The sand gradually coloured red as the fluid ran uncontrollably from the corpse.

Stepping forward, two girls unashamedly planted their black flags firmly in the sand at either side of the victim's carcass. There was no doubt they wanted the cold blooded murder to be directly attributed to the flags they bore.

Both black flags carried words written in white, and in Arabic – *'La 'ilaha 'illa-llah.'*

Mindful of the true status of a woman in the Islamic faith, one of the men waved the girls away as if they were an irrelevant nuisance. Then, making an impression on his elders, he ushered them away more forcibly with both hands. Warriors of a kind, some might say. But the girls' job was finished.

In a building affectionately known as 'the Doughnut' in Cheltenham, Gloucestershire, the men and women of GCHQ (Government Communications Headquarters), monitored electronic traffic from terrorists and spy agencies around the globe. Agents on one desk watched the video on a 'live feed' monitor merely because the frequency on which it was being transmitted had been used by Islamic State previously.

'The bastards have done it again,' voiced Tim, one of the intelligence officers. 'I wish I could push a button from this very desk and obliterate the swine. There should be no room for such barbarism in this world.'

'My sentiments exactly,' agreed Robin nearby. 'It's the Fourth Reich. It could never be worse than the Holocaust but it's as bad as Hitler ever brought upon us. That poor man didn't deserve to die like that. They deliberately humiliated him before they killed the poor sod.'

'What's that on the flags?' asked Stephen, one of the more inexperienced watchers.

'*La 'ilaha 'illa-llah.* It's Arabic, my friend,' explained Tim.

'Yes, I know that but what does it mean? I've not seen it before,' asked Stephen.

'Sadly, you'll probably get used to it and will no doubt see it quite a few times before all this is over,' declared Tim. 'Literally I think the translation means there is God, and then there is the messenger of God. I've seen it often enough. If memory serves me well then I do believe it really means something else. The Arabic words across the top of that flag mean there is no God but God, and the white seal beneath those words imprinted in what you might call a speech bubble reads God Messenger Mohammed. But to translate it into something the English can understand I can tell you that it says Muhammad is the Messenger of God.'

'Okay, thanks. Why do they make the writing so damned complicated then?'

'I don't know. For what it's worth the script is less elaborate than other flags with similar messages. The white seal is meant to resemble the official seal of the Prophet Muhammad, though lots of self-professed experts on the Islamic faith have debated what the seal actually looked like.'

Another voice, this time Roberta, a female, asked, 'Gentlemen, do we know who the victim is? He is much more important than the flags.'

'I think it will be a French-Canadian journalist living in Ottawa but on assignment for a news magazine based in Paris,' suggested Robin. 'It's not our job to identify the victim. That will fall to someone else but, for what it's worth, sometimes we have to switch the conversation around the way we do. It helps when your job is tracking these things down and waiting for the inevitable to happen. Sorry!'

'No problem, I understand,' offered Roberta.

'By the way, here's a list of journalists and aid workers kidnapped by Islamic State over the last three years. I think it's the third name down, Roberta.'

The document moved from one hand to another before Roberta's finger ran down the list and she announced, 'They didn't pay the ransom. They stood up to terrorism and paid the price. Let's hope his death is not in vain.'

'It's a long and bloody battle but we shall win the war,' commented Tim.

'Give me some good news, gents. What's today's trawl looking like?' quizzed Roberta.

'We're on it,' replied Tim. 'There's a lot of encrypted stuff as usual. Electronic traffic is heavy from the Tikrit and Mosul areas according to CAST- the crime analytics software: terrorism system. Unusually, we've picked up a lot of open speech from IS.'

'They're on the run from the Shia, that's why,' suggested Robin. 'What's the betting some are phoning home?'

'Where are we with the latest batch?' asked Roberta.

'Everything is with the analysts,' replied Tim. 'Give us time and we'll be able to sort out what's good, what's bad, and what remains just a downright mystery.'

'I'll tell the chief what we have,' revealed Roberta taking the list with her.

By the end of the day a video had gone viral on You Tube and other social media networks. Such was the power of communication in the modern age

In a gym in the basement of New Scotland Yard, Boyd and his team were involved in a training session. A row of treadmills were rolling well, a weight rack was in good use, and a splash of pure perspiration hit the floor when a phone rang.

Boyd wiped the sweat away, unhooked the phone from a wall mounting and said, 'Boyd!' He listened for a moment and replied, 'Ten minutes, sir.'

Replacing the phone, Boyd turned to the group and said, 'That was the boss. He wants to see me in his office. I'll catch you guys later.'

There was a wave and a nod before Boyd showered, changed, and took the lift to the Operations Centre. A short time later he was in the secure complex of the Special Crime Unit. He was in time for his appointment with the commander.

Alone in his office in New Scotland Yard Commander Edwin Maxwell QPM thanked his contact in the Security Service and replaced the telephone.

As Commander of the controversial Special Crime Unit, Edwin was an experienced London detective. He had served in the West End where he had forged a name as a good hardworking detective; the East End where he was a feared gang buster, the anti-terrorist branch as a source handler, and, more recently, as a senior supervisor in Counter Terrorist Command in charge of the international desk. Recently promoted and appointed to replace Commander James Herbert, Edwin Maxwell was something of a legend in London's Metropolitan police. He was dogmatic when he needed to be yet very popular and considered by many to be a proper gentleman. Yet those who had worked with him would be the first to remind others that he had reached the dizzy heights of the police service because he knew the job inside out. At the end of the day, he was a coppers' copper who had learnt how to wheel and deal in the corridors of power, and defeat the crooks on the streets at their own game. He had his enemies it was said, or was it just a jealous rumour from those who thought they should have been picked for one of the most important jobs in the nation's police service instead of Edwin. Either way, it was little surprise that he had been recently awarded the Queen's Police Medal for Distinguished Service. Above all, Commander Edwin Maxwell was a London copper through and through.

Admitting Chief Inspector Boyd into his office Commander Maxwell greeted his colleague with, 'Keeping fit, chief inspector, or are they tears I see on your forehead?'

'Good old fashioned sweat, sir,' replied Boyd. 'The team will be on station shortly.'

'Good!' replied the commander. 'We need them fit and capable. Tea or coffee?'

'Coffee, please, black,' responded Boyd. 'No sugar!'

'Take a look at this, William,' suggested Commander Maxwell pouring from a coffee percolator. 'I'll warn you now it's not very pleasant but it's a timely reminder why we do what we do and why we need to be constantly on top of the job. The perpetrators of such violence need to be hounded down, destroyed, and removed from the world in which we live. They are the scum of the earth. Their faith, their religion, their very being, offers no real apology and no sound reasoning for these atrocities. It is a battle we must win at all costs.'

Nodding, Boyd sat down when the commander switched on a computer screen on his desk. In silent acquaintance they recapped the video and dialogue before Boyd remarked, 'Nasty! And here was I thinking the Irish problem was about to start up again. It makes you wonder just where the threat really does lie. The desert is six or seven thousand miles away and our Irish enemies are virtually on our doorstep.'

'Quite, William, I couldn't agree more with you and both organisations behind these threats are game players. Our problem of course is that we have countless Islamic extremists living on our shores as well. If the job we do is countering the threat then I sometimes ask myself which threat we should tackle today. Cyberattacks, Islamic State, hostile enemy countries trying to infiltrate our defence system, serious organised crime, or just horrible people intent on making a name for either themselves or their organisation to the detriment of others. Which comes first when you're at the sharp end of policing? I sometimes wonder what the man in the street would do if he knew the truth. The reality is that the general public has very little knowledge of the threat we live with every day. They only get twenty second blasts from a biased television report when something really tragic happens. Otherwise they assume everything is alright.'

'Yes, it is disturbing,' agreed Boyd.

'Okay, William, update the troops on the video we've just watched. It's a good example of Salafist Jihadism.'

'That's a mouthful,' remarked Boyd. 'I've heard the term before, commander but remind me what it means.'

Taking a sip of coffee, Commander Maxwell then explained, 'Our friends in the Security Service believe that the individual behind the video is believed to be a member of Salafist Jihadism.'

'Ibrahim Hasan al Din?' suggested Boyd.

'That's the man,' agreed the commander. 'The Salafist Movement is the most serious and immediate terrorist threat to Europe. It's climbing up the league table of threats to the western world.'

'I see,' replied Boyd. 'The overall situation has got worse then?'

'It certainly has,' answered the commander. 'The movement is a transnational religious-political ideology based on a belief in violent jihad and the desire to return to 'true' Islam. The Salafi movement is a doctrine that lies within Sunni Islam. It imitates the Prophet Muhammad and his earliest followers. In fact, William, Salafi is all about copying the first three generations who came after Muhammad.'

'Why? That would take us back to before the Dark Ages.' suggested Boyd. 'It is the Twenty First century.'

'They are trying to copy their forefathers, William. The movement supports the implementation of sharia law but it can be divided into three categories: the largest group are the purists who avoid politics. The second largest are the activists, who do get involved in politics. And the smallest group are the jihadists, who form a tiny, yet notorious, minority. The jihadists are closely associated to Al-Qaeda; its affiliates in the Arabian Peninsula and North Africa, Jabhat al-Nusra, Ansar Bait al-Maqdis, and Islamic State. They all subscribe to the same ideology we call Salafist Jihadism.'

Boyd yawned and Commander Maxwell asked, 'I'm sorry. Am I boring you, William?'

'Not at all,' chuckled Boyd. 'I think the gym got the better of me. Please continue, commander. If our working days are about defeating the evil amongst us then we must all know the basics of why people are evil, and I'd rather my team knew why they were fighting this particular threat.'

Commander Maxwell nodded, and continued, 'The Salafi Movement rejects other religions and seek to establish a Sharia-based Caliphate throughout the world. They proclaim that every Muslim should fight for the realisation of the Caliphate. You saw that on the video, William.'

'I did, sir.'

'There is evidence that Salafist networks cross European borders,' continued Commander Maxwell. 'The Millatu Ibrahim group, banned in Germany in 2012, for example, is known to have not only recruited German jihadists but also served to connect them to extremist networks in Austria, Belgium, and France. Similarly, the 16 January 2015 Berlin police raid on eleven addresses and arrest of two men suspected of recruiting fighters, arms and finance for Islamic State, came a day after the thwarting of a terrorist plot in Belgium and appears to have been part of a wider effort to disrupt a European network of Salafist extremists. Oh, what a troubled word we live in, William.'

It was never like this in the old days, William.'

'I don't remember such times, commander,' quipped Boyd with a sly smile. 'How long ago was that?'

Chuckling, Commander Maxwell replied, 'Oh I don't know, William. In my prime we knew who the enemy was. Now we tend to be introduced to our opponents by various television news channels. I sometimes think we are only scratching the surface of the many threats that face our nation. We are good at dealing with what we can touch and see but blind to that which we do not understand or are not aware of. The destruction of a peaceful democracy like ours will not come from those who attack it by the path of evil. Peace will be destroyed by those who only sit and watch, and fail to stand up and crusade against the wrongdoers. We must continue our crusade, William.'

'I agree, commander,' replied Boyd.

'That's why I sometimes cringe at the apologetic outbursts of some our politicians and public sector leaders. No-one wants to tell it like it is for fearing of upsetting our diverse opinionated society and risking their job. Our so-called leaders thrive on focusing everyone on one subject at a time leaving many of the real problems unresolved and unchallenged.'

'That includes our mob some of the time,' remarked Boyd. 'The apologetic mealy-mouthed murmuring from our senior ranks is sadly not yet challenged by the rank and file – present company accepted of course, commander.'

'It's time, William,' nodded the commander checking his wristwatch. 'I think it's only right that we get this over with.'

'Yes, I know,' replied Boyd.

'Good! Come, walk with me,' dictated the commander rising from his seat. 'As you know, I'm sorry you didn't get the job. For what it's worth the commissioner made the decision and between you and I it's my belief he wanted you to remain in post since we really don't have a suitable candidate to take your place. And you are Head of Covert Operations, William, and will remain so for the foreseeable future. Still, perhaps another time.'

'Yes, these things happen, commander,' suggested Boyd. 'But I'm not upset if that's what you're driving at.'

'Good, I didn't think you were. Come on, it's time you met the latest acquisition to our unit – Detective Superintendent Sandra Peel. She starts work with us tomorrow but has popped in for an hour or so to find her bearings.'

'Of course,' replied Boyd. 'High time we had a superintendent in the saddle.'

The two men left the commander's office and walked down a corridor into a large open plan area where, at the front of the space provided, a woman in her early fifties was unpacking the contents of a briefcase onto her desk. Dressed in a dark two-piece knee length business suit, Sandra cut quite an imposing figure. Slim and six feet tall, she oozed self-confidence.

'Superintendent,' interrupted the commander. 'I'd like to introduce you to Detective Chief Inspector Boyd.'

'When will my office be ready, Commander Maxwell?' she barked. 'I'm a senior officer and your immediate deputy. I need privacy and space relevant to my status in the organisation.'

'Soon, Sandra,' replied Maxwell. 'Quite soon, so please calm down. I'm told it will be ready by the end of the week at the latest.'

'Good,' she mellowed before adding, 'I suppose that will have to do.'

'Yes it will have to do actually,' smiled Commander Maxwell.

'Of course, thank you!' Turning to face Maxwell's companion Superintendent Sandra Peel delivered, 'So you're Boyd. I'm pleased to meet you. Billy is it, or William?'

'Boyd will do nicely,' the chief inspector replied reaching out to shake hands. 'Everyone calls me Boyd. Welcome to the unit. I hope you enjoy your stay with us.'

'You may call me Ma'am, chief inspector,' insisted Peel ignoring a hand offered.

'Of course, Ma'am,' agreed Boyd awkwardly.

Detective Superintendent Sandra Peel paused momentarily and studied both men as well as the office they occupied. The walls were covered with maps of various parts of the world, photographs of wanted terrorist, and a collage of departmental images compiled from various office functions.

With over thirty years policing experience Sandra had served in various departments including Traffic, Community Support, Crime Prevention, CID, and the National Crime Squad. She was known to be as hard as nails with her staff, somewhat abrasive at times, and demanded high standards from those with whom she worked.

'I'll need to assess you in due course, Boyd,' she explained. 'I'm sure you are well aware of the staff appraisal system but we can cut a little slack this time round. I suggest a formal interview with everyone in the office will suffice. I need to get to know everyone and decide whether their capabilities match my standards. An hour apiece I'd say. I'll get my secretary to organise it?'

'Secretary?' interrupted Commander Maxwell. 'You will have no such luxury here. We have a pool of civilian typists and assistants who keep the wheels of our machine well-oiled and they support all of us when required. Furthermore, I think you'll find our selection procedures are second to none, superintendent. We select the best there is. Appointment to the unit is by invitation only. I think you'll find everything that needs to be done has been done in that area. And may I remind you, superintendent, that I have the final decision on everything in this unit and no-one else.'

'I see,' countered Peel. Unafraid she continued, 'I understand your position, commander. Nothing is ever taken for granted on my watch.'

'Mine neither,' commented Boyd still reeling from the news that he might have to undergo some kind of interview or appraisal to keep his job.

Commander Maxwell smiled tactfully at Boyd and offered, 'Relax the pair of you. The enemy is outside these walls not within

65

them. I need a team on the same track not a couple of clowns trying to score points over their opponent.'

'I agree,' admitted Boyd looking directly at Superintendent Peel. 'All newcomers should be allowed a little space to test the water. Hopefully I can introduce you to some of my team later today.'

'Yes, perhaps,' acknowledged Peel returning a diplomatic smile.

A red telephone rang in the office interrupting proceedings. It was immediately answered by Detective Constable Terry Anwhari. The unit fell silent as Terry listened, returned an acknowledgement, and slammed the phone down shouting, 'It's on. The source indicates they're on their way to the post office now. It's going down in fifteen minutes – Bethnal Green – and it's a trigger operation.'

'Hit it!' replied Boyd. 'Team Alpha - Let's go!'

There was an immediate reaction from part of the office when Boyd's order was given.

'Coming?' asked Boyd engaging Sandra Peel.

'What is it?'

'A post office robbery,' disclosed Boyd. 'One of Terry's informants tipped him off some time ago. A couple of suspected Islamic extremists have been planning an armed robbery at a post office for a while. We've had their apartment covered technically ever since. It's one of the things we do as you know. That call was from the listeners. The suspects are on their way to do the job.

'Thanks for the offer, Boyd, but I think not,' Peel replied. 'I'll start work properly tomorrow. I need to settle in first but I wish you luck.'

'Ahh, you're a pen pusher then,' joked a grinning Boyd. 'You should remember miss, madam or is it Mrs that respect is a two way street. People in the lower ranks often like the opportunity to appraise those in the higher ranks. It's the latest management model, you know. Two way assessment! Staff will only look up to you if you show them you can do the job and earn their respect.'

'Boyd,' snapped Commander Maxwell, 'The superintendent has a truly splendid record.'

'I don't doubt it, commander,' admitted Boyd. 'But we've a saying here on the unit. You're only as good as your last arrest.'

'It's Mrs actually, Boyd, although I am in the process of a divorce. Not that that is any of your business. As for recent arrests - yours was for a petty theft in Carlisle city centre I believe,' suggested Peel. 'Where is Carlisle by the way - Scotland, isn't it? Not to worry, my last arrest was for historic child sex exploitation leading to the arrest and conviction of thirty two people.'

'Any of them armed with a knife or a gun?' asked Boyd withdrawing a firearm from a wall safe and handing the 'Approvals Register' to the commander. 'Or were the cases so old that you might really ask the question what's more important - something that occurred a couple of decades ago or something from yesterday that is a serious threat to our nation? That's our job in this unit – dealing with the threat today, not yesterday.'

'I take exception to your tone of voice and attitude to historic investigations, Boyd,' barked Peel. 'You're beginning to annoy me and you'd certainly upset a stack of victims I can think of. Now I know why some of my colleagues think this department is controversial. It's the people in it, don't you think?'

'You're welcome, Ma'am,' replied Boyd. 'But the harsh reality is we don't have enough manpower to do the job we're supposed to be doing now. The job is getting side-tracked every day of the week into stuff that happened so long ago that someone needs to call time on the subject. Half the suspects are either dead or dying and half the victims are chasing compensation as much as they are justice. The only people making a success of historic investigations is a bunch of lawyers specialising in compensation. We've more resources working on history than we have working on today's problems.'

Boyd presented an empty Gloch pistol to Commander Maxwell who nodded and handed Boyd sufficient ammunition before signing the register.

'What you're really saying is that you don't care about the victims,' declared Peel.

'Enough,' roared Commander Maxwell angrily. 'You're like a couple of kids in the playground arguing over whose turn it is on the slide! Boyd - Get a move on and get the job on the road. Peel – Unpack and can it. You are beginning to annoy me. In fact you're both beginning to annoy me. I want today's operation to go successfully and without irrelevant argument in between. You're carrying firearms, Boyd. Focus or stand down!'

'Of course, commander,' replied Boyd.

'Concentrate on the job in hand,' snapped Commander Maxwell. 'I'll contact the borough commander and warn him of the operation. We'll throw down a red blanket. It will be a quarter mile radius from the post office. You will be the only officers in that blanketed zone and I will plot containment with the local commander.'

'Why do you do that?' bickered Peel.

'Give me strength!' barked Maxwell. 'To prevent a blue on blue. This might be your first day, superintendent, but I did advise you to study our procedures manual prior to starting work with us.'

'I needed to close down my last post,' explained Peel. 'I'll read it tonight, commander.'

'Take heed as follows, superintendent,' growled Commander Maxwell, his displeasure apparent upon realising oil and water weren't mixing well today. 'Day one, lesson one – All officers in this unit are trained to a high standard and are experts with firearms. Each officer has received a standard regulated briefing about when firearms can be used, when they can be carried, and when they can be discharged. On occasions when time permits we have full-on operational briefings but our problem is we are a 24/7 response unit and are often called to incidents as they are happening or are about to happen. Whenever present either you or I will authorise the issue of firearms relevant to each case. Read the unit's manual. For your information we've been waiting for that telephone call for about three weeks. In an emergency when we are not present Boyd has my authority to issue firearms here or anywhere in the UK.'

Boyd's team stepped forward and took charge of their weapons from Commander Maxwell. As each officer stepped forward Boyd introduced them to Sandra Peel.

'This is Detective Inspector Anthea Adams,' said Boyd. 'Second in command of S.C.U.S.T - our surveillance team - and recently promoted. Anthea is married to Raphael: a senior detective in Portugal. Inspector Adams is a crack shot and doesn't suffer fools gladly. She's also my deputy.'

Anthea checked and then holstered her weapon. Her auburn hair flowed to her shoulders and no further. An intrepid member of the unit, she occasionally spoke her mind. Intelligent and extremely competent, Anthea looked forward to a weekend flight to Lisbon whenever she could. Sporting a denim trouser suit and a black silk scarf, Anthea tightened her belt. She ignored the superintendent as she donned her bullet-proof vest, signed the commander's firearms' register, and then briefly made eye contact with Sandra Peel.

'Janice Burns,' continued Boyd issuing another firearm. 'A feisty Scot from Greenock if ever there was one. Janice is an expert in housebreaking and pickpocketing, as well as one or two other things that we don't necessarily advertise.'

'Lang may yer lumb reek,' cracked Janice.

Sandra Peel replied, 'Quite!' but received only a stark glare from Janice as she spoke to the commander saying, 'Dinnae forget I'm authorised for shotguns, sir. I'll take a Viking up and over if you've a mind.'

'Of course,' replied Commander Maxwell.

69

'Terry Anwhari,' introduced Boyd. 'His parents are from Pakistan but he was born in England. Terry speaks Arabic - Farsi - and has an excellent record as a detective in the West Midlands. He made significant inroads into the Muslim community and earned their respect and admiration despite the fact that he has no religious beliefs himself. This is his job. His informant tells us the proceeds of a successful robbery today will be used to finance terrorism abroad – probably sending youngsters living here to fight for Islamic State in the Middle East.'

Terry brushed past everyone and made for the door declaring, 'I'm riding point, channel twenty one.'

'Cheers, Terry,' acknowledged Boyd. 'Ricky French,' revealed Boyd. 'He's ex Flying Squad with a lot of informants in the criminal underworld and one or two tricks up his sleeve. He's the newcomer to the squad and, for your information he's studying a Master's degree in criminology. Not bad for a man in his mid-twenties.'

The register snapped shut. The job was on. They were gone from the office bound for Bethnal Green.

When the door finally closed and only a hinge squeaked, Detective Superintendent Sandra Peel eyed Commander Maxwell and proposed, 'Boyd and his cohort don't mince words do they? I see I'm going to have my work cut out with that individual. Where did you say he was from – Cumbernauld?'

Softening his voice slightly, Edwin Maxell replied, 'Cumbria, not Cumbernauld! I've never actually worked with Boyd before this posting, Sandra, but I'm told by my predecessor - Commander Herbert - that Boyd is something of an exception when compared to your average detective. He is quite unique apparently, something of a lone ranger and almost definitely a crusader in one sense of the word. Yet he is also an individual who carries the entire department with him. Have you read his personal file yet? His achievements are quite astounding and between you and me, I have quite taken to him.'

'Really!' remarked Peel. 'We'll see. I'm his first line supervisor now. I'll familiarise myself with the firearms procedure. I see no reason why a chief inspector should have such power particularly when I am a superintendent and responsible for him.'

'It's an agreed procedure with the Commissioner of the Metropolitan Police, all chief constables and the Home Office,' explained Maxwell. 'This is the Special Crime Unit. They work all over the country, superintendent and certainly haven't time to call at every police force in the United Kingdom to tell the relevant chief constable that they are carrying firearms.'

'I see,' accepted Peel. 'Tell me, commander, is Boyd a complete self-opinionated idiot who also happens to be a plain and simple racist?'

'I think not,' replied Maxwell. 'His wife is a former nursing sister and they have many friends from different cultures. In fact I think you'll find that they called his daughter Izzy after the doctor who delivered her: Doctor Ismail Farooq, I believe.'

'And the boy,' probed Peel. 'Did they call him Buddha by any chance?'

'Now who's being self-opinionated idiot?'

'A slip of the tongue, sir.'

'This is no ordinary office, Sandra. These officers do an extraordinary job. They are under-funded and short staffed but they will still bite your tongue off if they've a mind to.'

'Will they indeed?'

'Yes, but then you might like to know that Boyd called his son James after the last commander who retired recently – Commander James Hebert - They were great friends apparently.'

'I see,' replied Peel. 'Well I don't necessarily do friendship if it interferes with work, sir. I'll keep a fresh mind and may come up with some new ideas.'

'Of course, be my guest,' agreed the commander. 'Sadly, the unit hasn't had a superintendent for a while. Poor Mac died some years ago and we had immense trouble trying to find someone to fit the bill.'

'Then I came along.'

'Precisely! You were available as they say, and the commissioner decided we needed a superintendent.'

'I may need to rattle some cages, commander.'

'So be it if that is the case,' agreed the commander. 'My advice might be to keep your mind in gear and your tongue in neutral for the time being. You've been warned and you've already seen how they react.'

Dodging through the capital's traffic towards Bethnal Green, Anthea drove whilst Boyd radioed instructions to his team. Eventually, he turned to his colleague and revealed, 'Anthea, I've got a little job for you. It's your speciality.'

'Such as?' she probed. 'Pick my replacement?'

'No, not yet! Sandra Peel, the new boss?'

'No!' snapped Anthea shaking her head. 'The pips on my shoulder took a long time to get and now you want me to risk them on some crazy whim of yours about the new boss.'

'I…' voiced Boyd before he was cut off.

'Don't,' suggested an abrasive Anthea. 'I don't care if she's a spy from an internal investigation unit. I don't even care if she's a spy for the Home Office. It's a no. No-one is taking the Bath Stars from my shoulder and that's all there is to it.'

The drove in silence for a few minutes before Anthea added, 'And my pension.'

The persistent Boyd eventually mentioned the subject again.

'I need to know everything there is to know about her – Everything,' revealed Boyd.

'No! Not again! No!'

'Look she's been vetted by the top floor and everyone in between but she's a new broom and I want to know where she's likely to sweep, that's all,' explained Boyd.

'It's not ethical,' countered Anthea.

'No, she's not,' replied Boyd.

'I mean making enquires about the new boss doesn't seem right,' twisted Anthea uncomfortably.

'Anthea?' delved Boyd.

'When do you need to know?'

'As soon as possible!'

'Do you know I haven't been to that Portuguese restaurant in Euston for ages,' suggested Anthea conspiratorially.

'I'll pick you up Thursday night, about 8 o'clock,' suggested Boyd.

'Absolutely! Leave it with me, Boyd.'

'Thanks, I knew I could count on you,' replied Boyd.

'Give me strength,' whispered Anthea.

A wireless buzzed quietly in the background as Boyd punched buttons into a console and a map of the area came to life on the dashboard.

'Terry?' radioed Boyd.

A mile ahead, Terry Anwhari replied, 'At scene, our two tangos are on the plot outside. The getaway car is parked outside the post office. Tango three is the sole occupant. It's a three litre silver Mercedes just like the source said it would be.'

'All received,' replied Boyd. 'All units Tango One and Tango Two are at the scene. Tango Three is the driver of Victor One parked outside the post office. Break! Break! Break!'

The unit broke ranks and began to approach the post office from different pre-determined angles. At first they turned into side roads and ran parallel with each other as they approached the target, but then they split and converged from different directions.

Spinning back into the main road Anthea hit the brakes when a protest march of some kind took up the carriageway. About a hundred people occupied part of the roadway and marched towards them with flags and banners.

'What the hell is this?' bellowed Boyd. 'There's no March or demonstration on today's route planner.'

'It looks like a march in support of the Ukrainian war effort against the Russians,' explained Anthea.

Unable to translate the language emanating from the crowd Boyd saw the flag waving and singing and presumed they were in support of the Ukraine.

'Back her up, Anthea,' said Boyd. 'Take another route!'

But Anthea had other ideas, lowered the driver's window, placed a metallic blue light on the car roof, switched the car headlights on full, and ploughed down the offside of the road against the flow of traffic.

'I don't do reverse,' she quipped, snatching a lower gear. 'We need to be first in line not second.'

Approaching traffic veered to the nearside and mounted the pavement providing Anthea with an opportunity to floor the accelerator. Within moments the singing flag waving marchers were in the rear view mirror.

'Jeez,' murmured Boyd. 'I should have stayed in the office with the new super and the boss.'

Anthea took a left and then a right down an alleyway before gently bringing the car to a standstill opposite a post office in Bethnal Green.

'We're in position,' she radioed and then advised, 'Terry, we see you at our two o'clock.'

'Roger that! Tangos One and Two are inside,' radioed Terry. 'Victor One has its engine running with Tango Three at the driver's wheel, more soon.'

Janice burst onto the radio with, 'I'll take Victor One out as instructed. I am in position.'

Last to arrive at the scene, Ricky French radioed, 'At the rear and in position.'

Looking at Anthea, Boyd asked his inspector, 'Ready?'

'Ready,' she replied, dipping the throttle slightly.

Boyd radioed, 'This is Boyd. We are in position. Terry, you have control.'

'Roger that,' replied Terry Anwhari. 'All units, I have control. Stand by!'

A police helicopter appeared high in the sky and joined the radio conversation confirming the crew was providing coverage, videoing proceedings, and able to assist should the need arise. A bus came to a standstill nearby to discharge its passengers about thirty yards from the post office. Otherwise the street was fairly quiet for the time of day. The post office was situated in a building at the end of a terrace. Outside the building there were two red post boxes and a stamp dispensing machine. The corner was protected by a metal pedestrian barrier dividing the carriageway from the footpath.

'Stand by! Stand by!' radioed Terry Anwhari. 'I hear screams from inside the building. I'm taking a closer look. Wait! Wait! Wait!'

Somewhere in a surveillance car a heart began to beat a little faster, adrenalin gathered for the next rush, and a throttle dipped when Anthea's foot tickled the pedal.

'Looks like we made it just in time,' whispered Anthea.

'Well done! Here goes,' murmured Boyd waiting for a radio signal.

Terry Anwhari removed an extendable monocle from an inside pocket and raised it to his good eye. With a slight focus the images intensified and he swept the interior of Bethnal Green post office. He reported, 'Two tangos armed with sawn offs; two staff behind the counter, a woman and child in the corner at my two o'clock and one elderly male now moving to the opposite corner. Be advised two tangos and five victims. Stand by!'

Inside the post office Ahmed Massoon and Khair al Din Mustafa held their sawn off shotguns at waist height as staff filled a large black holdall with bank notes. Terrified, a woman and child cowered in one corner of the room whilst an old age pensioner froze by the counter completely traumatised by the whole affair.

'Hurry up!' ordered Ahmed thrusting his weapon towards the sub-postmaster in a threatening manner.

In the street outside, Ali Waleed sat patiently with his hands on the steering wheel of a stolen three litre Mercedes waiting for his colleagues to appear. The nearside doors were unlocked and partially open and had been so arranged to give the trio a good advantage when they left the scene. Escape in this scenario was all about leaving the area quickly.

Ali became suspicious when he saw Terry Anwhari looking through the post office window with what appeared to be some kind of tubular device.

With a click of a radio switch, Terry radioed, 'All units, Strike! Strike! Strike!'

On the first shout of strike Janice Burns surged her gun metal grey BMW series five down the tarmac headlong towards the waiting Mercedes. On the second shout of strike Ricky French entered the rear of the premises by the back door. On the third strike call Boyd and Anthea raced their Volvo T5 straight towards the front door of the post office.

When Ahmed and Khair stepped backwards from the post office counter with their loot secure in a holdall they turned to see Janice Burns stepping out of her BMW holding a shotgun.

Immediately, Ahmed swivelled his weapon around.

Ali saw Janice approaching. She was carrying a shoulder-high pump action shotgun. Deciding his freedom was more important than that of his friends, Ali slammed the Mercedes into reverse.

Janice tightened the shotgun into her shoulder and pulled both triggers. A couple of slugs raced from the barrels, penetrated the radiator, and blew a hole in the Mercedes engine block rendering it useless. Calmly, Janice walked towards the Mercedes totally oblivious to all around, reloaded, and fired two more slugs into the engine block. Twenty yards later, still trying to escape in reverse, and at a pathetic crawl, the Mercedes finally ground to a halt. An explosion of hot steam liberated itself from the radiator and, complimented by a noisy rattle from the remnants of the engine, finally signalled surrendered.

Janice swiftly reloaded and broke into a steady trot with her shotgun held at waist height. Ignoring the scene developing behind her, Janice shouted, 'Armed police! You are under arrest! Hands! Show me your hands!'

Reluctantly, terrified of this formidable woman running towards him and threatening his very existence, Ali, the Mercedes driver, thrust both hands out of the driver's side window as Janice approached him. Firmly, the Scot radioed, 'Victor One is down. Tango Three is compliant. Stand by!'

Approaching the car door, Janice levelled the shotgun at the man's head and snarled, 'Don't you even twitch, ma bonnie lad.'

Meanwhile, Anthea had gunned the Volvo straight across the carriageway and onto the kerb outside the post office. Both she and Boyd jumped from their car, used the doors as shields, and withdrew their weapons.

Simultaneously, Terry was at a side window looking directly into the building. He shouted, 'Armed police! You are surrounded! Drop your weapons!'

Immediately, Ricky burst into the post office from the rear door and took cover behind the counter. With his gun drawn he screamed, 'Armed police! Down! Throw your weapons down!'

Ahmed and Khair were stunned to realise their escape route was blocked by the front bonnet of a blue Volvo and four armed police officers pointing guns at them.

Dropping his shotgun Khair immediately held his hands up.

Ahmed retreated towards the back door, raised his sawn off, and pulled the trigger.

Simultaneously, Ricky French pulled the trigger but his weapon misfired and all he could hear was a dull 'Click!' when the trigger mechanism failed to respond. Glass above the wooden counter shattered into a thousand pieces and littered the floor. The female customer threw herself across a child and acted as a shield.

Taking advantage of the Volvo's armoured car doors, Boyd and Anthea levelled their weapons before Ahmed spun round to face them with his shotgun. Anthea immediately drilled a bullet into Ahmed's thigh.

They raced forward when Ahmed was thrown back with the force, screamed in agony, dropped his shotgun, and clutched his thigh.

Anthea kicked away his shotgun, overturned Ahmed, and handcuffed him as Ricky took Khair to the ground and manacled Ahmed's co-conspirator.

Outside, Janice engaged the Mercedes driver again. 'Lie face down on the ground now,' she shouted before Terry moved in and applied the handcuffs.

'Clear!' shouted Ricky.

'Clear!' shouted Anthea.

'Clear!' echoed Terry. 'We are all clear. You have control, Guvnor.'

'Roger, I have control,' radioed Boyd. 'Boyd to base, shots fired. One Tango injured, ambulance and senior supervisors to scene. Three Tangos in custody. We have control. Lift the blanket.'

'All received Team Alpha,' radioed Commander Maxwell from base. 'Lifting the blanket! Stand by for local back up.'

Three minutes of manic mayhem ended but the wireless signal had hardly diluted into the ether when wailing sirens filled the air. Local borough personnel whistled into the area and dominated the street.

Moments later two prisoners were in police vans, weapons and cash had been recovered, and an ambulance containing an escorted prisoner was on its way to a nearby hospital.

'Congratulations, Terry,' said Boyd. 'Excellent execution!' Turning to Ricky, Boyd probed, 'What happened to you? Did your weapon misfire or did you freeze?'

'The gun, Guvnor,' explained Ricky awkwardly. 'It misfired. That's never happened before.'

'There will be an enquiry,' advised Boyd. 'Internal Discipline and Professional Standards will be all over us as usual. They'll want to know why we planned it the way we did, why shots were fired and someone was hurt, and why your gun jammed.'

'What did I do wrong?' asked Ricky.

'Yeah, we took the escape car out first and contained the building. What's wrong with that?' asked Terry Anwhari.

'Nothing as far as I can see,' replied Boyd. 'But experience suggests someone will recommend we should have put half a dozen uniforms outside the post office and stopped the robbery in the first place. Not to worry, it's standard operating procedure when weapons are used. Be assured someone somewhere will present an infallible plan and tell us this is what we should have done. Problem is we seldom have time to plan perfection and the opposition have a bad habit of not coming quietly.'

Placing a consoling hand on Ricky's shoulder Boyd looked at them both and advised, 'You'd best get used to this because our commander will already have told Internal Investigations that we've just conducted a trigger operation. Just remember that today you dented plans by Islamic extremists to raise money for terrorism. That's what the job is about. We know we're going to be scrutinised now, probably by someone with a rule book as thick as Encyclopaedia Britannica. It's the price we pay for a peaceful democracy, my friends.'

A squad car pulled up and a superintendent stepped from the vehicle towards Boyd saying, 'I'm the investigator appointed by Internal Discipline and Professional Standards. I've been tasked to report upon your operation today since weapons were fired. Which one of you is in charge?'

'That would be me,' replied Boyd.

'Your weapons please?' demanded the investigator.

'Of course! Anything to oblige,' replied Boyd with a cheeky smile. 'You were quick to attend. Our adrenalin hasn't settled yet.'

On a map of central London a finger might move no more than an inch from Bethnal Green to find Whitehall. It was a mere four miles away.

It was here that Ivan Pushkin walked the streets. Dressed in dark corduroy jeans, a roll neck sweater and black leather blouson jacket, Ivan strolled casually towards Whitehall.

On the corner of the street Ivan paused apparently waiting for traffic to ease. In his late thirties, his home was situated a short drive from the centre of Moscow in the township of Kaluga, south west of Russia's capital city. Academically sound, Ivan had studied hard at school and was considered a bright young man. It wasn't long before the State Intelligence apparatus realised his potential and recruited him into the GRU – *Glavnoje Razvedyvatel'noje Upravlenije* – the Main Intelligence Directorate of the General Staff of the Armed Forces of the Russian Federation. It was the job of the GRU - the Russian equivalent of MI6 - to gain intelligence from potential enemies in foreign lands.

Ivan Pushkin was a Russian spy who had worked throughout Europe and America, often as a member of a legitimate Russian trade delegation or company representative.

Today, Ivan wasn't wasting his time sight-seeing in the capital city. Neither was he pretending to be interested in the latest technological advances of some western business concern. He was doing what he enjoyed most: spying on the comings and goings at the front door of the Ministry of Defence.

Pausing to light a cigarette, Ivan used a tiny camera hidden in his cigarette lighter to capture an image of a man walking down the steps at the entrance to the Defence Ministry. The subject carried an umbrella and briefcase but was dressed in a two piece suit and bowler hat and assumed an air of importance in his bearing.

Eventually, Ivan casually circumnavigated the entire building remembering the lay out of the structure. He studied the thickness of its walls and the depths of its windows looking for weak access points. For Ivan, it was one thing to study aerial photographs of a building inside a city that you did not know too well. Yet it was quite another to be able to be on the ground where you could touch and feel the target, and get a taste of the enemy's stronghold. Glancing upwards he saw a CCTV camera angled in his direction. He did not change his demeanour because the camera held his pose. Neither did he worry that his image had been captured in digital form. It was immaterial to him for he knew that he would not be the only one framed for eternity by the Ministry of Defence security personnel. Whitehall was alive with people.

Turning from Whitehall Ivan made his way towards some shops where he entered a newsagent and browsed the tourist maps on display. He finally selected a fold up Ordnance Survey map of Surrey and paid in coin at the counter.

With the shop behind him Ivan made the street and studied passing traffic and people walking about. Oh how I love this place, he thought. It's so different to home. I can buy things here that I can only dream about in Moscow. The standard of living in London is so much higher than in Russia. Here I have fine restaurants, health spas, beautiful women, fast cars, casinos, and a hundred different cultures all brought together in one place. Back home I have…. Russia!

Deadpan, without a trace of emotion on his face, Ivan reflected on his assignment as he began walking along the footpath. It was an assignment that lay at the heart of the Russian Intelligence Directorate.

Of course, Ivan knew the GRU gathered human intelligence through military attachés and foreign agents. It also maintains significant signals intelligence (SIGINT) and imagery reconnaissance (IMINT) as well as satellite imagery capabilities. The

GRU Space Intelligence Directorate has put more than 130 SIGINT satellites into orbit. He knew all that.

And yet, despite all that technology, Ivan's mission was a crucial part of Federation plans in the event of war. It was worrying for the intelligence services of the west because the GRU were known to supervise about 25,000 Special Forces troops known as *Spetsnaz*. Whilst there were many ways to gather intelligence about the enemy, one method was to deploy personnel in the field and learn more about one's adversary. The other was to subvert the target population. In the event of war, the first strike might not come from a nuclear missile, thought Ivan. No, it might come from a *Spetsnaz* assassination squad briefed by the GRU to kill the enemy's leaders prior to all-out war or invasion.

Ivan Pushkin was well aware of an individual who lived in Surrey. He had studied his targets well. His next visit would be to Epsom in order to carry out reconnaissance on the home of the Secretary of State for Defence. Such a person was on the list – a list of leaders to be assassinated in a first strike non-nuclear war between the United Kingdom and Russia.

It was just a game, thought Ivan. MI6 in Moscow will be sat watching the comings and goings at the Kremlin, and probably doing the same thing – Gathering intelligence.

Satisfied with his day's observations so far, Ivan pocketed his map, smiled at a young policeman patrolling the street, and made his way towards Grosvenor Square and the American Embassy. His list was long; his assignment on-going. The brief was simple. Find out where Britain's leaders live and update our files. Provide the *Spetsnaz* assassination squads with up to date intelligence. They would pull the trigger when called upon to do so.

Twenty five thousand feet above sea level two Bear bombers from the Russian Air Force suddenly changed direction and swept across the North Sea into British air space.

Moments later, a pair of Tornado F3 jet fighters attached to the Quick Reaction Alert squadron were scrambled from RAF Lossiemouth in Moray, north east Scotland and raced into the grey clouds to escort unwelcome invaders away from British soil.

The Cold War was over, but the daily business of collecting intelligence and / or reacting to the threat was still very much alive.

In the Baltic Sea, the wind howled. Waves hurled themselves over the bow of a Russian Cruiser as it carved its way through the tempestuous water escorting a destroyer. A hundred miles away, two Russian submarines changed direction and made their way to join the fleet. One was a newly commissioned Yasen-class submarine. It was a nuclear-powered multipurpose attack submarine armed with cruise missiles. The other submarine was a Russian Delta class with similar capability. Both vessels were normally stationed in the Crimea. Their formidable weapons were capable of destroying a target with supreme precision many thousands of miles away.

In his cabin, Richard Maynard enjoyed a private moment following a half hour nap. Checking a family photograph by the side of his bunk he wondered how his wife and daughter were getting on. He kissed the photograph and resettled it on the table before hurling himself onto his feet. He squared away his cap, checked his tie, and made for the bridge.

The course of the Baltic Fleet was unchanged. Captain Maynard's NATO force played out their exercise and the might of the Russian Baltic Fleet powered south towards them. Here and there radar screens gradually became peppered with the tell-tale locations of competing vessels.

'Lieutenant,' suggested Captain Maynard. 'Have you seen this? It looks as if the game is well and truly on.'

'It surely does,' replied the lieutenant. 'But how far will they go this time? That's the question.'

In Cumbria, in the north of England, Dina Al-Hakim searched the internet until she found a website she had heard about at the local mosque. It was a site that would only interest those of the Islamic faith an Imam had said. But the Imam had also warned that such a website was an insult to peace-loving Muslims for it carried messages of hate and gave lessons on how travelling a path of evil might result in the destruction of infidels in the west.

On a table beside her Dina studied a photograph of her older sister, Azma. When translated her name meant the 'Blessing of Allah'. Oh how Dina loved and respected her sister. Azma was an inspiration to those who would follow the warriors of Muhammad. Dina studied the photograph which depicted an image of a beautiful young woman wearing black fatigues.

Azma was sat astride the remains of an armoured personnel carrier. The rusting vehicle had been hit by a rocket launcher at close range and completely destroyed. This once proud weapon of war had been consigned to the dustbin and was merely one of many trophies captured in a long and bloody battle.

Kissing the image of her sister, Dina reverently pushed it to one side and reflected on how Azma was one of Muhammad's true warriors. She deserved love and respect. Azma was a heroine.

Opening a notebook, Dina rolled a pencil closer to her as she planned her evening. Only the smooth progressive tap of a keyboard could be heard inside her home in the apartment block on the banks of the River Caldew in Carlisle. Ignoring those towering castle ramparts on the opposite side of a river, Dina eyed her computer screen.

Guiding the mouse, Dina clicked on a link to an evil page that had been spoken of and entered the forbidden chat room. As her evening progressed, Dina began to make notes.

In an office in central London the Head of Barclays Bank Fraud Squad, John Spooner, stared at his computer screen. The bank's main website was frozen and there wasn't a thing his

Information Technology Department could do about it. He'd been told they'd received so many emails and social media communications that their system was clogged. It hadn't been hacked and no data had been stolen, they had told him. Yet it was a wretched state of affairs and the bank's telephone lines were red hot with irate customers unable to access their accounts.

John shook his head in disbelief and looked out across Canary Wharf below. Then he started to laugh. Here I am in Churchill Place, Canary Wharf: the centre of the British financial system. And Churchill Place, presumably it was named after one of the nation's greatest prime ministers: the war time leader Sir Winston Churchill? So here I am standing at the top of a building which can be seen for a hundred miles in any direction. Everyone in London can see this building and its two friends standing alongside it. It's an iconic view of the capital and all the financial wherewithal that goes with it. Yet I can't make a mouse move and I can't even log into my bank account. What's more our phone system is knackered too. It's a joke gone too far, he decided.

It was an anomaly he had some experience of. Generally speaking, he reminded himself, the volume of customers had reached a point where more server capacity was need to cater for the internet cravings of the bank's customers. But then again he was no fool. It might also mean that the website was being surveyed by a criminal cyber-gang. He wasn't sure which way to turn.

Without more ado John Spooner spun round, grabbed the telephone, and rang the National Cyber Crime Unit which sits within the National Crime Agency in South East London.

The number rang out as John glanced idly through the window of the tall elegant building to see a drizzle of rain begin its downward pattern on the glass.

Out in the desert there was no sign of rain.

It had been a long walk through the heat of the day and the chill of the night but Salman was nearing the pick-up point now.

He'd deliberately avoided all main routes and gradually negotiated a network of low wadis to stay hidden and out of sight of prying eyes, aeroplanes, and enemy drones. Using these gullies and dry riverbeds Salman had escaped the horrific insanity of war-torn Tikrit. Now he neared salvation, an amphora of cold water, food and fresh clothing, and a new challenge.

Shouldering his rifle Salman dropped to the ground when he heard the scrape of a boot on nearby tarmac. Belly down he hugged the ground before furtively crawling forward. He used the natural lie of the land to his advantage. As the desert gradually rose an inch, Salman lifted his head and presented the smallest target possible. Then he saw his contact and dropped back down again.

The man who would drive him quickly to the next stage was standing near his jeep smoking, and blethering idly on his mobile phone.

Salman moved position, listened, and crept closer watching his contact. Eventually it dawned on Salman that his contact was totally unaware of his presence. An amateur, thought Salman. I ask for professionals and they give me camel droppings to work with.

Five minutes later, the contact was still gossiping aimlessly on his mobile phone.

Salman had observed his contact long enough. He crawled most of the way, approached from the rear, and then suddenly stood up and cupped the man's mouth with his hand. Simultaneously, his dagger caressed the contact's throat when he said, 'I am late but you have no eyes and no ears. You are an imbecile who has no desire inside to win. You are a loser, my friend. You are not worth bartering for camel droppings. Do you live or die?"

Sweating, trembling, a cigarette fell to the ground and the contact pissed himself before nodding and flashing his eyes in an attempt to make contact with Salman.

Gradually, Salman withdrew his blade and said, 'No more of this. Take me to the rendezvous and keep your eyes and ears open all the way. I promise you that Allah has empowered me to kill any man who cannot fulfil the task for his warriors. You do understand don't you?'

Terrified, the Arab contact jumped into the driver's seat of a Jeep and fired its engine.

'Now drive,' ordered Salman. 'We know where we are going. Take me there and do not speak to me for I have nothing to say to a man who may have no tongue when the journey is done.'

Meanwhile, someone somewhere switched on a television set to catch up with the latest news. A programme informed the audience that Barclays Bank was having a 'slight problem' with its website and wished to apologise to their customers. Normal service would resume as soon as possible. It was just a minor technical glitch that would be resolved shortly.

Another individual tuned in the radio to listen to the sports news. Others read a newspaper to consider the latest promises from the political heartland. Many merely tuned in to get their regular dose of soap opera.

Residents of the United Kingdom continued their daily routine. The majority were totally oblivious to the true meaning of a day in the life of a nation at Threat Level Three.

*

Chapter Four
~

The Republic of Ireland
The following day
Threat Level Three - Substantial

Touch down at Dublin airport was smooth and without incident when Antonia Harston-Brown travelled to meet one of her primary sources of intelligence in the Republic: her agent, the Quarryman. Wearing a dark coloured trouser suit she looked something of a business woman as she made her way to the terminal building carrying only a shoulder bag. Her red hair billowed in the breeze as a door opened automatically and she entered.

Passing quickly through customs and passport control Antonia presented herself at a hire car desk and explained she had come to collect a car. She produced a passport and driving licence which were not in her name but did carry a photograph of her taken about twelve months earlier. Producing a copy of a hire agreement, Antonia waited whilst the female receptionist slipped away for a moment or two before returning with a gentleman wearing a grey three piece suit.

Every inch a businessman, the man spoke in a deep Irish accent and promptly handed Antonia a set of car keys and a complimentary map of Ireland. Moments later, he escorted Antonia through a marble esplanade into a car lot where he pointed to an area saying, 'Row C, Bay 61, take care and enjoy your trip.'

Antonia expressed her gratitude and made for the car which she unlocked. Adjusting the driver's seat, she then threw the map in the glove compartment and felt beneath her seat.

Smoothing her hands beneath the frayed leather, Antonia felt a handgun taped to the bottom of the driver's seat. With a slight tug, she gathered the weapon into her possession, checked it was loaded, and slid it into her rear trouser band. She reached again to the underside of the seat, found extra ammunition, and pocketed it.

Driving off northwards, skirting Swords, Antonia left the airport behind her and made for a coast road and a highway that guided her towards the six counties of Ulster. Close to Dundalk, still in the Republic, Antonia moved inland towards the border and the predominantly IRA county of South Armagh.

Weaving through a bizarre network of narrow minor roads that criss-crossed the border with Northern Ireland, Antonia eventually guided her vehicle towards a village located close to the border. The area was well known amongst the angling fraternity since it boasted some good fishing locations for those dedicated to their hobby.

Antonia slowed her vehicle and retrieved the gun from the trouser band at the small of her back. Double checking that it was loaded she slid it under her right thigh so that the weapon was immediately accessible to her. On reaching the crossroads at Crossnalogan she took a left towards a river. A few miles further down this road, as arranged, she located the Quarryman walking towards her carrying a fishing rod and a box of fishing tackle.

Tall and muscular, the Quarryman, Donal McArthy, looked every inch a lady's man. His long blond hair and deep blue eyes merely added to his natural good looks. A long-time supporter of the IRA, Donal had once been a member of an active service unit in the Province some years earlier. Now, disenchanted with an organisation who, in his eyes, had failed to accomplish total freedom from the British, Donal happily provided intelligence on the Republican Movement in exchange for cash. For Donal, it was purely a financial arrangement that drove him to collate information and pass it on.

Antonia, who prudently accepted such insider knowledge, realised it was a constant challenge to remain discreet at all costs. Personal security and the safety of her source were upmost in her mind for she knew it was incredibly dangerous for people like

Donal to work for the intelligence services. Informants uncovered by the IRA and its offshoots were considered to be traitors to the cause and often murdered by their colleagues. Yet Antonia knew that the biggest chink in Donal's armour was not a reluctance to carry out personal security to safeguard their clandestine operations. Rather, it was something quite worrying to Antonia for she knew that Donal McArthy was a womaniser who couldn't be trusted.

Checking her mirror Antonia drove past her agent. About two miles further on, she turned around and headed back in the same direction. This time she scrutinised the fields and passing places that might harbour her enemy, or anyone suspicious of the Quarryman and herself. Vigilantly she studied her rear view mirror, and the fields and countryside on both her nearside and offside. Eventually, Antonia eyed the man as she approached him for the second time but she drove right past without acknowledging his presence.

Satisfied it was him, and not a stunt double, Antonia slid into a parking area and waited.

Moments later the Quarryman opened the nearside door and climbed into the vehicle beside her. Snatching first gear Antonia immediately drove off.

'Donal,' said Antonia, 'How are you, my friend?'

'Good, so I am,' he replied, 'And you, good lady?'

'As well as can be expected in the circumstances,' replied Antonia. 'You wanted the meet, Donal. Now please cut the references to 'good lady'. It means you want something. What have you got for me?'

'What have you got for me?' countered Donal.

'The usual, a sum of money as previously agreed between us has been deposited in your private account. It all adds up and it's interest bearing. One day it will be yours to do with as you please. Now tell me what is so important that you insisted that I came across the water to see you?'

'I need to get out soon and I've been around long enough to know that you're the only one I can trust to help me do it. I want you to do whatever you need to do to free up the money in my account and get me out of here safely.'

'Why?' asked Antonia. 'What's happened?'

'My brother in law, Seamus, is suspicious,' explained Donal. 'I've decided it's time to make the break while I still can, so I have.'

'Suspicious?' probed Antonia checking her rear view mirror.

'No, not of us,' declared Donal chuckling. 'Callum Finnerty knows I'm seeing another woman, so I am.'

'You've had affairs before, Donal. They usually last a month or so before you come to your senses.'

'This time it's different,' offered Donal.

'I thought you were happily married to Seamus's sister? What's her name – Colleen?'

'Hi, Colleen it is. But sure now, I met someone else,' offered the Irishman. 'The problem is Callum Finnerty has told Seamus I'm having an affair. It's time for me to pack up and get out before things come to head, so it is.'

'Does Colleen know?'

'No, and I'll not be telling her.'

'You've chased women before, Donal, but never had a problem. Can't you pass it off as a one-night stand?'

'No! Can you help me or not, woman?'

'It's not that easy,' explained Antonia. 'I can't make it happen that quickly for you and in any case I'm not best pleased you've brought me all the way to the back of beyond to tell me you're chasing another woman. I came because I thought you had something important to tell me, not to sort out your love life and a failing marriage.'

'Oh there's that and all, so there is,' revealed Donal. 'London soon!'

'Bollocks!' snapped Antonia slipping into a lower gear and slowing the vehicle. 'I could have got change out of a pound in

Kilburn or Brent for information like that. London? Wow! Get out, Donal. You've had a free ride but I've just called time. Now move it because you're just a conman trying it on with the wrong person.'

'Okay! Okay! I'll tell you what I know,' offered Donal with a slight hint of panic in his voice.

'Where, when and who?' probed Antonia angrily as she squeezed the accelerator.

'Shopping centres in central London,' volunteered Donal. 'But there's talk of hitting someone at the very top.'

'Do you mean the Prime Minister or someone else?' asked Antonia.

'Your guess is as good as mine,' replied Donal. 'It could be a military chief for all I know. I'm not as well connected as I would like to be. But it's a family thing.'

'What do you mean a family thing?' queried Antonia.

'Seamus Logan is the man pulling the strings on this one,' declared Donal.

'Yes, you've spoken of him before,' Antonia admitted. 'I'd like to know more about him.'

'And so you should,' remarked Donal. 'His brigade, if you can call it that, is his family and a bunch of carefully selected family friends. Take the Teacher, for example. He's an older brother of Seamus yet no-one seems to know his real name. Whenever someone queries the name they are blanked or are told not to ask such questions. And then there's his cousin Declan.'

'We are aware of the Teacher,' commented Antonia. 'But I'd like to hear everything you know about him today. We'll make time, Donal. Now what can you tell me about this man Declan?'

'Find Declan O'Malley and you'll find out who the true target of Seamus Logan's mind-blowing plot is. O'Malley is over the water watching and looking out for Seamus, the Teacher and the rest of their family. I think you'll find O'Malley in London, so I do, but I can't be sure. All I know is that O'Malley is no longer an active soldier in the sense of being the one who pulls the trigger.

Sure, these days he's a spotter for Seamus and the boys. All I'd say is that O'Malley will know who the target is because it's O'Malley who has marked the target if you understand me?'

'Oh yes, a carefully selected target reconnoitred by a volunteer and earmarked for demolition,' defined Antonia.

'Sure, that's it, so it is,' replied Donal.

'The time frame?' probed Antonia.

'Soon, that's all I've heard. For what it's worth, I'd say within the next or week or so but you never know. It could be tomorrow the way they work.'

'And the method?' asked Antonia.

'Today the Teacher taught us about a command line explosion. He ran a wire from explosives beneath a car, fixed them to the plunger, and blew a car sky high. He told us he used four pound of Semtex. Tomorrow he's teaching us how to use a long range sniper rifle. You can take your choice. Sure, I wouldn't know how it will be done.'

'That's a big help,' said Antonia shaking her head. 'No help at all as well you know. What are the chances of you being selected to be in the team that carry out the attack or even volunteering for it?'

'Slim,' revealed Donal, 'Very slim! Seamus is a clever man, so he is. I think it's possible that some us that are taking lessons from the Teacher might be in the next wave but it's a family affair right now, and I'm not family. Apart from that I want out now.'

'Do you think they know you are a tout?'

'No, I'm safe that way,' revealed Donal. 'But Seamus won't like it when he knows I'm leaving his sister.'

'Okay, let's give this some thought. Now tell me everything you know about the Teacher, Seamus, Declan, and all those people the Teacher is training. I want to know everything, Donal.'

Donal nodded and Antonia activated a recording device. The redhead drove. Donal talked. An hour later, they returned to the crossroads where they parted company. Job done, Antonia headed for the airport whilst Donal returned to his fishing.

Back in the office of the Special Crime Unit Boyd debriefed the team in the presence of Commander Maxwell and Superintendent Peel. He explained how the robbery and shooting would be the subject of an enquiry from Internal Discipline and noted how both of his supervisors agreed with the standard operational procedure. That said, some wondered why the State authorised police use of firearms to uphold the law and then put in place such stringent procedures every time they were used.

When the telephone rang it was Antonia who updated the unit about news of the planned attack. She explained her written report, and a transcript of a conversation with her source, were in the pipeline. Intelligence had been gleaned from the Quarryman but how true was it, she wondered, and how much of it could be checked out and validated?

Half an hour later a formal print out of Antonia's report hit the commander's basket.

Boyd asked of Commander Maxwell, 'In view of Toni's report, commander, where do you see the primary threat coming from today – Irish terrorists or Islamic extremists?'

'Today, tomorrow, this week, next week, I don't really know at this precise moment, William,' replied Maxwell. 'It's one thing to know or suspect something and quite another to be able to prove it. I think we need to have a careful look at this and see what else we have on the subject. Meanwhile, I'd like to try and find this Declan O'Malley as a matter of urgency. Begin with the usual formal sources – national insurance, employment, benefits, that kind of thing. Is he living on the mainland overtly or has he disappeared into the woodwork? I suspect the latter but we'll need to start somewhere. Jump on it now please.'

'We might already have a file on him, sir,' suggested Boyd. 'Leave it with me, commander. I'll see what we can shake up.'

'Soon,' snapped Sandra Peel officiously. 'Indeed, now!'

Boyd replied with a stark stare.

Commander Maxwell answered a phone ringing on his desk, introduced himself, listened, and turned to his colleagues saying, 'That was the commissioner. Our unit has been earmarked to bolster security at the forthcoming G8 convention in Shanklin on the Isle of Wight.'

'Wonderful,' replied Boyd. 'I thought that was essentially a crowd control thing for the uniform section – riot control officers and the like - Why us, commander?'

'Because it's our turn, William,' explained Edwin Maxwell. 'The commissioner tells me it's a threat to the security of the nation. He would like us very much to be aware of the event and get involved as necessary. I knew you'd be pleased.'

'What exactly is G8, sir?' asked Peel.

Commander Maxwell chuckled sarcastically and replied, 'Oh dear! You really do need some savvy of global politics to work in this office effectively, Sandra.'

'I'm beginning to see that,' replied the superintendent. 'But G8 is the kind of organisation that you hear about from television. It goes in one ear and out the other, sorry!'

'I'll try and put it in a nutshell,' explained Maxwell, 'The Group of Seven - G7, formerly G8 - is a governmental forum of leading advanced economies in the world. It was originally formed in 1975 by six leading industrial countries – France, West Germany, Italy, Japan, the UK and the USA. Then Canada joined a year later and it became G7. It became G8 when Russia joined in 1998.'

'Confused?' queried Boyd of Peel. 'I am.'

Superintendent Peel shook her head in dismay.

Commander Maxwell withdrew a file from his desk drawer and handed it to Peel. Removing a pair of spectacles from her handbag she began reading the document as Maxwell continued with an explanation.

'Politicians never make anything straightforward, William,' suggested Commander Maxwell. 'Anyway, Sandra, Russia upset everyone with their invasion of the Crimean Peninsula in 2014. When they wouldn't pull out of the Ukraine the group suspended them and various sanctions have been imposed on the Russians ever since. I suspect that's why they get awfully upset with us from time to time. Presently, the G8 in effect comprises seven nations and the European Union is the eighth member.'

'What's in the job for us?' asked Boyd.

'Historically,' revealed Maxwell, 'Antagonists complain that G8 do not do enough to help global problems such as Third World Debt, global warming and the AIDS epidemic. That's all to do with the fact that developed countries operate strict procedures when it comes to medicine patent policy and suchlike. Over the years it's attracted every Tom, Dick and Harry in the world to come and protest about anything and everything. I'm sure we'll be called in to assist surveillance on some of those with more anarchistic views than the rest of society.'

'That's all we need,' remarked Boyd. 'We've enough on our plate at the moment. I heard on the radio today that the banking system seems to be the target of some sort of cyberattack from an unknown enemy. I presume the computer whizz kids are fighting that one, commander?'

'Oh it gets much worse, William,' declared Commander Maxwell. 'Intelligence analysts suggest an attack on the stability of the county is highly likely. We are in the middle of a cyberattack on out infrastructure, an increased threat from the Russians which Antonia is now aware of, and a whole host of other titbits of intelligence that don't paint a nice picture. Accordingly, the national threat level has been raised to Threat Level Two.'

'Russians?' queried Boyd. 'Antonia is handling some kind of Russian case by the sound of it, sir?'

'Of course,' replied the commander. 'It's what the Security Service do best. She'll call when she wants us, Boyd. The lady knows what she's doing.'

Boyd nodded and made a mental note of another threat in the pipeline.

Out in the desert, many miles from Tikrit, a black muddy Jeep backfired noisily before pulling up in a shallow riverbed. Weary, Salman yanked on the handbrake and got out of the vehicle. He dropped to his knees and filled a water bottle from the sparsely trickling stream. Cupping both hands, he drank his fill. Eventually, Salman stood up, shaded his eyes with the palm of his hand, and made out the settlement ahead. He did not look back but set off at a fast pace with his eyes firmly on the path ahead. He would be there by nightfall.

Behind him, in the driver's seat of the Jeep, a volunteer of Islamic State lay slumped in the front seat of the vehicle. His throat was cut from ear to ear and his tongue had been pulled through to hang grotesquely on his chest.

The man would not speak again either in person or on his mobile phone. The contact was a victim of an assassin who took no prisoners in the war that he fought.

Salman had decided that the risk of discovery was too great. The man had paid the price of speech.

*

Chapter Five
~

London
Early the next day.
Threat Level Two - Severe

Dawn tinted the sky a feeble purple haze but eventually left a damp clingy atmosphere to haunt the capital's streets. Undaunted, the morning rush hour shrouded the highways leading into London. Tube trains also shared the brunt of the daily commute to work. They were at full capacity when they arrived at various underground stations and surrendered their human cargo onto the packed platforms. Such was life in the race to reach the office; the factory, or the shop as people hurried and scurried in different directions. The city was alive with people tied up with their own personal thoughts, their hopes, aspirations, dreams, and fears for the day ahead. Life in the twenty-first century was all go.

A grey Skoda Octavia was the first to arrive in the fast food drive-through restaurant car park that morning. Its driver selected a vacant spot in the middle of the parking area, locked his door, and walked away. Aged in his mid-fifties, he wore dark trainers, denim jeans, and a dark hooded top which he pulled close to his face.

Simultaneously, a light blue Hyundai negotiated a ramp and climbed to the fifth floor of a multi-storey car park overlooking central London. The car park boasted ten floors. The driver collected a ticket on entering the car park but left the scene on foot. He too wore dark trainers, denim jeans, and a dark grey hoodie pulled tight to his face.

Both car parks soon filled up as commuters and shoppers gradually slotted into vacant parking bays and went about their business. It was breakfast time for some and work time for others.

Forty five minutes after the vehicles were parked, John Carter ordered an all-day breakfast at the drive-in restaurant whilst Pat Bainbridge parked on the fifth floor of the multi storey ready to walk the last three hundred yards to the office. Neither was prepared for what happen.

The two vehicles exploded within three minutes of each other. It was carnage!

One person was killed walking across the car park of the fast food restaurant going to meet John Carter inside. Another twenty five were injured. Six vehicles in the area of the car park were severely damaged. Glass at the front and sides of the restaurant sprinkled the tarmac area when the undercar bomb exploded with an almighty bang.

When the car bomb detonated in the multi-storey car park an attempt to bring down the sixth floor on top of all the vehicles failed. Yet the South Korean engine block was blown out of the Hyundai and, with the force of four pounds of Semtex explosives behind it, embedded itself in the ceiling of the fifth floor close to Pat Bainbridge's Vauxhall. No-one was killed in the area but twenty two individuals were hospitalised from falling debris and cuts from falling glass fragments. More than twenty others suffered from severe shock.

The first police officer to respond to the fast food restaurant bomb was driving there for his breakfast too. With six months service in, Constable Lenny White was physically sick at the sight of death and severely injured people in amongst the destruction. No amount of training at Hendon Police College would have prepared him for such an event, said his colleagues.

As emergency calls flooded the 999 system, a fleet of ambulances rushed to both scenes. Two local hospitals were put on a high state of alert when the expectation of patients soon became a reality. It was no sudden routine drill. It was the real thing. Beds, doctors, and surgeons, became an urgent priority.

The first responder to the multi-storey car park bomb was a veteran traffic patrol officer with twenty-seven years' service. Bob Russell's experience and training reminded him to close down the car park immediately and protect those in the immediate vicinity from falling debris and the possibility of building collapse. Bob's colleagues reported that his actions probably saved dozens from death or injury when a section of wall eventually dislodged and fell from the fifth floor to the ground below ten minutes after the explosion occurred. The brickwork collapsed into an area the veteran had closed off with three hastily deployed traffic cones and a hazard warning sign. Eventually, both locations were designated major crime scenes and experienced forensic teams moved in.

Detectives established at an early stage that the two vehicles had been stolen from the Watford area during the previous month. No effort had been made to change the identity of either vehicle. Search and Evidence teams soon located registration plates near the scene of the explosions and quickly confirmed the authenticity of the vehicles.

One hour after the explosions a telephone rang in the office of The Times newspaper. An Irish voice claimed responsibility for both car bombs stating they were the work of the New Front for Irish Independence. The caller was male and gave the registration number of both vehicles involved in the incident in order to authenticate his call. He then used a password and made it clear the same password would be used in the future. It was a clear signal that this was the start of a new campaign and not a one-off occurrence. The line went dead before the reporter could ask a single question. Five minutes later the same voice made an identical call to the Control Room of New Scotland Yard in Broadway, Victoria and the same conversation took place. Both calls seem to have been made by the same person from the same telephone box close to Euston Railway Station.

Superintendent Sandra Peel attended both bomb scenes and was appointed Senior Investigating Officer. She took immediate charge of the investigation. Assisted by Inspector Anthea Adams, Peel made it clear from the start exactly what she wanted and how determined a lady she was.

'Anthea, I need a bomb scene search team to do a fingertip search of the immediate area with a back-up squad to collect all the evidence. I want a dedicated exhibits officer who has a lot of experience in this type of work. Then I want a team to interview everyone working in the fast food restaurant, a team to trace and interview the people of every car on the car park this morning, analysis of CCTV inside the restaurant and in surroundings shops, offices and buildings. I want a road check here every day for the next seven days. I want everyone who uses this route on a regular basis traced and interviewed. Someone saw our bomber drive here and walk away. I want to know which route they used to get here and which route they used to walk away. At the multi-storey I want the same response. That car park is used every day. I want to know by whom and what they saw. I want these bastards traced and put where they belong.'

'I'll make a start, Ma-am,' acknowledged Anthea.

'And I want Janice to liaise with the forensic team and Richard and Terry to put a team of local detectives together and push the investigation onwards,' continued Sandra. 'I want every door in this neighbourhood knocked and the occupants spoken to. Someone planned these atrocities and made a reconnaissance of the area. Someone must have seen something. I want to know who saw what? And I want the area turned upside down until we find something that puts us on the right track. Shake it down! Okay?'

'Got it,' noted Anthea.

Peel stepped away for a moment, turned to Anthea thoughtfully and said, 'It's only a few months since my bomb scene management course in an army camp in the north. It seems like years ago now. This is my first one with the unit, Anthea. It's a completely different type of job to what I'm used to. How am I doing and what have I forgotten?'

Checking her notes, Anthea looked up and replied, 'You're doing fine but can I suggest something?'

'Go on, I'm listening?'

'On the fast food car park the driver just drove straight onto the plot and walked away. We may or may not turn up CCTV but I'd be looking for oil patches on the tarmac because I'd want oil samples for future analysis and I'd want to see if he or she had left their footprints in a particular oily patch. It's a popular site and the answer might be on the doorstep for all we know. In the multi-story car park the driver stopped his vehicle and took a ticket out of the machine. The barrier lifted and he drove in. There are priorities that I can see.'

'What are you getting at?' asked Peel.

'Two things,' replied Anthea. 'One – We can find out the precise time when the bomb car entered the multi-story and then check to see if someone was leaving the car park at the same time. Someone leaving may have stopped on the other side of the barrier at the same time our bomber was entering. They may have looked each other in the eye. In any event it enables us to be more specific with the time factor when we add in all the other lines of enquiry we are about to do.'

'That's a couple of long shots,' declared Superintendent Peel.

'The secret of our success often lies in a long shot or two,' suggested Anthea, 'Sometimes three!'

'And the second?' queried Peel.

'The diver took a ticket from the machine when he entered. Is his DNA on the machine or did he throw the ticket away when he left the car park because he didn't need it?'

'I'll make it a priority,' replied Peel. 'Anything else?'

'Maybe I forgot something,' offered Anthea. 'No-one is perfect. I'd run it all through Boyd and Commander Maxwell and not take it too personally if they suggest something new to you. Woman to woman I can tell you that we're not hot on overbearing discipline in this team, Sandra. If you don't mind me saying so you're on track to upset a few people on the unit because you have an overbearing attitude. Lighten up, Sandra. We've got enough problems from government intent on using us as a political football and trying to prove we're a good case for the austerity cause. We're good at our job. We don't need jumped on by a new boss who is still learning the game. People died here today. They were killed by our enemies – the enemy of the State – the dead aren't interested in your status and discipline, boss. Their loved ones just want justice. That's what we do. That's all.'

Detective Inspector Adams walked away.

Sandra Peel was at a loss for words as she stared at Anthea's back. Blinking her eyes, Sandra suddenly jolted and took a step forward before holding her ground.

'Anthea!' shouted Peel. 'Just call me Sandy if that helps. I got off on the wrong foot the other day. I'm learning fast but it's a rough place to start.'

'We'll get you there, Ma-am,' replied Anthea.

Sandra Peel watched Anthea walk away carrying a list of actions to begin and then shouted, 'Anthea! Thanks!'

Anthea Adams didn't look back as she reached for her mobile phone to sort her priorities out. She just offered a casual wave as she pondered on how relationships change when unexpected factors in the kitchen turn the heat up.

Later that day Sandra Peel and Anthea Adams interviewed a CCTV operator working close to the multi-story car park

By that time the two detectives had worked out from data supplied by the ticket machinery that the blue Hyundai had entered the car park at seven forty six in the morning. They allowed two minutes for the driver to park on the fifth floor and four minutes for the driver to walk out of the car park. Absorbed in their enquiry they studied a CCTV image from a car dealership situated directly opposite the multi-storey car park. The image caught a man walking from the car park at seven fifty three. He was wearing a 'hoodie' and was of average height and build. The male walked with a slight limp and dragged his left leg.

Peel designated the subject, 'Suspect One'.

103

Suspect One appeared on camera for no more than two seconds but during that time he walked past a lamp standard. Janice re-enacted the suspect's walk for Peel and Adams and then measured the supposed height of the suspect using his image against the lamp standard. Janice measured the supposed height of the suspect on the lamp standard and calculated he was approximately five feet nine and one half inches tall.

Intelligence sources in Northern Ireland were able to identify the subject as Patrick Brendan O'Malley: a known member of the IRA who had been wanted for terrorist related offences for some years. His medical history revealed he walked with a limp as a result of falling from a roof many years earlier. It was thought that he was watching an army base at the time he suffered the fall. MI5 analysed images of the suspect and revealed he had a brother who was also missing from their radar. His name was Declan O'Malley – present location unknown.

House to house enquiries by the team resulted in information suggesting numerous persons of a similar description were seen in the area. All of them were possible witnesses but none were specific. Examination of further CCTV recordings revealed a man with a slight limp, presumably Patrick Brendan O'Malley, also appeared a short time later about half a mile from where he had parked the Hyundai. He made a call using his mobile phone. The detectives believed this second call detonated the bomb in the fast food drive through restaurant.

Peel and the team were jubilant, but there was still much to do. They had to advance 'knowing or suspecting' to 'proving'.

There was no coded warning from the Active Service Unit when the two car bombs went off in central London. They had been activated by mobile phone in a sophisticated manner that suggested an experienced bomb maker was involved in assembling the bombs. The devices may well have been planted by the O'Malley brothers and detonated by Patrick Brendan O'Malley but they had all the hallmarks of having been designed and put together by a man known as 'The Teacher.'

In the afternoon jubilation at identifying the suspects took a sideways jolt when the Control Room at New Scotland Yard received a telephone call from an unknown caller. The message was short; the threat unsavoury. A caller, purporting to be a member of 'Anarchists Unite', threatened to 'bomb' the Crown Hotel in Shanklin on the Isle of Wight if the G8 conference was held there.

National intelligence sources compared the caller's voice with colleagues in the FBI in America. The Americans confirmed the voice print out was similar in pattern to an unidentified subject who had made threats against the G8 in America and Italy previously.

Later that day, in Commander Maxwell's office at the Yard, Boyd asked, 'Who on earth are Anarchists Unite?'

'I think we are about to find out,' responded Commander Maxwell. 'According to our friends in the FBI they will use everything at their disposal to prevent the G8 conference going ahead. In any event, they are likely to provide an extremely disruptive element at the scene of the conference. If we cannot nullify them then we need to investigate them and penetrate them. In our country they are not on our radar and are an unknown threat but in America, and elsewhere, they seem to have built up a reputation of being violent.'

'The conference is on an island for God's sake, commander,' suggested Boyd. 'They'll never make the ferry from Southampton. We'll block it with uniforms.'

'And the waters surrounding the island is an obvious natural barrier,' remarked Anthea.

'No, they'll use boats or anything that floats,' remarked Peel as she filed a report into the commander's tray. 'Maybe even aeroplanes; you know – those private two-seater things that buzz around the countryside.'

Swivelling his head suddenly, amazed at her comment, Boyd said, 'Yes, Ma-am! Yes, of course they will. We'll have to suggest a 'no-fly zone' is implemented for the duration of the event.'

Smiling, Anthea remarked, 'You should always trust a woman's intuition, gentlemen. Always!'

'By the way,' offered Boyd. 'Good result today, Superintendent Peel. Well done!'

'Really,' replied Peel. 'Was that a condescending remark or truly from the heart, Mister Boyd?'

'It was a truly well done from the heart,' offered Boyd. 'I assure you.'

'Thanks, I'm getting there,' declared Peel. 'But I'd prefer if it you'd all call me Sandy. I need to fit in and we need to catch the O'Malley brothers wherever they may be.'

'And the Teacher,' reminded Boyd.

'Oh yes, this student would dearly like to catch the Teacher, believe me,' voiced Peel.

'No disrespect intended, Ma-am,' suggested Boyd. 'But it's time you met Toni.'

'Toni?' queried Peel.

'Antonia Harston-Browne!' revealed Boyd. 'We call her Toni. It's short for Antonia, obviously. She's our main contact in the Security Service and a senior intelligence officer. Toni is also assigned to our unit. Her speciality is running agents into terrorist organisations. I recommend her to you without reservation. She is a crucially important member of our team and, by the way, I think it's time to tell you that she has a source close to the Teacher. You need to talk and, if the commander will permit me, we are invited to Thames House for an important meeting.'

Superintendent Peel paused for a moment, considered the implications and replied, 'When? Why didn't you tell me earlier?'

'Because I work on the 'need to know' principle and I need to feel secure in my own way. I want to be able to tell my colleagues something that stays inside our unit. I don't trust everyone that wears a police uniform or joins Counter Terrorist Command. Being part of the club doesn't necessarily give you all the membership privileges you might expect. I didn't join the force to spend my entire career dishing out speeding tickets. No disrespect, Sandy, but you are the only person in the unit who wasn't handpicked for the job. You got the position because the commissioner decided we needed a superintendent and no-one applied for the job. You got it because you were the only one available and with a CV that came somewhere near to what we want. You were deployed by senior management not selected by the commander and the unit.'

There was a silence that filled the room: an uneasy atmosphere that brought an element of heated claustrophobia to the gathering.

'Begging your pardon, commander, but it needed to be said,' suggested Boyd. 'It's long overdue and we're too busy to play games. A bit of reality never goes amiss.'

Commander Maxwell smiled and said, 'Good! That's the air cleared then. I have a habit of taking a drink to celebrate a good day's work - A glass of port perhaps?'

'Sounds like an acceptable habit, commander,' laughed Boyd. 'And I think it's high time we buried the hatchet.'

'Tinoco!' remarked Commander Maxwell. 'Courtesy of Anthea's husband Raphael, it's a quite wonderful little port which I heartily recommend to you.'

'In which case it would be bad manners to refuse,' chuckled Boyd.

Commander Maxwell poured the port.

Sandra Peel raised her glass, turned to Boyd and commented, 'Hatchet? I don't know what you mean, Boyd.'

'Me neither, Sandy,' replied Boyd. 'Cheers! Here's to your success.'

It was only a sip, a brief taste of Raphael's best from Portugal but as Peel engaged Commander Maxwell Anthea sidled up to Boyd and whispered, 'Forget the dinner in that Euston restaurant, Guvnor. We're going to be too busy. In any event, the boys tell me the office gave her a nickname on day one – Sandy.'

'Sandy?' queried Boyd. 'Of course, it's short for Sandra, I suppose.'

'No! It's short for sandpaper. The superintendent is a little abrasive when it comes to dishing the orders out apparently.'

'Ouch!' shivered Boyd.

'For what it's worth, Guvnor, she can do the job,' delivered Anthea. 'And deep inside me I think she might be just a big cuddly soft teddy bear. That's all.'

'A teddy bear?' questioned Boyd.

'Well, you know what I mean, soft inside,' replied Anthea.

And?' queried Boyd. 'Today?'

'She did well today,' announced Anthea. 'She's going to be fine, just fine!'

Peel finished her drink, ignored Boyd, and said, 'Thank you, commander. That was a nice break but I'm going to check the scene and see what has been done and what still needs to be done. It's heartening to stand here knowing we have a very strong line on those responsible. But we've also got a lot of victims and grieving people out there, and a hungry media needing fed. Well, I'm not feeding the media but I am going to make sure those who have lost their loved ones receive the support they need. I'll touch base with Terry and Ricky. I must say when you dish out the orders here everyone is off like a rabbit. They're working flat out without any supervision. Then I'm going to draw the files on the O'Malley's and the Teacher and see what we need to do to catch them. I think it's time to tell you that I don't care how I got the job. It's mine and you'd better get used to it because I want to make a difference. That's why I joined.'

'Of course,' replied Commander Maxwell. 'By the way, Terry and Ricky were handpicked for that reason. They both work well with minimum supervision. That is what I expect from all my staff. Anyway, I must fly. I have a meeting with the commissioner in fifteen minutes. He wants to know all about the New Front for Irish Independence. But I'll tell him about the latest on the G8 too.'

Glasses collected, port stowed for the next celebration a nation's police service went onto full alert when news of the atrocities became known.

All ports, harbours and transport hubs were monitored when a massive investigative operation began.

There was no more time for celebrations, and the hatchet, for now, appeared to have been buried.

An up to date document from the latest trawl of electronic data obtained by GCHQ at the Doughnut, in Cheltenham, had been prepared by Cornelius Duke, senior intelligence analyst in the unit whose nickname throughout the intelligence community was 'The Duke'. His summary of intelligence from the Middle East revealed a substantial increase in electronic traffic emanating from the areas of Tikrit, Mosul, northern Iraq and the Islamic State stronghold and headquarters - Ar Raqqah. In itself, this was not unusual for this was the centre of fighting at the present time.

Whilst much of the traffic was encrypted some sensitive and technological intelligence could be obtained from CAST, suggested the Duke. CAST was an abbreviation for 'Crime analysis software – terrorism.' Yet the Duke also noticed an increase in overt speech data where non encrypted data had been plucked from the ether – cyberspace - in accordance with the legal guidelines governing the work of GCHQ.

Cornelius Duke continued his appraisal. Half way down a page reference was made to an individual named Salman. The Duke highlighted the reference since data indicated three electronic traces to Salman. It was said such a man was from Tikrit and was travelling west to assassinate western leaders.

Such information wasn't regarded as a golden nugget of intelligence in the eyes of Cornelius Duke. It was interesting and informative but not crucial when compared with other matters which could be more easily handled. Positive information that might lead to a successful drone strike, interception, disruption or arrest was much more sought after because it might bring a positive result. Cornelius knew that where millions of pounds were spent gathering and analysing intelligence, politicians expected and demanded results that justified expenditure. Salman was interesting but data was inconclusive. Salman who - from where - were the obvious questions posed by Cornelius. What historical data was held on a subject of the same name that might be the Salman spoken of was another. Nil was the answer. How might the intelligence of an unknown be assessed? The intelligence community would be unlikely to close down a thousand airports and border crossing areas in the hope that such an individual might be prevented from accessing a point of entry. In any event, Cornelius knew much from his extensive experience. For Cornelius, it wasn't surprising to find that warriors were told if they were captured they should give the opposition a false story that might confuse the enemy and throw them off the scent.

The man from Tikrit represented the entire amount of information held on the subject, noted the analyst. It amounted to a throw away comment made by an Islamic State warrior minutes before his death at the hands of a bullying tough nut Special Forces soldier. All that needed to be done had been done. The name Salman had been registered in the intelligence index for future comparison and analysis.

Midway down page three of the document Cornelius Duke pencilled a mark next to the word Salman. It bore the legend – 'Noted, inclusive, no further action…. The Duke.'

*

Chapter Six
~

Birmingham
That Night
Threat Level Two - Severe

A clumsy shuffle of leather along the tarmac was accompanied only by the heavy breathing of a private security guard nearing the end of his shift. It was close to ten o'clock at night when Ken Mossop heaved his sixteen stone frame across a low level wall and planted himself firmly on the paved area of his final call. Ken swore under his breath when he realised he'd accidently torn his dark blue uniform trousers but then put it to one side; he had work to do. Ken had no appointment. His was a random visit during unsocial hours merely to check site security and make a note in his duty schedule. But Ken was bored and hoped to find a couple canoodling in the dark using the shadows that this magnificent Hebrew building provided. Devious, perhaps a little bizarre at times, he'd decided to enter by the back way. It was his last visit of the night.

Taking a deep breath, Ken removed the wrapper from a chocolate bar and took a huge bite before discarding the paper on the ground. He belched, wiped his mouth with the back of his hand, and tightened his belt so that his stomach hung loosely over the trouser belt. Then he stepped carefully and quietly towards the rear entrance. Using moonlight shadows and passing car lights reflecting from the walls, he could tell the area was devoid of people. Ken knew the place so well. This was just another regular visit for him to record and then move on. He made towards the front door munching his chocolate and thinking of where he might buy a takeaway on his drive home to the other side of the city.

A brush swished smoothly across the front door of the synagogue daubing a swastika in red paint. Close by, another brush twisted the words, 'HOLOCAUST LIARS' and 'ISLAMIC STATE' in the same vivid blood red paint.

'More, Rashid,' a voice whispered, 'Finish it just like we agreed. Okay?'

'Are you sure, Abdullah?'

'Allah commanded me, my friend,' declared Abdullah. 'It is what we must do for the warriors of Muhammad.'

The letters 'AQ' duly blotted the tall wooden frame when Rashid completed his graffiti.

'AQ and Islamic State will frighten the life out of the blasphemous infidels.'

'Why didn't you just paint Al Qaeda?'

'I've run out of paint.'

'I've got some left.'

There was another swish of the brush when 'ALLAHU AKBAR' was daubed in large words across a wall next to the entrance.

Ken strolled round the corner and interrupted the vandals at work. Dropping his chocolate bar in total surprise, he stood motionless for a moment before screaming loudly, 'Gotcha, you little buggers!'

'Shit!' screamed Rashid. 'Let's go, Abdullah.'

A paint brush fell to the ground. A foot kicked a tin and a long smear of red paint raced across the paving to foul the synagogue entrance. The paint flowed from the top step and dripped scornfully onto a lower step like an unwanted malicious wound in a Jewish soul.

Two Asian teenagers with paint on their hands and hate in their hearts were up and away with an overweight out of condition security guard running after them.

The vandals were down the steps and making for the roadway at speed with Ken thundering behind.

Losing ground, and fumbling for his radio, Ken bellowed, 'Base! Base! Central Synagogue making for Calthorpe Park chasing two kids who have vandalised the place. Get the police!'

Panic set in with the rush to escape. Rashid stumbled, fell, and suddenly felt sixteen stone of revenge crash down upon him.

'Gotcha! You little bugger!' screamed Ken grabbing the teenager by the scruff of his neck and trying to subdue him. But Rashid screamed in fear of the huge man, kicked out, and struggled to wriggle his way out of Ken's clutches.

Looking back, Abdullah realised his friend had been captured. He returned immediately and began pulling Rashid away from the security guard.

Hanging on, Ken was determined to secure his prisoner, fumbled for his radio, and then felt Abdullah's boot thud into his face. Blood spurted from his lip when he released his grip and fell backwards.

Rashid broke free.

Abdullah kicked the security guard again in the stomach, then stamped on his head, and spat on the security guard. Finally, Ken Mossop rolled over and tried to shield his body from the worsening onslaught.

Satisfied, their captor had been nullified the two teenagers were on their feet again. They were across the road and into the park with all its greenery and rambling foliage before Ken Mossop revived enough to radio, 'I had one. He got away. He...'

Then Ken drifted away again and rolled into the paint, slid ungracefully down the steps in pain, and faintly radioed, 'I've lost them. They've gone to ground in the park.'

In the company's control centre some miles away an operator sensed something was wrong and called the local police. By the time they arrived, the two Asian youngsters had made good their escape. An ambulance was called and local detectives began an investigation into vandalism at Birmingham's Central Synagogue and a subsequent attack on an overweight security guard.

A search of nearby Calthorpe Park was made with negative result. There was a strange almost bizarre irony about the case, thought local police. Calthorpe Park separates Birmingham's Central Synagogue from the city's Central Mosque. One establishment is the focal point of Jewish worship and the Hebrew community, the other is one of the largest Mosques in Europe and is loved by Muslims throughout the city and beyond. Walking between the two would take one on a trip of slightly over a mile, about ten minutes. There is little to separate the two buildings except the park, thought the police.

The area was Balsall Heath, Birmingham: a great city known for its diversity, culture and – on this day – an anti-Semitic, anti-Jewish act of vandalism carried out by two violent teenagers in the name of Islamic extremism.

Standing on the paint-stained steps of the synagogue a police officer peered out towards the park and said to a colleague. 'Looks like those two are home free.'

Turning to inspect the paintwork, he said, 'Allahu Akbar! Really? If that God of theirs is so damn great why do they have to harm others to try and prove it?'

During the night, and in accordance with procedures, details of the attack on Birmingham's Synagogue and the security guard were forwarded to the Special Crime Unit in New Scotland Yard where it was read by Antonia Harston-Browne, and others, on a 'ticker' intelligence system.

The case would be forever undetected but the details were loud and clear. The Islamic threat was not confined to British interests in the Middle East. It was alive and well in the West Midlands, and in danger of thriving.

In a village close to the Turkish border, Salman jumped from an orange coloured Toyota pick-up, waved away the driver, and waited for the vehicle to disappear over the horizon. When the coast was clear Salman walked across the highway, climbed a slight incline, and then dropped into the valley below.

Moments later he entered a makeshift wooden hut. There he met a woman who fed him and clothed him before making herself available for the man she had been told was a warrior of Mohammad.

Salman slept and waited for the dawn border crossing.

*

Chapter Seven
~

Cheltenham
The Following Day
Threat Level Two - Severe

At the 'Doughnut' in Cheltenham, GCHQ officers were alerted to a transmission on a frequency they were monitoring.

A video suddenly burst onscreen to reveal a middle-aged unshaven man being dragged from a cave by three younger men. He was screaming and using every ounce of pitiful energy to struggle free. His clothes were torn and ragged whilst a belt securing his trousers seemed to be far too big for his waist.

'His clothes are too big for him,' remarked Tim; one of the GCHQ audience. 'Look how thin he is.'

'I'd say he'd lost a lot of weight,' suggested Stephen. 'He's skinny. They've kept him alive long enough for this show. Are we recording?'

'We are,' declared Tim.

The prisoner was a sad pathetic mixture of rag and bone such was his scruffy unhealthy condition. A couple of weeks of untrained stubble had forced a beard from his chin and his hair curled unwieldy over his ears and down his neck. Tired and distressed, an emaciated appearance scarred his features. His fragile cheek bones were pronounced and taut across his face in a bizarre alliance with a gag suddenly thrust into his mouth to prevent him speaking.

'Good,' replied Stephen. 'I fear the worst. They've shut him up for the speechmaker.'

The gag must surely have provided more pain and anguish for the victim. Yet from somewhere within his body and soul he found the strength and courage to continually struggle in an attempt to free himself from his captors.

Unexpectedly, there was a sickening crunch when the man's head deliberately collided with the bodywork of a Toyota pick-up and his hands were tied to the tow bar of the vehicle.

'Here he is,' remarked Stephen watching from the comfort of an office chair thousands of miles away. 'And that means bad news.'

A dark figure emerged from the cave. His image gradually cleared to reveal a man wearing grey robes. He was in his sixties and wore sandals whilst sporting a full greying beard and moustache. The elder carried a long ugly scar down the left hand side of his face and the fingers of his right hand were crooked and gnarled.

Stephen remarked, 'Ibrahim: their leader.'

'Are you sure?' asked Tim.

'His hand - He's arthritic,' revealed Stephen. 'His fingers are bent and twisted. We know he has arthritis and the scar confirms it for me. That's him, no question.'

Ibrahim Hasan al Din stepped purposefully into the shot and checked that the man's hands were securely tied to the tow bar. The leader of this group of Islamic warriors did not pause to offer sustenance or advice. He merely checked that the man's arms were taught before gesturing to the cameraman to get a close-up shot of the knots. Then he pointed to a second Toyota and instructed the guards to secure their prisoner's feet to its tow bar.

It was as if Ibrahim Hasan all Din - the elderly leader - had visited the scene to witness proceedings but then decided to guide, advise, and inspire those behind the debacle.

Checking the ropes once more, Ibrahim nodded in satisfaction before removing a gag from the victim's mouth and walking away. Such a minor action was coldly calculated. The prisoner immediately screamed in terror before pleading for his life.

'It's the same people as last time,' suggested Tim. 'Stephen, it's the Fourth Reich get Roberta quickly please.'

Swivelling in his chair, Stephen picked up a phone and punched the digits as Robin approached and hovered nearby. A group then began to gather and stood behind Stephen watching the events in the desert unfurl.

Replacing his phone, Stephen said, 'Roberta is on her way.'

They turned to watch the transmission aware that it would be on various social media platforms within the hour.

One of three bearded men, supported by two girls carrying the black flags of Islamic State, stepped forward and presented himself to the camera.

'I am Hassan Waheed from Blackburn in England. I call upon all Muhammad's followers to rise against the kefirs of the west. It is time to destroy these infidels.' Drawing a dagger from his belt Hassan raised it high in the air and continued, 'It is time to remove the leaders of America, Canada, Britain, Australia and Europe so that Allah can be the one voice – the one true voice that is above all others.'

Arriving out of breath, Roberta enquired, 'Am I too late? Have I missed anything?'

'Just in time for a rallying call, I think,' replied Stephen. 'The young man has just introduced himself as coming from Blackburn. Mind you, they may be in Iraq but that Lancashire accent shines through loud and clear. Now that will certainly help us to identify the crew but it's not looking good otherwise.'

On screen, the victim's hands and feet remained tied to the tow bar of two Toyota pick-ups as the Islamic tirade continued.

'One day Allah will rule the world,' explained Hassan in his harsh Lancashire accent. 'Not the President of America, not the Prime Minister of Britain, or the leaders of Canada, Europe and Australia. Our God is the greatest. Allah is higher than the presidents, kings and queens of the world. We must bring them down. Allah is above all other Gods. It is time to put Allah at the very highest pinnacle of our thoughts. Now, oh warriors of Muhammad, now is the time to rise and strike down the leaders of the infidels.'

At a nod from one of the bearded men, one of the girls lowered the black Islamic flag signalling the two Toyota drivers to pull away from each other. As they did so, the man's body stretched tight and held in an agonising pose when he screamed for mercy.

Only the sound of a throbbing accelerator accompanied the screaming victim as the camera held the image for ten seconds or more.

'I can't watch it,' whispered Robin.

Ibrahim Hasan al Din instructed his warriors with the nod of his head.

Suddenly, violently and horribly, the body of the poor victim separated and dismembered when the two Toyotas accelerated out of shot and pulled away from each other. The video camera moved, focused, and captured only the terrifying image of a murdered man on the screen.

When the image on the screen went blank it was greeted in the Doughnut by stunned silence. A voiceless hush shrouded the gathering broken only by white noise from the computers.

A voice quietly suggested, 'I just hope these bastards roast in hell – Slowly – One rib at a time.'

'How do you tell someone's family what happened to them? What do you say to a family?' a voice asked. 'Oh the poor man, that is so inhuman. My heart goes out to him.'

'Maybe we'll just nuke 'em and have done with it,' stated another.

'Provided some misguided politician doesn't get rid of Trident; if they abandon our nuclear capability we will be without a good right hook,' offered Stephen.

'Oh get you,' remarked Tim 'What did they put in your coffee this morning?'

'Two doses of truth, one twist of reality, and an unhealthy understanding of the global threat. I wasn't brought up to kill people, Tim, so a nuclear missile is not on my Christmas list but until there is relative peace throughout the world, and the threat to our country is very low, we need Trident and an armed services to defend us.'

'Not everyone will agree with you. Why do say that?'

'Because one day these bastards will have a nuclear capability unless we stop them and then… It frightens me to think about it.'

'Have you heard the latest?' announced Roberta.

'What now, Roberta?'

'Our system has identified a new website put online by Islamic State.'

'Not another one!'

'I'm afraid so. The problem with this one is that it is aimed at Islamic extremists here in the UK. The website has a chat room where you can talk to Muhammad's warriors on the front line. They're giving lessons in how to destroy you, me, non-Christians across the globe, and the rest of the infidels who live here.'

'Can we close it down or have we got someone in there?'

'We're working on it.'

'Any traces yet?'

'A list is being drawn up. We've names on it from Aberdeen to Carlisle and from Newcastle to Luton, and none of them are a Smith or a Brown.'

'More work for 5, 6 and the anti-terrorist network.'

A telephone sounded on a desk close by; the screen flickered, and died. The gathering disbanded and returned to their desks. The work went on as a stack of computers captured another batch of electronic data for analysis.

An hour or so later, in Carlisle, Dina Al-Hakim smiled at the computer as she watched the latest video from Islamic State. Unconcerned with the victim, vehicles, or the horrendous manner of murder revealed, Dina only had eyes for her sister Azma. Dressed in black fatigues and carrying the black flag of Islamic State, Azma looked every inch a warrior of Muhammad when she planted her flag in the desert sand. She was beautiful and heroic, thought Dina. She is my inspiration and, reflected Dina, Azma knows my cousin Hassan and our great leader, Ibrahim Hasan al Din. A tear gradually formed in Dina's eye and trickled down her cheek when she blew a kiss to her sister and gently touched the computer screen.

Aloud, in the loneliness of her apartment, Dina spoke.

'I will not let you down, Azam. One day you will be proud of me, you'll see.'

Guiding her mouse, Dina opened a new search panel and entered the name of a website she had learnt of in the chatroom. Here she looked at the goods on display and decided if they would be sufficient for the work she planned in the weeks ahead. The colour, size and impact were important, she reminded herself. Money was no object.

'Oh yes,' said Dina speaking to Azam's photograph. 'I'll make you proud of me, my beautiful sister.'

Carlingford Lough is a beautiful glacial fjord or sea inlet that forms part of the border between Northern Ireland to the north and the Republic of Ireland to the south. On its northern shore is County Down and on its southern shore is County Louth. It is a truly beautiful and serene place.

On the banks of the lough a woman strolled allowing her Jack Russell terrier to wander away on his own to forage at the water's edge. She strolled happily along the edge of the water occasionally dipping her wellington boot into the lough pretending to be a child enjoying her first paddle by the seaside.

'Misty,' she shouted. 'Come on, Misty, it's time to go.'

But the dog had other ideas and she closed with the terrier leashing its collar and dragging it away from a clump of bushes near the water's edge.

The Jack Russell refused, dug its heels in, and, nose down, tried to pull his mistress towards the bushes.

Then the woman saw the corpse and screamed.

She screamed like she had never screamed before when she discovered the body of Donal McArthy. He had been shot in the mouth and dumped on the banks of the Carlingford Lough. The bullet had entered his mouth and egressed from the top of his skull

Fifteen minutes elapsed before the woman regained sufficient presence of mind to telephone the police. Within the hour, the area was marked out as a crime scene and a murder investigation by the Republic's police was underway. By midday details of the murder of Donal McArthy were in the media and with the intelligence services.

Later, Antonia sat in her office drinking coffee supplied by Boyd who was on the telephone. She was mortified.

'That's the second I've lost,' declared Antonia tearfully. 'All these years and that's the second time the other side have taken and killed one of my snouts. It's time to go, Billy. I'm doing something wrong. It shouldn't be happening. I've got to get out of this job.'

Boyd slammed the phone onto its cradle and countered, 'Don't be stupid, Toni. It's a precarious game we play and your playmates know full well the dangers. Anyway, that was the Irish office. The bullet used to kill your man Donal has identical striation marks on it to that of a bullet used in a murder a year ago. The same weapon has been used twice. A forensic examination of the scene reveals footprints.'

'Near the water's edge? You'd expect that,' agreed Antonia.

'The Irish police think the murder is domestic as opposed to terrorist,' revealed Boyd. 'They're looking for Seamus Logan: Donal's brother in law. Word has it he took Donal to task over another woman he'd hooked up with in preference over his sister. It looks like what Donal told you at your last meeting with him was right on the button.'

'That doesn't surprise me,' added Antonia. 'Women were always his weak point. Now you're telling me Seamus Logan is suspected of Donal's murder.'

'That's what the Irish police believe apparently. There's a suggestion that the Teacher may well have provided Seamus with the handgun that killed Donal,' said Boyd.

'Time will tell then,' offered Antonia. 'But we've lost a good snout with direct access into the New Front for Irish Independence.'

'Then we'll find another one,' declared Boyd.

'Were it that easy,' responded Antonia. 'It can take years to get where you want to be, you know that.'

'Sadly, I do,' stated Boyd, 'And good people to do it.'

There was a knock on the door and Anthea entered. She dropped a stack of files on Antonia's desk and said to Boyd, 'That errand you sent me on! I've a bit more if you're interested?'

'Excuse me, Toni,' offered Boyd to Antonia. 'I'll take five.'

Nodding in agreement, Boyd and Anthea stepped outside the office where he asked, 'Sandra Peel by any chance? What you got, Anthea?'

'Not much but I thought you'd like to know she plays the violin,' smiled Anthea.

'But does she play the field?' enquired Boyd.

'No, definitely not by all accounts,' reported Anthea. 'But her husband did. That's why she's in the middle of a messy divorce. She's the main source of income. Hubby is after the house, her pension, half of this, half of that. You know the score.'

'I've heard,' replied Boyd. 'Doesn't sound good for the lady, anything else?'

'According to a few I've spoken to who worked with her Peel is a very strict boss. She has no blemishes on her character that I can find. That said, I'd say she's loved and hated in equal passion probably because of her abrasive nature at times. She seems to like things her way only.'

'Otherwise she seems fine,' acknowledged Boyd.

'Absolutely,' agreed Anthea.

As his inspector walked away Boyd enquired, 'Does she really play the violin, Anthea?'

Looking over her shoulder, Anthea replied, 'Oh yes, she played in an orchestra in her younger days, I'm told.'

Anthea walked on as Boyd replied, 'Not the conductor though!' He tapped on Antonia's door and prepared to discuss intelligence with Antonia before a reply was made.

Delighted that Barclays Bank website was downed for the day Zhan Wen ignored the idle chatter pouring from the operators outside. Her eyes held fast to a computer screen as she browsed the internet in search of her prey.

Standing behind her an Indonesian tongue spoke gently and offered, 'My friends are very pleased with your recent actions.'

Smiling, Zhan Wen replied, 'And my friends out there are very pleased with their reward.' She moved a mouse, clicked a link, and disclosed, 'I'm in. I'll need to write out the protocol for my operators and then we can begin. Are you happy with this one?'

The Indonesian peered over her shoulder, tapped the screen with his forefinger, and offered, 'I think it is time we gave the banking system a rest, good lady. My friends would like you to survey this one as soon as possible.'

A piece of paper found itself liberated from a jacket pocket. Four greedy fingers and a thumb pinned the paper down to the desk and slid it gently in front of Zhan Wen.

Resting her hands on the table for a moment, Zhan Wen then turned the slip of paper over and read out in Mandarin the name of a British government website.

'Of course,' replied the lady. 'Now?'

'Yes, now please,' came the instruction.

Grinning cheekily, Zhan Wen asked, 'Who is this one for or am I not allowed to ask?'

'My client is a discreet entity. Some would say such a person or organisation never speaks. What you don't know you cannot divulge under interrogation if – God forbid – this enterprise is ever broken by the law. Don't ask, my friend. Questions that need answers do not foster a good business relationship between us.'

Nodding, Zhan Wen replied, 'Of course, how stupid of me. I apologise. I shall not be so stupid again. I was a little curious that's all. But if the truth be known as long as the money is in the bank then I don't really care who the client is.'

'Good, then let's leave it at that.'

Zhan Wen tapped details of a target website into her computer and pressed the 'enter' key. In the room outside a large screen burst into life and grabbed the attention of idle computer operators.

'Work!' declared a voice. 'Survey only at this stage.'

Moving to her office door, Zhan Wen announced to the assembly, 'The website is gov.uk. Here we will find various British government departments. As before, survey the site, penetrate the target, and await orders regarding delivery of a package to the target website.'

There was a clamour of excitement from the operators. A hand moved, a keyboard came to life, a browser fired, and a mouse guided the day's malice to the dedicated website.

'It's a big one!' someone suggested.

'With a huge pay check,' countered another.

'Proceed when ready,' ordered a smiling Zhan Wen.

As the cyberattack began an Indonesian gentleman lit a piece of paper bearing the name of the government website and then used it to light a cigarette.

'Thank you, Zhan Wen,' he offered. 'Thank you!'

Elsewhere, a sign at the entrance to a secure compound indicated that a building imprisoned by double palisade railings belonged to a utility company. A small car park ingratiated itself to two dozen private vehicles and a couple of company vans bearing rather dull company logos. The structure itself boasted a metal door at the front and an unusually high number of radio antennae sprouting from the low roof. Only a shrewd observer might decide that the bulk of the building stretched underground.

In this unobtrusive underground bunker in South East England, in the county of Kent, a government cyberspace unit was on full alert. A bank of operators sat at their desks with their computers working overtime and fully charged. Quietly, defiantly, they tracked incoming electronic signals, tried to decipher their origin, and made plans to counterattack in the hours ahead.

Determined, and with the enigmatic tapping of fingers on a row of black and white keyboards, the cyberwar began.

Chapter Eight
~

Thames House, London
The day after
Threat Level Two - Severe

They climbed the steps together. Two men dressed in smartly cut suits and a female wearing a skirt and a jacket.

'This is a first,' whispered Sandra Peel to Commander Maxwell. 'I never expected to be invited to the headquarters of MI5. Never in a million years.'

'What makes you think this is the real headquarters?' asked the commander.

Speechless, Peel faltered on the steps for a moment, and then replied, 'You mean…?'

Commander Maxwell smiled and said, 'My little joke, Sandy. Lighten up, you'll find they are quite normal in here. Come on.'

Boyd leaned towards Peel's ear and offered, 'The commander isn't joking, Sandy. This is the headquarters they show in all the Bond films. The televisions companies use it for the news programmes but it's basically a great big government call centre doling out unemployment benefit and welfare entitlements. The real headquarters of MI5 are situated in – Well, it's need to know and you don't need to know so I can't tell you. I'm sorry.'

'Boyd!' barked Commander Maxwell. 'Save your puzzles for those who solve them for a living.'

The two men stepped ahead of a bewildered Superintendent Peel, paused on the top step, and turned back to face her.

Sandra Peel wore a black collarless jacket over a silk blouse and a knee-length skirt, which she smoothed whilst studying the building.

'What now, Sandy?' enquired Boyd.

'The statues,' declared an intrigued Peel pointing to masonry on the Thames House building. 'Who are they?'

'One is of Britannia and the other is Saint George,' replied Boyd, 'Both of which say much about the building and those inside it before you even get through the door.'

'Warrant cards,' suggested Commander Maxwell. 'There's a security procedure and I don't want to be late for this meeting.'

'Yes, indeed, sir,' countered Boyd. 'JTAC awaits.'

Identity verified the trio were escorted to a conference room. Checking the agenda, Boyd placed a briefing document at each table place before returning to his seat to await other guests.

'I don't know any of the speakers or any of the attendees,' whispered Sandy reading through an agenda. 'Other than the Home Secretary and that's only because I watch the news on television.'

'You don't need to be acquainted with them,' murmured Boyd. 'Just read the card on the table in front of the speaker. That will tell you all you need to know.'

Sandy Peel scanned the table and read the place cards from MI5, MI6, GCHQ, Special Forces, the Foreign Office, and various departments she was not aware of.

The Home Secretary opened the conference when she said, 'Welcome to the Joint Terrorism Analysis Centre – JTAC – Let me remind you that JTAC is responsible for setting the threat level from international terrorism throughout the United Kingdom whilst the Security Service - MI5 - is responsible for setting threat levels related to Northern Ireland. We are a multi-source intelligence organisation headquartered here in Thames House providing advice to the government and companies within the Critical National Infrastructure on terrorist threats. We provide assessments to government departments, major companies and institutions, predominantly in the transport, financial services, utilities and telecommunications industries.'

Covering his mouth with his hand Boyd offered, 'You're in at the deep end, Sandy. Good luck.'

The Home Security announced, 'I'd like to introduce you to Sir Phillip Nesbitt, K.B.E. - Knight Commander of the Most

Excellent Order of the British Empire - Director General of the Security Service. He is our host for these proceedings.'

There was a ripple of polite applause before she continued, 'Phillip has enjoyed a long career in the Security Service and once handled matters on both the Irish desk and the International Terrorist desk before moving into realms of protective security and organisational administration.'

As the Home Secretary continued with her welcome speech, Boyd quietly studied the Director General. In his fifties, Sir Phillip Nesbitt was perhaps slightly overweight, of medium height, light brown hair and brown eyes, yet fairly nondescript in appearance. He held an air of confidence that had the potential to beguile the unwary and unprepared, thought Boyd. And I do believe he is in love with Antonia Harston-Browne, reflected Boyd. This is a man I need to know much more about, he decided as he made unintentional eye contact with the Director General.

Taking his cue from the Home Secretary, Phillip stood and revealed he would discuss the broader intelligence picture shortly. Then, without further ado, he introduced Commander Maxwell saying, 'I'm sure the commander will be able to outline recent events in central London and elsewhere and update us on the current threat to our country in relation to terrorism.'

Commander Maxwell addressed the meeting with, 'The paper in front of you represents our analysis of the threat from Islamic State. I'll begin with the Islamic threat here in London and the rest of the UK. Put simply, extremism on our streets is on the rise. The number of recorded incidents of racial extremism continues to grow at an alarming rate. It's quite worrying since I see no sign of reduction despite the efforts of all concerned. We are engaging with community leaders and religious leaders as well various local initiatives but we are not making any major progress.'

'Yes, that is a worry,' confirmed the Home Secretary. 'I'm sorry, commander. Please continue.'

Nodding, Commander Maxwell resumed. 'I'm aware you have seen the latest and most recent video from Islamic State. It is, I believe, ladies and gentlemen, a clear call to extremists across the globe to rise against non-Islamic countries and destroy the leadership as it pertains to each individual country. As far as the UK is concerned, I see a threat against our leaders. By that I mean the monarchy as well as our prime minister.'

'Surely you mean government ministers primarily,' suggested the Home Secretary. 'After all, that is where our governance comes from in practical terms.'

'No, I don't,' replied Maxwell. 'A careful analysis of what is said by the young man from Blackburn leads one to the notion that our monarchy is at risk since he clearly mentions kings and queens as well as other leaders.'

'I see, of course,' smiled the Home Secretary. 'I am aware of the constitutional arrangements. Your remark is supported by our senior analyst – the Duke. Tell me, have you identified the youth from Blackburn?'

'Yes,' replied Commander Maxwell. 'He is Hassan Ali – a third generation Iraqi born here in the UK – Elements of his family are known to us and the Security Service. But I'd like to bring you back to the threat from the video.'

'One moment,' interrupted the Home Secretary. 'Are you telling us this man was on your radar but neither you nor MI5 were able to prevent this man from joining Islamic State?'

'Correct,' answered Commander Maxwell. 'But it may be better to discuss that matter elsewhere. May I continue for the moment and suggest to you that the threat against our leaders extends to the Deputy Prime Minister, the Defence Secretary, the Foreign Secretary, and various key members of the Cabinet. They are all at risk too. I'd like to point out that the video is made in the company of one of their most respected leaders – Ibrahim Hasan al Din – His presence gives substantial weight to the threat made.'

'Well I shall pre-empt the security process and insist that every effort is made to double protection given to those at threat,' declared the Home Secretary haughtily. 'And these do include the Monarch, the Royal Family, and senior figures currently receiving protection.'

Smiling politely, but shaking his head, Commander Maxwell contradicted the lady when he contended, 'Home Secretary, some things might be better discussed in another place but if you insist then I will deal with the matter now.'

'Please do,' replied the Home Secretary abruptly. 'Indeed, commander, please do get on with it.'

Commander Maxwell declared, 'We have insufficient personnel to consider such protection, Home Secretary. Government has made so many cuts in police budgets that there isn't the numbers trained to the level required for such an operation. Furthermore, you are aware that level one protection on the scale envisaged will soon escalate to one million pounds per subject if we are to do the job properly. I'm talking about hardening security at homes and premises as well personal protective measures. I suspect that is not an option in these economic times. You have deployed financial resources everywhere except where they should be at the moment. At a time when both the police service and the armed forces are called upon to defend our country I remind you these services seem to be part of an austerity package that lacks understanding of the times in which we live. Is it a form of fiscal management? Forgive me, but I am confused by government practices.'

'I disagree with your claim,' growled the Home Secretary. 'You're merely another voice crying wolf! I recommend a reduction in the use of human resources and better use of technology. I also stipulate the increased deployment of volunteer officers from the special constabulary and a more focused use of police and community service officers. I think it is your service that perhaps ought to apply better standards of fiscal management, commander.'

Boyd chuckled and shook his head but was immediately rebuked by Commander Maxwell's penetrating glower.

'Why are you laughing?' demanded the Home Secretary.

'Me,' replied Boyd. 'Oh I just think my boss is right.'

'He's wrong,' bellowed the Home Secretary.

'I agree with Commander Maxwell,' argued Sandra Peel staring directly into the Home Secretary's eyes. 'He's right on the button. The first duty of government is to look after its people at home and abroad. Your government seems to look after itself first and others second. The people are last to be thought of at times and you have a record of not being averse to changing the rules to suit yourselves. Government demands and expects more and more but less and less is given in return. You can supply all the modern technology in the world to help fight crime and terrorism but policing is about reassuring people as well as having enough manpower to master and use technology. Policing is about catching everyone and everything that falls through the system. We are a safety net for all the other public services that austerity has destroyed. Dealing with lost and found property, missing persons, mental health cases, and a host of non-crime matters on a daily basis is bound to drag us down from what you perceive our real task to be. Policing is about much more than crime fighting. It's also about having enough feet on the ground to respond to the threat in real terms. At the present moment we are overwhelmed.'

The Home Secretary stared at the superintendent, expected Commander Maxwell to inhibit his officers, and eventually shook her head in a display of annoyance before remarking, 'Did you have to bring politics into this meeting?'

'I did suggest the conversation might be dealt with elsewhere,' explained Commander Maxwell. 'But since you mention it may I remind you that both national and international politics influence the nation's threat level. Moreover, volunteers and untrained amateurs are not the answer when it comes to protecting those who are at risk. You're in the driving seat, Home Secretary, but it is our duty to inform you there are insufficient trained personnel to do the job you request. Superintendent Peel is right.'

The room fell silent for a while before the Home Secretary scowled, 'It's not a request. It's an instruction.'

'Born of political and economic necessity or grounded in reality and common sense?' queried Commander Maxwell.

'Perhaps the military would be better placed to assist?' growled the Home Secretary turning her head towards Colonel Barnes of UK Special Forces.

'The British public are used to unobtrusive discreet protection when it comes to the Royal Family and our senior government ministers,' explained Peel interjecting. 'Throwing a ring of troops armed to the teeth around the vulnerable and unprotected is not the answer and will not reassure the public.'

Colonel Barnes of UK Special Forces nodded his agreement, coughed, and voiced. 'It's certainly not what the Special Air Service and Special Boat Service were established for, Home Secretary. There is a role we can play in certain circumstances, of course, but the kind of protection you speak of is not ours to give in the circumstances you describe. Apart from that, we have numerous secure operations already in place. Indeed, we too are overwhelmed both at home and abroad.'

'Commander Maxwell and his team are correct,' voiced Phillip Nesbitt. 'Yet it is not a matter for me to decide upon as well you know.'

'We'll do our best, Home Secretary,' offered Commander Maxwell. 'But it may not be enough.'

Phillip Nesbitt sensed unease in the relationship between the police and the Home Secretary and immediately intervened saying, 'I think this is an excellent time to introduce my counterpart in MI6. I'm delighted to introduce Sir Julian Spencer from MI6, the Secret Intelligence Service.'

Sir Julian Spencer K.B.E - Knight Commander of the Most Excellent Order of the British Empire - acknowledged his introduction. Six feet tall, the dark haired gentleman wore a dark grey suit, pristine white shirt and dark blue-grey tie.

Standing, he began, 'Thank you, Phillip. The matters to which I refer have little comparison with acts of terrorism in the UK. You need to be appraised of an emerging threat that may affect us all, particularly when discussing resources within the police, UK Special Forces, and the military. For example, China has agreed to supply Argentina with new fighter jets that will replace its aging fleet of Mirage planes.'

'Are you saying this is a significant development in the threat to our nation, Sir Julian?' asked the Home Secretary.

'I'm saying we need to be very much aware of it,' replied the Head of MI6. 'Argentina earlier sought to buy fourteen Swedish fighters from Brazil to upgrade its air force but our Foreign Office colleagues and European allies successfully blocked that deal. Some weeks ago, the Argentina president visited Beijing and secured a deal for the transfer of various articles of military equipment, including navy patrol vessels and jet fighters. As a show of support, China has repeatedly echoed Argentina's claim on the Falkland Islands and compared the rift to China's dispute on islands in the South and East China Seas. May I suggest that the threat from Argentina and her allies is raised? It is a good time to consider what response we are capable of if the Falkland Islands were invaded again particularly as defence cuts seem to be uppermost in the mind of government at the moment. Our military is too few, even the Americans have noticed that and have discussed it in military circles. It is, in fact, an open secret.'

'Interesting,' remarked Boyd. 'Whilst in Cumbria recently I witnessed a demonstration by Argentinians at a royal visit. It was noisy and eventually got out of hand.'

'Irrelevant,' remarked the Home Secretary. 'Please don't interrupt, officer. Anything else, Mister Spencer?'

'Russia,' replied the Head of MI6. 'Crimean ministers recently held a vote in their regional parliament to join the Russian

Federation and secede from Ukraine. The move comes as tensions continue to mount over the presence of Russian troops in the peninsula.'

'Why does Russia have a naval base in Crimea?' asked Boyd.

'Russia's capacity to reach the sea is limited by geography, so ports leading to the sea are crucial,' explained Julian. 'Russia leases the base at Sevastopol. The lease was due to run out in 2017 but the 1997 treaty extended the lease to 2042.'

'Why did they extend the lease?' asked a politician from the Select Defence Committee.

'As I say, the lease originally ran out in 2017 but in 2010 the Russians hiked up the gas price and Ukraine caved in. Basically, the Ukrainians need gas and the Russians want Sevastapol and the Crimean peninsula,' stated Sir Julian. 'Ukrainians can see the benefits of joining the European Union. They are a relatively poor country who would rely on the economic strength of the EU to bolster their finances. If they did join the EU they would immediately become members of NATO. Can you imagine the Russians giving the Crimea up so easily? NATO would be a stone's throw away from the doorstep of Russia. That would be far too close for Moscow's liking.'

'And there would be problems for a displaced Black Sea Fleet with nowhere to drop anchor.'

'Precisely!'

'Don't forget the Spanish claim to Gibraltar,' suggested Sandra Peel sarcastically.

'Really, superintendent,' voiced the Home Secretary. 'I think we have enough on our plate at the moment, don't you?'

"There is one thing that I cannot see on the agenda,' remarked Sandra.

'And that is?' queried the Home Secretary.

'The upcoming G8 conference on the Isle of Wight isn't mentioned.'

'That's hardly a threat to the nation, Superintendent Peel.'

'We have intelligence that bomb threats have been made in previous years. Such a threat to the stability of that part of the UK will surely have a direct bearing on the deployment of police resources to deal with it.'

Leaning forward the Home Secretary asked, 'And how many bomb threats against the G8 have been made this year?'

'One from Anarchists Unite,' replied Peel.

'You mean from the same source as all the other bomb calls that have been made over the years regarding the G8? The reality is that these are merely calls made to frighten us. There is no history of a successful bomb attack at such a gathering. I do wish people like you would get your facts right before you launch into things.'

'It's a credible threat,' replied Peel stiffly. 'And one we need to deal with by penetrating the target and nullifying the threat.'

'Quite,' replied the Home Secretary. 'Let's move on; Sir Julian, your comments please.'

Sir Julian stood up and said, 'There's been an increase in electronic traffic form the areas of Mosul, Tikrit and Ar Raqqah. These have been reported by our colleagues in GCHQ. I've been able to scrutinise some of the unencrypted data and draw your attention to the phenomenon we are calling the man from Tikrit.'

'Unencrypted messages make me think such a matter has little importance,' commented the Home Secretary. 'Surely an important message would be encrypted?'

'Most of the traffic intercepted is encrypted, Home Secretary but some reveal the 'man from Tikrit' is called Salman and he is on his way. The message is that Islamic State lost the battle but they will kill our leaders in retaliation for the defeat.'

'And the Duke's analysis?' queried the Home Secretary.

'Cornelius Duke suggests no further action but since then we have the video which does not mention Tikrit but does make a threat to our leaders,' explained Sir Julian. 'I think it may be connected but none of us can be sure. If I add to that a general analysis from CAST – our analytical software - I'd say we need to be very much aware of the man from Tikrit because the software reveals the amount of traffic relative to this subject.'

'It's what a detective calls a gut feeling,' remarked Boyd. 'No proof, but everything compels you in a certain direction.'

'Speaking of directions,' interrupted Sir Phillip, 'Barclays Bank was attacked very recently but no data was stolen. The cyberattack came from the direction of Indonesia and the South China Seas. It was a site survey so I expect the cyber warriors will return. I wonder if the origin of the attack is China particularly when I see a cosy relationship developing between the Chinese and Argentina. Both have claims on land in possession of other nations at this time. Perhaps they are scratching each other's backs. These cyberattacks on our national infrastructure continue to grow and we are thwarting attacks on own government sites on a daily basis. The matter is worsening. We need to improve our technological ability in this area.'

'I see,' remarked the Home Secretary. 'Is the man from Tikrit now on your radar?'

'Obviously the system is now aware of the man from Tikrit,' explained Phillip. 'But he has no real name, no description, and no face. He might not even exist for all we know. He might be a product of the imagination planted to send us off in the wrong direction. We don't know who we are looking for.'

'He's hardly going to arrive on a ferry at Dover riding a camel and wearing a Lawrence of Arabia headscarf,' quipped Boyd.

'Quite!' snarled the Home Secretary angrily. 'Thank you, now can I ask why the young man from Blackburn was not on your radar, Sir Phillip?'

'MI5 faces something of a deadly dilemma over terror suspects it has under surveillance, Home Secretary. The intelligence services are damned if they do and damned if they don't. We really need legislation that allows GCHQ to gain more access to emails, texts and transmissions from various electronic devices.'

'Not possible in this parliament, Sir Phillip,' remarked the Home Secretary. 'The electorate are worried about big brother and the nanny state.'

'The electorate,' remarked Sir Phillip, 'Are what politicians need to secure their jobs via votes. For the intelligence services the electorate are those we are here to protect.'

'Not quite what I meant, Sir Phillip.'

'There are groups within society that are more interested in liberty and freedom than security, and I understand that, but we face unprecedented times. We need an accepted operational command structure that allows the intelligence services in the UK to upgrade their legal access to electronic mail when the threat level is assessed at threat level three or above. Legal access to electronic material needs to equate to the status of the threat level and we must have authority over those who manage networks.'

'I doubt that will ever happen,' remarked the Home Secretary.

'The reality is we're not interested in what the electorate had for breakfast or what brands they follow on Facebook or Twitter,' stated Sir Phillip. 'At least six hundred British nationals are believed to have gone to Syria. It's a lot to study when you add those on the watch list, and those already subject to surveillance. They are communicating with each other and planning our destruction. We need to intercept specific communications. The nation is at war with terrorists. Who does the electorate want to win?'

'Okay, what can you do Commander Maxwell?' asked the Home Secretary. 'What is so special about your unit within Counter Terrorist Command?'

'The Special Crime Unit is a hand-picked team of detectives drawn from Counter Terrorist Command, formerly the anti-terrorist branch, together with some top detectives from all over the British Isles and some hand-picked individuals from MI5 and MI6 as well as other national agencies appropriate to our remit. They are all experts in some field or other and serve between three and five years in the unit,' explained the commander. 'In some cases they may serve longer. We select only the best of the best and will settle for nothing less than total loyalty to the unit. The unit's remit is to police, defend, and secure the freedom of the nation and its people from serious organised crime and national and international terrorism. The unit works from a secure area within the Security Service building. My officers only have access to this area within Thames House for obvious reasons relevant to security. They need only know that which concerns them. The very latest equipment is installed to prevent cyber hacking and we call our floor The Operations Centre. We have an identical area in New Scotland Yard. Detective Superintendent Peel is my second-in-command whilst Chief Inspector Boyd is Head of Covert Operations in the unit. His speciality is running a stand-alone response team capable of running any major investigation anywhere in the country, and if necessary elsewhere. The unit has one commander, one detective superintendent, one DCI who runs the covert ops team, and 4 other wings. Each is commanded by a DI with 2 DS's and 10 DC's. The total strength of the Unit varies between 60 and 70.'

'Can Chief Inspector Boyd define your work?' asked the Home Secretary.

Boyd replied, 'That depends on how we select what we do when we do. We are constantly juggling our operations because we should be at least twice the size we are. But I can define the threat today, as I see it, as follows - Islamic extremism against leaders and non-Muslims - Irish terrorism, the claim to the Falklands by Argentine supported by China, an emerging new Cold War with Russia over the Ukraine and the real problem of cyberattacks on our infrastructure, and, of course international serious organised crime aided and abetted by an unpoliced world wide web.'

'I agree wholeheartedly,' revealed Julian

'Seconded,' agreed Phillip

'I couldn't have put it better myself,' suggested Maxwell

'I do not think we have any other option but to seriously consider raising the level to Threat Level One,' declared the Home Secretary. 'But I must ask your Mister Boyd to review security for our Royal Family and the Prime Minister. I intend to call upon the Commissioner of the Metropolitan Police with a strong recommendation that he attach this particular covert unit to the Royalty and Diplomatic branch for the foreseeable future in an effort to highlight security flaws. I want your self-appointed self-styled best of the best to beef up protection whilst at the same time providing a highly skilled investigative team in situ, so to speak.'

'I'd rather not,' beseeched Boyd.

'But you will,' declared Superintendent Peel. 'If the intelligence has been assessed correctly then an attack will be imminent and our unit will be at the forefront of protective and investigative measures.'

'We are only as good as the weakest link in the chain,' said Boyd. 'No-one ever succeeds alone in this business. We have to work closely with everyone else involved in reducing the threat. And it's far too late to increase manning levels when we need them now not in six month time. All this will do is to increase our juggling expertise.'

'Then see to it,' ordered the Home Secretary.

'Of course, Home Secretary,' agreed Peel.

'Thunder and lightning,' murmured Boyd. 'Maybe they'll both strike down the man from Tikrit that I need to find.'

Nods around the table signalled Sir Phillip to state, 'Thank you, ladies and gentlemen, now if I may have your attention. We are all agreed that an attack is expected imminently. Our combined response should be exceptional in the circumstances we have just discussed. Maximum protective security measures should be put in place immediately to meet the specific threats discussed and to minimise our vulnerability and the risk factor. I think I should also remind you that Threat Level One means the level is critical. Another Cold War looms and we need to be vigilant. There is no good news from this meeting. I note from those around the table the diversity of opinion that is in the air. For example, terrorists are waging war on democracy; our intelligence community is overwhelmed by the threat, a broken police service is at odds with a government it perceives to be corrupt and incompetent, and our country is at war with itself. It is time to meet the threat head on and win. We cannot do that divided. We must forge links between us that are strong and unbreakable. Now I ask you all to return your posts and do what you do best. We are at Threat Level One. The future of the nation is in our hands.'

The Home Secretary approached the police trio, handed Boyd a business card, looked scornfully at Sandra Peel, and said, 'Chief Inspector, you will ring me immediately you perceive a direct threat to the monarchy. I want to hear such information right from the horse's mouth and not via a third party.'

'Then I'll pass it to the mounted section,' suggested Boyd. 'They have the horses, not me.'

There was a smile or two from around the table before Boyd exchanged cards with the Home Secretary.

Delegates adjourned their meeting for a month. The threat was always live to such people and often subject of heated debate. It never went away despite whatever level it attained. The threat lived, breathed, evolved and dissolved on a daily basis. It was at the heart of the intelligence community.

As they walked through a corridor, Antonia caught up with Boyd and remarked, 'Good meeting! Sad times! And you're on a very thin tightrope carrying her business card with you. You've just given her a scapegoat because you'll get the blame if things go wrong.'

'What again?' laughed Boyd. 'That won't be the first time, will it?'

'Look, Billy, I need a word,' suggested Antonia

They stepped into a vacant office where Boyd asked, 'What's wrong, playing politics with the Home Secretary? Look,

Toni, I'm a policeman. I'll go with anyone who supports the police whatever their politics. If I was a plumber, a doctor, a nurse, or an airline pilot I'd fight for my corner wherever and with whomever.'

'No, it's Phillip,' replied Antonia. 'There's something not right and I don't know who to turn to. The service isn't famous for whistle blowing, Billy, but I'd appreciate your help.'

'Go on,' replied Boyd sympathetically.

Pursing her lips for a moment, Antonia exhaled loudly before saying, 'He's visiting historic castles on a regular basis.'

'What? Is that all?' exclaimed Boyd. 'Hardly earth shattering, Toni. Perhaps he just enjoys time out to relax on the castle battlements? It's a stressful job he has, you know.'

'It's every six weeks or so.'

'I see!'

'Yes, and it's not right,' growled Antonia. 'There's something wrong. You're not the only one who has gut feelings you know.'

'What do you mean by historic castles, Toni?'

'Rambling old buildings owned by the aristocracy and dotted about all over England and parts of Scotland and Wales. You know the ones I mean. Some are owned by the rich and others are owned by the less rich who turn part or whole of the castle and estate into an aristocratic theme park of some kind or other. It helps pay the rent and death duties apparently.'

'I don't think I know anyone from the aristocracy,' mused Boyd. 'Any household names I should know, Toni?'

'Not that I know of; he's not said a word which is most unlike Phillip. I can tell you the castles are sometimes occupied by a Duke, Marquis, Earl, Viscount, or Baron. Some of them insist they are sixty first in line to the British throne or whatever. He stays overnight and returns directly to the office the next morning. What's more, he won't discuss what he's doing whilst he's away.'

'Another woman?' ventured Boyd.

'I don't know,' revealed Antonia somewhat saddened. 'Whatever it is, he prefers someone else's dungeon to mine.'

'Phillip doesn't have a reputation for chasing women, Toni,' stated Boyd. 'So my suggestion would be that there's someone special involved or something special involved. Sorry but from what I know of Phillip it won't be a stamp collecting club.'

'Damn you, Billy,' snapped Antonia. 'You're no help at all.'

Stepping towards the door, Boyd took hold of the handle, and paused. Then he turned back to face Antonia and said, 'What am I thinking about. I'm always here for you because over the years we've been through so much together.'

'Which is why I thought you might help,' delivered Antonia.

'Why haven't you reported it through your security channels? Don't tell me you don't have a whistle blower system, Toni. I know more about your mob than you'd ever imagined. We work with you and the service works with us but that's as far as it goes. You will never be police and I will never be MI5. I don't complicate my position by thinking of myself in any other way than being an ordinary copper working with a great bunch of people. But you guys at your level are intellectual practitioners. I'm not. That said, Toni did you ever see me walk down a blind alley not knowing who was behind me?'

'No, I haven't reported it to the security branch,' admitted Antonia. 'And you undersell yourself. But tell me, Billy, what if I do tell security and Phillip is up to something illegal?'

'Then he's the wrong man for you and the wrong man to be Director General of the Security Service,' delivered Boyd.

'So?'

'So ditch him now and walk away or…'

'Or what?' enquired Antonia.

'Talk to your friends in the city. You've some wealthy well-placed friends in the establishment, Toni. Call some favours in. You've done it before to achieve an objective. Now do it again for yourself.'

Walking away for a moment, Antonia thought things over before replying, 'I can't. I need to keep that side of my personal life out of my professional life.'

'In that case there's only one thing to do if you're not going to go legal,' suggested Boyd. 'And I'll do it because I wouldn't ask anyone else to do something like this.'

'An investigation into Phillip?' queried Antonia. 'You'd run a covert operation against the Director General of the Security Services?'

'Of course not,' replied Boyd. 'It would be illegal to copy the sim card in his mobile, listen to his landline, and place a listening device in his apartment without legal authority. I'd need a key to get into his apartment or a copy and then I'd need…' Boyd paused, studied his colleague, and said, 'Of course I wouldn't do that, Toni.'

'You do know they will sack you if you are discovered,' delivered Antonia. 'In fact, they will probably hang draw and quarter you.'

'And I will tell them it is my job to protect the realm at all costs – no-one is above the law – no-one, it's my decision,' revealed Boyd.

'You love your country that much?'

'Yes, it's just the people who live in it who are the problem.'

'Then it is a path you must walk alone,' suggested Antonia.

'Will you watch my back, Toni?'

'Yes,' responded Antonia slowly. 'But I was never with you.'

Looking quite serious, Boyd stepped out of the office and immediately walked into Sandra Peel.

'Ahh, there you are. There's a job on and it's ours.'

'What now with me in my best suit and you in your best bib and tucker?' quipped Boyd.

'Yes, the office rang,' explained Superintendent Peel. 'Crimestoppers got an anonymous call from someone saying they were calling from Northern Ireland. The caller said Patrick Brendan

O'Malley is living in a flat in Walthamstow, address given. Actually, the call was made from a box on the Irish border because the caller seems to have deliberately forgotten to replace the handset onto the cradle. I'll guess it's been made by someone who is not in favour of the New Front for Irish Independence.'

'That's a good guess in my book. Does he walk with a limp?' enquired Boyd.

'Apparently!'

'Brilliant, let's go, Sandy' decided Boyd. 'Anything on his brother?'

'Not a thing. What do you think of it?'

'I think the New Front for Irish Independence have upset the Republican Movement, Sandy,' remarked Boyd. 'They don't like opponents and we might end up taking the biscuit. Is it verified?'

'Inspector Adams is in charge at Walthamstow, Boyd. She tells me the flat is occupied by one Irishman who fits the description. Do we go in or do we wait for him to come out?'

'Interesting,' puzzled Boyd. 'What does Anthea think?'

'She's on channel thirty-six,' replied the superintendent. 'Why don't we ask her?'

*

Chapter Nine
~

Walthamstow, North London
A short time later
Threat Level One - Critical

Casually parting the curtains with his free hand, Patrick Brendan O'Malley checked the street outside whilst stirring sugar into a mug of coffee with the other. Satisfied all was well, Patrick took a mouthful and then pushed the mug to one side of the table.

'Too much sugar, damn it!' he voiced aloud.

On edge as a result of life at the sharp end, Patrick had spent too many days hiding from police, British Intelligence, and those who might be their informants. They'd taken their toll on a man like Patrick, for he was no ordinary man.

In his forties, Patrick stood no more than five feet ten inches tall. A mop of unruly light brown hair sprouted from his skull and did little to compliment his fairly solid body frame. His limp defined his appearance since he had a tendency to drag his foot when he was tired. Yet he was proud of his limp in a bizarre kind of way. He'd inherited it falling from a roof whilst preparing to carry out a sniping operation at an army base near Crossmaglen in Northern Ireland. Dressing like a member of the travelling community, he bore a close resemblance to his brother Declan yet the limp was the obvious factor that separated them. Patrick was a man who lived in a world of his own creation: a world of ducking and diving from those who would gladly see him imprisoned or dead. Loved by some, a hero too many, he lived on the dark side of the street where kneecapping, shooting, bombing and killing were almost a staple diet to a man dubbed a 'domestic terrorist' by the nation's media.

Patrick reflected that if he lived in France he be reported upon by the media as an international terrorist. He tried the coffee once more and this time managed to swallow a mouthful.

Patrick stared at the empty house on the opposite side of the street once more. Studying the upper windows carefully he challenged his eyesight when he honed in on a dark patch in their symmetry. Shadows! He wondered. Can I see shadows or is it just that those curtains are old and faded. Lace curtains, he thought. Who would have thought lace curtains still existed in this day and age. Still, better to see the shadows than not, he decided.

Then Patrick laughed and told himself he needed a rest. He was seeing shadows behind lace curtains when there were no shadows to see. He turned to a table in his lounge.

Delicately, the master craftsman went about his work. He pulled on a pair of long plastic gloves, smoothed the fingers tight to his skin, and gathered all the pieces of a bomb together. He knew it would take time but gradually his mix of bits and pieces would combine to devastating effect. He understood what he was doing. It wasn't the first time and he planned that it wouldn't be his last.

Stretching the gloves as tight as possible across his hands, and up both forearms, Patrick ensured no part of his skin was visible. He'd worked out there was just no way he was leaving fingerprints or DNA anywhere on this little package.

Smoothing one end of a dowel pin with a fine piece of sandpaper, Patrick eventually inserted it into a circular hole along the side of a small wooden box. Virtually rectangular in shape, the box measured the size of a ten inch netbook. The hole he had created would be where a USB port might have been had it been a real netbook.

Warily, he attached the dowel to a timing device inside the box and added a small quantity of home-made explosives. Gradually, he packed the box with more explosives and used his gloved fingers to push the substance flat so he could cover it with a lid. Finally Patrick introduced a detonator, which he didn't connect.

Sitting back to check his handiwork he went over the bomb diagram imprinted in his mind. Yes, he reminded himself. All the pieces do need to be connected properly. He was happy with his new project. It was just an old and basic design altered slightly to accommodate the host package. And he knew it worked. Another bomb was nearly ready. It would travel well and wouldn't take long to assemble. It was compact, easy to carry, and very powerful.

One more completed, he thought. Patrick placed it in a cupboard with the others.

Yet one of the founder members of the New Front for Irish Independence remained suspicious of the premises opposite. Sure there was a 'For Sale' sign in the front garden and the name of an estate agent was clear for all to see, he realised. But he hated the possibility that he was being watched and, from long experience, considered the empty house to be a hazard until such time that the vacancy was proved. He reminded himself that it was tiny things like this that had kept him free for such a long time.

Patrick gently parted the curtains a tad once more before sliding an overcoat carefully across his shoulders and checking a pistol in the inside pocket. Then he moved towards the door, paused, connected a string loop to a door handle, and tied it to a shotgun trigger a few yards away. Making sure it was pointed in the right direction he mounted the loaded shotgun onto the back of a leather sofa and propped it up with cushions. Patrick made sure the line was taut and stepped back. It would do the job he intended and if need be.

His fingers smoothed over the cold metal of the gun barrel before he approached a cupboard and opened it to inspect his lair. Patrick shook his head, unsure, and perhaps stressed out more than usual.

Leaving the cupboard open, Patrick stepped towards the window once more, opened the curtains wide, and checked the street both ways. Not a car or person to be seen, he thought.

A finger clicked a camera and captured his image from fifty yards away. A voice in a covert observation post radioed, 'That's

Target one. Positive confirmation at the target address! No sign of Target Two. Stand by!'

Yes, this is it, Patrick decided as he showed himself in the window. It's just not right out there. What did I miss, he mused. I should have checked the street first thing when I woke, he reminded himself. Where is the postman and next door's dog? Where is the lady from number twenty seven who likes to titivate her garden every day? And why is that plumber's van parked where it is – abandoned?

Patrick looked both ways and smiled to his unseen audience. That should do it, he decided. They've had time enough to see that it's me if that's what they are looking for. Or am I crazy? Have I dropped over the edge from living on that very edge for so long?

Rummaging in the cupboard, Patrick removed a hand grenade and then checked his wristwatch. Forty five minutes, he decided. Then he returned to the cupboard and connected a detonator to one of the devices inside. Carefully, he activated a timer and set it at forty five minutes. Maybe I'm wrong; maybe I'm right, I don't know, he thought. But I can always disconnect the detonator before it explodes. I made the bomb. I know how to kill it. He closed the cupboard door and stepped away.

Opening an adjoining door into the downstairs kitchen, Patrick stepped through into a corridor. Locking the door with a key, he helped himself into his overcoat properly, turned the collar up, and made for the street outside.

It was just a precaution, thought Patrick. They will follow or break into the house, he decided. If they break into the house they'll get a surprise. So now we shall see if the shadows are real or a figment of my tired imagination. In any case, I'll take a stroll and fifteen minutes exercise before going back to it. That will give me thirty minutes to defuse the bomb if I need to. Maybe I should call

149

it a day soon and retire from the business. Perhaps somewhere warm would be nice, he thought. Maybe South America!

Traffic was light and only occasionally hindered the view from Anthea's surveillance position: a front bedroom on the first floor of the vacant house situated across the road from Patrick O'Malley's rented accommodation.

Yawning, Anthea and Janice took turns to man a huge pair of binoculars set on a tripod and focused towards O'Malley's front door. Terry Anwhari dosed on a nearby sofa waiting for his shift as observer.

'How long?' asked Janice. 'Or do we wait for the technical guys to give us audio visual later tonight?'

'Under the cover of darkness?'

'Yes,' replied Janice.

'I hope we have something by nightfall, Janice. If he goes for a walk we'll go with him,' announced Anthea. 'But that's him. Check the Polaroid again. This is the man, don't you think? He almost posed for it which I find quite strange.'

'Probably hasn't a clue we're onto him,'

Anthea handed a photo of Patrick to Janice who viewed it. The snap was still slightly damp and obviously new. Janice replied, 'He has the eyes of Hannibal Lector!'

'On the other hand if he gets a visitor we'll know a little more about his associates and hopefully a vehicle will turn up at the house,' explained Anthea. 'But if he stays inside we'll either have to talk him out or go in and get him.'

'Aye, I suppose we could always just go and knock on his door,' suggested Janice with a sarcastic smile. 'Give him a wee bit of a sing song like carol singers.'

'We might do that if there's no movement today,' replied Anthea. 'Did anyone tell you that you look like a door to door perfume saleswoman? You might be the one to knock on the door and make contact. Do you think you can get him to answer the door with a saucy smile and the whiff of a new perfume?'

'Probably, I just cannae remember that happening in Glasgow,' chuckled Janice. 'I'll need to find out about after shave as well, I reckon. But tell me, Anthea, do you think both our men are in there?'

'Funnily enough, yes,' replied Anthea.

Boyd and Peel approached in a vehicle but when they were about a mile from the scene, Boyd drove towards two armed uniform officers blockading the highway at an outer cordon. Whilst Sandra Peel jumped out and introduced herself to the officers, Boyd radioed, 'This is the boss car. We are at the outer cordon. Who has control?'

DI Anthea Adams replied, 'I have control. This is a red blanket zone. Target One is in situ at his home address. Positive identification made. We have the premises under observation and a covert evacuation operation is in progress.'

'Looks like we're going in,' suggested Sandra Peel closing the car door and unlocking a secure part of the dashboard. She rummaged for a moment, withdrew a handgun and holster, and queried, 'What about vests?'

'Not yet,' replied Boyd. 'It's a mix of terraced houses as well as semi-detached homes. Some are student flats; some are two or three bedroomed houses lived in by older people. They're nearly all rentals in this area. Anthea is covering all the bases. Give her time. We'll go closer and help in evacuating the locals if we have to.'

Two members of the unit had gained access to surrounding houses and furtively removed the families present. Gradually, the immediate area was cleared.

Anthea radioed, 'Boss car – Guvnor - I have control. Come to the inner cordon and stay!'

Boyd and Peel pulled up a hundred yards short of the target premises and switched their car engine off.

'I see you,' radioed Anthea. 'Now stay!'

'That's us told,' murmured Boyd switching a CD unit on.

'We should take control,' suggested Peel.

'No,' suggested Boyd. 'Leave it to Anthea. You might be the new superintendent but she's the new DI and she's no fool. If it is Patrick O'Malley Anthea knows he won't come quietly. The lady has been on hundreds of jobs like this. She's an expert in what she does. Anthea has set up an outer and inner cordon of firearms officers. She has control. That's what we do on this unit. The controller controls irrespective of rank. Now let her control, Sandy.'

Sandra Peel nodded, exhaled with dissatisfaction, and looked out of the window for inspiration.

Pressing the 'talk' button on his radio, Boyd replied, 'Boss car received. We are in a back-up static position at the outer cordon. You have control. Out!'

They watched and waited and listened to the sound of a saxophone softly playing from Boyd's CD.

'Relax,' advised Boyd, 'Deep breaths and soft music before we're needed.'

'Really?' queried Sandra.

'It has a calming effect,' suggested Boyd.

'You're all mad,' muttered Sandra.

Leaving his house by the rear door Patrick stood in an enclosed yard for a few moments. He listened to the sound of traffic, of birds singing, and of nothing else. No sounds from television or radio from the neighbours, he thought. Warily, he walked round to the front and stepped onto the pavement.

'Contact! Contact! Contact!' radioed Janice on the binoculars. 'That's definitely our man, Anthea. He has the limp as well as the look of the man in that Polaroid.'

Anthea checked the photograph, nodded her agreement, and replied, 'Let's go. We'll follow him for a while and gather the troops around him. 'Terry,' she shouted. 'You're up. We're on the target's tail.'

Swinging his feet onto the carpet, Terry Anwhari stepped forward and immediately took charge of the binoculars. 'I'm on it,' he voiced.

The two ladies made their way downstairs to the back door whilst Anthea radioed, 'All units Target One is out of the target premises and onto the pavement walking north. Stand by for follow and capture. We'll surround him and take him to the ground.'

With a radio buzzing with acknowledgements, Janice swiftly moved into a positon behind Patrick on the same side of the street. Anthea walked slightly behind but on the opposing pavement. Activating her throat microphone, she radioed their position and tightened the cordon around Patrick Brendan O'Malley.

Strolling casually, Patrick had one hand in his pocket whilst the other swung freely by his side. But his eyes were alert as he approached a white Transit van that was parked close to the kerb. It was the plumber's van.

Deliberately, Patrick faltered at the front of the van as if he were searching his pockets for something he might have forgotten. His fingers entwined the trigger guard of his pistol. Yet Patrick took the opportunity to study the windscreen on the Transit van and realised the sun was in exactly the right position for his needs. He noticed the reflection of Janice and Anthea walking on either side of the street. Patrick studied the two women for a moment, and then walked on.

Nah, he thought. They wouldn't send a couple of women after me. No chance! Five steps further and his mind worked overtime when he reminded himself never to underestimate his enemy.

Patrick stopped abruptly and looked around him.

Ricky French walked at right angles along an adjacent street. They would meet soon. Patrick set off slowly once more, shortened his stride to a casual stroll, and reduced speed whilst keeping an eye on Ricky French.

Suddenly stopping, Ricky blew his nose, and then continued.

I don't like this, thought Patrick feeling for the grenade in his pocket. I'm going to walk straight into the guy at this rate - and those two women - are they or are they not police or MI5?

Spinning on his heel, Patrick returned towards his house with his limp becoming more pronounced as his leg began to drag slightly on the ground.

'He's sussed us,' radioed Anthea. 'STRIKE! Let's take him.'

On his toes now, with adrenalin bursting through his veins, Patrick deliberately glanced over his shoulder towards Ricky before crossing the road and heading directly for Anthea. Then he heard a car engine burst into life. A split second later he heard the sound of two more car engines throbbing loudly and obviously coming his way. He couldn't see them but he could certainly hear them. A glance at Janice caught her eyes watching him. Anthea was talking but there was no-one there to hear her voice.

The woman is on the radio, he decided. Patrick began to run towards the house.

Boyd and Peel heard the signal 'STRIKE' and roared into the street to find three detectives chasing Patrick down the middle of the road.

Unfazed, Patrick took everything in his stride and ran towards Boyd's approaching car.

Boyd hit the brakes and slewed to a halt.

Mounting Boyd's car bonnet, Patrick stepped across the roof, and then down onto the boot. He stumbled awkwardly when his feet hit the tarmac again but then regained his feet before legging it down the street.

Seconds later, Ricky French brought Patrick down with an unorthodox rugby tackle. He grappled the Irishman around his chest and dragged him to the tarmac.

A struggle followed when Patrick tried to break loose. The two men rolled over on the ground. Patrick struck his knee into

Ricky's groin and heard Ricky wheeze in anguish. Patrick rose to his feet whilst Ricky remained on the ground in obvious pain.

Suddenly, Patrick O'Malley snapped his arm through the air like a whip. The speed of his manoeuvre triggered an elasticated cord mechanism which released a Browning semi-automatic 9mm pistol from his shoulder holster. The lethal weapon was suddenly in his hands

In the split second that followed Patrick raised the gun to waist height, curled his finger round the trigger, and fired towards the women.

Anthea and Janice dived into a hedge when a couple of rounds scorched the air between them.

Ricky French struggled to his knees and drew his firearm.

Spinning on his heel Patrick lost his balance, turned, and was about to fire again when Ricky dropped him with a double tap to the chest. The Irishman's Browning flew into the air when the force of two shots in quick succession threw O'Malley backwards.

A deluge of blood poured from the Irishman's chest cavity.

Anthea ran to Patrick's side and shouted, 'Declan! Where is he?'

There was a cough from O'Malley and a splurge of blood escaped his mouth.

'Where is he?' yelled Anthea.

O'Malley laughed as his hand fumbled inside his clothing. Stretching out, his fingers brushed the rounded edge of a grenade as he reached for the pin that would detonate the device.

Suspicious, Sandra smothered his wandering hand with her foot.

Kneeling on the ground beside the dying man Boyd pleaded, 'If you can do one thing for your fellow man before you die, Patrick, tell us where your brother is so that we can take him quietly. We're not looking for his blood and no man should die on a cold piece of tarmac on the streets of London. But we do want you and your brother.'

Patrick glanced at the detectives and then grinned broadly. Then he laughed through the blood and mucus escaping his mouth. Eagerly, he snatched hold of Boyd's jacket, with his free hand, pulled him closer, and muttered, 'Declan, you say. Declan! Why he's in the house, so he is. Aye, he's in the house.'

'Your house?' asked Boyd suspiciously.

'Aye, just there, yer stupid bastard Brit. He's asleep just now. Aye, he's asleep, so he is.'

Patrick coughed again. His chest heaved upwards and then sunk down. He died in a pool of blood on the streets in a city he hated with all his heart and soul.

'Are you alright, Ricky?' asked Anthea.

'Oh yeah, I've got balls of fire that's all,' replied the detective doubled up in pain.

Normally, a laugh or two might have been appropriate but the team knew they were vulnerable.

'Shots fired! Shots fired!' bellowed Anthea into her radio. 'Target down! I repeat target down. Ambulance required.'

'Roger!' radioed Commander Maxwell back at base. 'All received. Red Blanket is still down. Do you have total control?'

'Watch your back, Anthea,' advised Boyd. 'Where is his brother?'

Nodding quickly, her mind racing overtime, Anthea radioed, 'Partial control is established, commander. Target One is deceased. Target Two - his bother - may be in the vicinity. I have control but keep the red blanket down. We are evolving, over!'

'All received,' replied the commander. 'All units hold the cordons and await further instructions. Red blanket is down. I repeat the red blanket is still down and the operation is live. Proceed with caution.'

Sandra Peel knelt beside Patrick and began searching his pockets whilst suggesting, 'I know this might sound crazy, guys, but are we sure we got Patrick and not his brother, Declan?'

'I'm sure,' replied Anthea.

'What you got?' asked Boyd watching the superintendent.

Sandra Peel detached the Browning from the deceased's hand and elasticated cord. She padded the body down whilst trying to ignore a pool of blood gathering on the ground and spoiling her best skirt. She produced a hand grenade from his trouser pocket and laid it carefully on the ground beside his body.

'Pin attached,' she remarked.

Boyd zeroed in and agreed, 'Confirmed!'

Sandra then produced a wallet containing a driving licence and passport. Both were in the names Patrick Brendan Lynch. Then she found another pistol tucked down Patrick's trouser belt close to the small of his back.

'Some cool cookie this one,' suggested Sandra. 'He's an arsenal waiting to explode. I'm glad we took him in daylight.'

Boyd nudged Patrick's ankle, bent down and found something else. 'Another one,' he offered. 'His limp was made worse by the handgun in his ankle holster.'

'The man really is a bloody walking arsenal,' shrieked Ricky.

'Not anymore,' replied Boyd recovering a pistol from the holster. 'No gun jamming this time, Ricky?'

'Just as well,' Ricky replied.

In the moments that followed Anthea's brain went into overdrive when she said, 'Take cover everyone. If Declan is in the house then he heard the shooting and is either making a run for it or about to take us out. Take cover. Now!' she bellowed.

The team scattered, rolled behind cars, under the Transit van, and behind squad car doors.

'Good shout,' declared Boyd. 'And we are too exposed.'

'Wait one,' shouted Anthea. Engaging her wireless she radioed, 'Terry, what have you got?'

A couple of seconds elapsed before Terry Anwhari replied, 'I have eyeball on the target premises. No movement detected. Standby!'

In the bedroom of the observation post Terry Anwhari took a bite from an apple, refocused, panned and zoomed, and then replied, 'No change! No movement!'

'Now what?' asked Ricky lying tight against the plumber's van. 'I feel like a coconut at a fairground just waiting to be knocked off. Is there someone in the house or not?'

Anthea radioed again, 'All units at the outer cordon keep your eyes peeled. We may have Target Two on site. He may be in the immediate area. Exercise extreme caution.'

Turning, Anthea looked down at her denim jeans and said, 'Damn it, they're torn and I only got them last week.'

'Typical,' remarked Boyd shaking his head. 'We're under fire and you're bothered about the fashion police.'

'Okay, boys and girls,' said Anthea ignoring Boyd. 'Is Declan watching us? Is he still in the house? Does he have a sniper's rifle? Or has he gone?' Then she radioed, 'Terry what can you see now?'

'No change,' replied Terry. 'I can see no movement at the house.'

Boyd glanced at Anthea and then Sandra before asking Ricky, 'You got your breath back?'

'I'm fine now,' replied Ricky.

'Janice?' queried Boyd. 'You okay?'

'Och aye,' replied the feisty Scot. 'My money says we've an empty house.'

'Sandy?'

'The day can't get any worse. Best clothes ruined and I'll never get this blood out of the jacket. It's going in the bin. Anything else I can help you with?'

Boyd returned a smile and said, 'It's your call, Anthea. You have ground control.'

'Years of training and classroom scenarios don't count for much when you're sat wondering whether some bastard is waiting to shoot the top of your head off your shoulders,' announced

Anthea. 'I'm with Janice on this one but I might be wrong. What do you think?'

Boyd replied, 'Not sure, Anthea, but we can't stay here. Potentially, he's got us pinned down if he's there. We're like sitting ducks in a shooting gallery. I suggest we make a move soon. Ricky? Sandra?'

Reloading his handgun Ricky French replied, 'If we all go together we'll soon find out.'

Shaking her head Sandra suggested, 'Well, just point me in the right direction and I'll run all the way.'

Anthea looked directly into Boyd's eyes and said, 'Billy, you take it.'

'Are you sure?' asked Boyd.

'Control,' radioed Anthea. 'We have evolved. Boyd has control. Over!'

'Roger,' from the commander's voice. 'All units, Boyd has ground control. Stand by!'

'Yeah, good one, Anthea,' chuckled Boyd. 'I've never been in this position before. Damned if we do and damned if we don't.'

'I'll be with you all the way,' replied Anthea. 'But this is your speciality, Guvnor. It's your call.'

There was a silence that penetrated the air: an uneasy atmosphere that gradually calmed when Boyd decided, 'Okay, my call. Make sure you're all fully loaded.'

There was a check of weapons before Boyd radioed, 'Terry, we need your eyes wide open, okay?'

'You got them,' came the reply. 'No change! No movement!'

'Take a deep breath everyone,' said Boyd softly. 'Settle the heart and cool the temper. If he's there then he's chosen not to shoot just now. If we move slowly he might take a couple of us down. So when we get our breath back and we're all in the same boat we'll go. We're going to hit the house on the count of five, okay?'

The team nodded their understanding before Boyd radioed, 'Terry, we're going in on my five. If you see the slightest movement...'

'I got you, Guvnor,' replied Terry. 'No change at the target.'

'All units,' radioed Boyd. 'Stand by! Team Alpha are about to hit the house.'

Checking his handgun once more, Boyd declared, 'Okay, let's make a move. There's five of us. We are a hand with four fingers and a thumb. On five we'll make the house and hit the wall. Spread out on my command and run as fast as you can to the target. I want our hand on that house wall – spread out - Understand?'

The team nodded in agreement.

'All happy?'

Janice, Anthea, Ricky and Sandra all nodded and readied themselves taking deep breaths and sneaking a glance at the target.

'Okay,' replied Boyd. 'Terry, on five!' he radioed.

'No change at the target,' radioed Terry. 'Come!'

Adrenalin surged, blood rushed, pulses raced when Boyd radioed, 'Five... Four...'

'No change at the target. Come!'

'Three... Two...'

'No change at the target. Come!'

'One...'

On 'One' all five detectives sprinted towards the target house with their weapons drawn.

'No change,' radioed Terry. 'No change!'

Boyd hit the front wall first followed closely by Janice and Anthea. Sandra was a second behind with Ricky bringing up the rear. They were spread out occupying five different positions across the house wall.

'So far,' radioed Boyd looking up at the bedroom windows. 'Terry?'

'No change at the target premises,' radioed Terry from the observation post.

The adrenalin rush paused. A pulse slowed down. Sweat receded. A finger curled round the trigger guard and eyes scoured windows and doors downstairs.

'Anyone see anything?' demanded Boyd.

Silence greeted his comment so he pronounced, 'It's empty. That was the best chance he had. Wait one!'

In the short thinking time that defines elite courage and true leadership Boyd said aloud to his team, 'No shots! Patrick urged us to do the house! There's no Declan here as far as I can see unless he's hiding in there! Why did the man want us to hit the house?'

Ricky French buzzed, 'He was a walking booby trap, Guvnor.'

'Yeah, wait one,' ordered Boyd. 'Maybe the house is too. He was keen enough to offer us Declan inside.'

Holstering his weapon, Boyd dropped to the ground and crawled to the nearest window before radioing, 'Terry?'

'No change,' replied Terry Anwhari. His eyes were glued to his binoculars when he reported, 'There's not even a fly on the windows, Guvnor.'

Peering inside, Boyd made out the distinct profile of a shotgun supported on the back of a sofa. The trigger was looped and tied to a length of string that seemed to trail away to the door handle.

'Booby trap,' declared Boyd. 'Boyd to base,' he radioed. 'Commander, I need a specialist entry team and a bomb disposal unit at this location. There's a booby trapped shotgun at our point of entry and, in view of what we know about Target One, I reckon the house could be booby trapped too.'

Inside a cupboard, the hand of a clock moved on and neared that part of a device known as a detonator.

'All received,' replied Commander Maxwell. There was a short period of silence before the commander radioed, 'Billy, if you're able I'd get out of there as safely as you can and as quickly as you can.'

'Yes, sir,' replied Boyd. 'I'm backing away now.'

Ducking low, Boyd said to his colleagues, 'Follow me.'

With his weapon pointed at the windows and Terry Anwhari persistently confirming inactivity Boyd gradually backed away from the house and took up a static position locked on an upper bedroom window.

'Come now,' he ordered.

One by one, using Boyd for cover, Sandra, Ricky, Anthea and Janice retreated from the house. They aimed their weapons at the windows before reaching the street where they took cover behind the plumber's van.

Eventually, Boyd stepped backwards from the house, holstered his weapon and said, 'Ever felt like an absolute fool? Now I'm just asking myself where the hell Declan O'Malley is.'

Two steps later a sliver of metal kissed the tip of a detonator which sent an electronic pulse down its spine into the explosive package. The flash became an explosion when a dozen bombs in a cupboard suddenly erupted in a ferocious display of flame and destruction.

A cupboard door blew off its hinges. The surrounding brickwork crumbled, brought down an interior wall, and did little to stop a huge explosion rumbling through the empty house. A rapid succession of violent thunderclaps rippled through the room blowing glass from the windows and causing an immense fireball to fly into the air and destroy everything in its path.

Boyd felt the force of the bomb hit his body as he made the roadway. Seconds later he was unconscious on the tarmac bizarrely lying next to the body of Patrick Brendan O'Malley.

'Officer down,' radioed Anthea. 'Ambulance required! Officer down!'

'On its way,' radioed Commander Maxwell. 'Is Declan O'Malley on site?'

Faraway in the north of England, a cold breeze invaded the marshland and bit into Declan's exposed skin. A drizzle of rain fell and swept brutally into his face. He wiped away the dampness as if it was unwanted tears.

Wet soil did not deter Patrick's brother from his task. Declan powered onto a spade and gradually dug an iron box from the sodden ground as the sun hid behind a dark cloud and night began its long journey across the Solway Firth.

Sweating now, Declan heaved his box from its lair and pulled it away from the hole he had dug. Eagerly, he removed a key from his jeans pocket, cleansed the padlock with a dry rag, and opened his box.

Declan checked the contents of his box and withdrew all the weapons and explosives he needed for the days ahead. He placed them into a dark blue leather holdall which he zipped tight before returning the iron box to its hiding place and covering it with soil. Before leaving, Declan arranged the turf. Satisfied the hide was well concealed he hoisted the holdall onto his back and made for the car parked nearby.

Behind him the cold breeze became a treacherous howl, drizzle turned to heavy rain, and the Solway Firth gradually began to breach the marshland.

Declan O'Malley was more than three hundred miles from the bloodstained streets of London, and he was on the move.

Later that night Boyd walked into his office to the applause of the unit.

'Slight concussion?' suggested Anthea.

'Yes, precisely,' agreed Boyd. 'A check up in casualty and they let me out. I'm fine how about everyone else?'

'Tired! A bit shell-shocked like you but no injuries,' reported Sandra Peel handing over a document. 'Here, I wrote the operation up for you and Anthea. What do you think?'

Taking the papers Boyd settled onto the edge of a desk and began reading the superintendent's report asking, 'Has Anthea read this?'

'She has,' replied Peel. 'I have to start somewhere with paperwork, Boyd. It seemed like as good a place as any. And I see you have a tray full of reports to sort out.'

Nodding in agreement, Boyd turned a page over but was aware of Anthea's presence.

'Guvnor, I just wanted to say thanks,' delivered Anthea.

'We're a team, Anthea. It's what we do,' replied Boyd. 'Except this time I made the wrong decision. Thankfully, we got lucky.'

'Wrong decision or not we got our man and no-one got hurt,' replied Anthea.

Turning another page Boyd engaged Sandra Peel and said, 'Has the commander seen this?'

'Not yet, why?'

'Because I'm jealous, Sandy,' explained Boyd. 'You've a way with the words. It would take me hours to write it up like that. How have you managed to keep it out of the hands of the media?'

'I've done a deal with them. I've promised an exclusive on the entire operation in return for silence on this one. I've told them we've one outstanding and press coverage may well prevent us from finding him since it might just set him on the run. Otherwise it's a legal request for a prohibition notice. They're all over us but at the moment they're on our side.'

'And that's in your report?' asked Boyd.

'Yes,' responded Sandra. 'Actually, I've always been good with paperwork, Boyd. Now I just need to get up to speed with operational procedures and I'll be more useful around here.'

'A new outfit might help,' mocked Anthea impishly.

'Aye, one that doesnae stop yer frae running across the road like a frightened wee rabbit,' laughed Janice.

'A wee kilt perhaps,' teased Peel in a scots accent.

'Or tartan trousers,' added Boyd. 'Look, Sandy, this is no ordinary police station with a hundred or more youngsters running around with minor crime reports and a dozen Saturday night assaults to sort out. The job doesn't get any sharper than this. Don't put yourself down. You'll get the hang of it, don't worry. And as for dealing with the press – now that's what I call class.'

Returning the report to Peel, Boyd made for his office.

'Boyd,' remarked Peel following on behind him. 'What you did today was quite remarkable. It took everyone's breath away. You used yourself as cover for the rest of the team. That takes guts. When the press know they can print that they'll make you a national hero. It's time they had one and they're short in supply.'

'It wasn't brave of me, Sandy. And I don't want to be a national hero for a week until the next news bite comes along. No, I had a mental blackout,' suggested Boyd. 'We were lucky it turned out the way it did. I made a mistake, Sandy. I should have called in the Met Firearms Specialist Squad and left it to them. A few ballistic shields and a little bit more brainpower were required. We went on a wing and a prayer. If something had gone wrong it would have been my fault and it won't take long for your friends in the media to work that one out.'

'You underestimate yourself, chief inspector,' replied Superintendent Peel. 'By the way I have no friends in the media. I just gave them a deal they couldn't refuse. And as for your part - we took out O'Malley because he presented himself and he's a wanted man. Plus, he's one of Europe's most dangerous terrorists. At least he was until Ricky ended his career.'

'We were lucky, that's all,' argued Boyd.

'I'm not a surveillance expert, Boyd,' stated Peel. 'But I learnt today that you can plan what you would like to do but it's the target that makes all the running. The surveillance target has ground control, not us. Anthea blew the whistle because she thought we were in trouble. But then she left Terry with his eyes on the house and counted on you because she trusted you to make the right decision. I don't know anyone who has been caught in no man's land in an operation like that, chief inspector. In fact, to tell you the truth, your team would have run through a wall for you today if you'd asked them, Boyd.'

'Maybe today; maybe not tomorrow,' remarked Boyd.

'Look,' suggested Peel. 'I need half an hour's chat with you later. I'd like to discuss the job in more detail, maybe a drink at the Feathers?'

Swinging into his office, Boyd snatched a note from his desk, read it, and stuffed the slip of paper in his pocket. 'Sorry, Sandy, I'd like to but something just came up, perhaps another time?'

Disappointed, Peel replied, 'I hope she's worth it.'

Raising his eyebrows, Boyd countered, 'I think you have the wrong end of the stick, Sandy. Now if you'll excuse me I need to get changed.'

'Of course,' replied the superintendent. 'I'll drop the report off at the commander's office.'

Moments later, Boyd withdrew that slip of paper from his trouser pocket. He memorised the address and burnt the note before changing into black jeans, a roll neck sweater, and a black hooded fleece. He snatched his car keys from the desk, took the lift to the back stairs, and left the building by a side door.

Later that night, Boyd pulled off the main carriageway, abandoned his car, and took a bus into the Epping Forest area of North London. Sitting alone on the top deck Boyd noticed the location was semi-rural with a series of detached houses spread out evenly to afford a fair amount of privacy to each individual plot. The estate was huge with each detached home extending an acre and enjoying well-established, well-kept woodland at their back door. Ten minutes later he made his way downstairs and got off at the next stop.

Stepping onto the footpath Boyd walked straight into Antonia and almost knocked her over. Smiling briefly he joined her for a while as they walked further into the housing estate.

Her red hair hung loose when Antonia murmured, 'You didn't really think you'd be alone, did you, Billy?'

'No,' announced Boyd. 'Not really. I expected you to be here as arranged. I've seen the house. It's deserted. Did you bring the gear?'

Antonia replied, 'Officially, I'm not here but I'll watch your back as discussed. I'll ring your mobile if there's a problem. Make sure it's on vibrate.'

'Done,' replied Boyd. 'But did you bring the stuff with you?'

'Sorry, yes, of course,' replied Antonia. 'Did you read my script for the timings?'

'Yes! When I enter I must assume the silent alarm has gone off and a response from the police is on the cards. I have four minutes to do the job and get out of the house before they arrive.'

'That should be long enough,' suggested Antonia.

'What about his mobile?' asked Boyd.

'I presume he has his main one with him but he has a couple of private ones that I know of. I doubt they are hidden anywhere. You know what to do if you find them?'

'Yes, of course, any paperwork?' queried Boyd.

'No,' she replied.

'Good, it's illegal then,' suggested Boyd.

'Only if you get caught and the plan goes wrong,' smirked Antonia.

Removing a rucksack from her back, Antonia handed it to Boyd who hoisted it onto his shoulder and asked, 'Everything there?'

'Of course,' replied Antonia.

'And the key?' queried Boyd.

'Here,' responded Antonia handing a door key over. 'It's a copy. I made it myself.'

'The CCTV?'

'Is poor quality at night,' advised Antonia.

'Wonderful, Toni, are you sure?'

'Just don't hang around in the driveway, Billy.'

'Security lighting?'

'Will light you up but that's all.'

'It's a breeze then?' offered Boyd.

'We'll know all we need to know in twenty four hours, Billy. Trust me! If the wheel comes off I'll put it back on again.'

'And the man himself, where is he?' asked Boyd.

'If he's to be believed he's in a castle in Wales,' remarked Antonia.

'I'll go in exactly on the hour,' revealed Boyd.

'Good luck, Billy.'

'Catch you later,' replied Boyd. 'Twenty minutes! Be on the bus.'

'I'll be watching,' the lady replied.

'Time?' remarked Boyd checking his wristwatch.

'Three, two, one... mark,' announced Antonia. With watches synchronised the two peeled away from each other as Boyd made his way towards the target premises.

When Boyd's watch neared nine o'clock he moved in.

Brazen was the only word that Boyd would attribute to his method of entry. He removed a peaked cap and sunglasses from the rucksack and put them on. Disguised, he then pulled a hood down and tightened the draw strings across his face. There was the slightest crunch of gravel underfoot as he made his way down the driveway of the target house. As he drew nearer he lengthened his stride and quickened his pace. Once he was at the front door, Boyd inserted a key and entered the empty house.

Time was of the essence. Boyd checked his wristwatch and then removed his shoes. Careful not to bring either gravel or soil into the house, he placed his shoes in the rucksack and stood in his socks. Then he replaced the sunglasses and cap and squinted his eyes. Heart thumping, adrenalin racing, Boyd took a couple of deep breaths and allowed his eyes to become accustomed to the dark. Rummaging inside, he removed a torch and a pair of leather gloves. He eased the gloves on and then switched on the torch. He adjusted the torch beam so that only a thin beam of light showed the way forward. Working fast now, he visited all the downstairs rooms quickly scanning the contents. In the kitchen he smiled when he spotted two mobile phones on the table. He eased the back of the mobiles off, inserted a sim card copying device into the compartment, and replaced the backs with a careful 'snap'. Smoothly moving through the lounge and dining room, he found the main telephone point and traced the wiring to an ornate telephone on a coffee table.

Pausing for a moment, Boyd studied the layout of the lounge area and then approached a television set which was fixed on a low tripod stand. He tipped the set backwards slightly and found a hollow where the three legs of the stand met and took the weight of the television. It was here that Boyd planted a listening device before he tipped the set back into its correct position. The device was thin, quite small, and held a battery that would expire in about ten days. Making sure he hadn't left anything behind, Boyd retraced his steps, replaced his shoes, returned the torch to the bag, and donned his disguise once more. Then he locked the front door behind him and made his way in the dark along the drive and into the estate.

A bus drew up in the lay by and Boyd jumped onto the platform. A police car with a flashing blue light drove by at speed. Boyd paid for his ticket and then went upstairs.

Antonia ignored him but Boyd sat beside her and placed the rucksack on the floor between them. At the next stop, Boyd got off the bus leaving the rucksack in Antonia's possession as she looked out of the window.

Only two members of the Special Crime Unit – one from MI5 and one from the police – knew they had successfully copied data from mobile phones belonging to Sir Phillip Nesbitt K.B.E. They were only ones privy to the planting of a listening device in the home of the Director General of the Security Service.

There was no authority, no paperwork, and no written trace of the operation they had carried out. Involving minimum planning, it was a hurried attempt to gain intelligence on a man who lived and breathed security.

Boyd wondered how long it would take the system to find his listening device. Would the authorities suspect such an attack? Would they find evidence of an unlawful entry? Might they sweep the house electronically? Or would they merely recognise the alarm as a fault on the line and mark the incident down as a false alarm with good intent?

Driving back to his hotel Boyd wondered how he might explain his part in the operation if he was ever identified as the burglar from the CCTV footage.

In an airport lounge in Turkey a smartly dressed man in his late twenties emerged from the prayer room. He straightened his tie and stepped forward before handing his ticket to the flight desk attendant. The lady flicked through the pages of his passport, nodded, checked his ticket, and then asked him if he had any luggage.

Other than what he was carrying, the smartly dressed gentleman had nothing to declare.

Smiling politely, the attendant allocated the man a seat, returned his documents, and beckoned the next customer forward.

Salman was on the move. His flight to Paris awaited him.

*

Chapter Ten
~

The Operations Centre, Special Crime Unit,
New Scotland Yard. The following day.
Threat Level One - Critical

Refreshed from a good night's sleep, Boyd was in the office early to meet the latest acquisition to the unit – Bannerman – the new DI. Of course, both men knew it was a temporary assignment due to the newly designated threat level. But Boyd was anxious to welcome an old friend from Cumbria since they had worked there together many years earlier.

Detective Inspector Bannerman had been drafted in from the Special Escort Group of the Met's Royalty and Protection Squad to the Special Crime Unit. His brief was to work with Boyd towards the enhanced security of the Monarch and other senior Royals.

The two men shook hands, embraced, and stood back from each other waiting for the other to speak.

Bannerman shuffled his feet impatiently. The feet wore size ten shoes and he stood six feet five inches inside them. Broad across the shoulders, he was quite muscular despite a slight paunch around his midriff. A chiselled square chin gave him the appearance of a man older than he actually was whilst a crop of microscopic ginger hair sprouted from a rounded skull and crept dangerously towards his ears. His mouth engaged in most of the action for at times he gabbled on endlessly about the most unimportant of things. From a distance, he looked almost bald. Up close, no one told him so. His friends called him 'the big man' but his enemies called him 'the screaming skull'.

The ex Cumbrian officer spoke first saying, 'Boyd, we meet again. How cool is that?'

'You've done well, Bannerman,' remarked Boyd. 'They tell me you're the man who trains the royal protectors. In fact, they tell me you are the king of all protectors.'

'I do my bit,' smiled Bannerman. 'They tell me you upset the Home Secretary and ended up working with me for your troubles. That'll teach you to keep your mouth shut next time.'

'Yeah,' nodded Boyd. 'That's what the commander told me too. Have you met the big boss yet?'

'A number of times,' replied Bannerman staring down at the shorter Boyd. 'The commander knows I'm here. Do you think we can make this work, Boyd?'

'Of course we can. Let's make a start. Who do you see as the biggest threat to the security of the monarch and these royal events?'

'That's an easy one, Boyd,' replied Bannerman. 'Ask any of the royals and they will all tell you that one of the worst problems for them is a 'follower'. By that I mean, not a terrorist or a heckler but a potentially weird character that lives and breathes the monarchy and would go to the ends of the earth to be close to one of the royals.'

'Someone from the Press?' queried Boyd.

'No, although they are a worry at times.'

'A follower, Bannerman?' questioned Boyd. 'Do you mean someone who just really and truly supports our monarchy? Isn't that a good thing?'

'Yes, it is in a way,' explained Bannerman. 'But then the same people can frighten the life out of everyone when they try to get into everything from royal cars to palace bedrooms and garden parties without an invite. I could go on, Boyd, but the point is they can be anyone you meet in the street. They love the royals but they are a real pain in the arse to our protectors, problems, problems, problems, all the time!'

'Not would-be assassins and terrorists then?' queried Boyd.

'Distinguishing between the two and defining the term 'Royal follower' is the problem, Boyd.'

'I just knew this wasn't going to be easy,' laughed Boyd.

There was a brief knock on the door and Sandra Peel entered. Boyd conducted the introductions and an exchange of pleasantries before Sandra asked, 'How are we going to add extra protection to the monarchy, gents?'

'We're working on it,' replied Bannerman. 'But we need to get some basics out of the way first.'

'Good,' smiled Sandra. 'It worries me as to how we can improve on the present situation.'

'The present situation can always be improved,' remarked Bannerman. 'Don't you agree, Boyd?'

'Yes, but you are better placed than me to answer that one,' responded Boyd. 'My idea is to consider every event the senior monarchy attend and then examine what problems we have in the area. You know, how many people are on the watch list in that area; who might be a threat and what steps we need to take to counter any perceived threat.'

Shaking her head with a grin creeping across her face, Sandra commented, 'Oh that shouldn't take too long then. There's only how many thousand suspects to put through the system?'

The trio laughed and Boyd replied, 'Seriously, Sandy, can you set us up with a direct contact with someone at GCHQ? And I'd like a twenty four watch on our ticker intelligence system if possible. I'd like some real time analysis of what is on the CAST and ticker systems. By that I mean I want someone on site checking data that comes through and trying to prioritise it. '

'Yes, I'll speak with Commander Maxwell. I'm sure we can make the necessary arrangements but it sounds like a two-man job.' Sandra Peel turned to go but then added, 'By the way, I think I'll take first shift on the ticker system. If I'm going to be any good at this job I really should start at the beginning.'

'Well, that's a first,' chuckled Boyd. 'I don't think we've ever had a superintendent manning ticker before.'

'Before you know it,' added Bannerman. 'We might have the good lady on the protection squad with us.'

Peel chuckled as she walked away saying, 'One thing at a time gents; one thing at a time. And you sure as hell don't want a piece of sandpaper being abrasive to the royals, do you.'

Stunned for a moment, Boyd watched the lady go and listened when she turned and said, 'Oh, yes, boys, I do know why they call me Sandy – But I'm working on it.'

Bannerman glanced at Boyd and murmured, 'They call me the screaming skull. Here, let's get on with it, Boyd. We can make a start now and pull it to pieces on our way to Cumbria later this morning.'

A notebook hit the desk followed by a pencil. The two detectives were up and running, and making notes.

In a detached house on the edge of Epping Forest Phillip Nesbitt yawned as he pulled his dressing gown tighter around his body and walked into the lounge to answer the telephone.

Tired from the previous night's exertions, he rubbed his eyes and then snatched the phone from its cradle answering with a crisp, 'Good morning!'

Listening to the caller, Phillip stepped towards the television as he began his conversation.

'Yes, of course,' he stated. There was a pause before he continued, 'Well, that's exceptionally kind of you. Do you really think it's gone that far?' he asked. Moving closer to the television, he shook out his neck from a stiffness creeping in, and said, 'I'd be delighted to accept. Yes, please proceed.'

Standing, staring at his dull reflection in the dark screen of an off duty television, Phillip Nesbitt smiled and said, 'Of course, I'll be there. I wouldn't miss it for the world.'

Gently replacing the telephone on its cradle Phillip ended the conversation, switched on the television, and settled down on the sofa to watch the morning news.

According to Commander Maxwell, thought Sandra Peel, superintendents don't normally work on the ticker intelligence system. But then the unit normally recruits specialists and experienced analysts for this kind of work. Intelligence analysis isn't my forte, she mused.

'So how does it work, Antonia?' asked Sandra.

'The team call me Toni, Sandy. Did you forget?'

'Yes, of course,' replied Sandra settling spectacles on the bridge of her nose. 'It's just that I see a computer screen with our logo on it and then every ten seconds or so a brief intelligence report trickles across the screen three times before it disappears into where?' And who loads the reports to start with, Toni?'

Antonia Harston-Browne's long red hair swung across her shoulders and gently settled when she took a seat next to Sandra Peel.

'That's right. Basically, our partners in the intelligence community from America, Canada, Australia, various parts of Europe, and elsewhere, all contribute to the effectiveness of the system. Once an intelligence officer – from the police counter terrorist agencies, the military or intelligence services – is authorised to use the system they are up and away. It is so easy to use and each operative has password entry to the system. What we have is a worldwide collection of intelligence data being sent to the system by authorised personnel only. The people sending it don't necessarily have access to read anything on it. Various analysts have different levels of security access. The higher your security clearance the more you can read about what's on the system.'

'So everyone contributes but only a few actually know what's in the ticker?' suggested Sandra.

'Exactly!' replied Antonia. 'It's computerised need to know in one way. Every ticker report lies over a comprehensive report so we can read more when we want to by just clicking on a ticker report as it passes across the screen on its way to the security data warehouse. The report then opens up and takes you to a separate file. Once it gets to the data warehouse it is kept for reference and analysis before being disseminated as appropriate.'

'That sounds like an expensive toy,' ventured Sandra.

'It is the most advanced system of its kind in the world. It took years to design and cost millions to put in place across secure partner sites,' revealed Antonia. 'The most technically advanced 'secure, search and analyse' software is in position. It works in conjunction with CAST – crime analytics software for terrorism - They tell me it's impregnable due to the multi facet encryption embedded in the system.'

'How do I turn it on and off?' asked Sandra.

'You don't. I do,' laughed Antonia. 'Once you've settled in the commander will tell me to instruct you properly in its use. Just at the moment we're too busy to do that but you're security clearance allows you to work with me on this as a reader. Look, don't fuss yourself over the need to know jargon, Sandy. It works and it's a great piece of kit. All you need to know at the moment is that we've got it and I've set it to display everything relevant to our targets and brief.'

'You can set it to read things?' queried Sandra.

'We can set it to show us on ticker everything relevant to Islamic State and Al-Qaeda that is going through the system right now,' admitted Antonia.

'That is a Rolls Royce,' whistled Sandra. 'We are well and truly ahead of the game.'

'The computer is,' agreed Antonia. 'But Boyd is right. We need people to read it and make sense of it and that isn't as easy as it seems. We're short of the right people to do that and we're often behind the game actually. This does its bit to try and even up the score. The problem is, practically, the enemy makes the running. We have to do the catching.'

'Can I play with it?' asked Sandra.

'Only when you've made the coffee,' smiled Antonia.

Half a dozen mugs of caffeine later, Sandra Peel was well into the system. Placing an empty mug on a table, she engaged Antonia and said, 'Am I using this right, Toni?'

'What's wrong?'

'Well, if I've done this right, I think I've found Declan 'O'Malley.'

Antonia instantly swivelled her chair round and said, 'What? Declan O'Malley! You're kidding. What have you done?'

'Because I have limited access I recapped ticker and went into the reports concerning the Patrick Brendan O'Malley arrest.'

'History,' remarked Antonia laughing. 'There's nothing there that takes us to Declan. But what did you do to my computer? I hope you haven't broken it.'

The ladies exchanged another cautious chuckle before Sandra explained, 'Patrick Brendan O'Malley also used the name Patrick Lynch as a falsehood to gain a passport, driving licence, and necessary paperwork to live here without being detected by normal means. Agreed?'

'Agreed,' admitted Antonia.

'So when I reviewed the brief ticker report on the arrest I clicked into it and the system took me to our more comprehensive reports in the background. That's when I started to dig around.'

'What did you find?' asked Antonia.

'Nothing!' replied Sandra. 'Other than there is absolutely no recorded data anywhere on Declan O'Malley other than he is wanted by ourselves for terrorist related offences, and his current intelligence file which hasn't been updated for quite some time.'

'So what are you driving at?' queried Antonia.

'I wondered how close these brothers were,' explained Sandra. 'Then I wondered if Declan O'Malley was using the name Declan Lynch. Guess what?'

'You found hundreds of Declan Lynch's on the computer system and found yourself back at square one?'

Nodding, Sandra replied, 'Yes, but I also found a Declan Lynch using the same date and place of birth as Declan O'Malley. He has a current passport issued in that name and it carries his photograph. According to the passport office he has an authentic address but when I checked I discovered the house was demolished three years ago to make way for a supermarket. He has a driving licence in the name Lynch which also carries his real O'Malley photograph. Toni, he is a copycat of his brother, Patrick. He's done exactly the same as Patrick in every area. Main thing is he's duplicated his entire life in the name Declan Lynch. It's so obvious we missed it.'

Antonia glowered over the computer screen, moved a mouse, clicked into a file, read, and then allowed a massive grin to invade her face.

'Tell me where he lives,' asked Antonia.

'Carlisle,' replied Sandra. 'According to my research on the ticker system and our partner websites Declan Lynch - also known as O'Malley - lives in a house that was demolished.'

'But he's gone to a lot of trouble to document his existence up there,' stated Antonia. 'These kinds of papers can change your identity to some degree. Who countersigned his passport?'

'His brother,' replied Sandra.

Shaking her head anxiously, Antonia replied, 'I bet he's there somewhere. Where's Boyd?'

'On his way to Carlisle,' disclosed Sandra. 'There's a royal visit there soon and he's setting up an investigative control room of some kind. He needs a local base where he can put people under the microscope if he wishes. He's looking at anyone who can be perceived as a possible threat. But he'll be taking time out to visit his wife and family as well I suspect. There's a military march pass, band, and all the usual trimmings. He's not expecting problems in the backwoods of Cumbria but he's using a system he's devised to try and cover all the bases.'

'Who's he with?' questioned Antonia.

'He's riding shotgun with Bannerman and the team,' replied Sandra.

Chuckling, Antonia hit the digits on her mobile phone and remarked, 'Millions of pounds worth of technology record everything you need to know but it still needs a pair of eyes and a brain to work it all out. Well done, Sandy! The coincidence is too big not to miss.' Antonia listened to the phone ringing out at the other end of the call and continued, 'And it's all gone to waste if the man on the ground doesn't answer his phone.'

In a police office on the outskirts of Carlisle Boyd pointed to a photograph lying amongst a dozen others on a table and said, 'That one.'

'Are you sure?' questioned the local event commander: Superintendent Jack Beardsley. 'We don't know much about the subject at all.'

'We soon will,' declared Boyd. 'From midnight onwards please.'

'It's just that you seem to have one clear target and a number of interesting ones that don't look very threatening,' suggested Superintendent Beardsley.

'I know where this one is,' remarked Boyd with his finger on a photograph. 'We're working on the others, that's why I've set up a temporary control room and drafted in some of my enquiry officers.'

'I see,' replied the event commander.

'Sir, the royal visit will be secure on my watch. Full surveillance with immediate effect, I'll take responsibility.'

Superintendent Beardsley looked into Boyd's steely eyes and then studied the photograph Boyd had indicated. Gradually, he turned his head and found Bannerman's eyes boring into him.

Bannerman nodded and, prudently, Beardsley replied, 'Okay, I think you're wrong, chief inspector, but, as you say, it's your decision and your responsibility. Just don't get in the way of my city personnel. They've enough to do and I don't want them running round like rabbits at the beck and call of a big city detective like you.'

'Wouldn't dream of it, sir,' smiled Boyd. 'And - with your permission – Bannerman will run the investigation from our temporary control room. We both know the city reasonably well.'

'Do you indeed,' suggested the superintendent as he walked away. 'Well, we'll see about that.'

The door closed behind the event commander's back and Boyd said, 'Welcome home, Bannerman. Jack Beardsley never changes! Don't you just love it when everyone remembers you from way back when?'

In Goussainville, a stone's throw from Charles de Gaulle airport on the outskirts of Paris, Salman stood in front of a mirror in the bathroom of a house rented by his French associates. He ran his fingers across his stubbly chin and rubbed fatigue from his eyes. Unexpectedly, he yawned and then shook his head. How tired am I from travelling, he mused. I must wash before I eat, drink, and prepare myself. I need to be strong and fit, he decided.

Allah, please grant me strength to finish my journey so that I may join you in the days ahead, beseeched Salman.

Taking an open cut-throat razor he carefully pruned rough hair from his gullet and worked upwards. Inch by inch, whisker by whisker, he glided the razor across his thin beard until it found skin beneath. Occasionally, he paused, dipped his blade into a basin of warm water, shook it dry, and began again.

Soon, he thought, I shall be a new man with a clean shaven appearance and the looks to go with it.

When he had finished shaving, Salman unscrewed a plastic bottle and poured a handful of lotion into a cupped hand. He set aside his bottle and carefully rubbed a colouring ingredient into his hair. Then he washed and dried his hands before turning to a wardrobe and laying out a brand new grey business suit, fresh white shirt, tasteful silk tie, and black polished shoes. Almost complete, Salman removed a bespoke leather briefcase, unlocked the combination, and checked its contents.

Rummaging inside, Salman found the American mail order catalogue he had insisted upon. He thumbed the pages, made a selection, and placed an order for delivery to an address in West Yorkshire, England.

Mail order brides, he mused. That will do, something slender and highly energetic.

Soon, he thought. Soon Allah's Warrior will be on the other side of the Channel. I'll be in and out before they know what hit them.

*

Chapter Eleven
~

Caldewgate, Carlisle
Cumbria
Threat Level One - Critical

Dina had completed her morning-prayer session, enjoyed a light breakfast, and left her apartment just as the ten fifteen train to London was approaching Carlisle railway station.

On foot, she made her way through a breezy Caldewgate and used a light-controlled pedestrian crossing to reach Caldew Bridge. A few yards later she turned sharply into a lane which led downhill to the rear entrance of Carlisle railway station.

Dressed in her favoured hijab, the dark grey headscarf covered her hair and shoulders but allowed her pretty face to be exposed to rugged city elements that bit savagely into her face. Fortunately, Dina also wore a dark chequered jacket and trousers that kept her reasonably warm. She also carried a small rucksack on her back as she stepped towards the entrance and onto the northbound platform.

Oblivious of those around her Dina Al-Hakim glanced at the large clock hanging from the station roof and quickened her pace slightly. Moments later she climbed a staircase and crossed from one platform to another.

'Subject is on the footbridge approaching platforms four and six,' radioed Terry Anwhari quietly.

As Boyd's surveillance team monitored her every movement Dina descended the footbridge onto platform four and approached the London bound train when it pulled up at the platform.

'I have the subject,' radioed Janice. 'It looks like she is about to board the train. It leaves in about five minutes. Who's with me?'

Sauntering through the front entrance Ricky French idled along the platform reporting, 'Ricky is with you, Janice.'

'Stand by, all units,' radioed Janice. 'Subject is stationary about to board. Stand by!'

On the car park outside, two detectives sat in a squad car listening to a saxophone plating softly on a CD.

Boyd killed the music and stretched his legs saying, 'Here we go.'

'A train! The London bloody train, Guvnor,' growled Anthea. 'That's not in the script!'

'It never is,' snickered Boyd lifting his radio. 'This is Boss Car if the target takes the train then I want Janice and Ricky with her. All others on foot to the main entrance please. Janice, you have control.'

'No change,' radioed Janice. 'Passengers have disembarked and others are now taking seats. Our subject is still at a carriage doorway on the platform. Stand by!'

'Why isn't the target getting on the train?' queried Anthea.

'I was just thinking that myself,' replied Boyd. 'She isn't doing any anti or counter-surveillance that I can see. If she's going to be a problem to us then it's because she's either a lone wolf operator or a member of a gang of extremists. She's puzzling me.'

'Mmm… One or the other,' suggested Anthea. 'But then she might just be worried about her sister. That would explain why she joined a chat room the Security Service are monitoring. Maybe we presume too much because of her sister.'

'Maybe,' admitted Boyd.

'Do we know what she's saying in the chat room and who she's talking with?' queried Anthea.

'I don't,' replied Boyd. 'And I don't expect the system will tell me the answer to that one. Toni's mob will want to protect the identity of their mole in the chat room. It's need to know and all we need to know is that she is of interest to those involved in national security.'

'Well, I'm pretty sure she hasn't a clue we're following her, Guvnor,' remarked Anthea.

'Which leads me to presume,' suggested Boyd, 'She might just be waiting for someone to get off the train otherwise she could have jumped on the train as soon as it arrived.'

'Maybe she's a train spotter,' suggested Anthea with a cheeky smile.

'Maybe,' replied Boyd. 'If she's not we'll get our team into the cars and charge down the road to the first station it stops at and then take it from there.'

'Why or why did we pick this one?' queried Anthea.

'Because Declan - the Irishman - isn't yet on the radar and this one is,' delivered Boyd. 'And this little lady has a sister fighting with Islamic State. She's worth a look, Anthea. We need to find out more about her and her friends.'

'Agreed,' replied the inspector chuckling. 'It's just a pity it isn't an offence to have a sister who is a terrorist.'

'Then we might just have a prison shortage,' joked Boyd.

'No change,' radioed Janice Burns.

Terry Anwhari descended the staircase onto the platform and immediately stopped beside a kiosk where he bought a coffee and a hotdog as he turned his back on Dina and blended into the scene.

Suddenly, Dina turned sharply from the carriage and approached the same kiosk earning a welcoming smile from the kiosk attendant. Dina bought a coffee and then stepped towards the main entrance. Moments later she emerged from the concourse into the street outside the railway station.

'We have the subject in Court Square outside the station,' radioed Anthea. 'I'm on foot.'

Exchanging understanding nods Anthea left the car carrying a shoulder bag as Boyd sneaked a camera onto the dashboard and began to focus the device towards Dina.

A minute later, eating a hotdog and drinking coffee, Terry walked across the street and stood close to a taxi queue. Janice held her position in the railway station whilst Ricky entered a newsagent in the station. Looking through the window he was able to watch Dina whilst browsing magazines and newspapers. Other members of the team criss-crossed the square, one entered a café, another took a seat in a garden beneath the imposing structure of Carlisle Citadel and relaxed on a bench amongst the flower beds.

We're all over her, thought Boyd. She's an amateur and has no idea we're here.

Janice radioed, 'A train from Newcastle has just arrived. Och, ye can expect a wee crowd emerging from the entrance soon.'

Moments later, a cold Carlisle breeze bit into the faces of travellers leaving the Carlisle-Newcastle train and wandering into Court Square.

'Hold your ground,' radioed Boyd. 'I have control. Two males are approaching our subject. Stand by!'

'I can confirm they got off the Newcastle train,' radioed Terry.

There was only the briefest exchange of looks but two males walked straight past Dina towards a café where they stood outside and read a menu. Dina ignored them and continued to drink her coffee only occasionally glancing in their general direction.

Dina knows them but they ignored her, thought Boyd who then radioed the description of the two new players.

Both were in their late twenties and dressed in trainers, denim jeans, and dark anoraks. Both sported full beards and moustaches but the taller of the two had jet black hair which was parted high on the left. He also carried a black leather holdall. The other had much shorter hair which was not as dark.

They look Asian, thought Boyd.

Then it dawned on the detective that the two men did indeed know Dina. Watching the body movements of the two men Boyd noticed they were looking at the café menu but weren't actually reading it. They were using reflections in the café window to see if they were being followed out of the railway station.

'All units Targets Two and Three are on their stalks,' radioed Boyd. 'These two are looking for followers. Hold your positions and stand by.'

Seizing a unique opportunity, Anthea walked between Dina and the two suspects, clicked a switch on her shoulder bag, and promptly began videoing the two males. Seconds later she killed the covert camera and climbed the steps into the Hallmark hotel. Within a minute, Anthea was sat at a window seat in the lounge with her shoulder bag again videoing the trio whilst she ordered morning coffee from a young waiter.

Choosing a magazine from the table, Anthea turned her back on proceedings as she slunk into her chair and began to read.

One of the males turned, walked the length of the pavement back towards the railway station, paused for a moment, and then finally approached Dina.

'Confirmed contact,' radioed Boyd. 'All three targets are now in conversation.'

The meeting was short, the speech brief. Dina smiled at the two males who nodded. The taller man carried a holdall which he handed to Dina. She accepted it. They walked away whilst she set off in the opposite direction.

'Ten seconds and out,' radioed Boyd. 'Okay we have our subject with a suspect holdall and two male targets returning to the railway station. Did you get that Anthea?'

'Everything,' replied Anthea repositioning her shoulder bag to catch images of two men returning to the railway station.

Boyd observed the men enter the railway station whereupon a short time later Janice reported the two had returned to the Newcastle train and were sitting on the offside of the middle carriage.

'Ricky, Janice,' ordered Boyd. 'Go with them. I'll arrange a reception committee at Newcastle. Prepare to link with Northumbria in due course. All other units stay with Target One.'

My team is divided, unarmed, and on a shoestring already, thought Boyd. And it's not even lunch time. What a good time to ring the Home Secretary and tell her I'm on to something but we've ran out of resources – but then again, I didn't have many to start with, thought Boyd.

The Carlisle-Newcastle train set off with Ricky French and Janice Burns on board sat in the first and third carriages watching the comings and goings of the targets in the middle carriage. The journey to Newcastle would last an hour and would pass without incident.

Meanwhile, Dina hoisted a rucksack across her shoulders and walked off with a mysterious holdall at her side.

Whatever it is, thought Boyd it has been brought to her by people from the Newcastle train and is now in her hands.

Dina stepped into the roadway and flagged down an empty taxi approaching the rank.

Boyd fired the squad car as Anthea emerged from the hotel and Terry left the newsagents heading towards him. Boyd slid across into the passenger seat allowing Anthea to take the driver's seat with Terry in the rear.

The taxi was through the traffic lights at a crossroads with Boyd and the remnants of his team held at a red light a hundred yards from the railway station.

'Do we take her now, Guvnor?' asked Terry.

'Anthea,' queried Boyd. 'Your views please?'

'We're all over her. She's going nowhere, Guvnor?' replied Anthea. 'What's the hurry?'

Talking on his mobile, Boyd said, 'Northumbria Police! Head of CID please.' Turning to his colleagues Boyd continued, 'I agree, Anthea. But here's one for you. Question, do we disrupt her now and search her holdall or do we stay on her tail until we know more about our two mystery men at the railway station? Answer, the latter; I reckon if Northumbria can house and identify the two Janice and Ricky are following we'll know a little more and we can make a better decision. Both courses of action might be right, both might be wrong. We just need to make a choice. If the royals were here now then we know what we'd do – we'd take a look in the bag – but the royals aren't here. This is preparation. Let it run. We have control and that makes a change.'

'Tempting to look in her bag though, Guvnor,' suggested Terry Anwhari.

'I agree,' replied Boyd. 'But as Anthea said, Terry, we're onto her. We need to house her and the holdall, wait, think, and then decide on the next step. Okay?'

'Fully agree but there's another problem,' reported Terry.

'Such as?' asked Boyd.

'Her taxi is now two hundred yards ahead and there are four sets of traffic lights that I can see,' declared Terry. 'No disrespect, Inspector Adams, but we're losing ground.'

Boyd closed his eyes, chuckled, and replied, 'Last time I suggested that she mounted a pavement and blasted her way through.'

'And I'll do it again if I must,' snapped Anthea. 'Right now she's held at the lights and we're gaining. No speech please. I'm driving.'

'Fair enough,' murmured Terry looking out of the window at the city shoppers. 'Just saying, that's all.'

Boyd got through to the Head of CID in Northumbria and arranged a surveillance team to support Ricky and Janice.

Ten minutes later the taxi swung into Caldewgate and delivered Dina to her flat. Pulling into the side of the road Anthea observed Dina leave the taxi carrying both a rucksack and the holdall. A short walk later and Dina was back home with Terry Anwhari scaling a set of steps to the rear of an empty apartment opposite Dina's. Letting himself into the vacant site he radioed Boyd saying, 'I'm in the rental, guys. Are you getting me?'

'Loud and clear,' replied Boyd.

Nearing a convenient window, Terry reported, 'I have an eyeball on the target's apartment. She's inside.'

Fifteen minutes later another team moved in to watch Dina when Boyd and his colleagues stood down to an office at the local police station.

Three hundred and thirty miles south, another police surveillance operation was taking place. Counter terrorist detectives assigned to protection duties at the home of the Minister of Defence had their eyes on a blue Ford Galaxy touring the vicinity.

Secreted in an old wooden shed in the garden the officers monitored all the vehicles passing by. Each vehicle was photographed, logged, and the ownership enquired into. The officers were used to seeing the same vehicles with the same drivers every day of the week. It was a natural occurrence for them. The watchers had a good idea of who was who. They knew the regular postman lived in the village and when off duty he drove a blue Seat. The local publican drove a black BMW; the village doctor favoured a classic Jaguar, and the local vicar drove a charcoal coloured Jeep to get around the parish.

When a blue Galaxy drove past for the third time in the same hour, they became suspicious and started to take bets on whether the car belonged to a local estate agent or a door to door salesman. Then they checked the registration number and realised the vehicle was being driven on diplomatic number plates. Enquiries revealed the plates were attributed to the Russian Embassy in London and the driver ascribed to the vehicle was a gentleman using the name Ivan Pushkin.

More telephone calls led to the Operations Centre in the Special Crime Unit and MI5. Pushkin was known to the intelligence community. He was reported as being a trade delegate visiting the country in connection with the proposed development of business opportunities between the UK and the Russians.

Damn it, thought Ivan. Why do these people live in the middle of nowhere? Yes, close to this village called Epsom, but it covers miles and miles of country lanes and takes some finding. Still, I have located and photographed the house where the Secretary of State for Defence lives. I've even drawn a plan for the troops. I can put a positive vision on the satellite images we have at the moment. There wasn't even a policeman in sight other than a couple of uniforms on the main gate looking bored and playing doormen. Realistically, mused Ivan, someone somewhere may well have seen my vehicle in the area. Do I care? No, my work is never ending. If they discover me, considered Ivan, what will they do to me in my diplomatic car and with my diplomatic cover? Imprison me or merely question me in a stinking cell for a day or two because I drove by a politician's house? Probably neither! Maybe they will panic, worry, or feel threatened. Actually, I don't really care because if I am discovered I am just a shot across the bows in the games of espionage and adverse diplomacy that we play. Now it's down to the *Spetsnaz* assassination squad when the order is given. And good luck to them, say I.

Chuckling, Ivan turned up the radio and listened to music blasting from the dashboard as he selected a lower gear and rammed the accelerator to the floor.

God I love this country,' thought Ivan. It's so green and luscious. These must be the leafy lanes the poets go on about.

Unaware he was being watched, Ivan drove on.

'Alpha One Three, I have him,' radioed a surveillance officer attached to the Security Service team. 'That was definitely a photograph he took as he drove by. I have him on the binoculars.'

'Alpha Six, we have had him inside the area for thirty minutes He's doing a reconnaissance not a drive by. He's on his way out towards the main road. Stand by, team.'

'Bravo Four Six, I have the subject timed at twenty two minutes on site and eight minutes stationery at the north east side of the premises.'

'Kilo Two Three, Let's take him back to London. I don't know about you guys but three weeks following this character tells me he's on the wrong side of the diplomatic fence. He's been to the home of every cabinet minister in the government.'

'Alpha One Three, does that mean you're in the chair tonight? I think it's your round.'

'Kilo Two Three, it sure does. Stand by he's turning onto the main road and heading east.'

Ivan checked his rear view mirror and confirmed he was not being followed. He felt as safe as houses as he slid into the offside lane and began to overtake slower moving vehicles.'

From a screen on the dashboard of one of the surveillance vehicles a light flashed on a computerised map. It gave comfort to the surveillance officers that the tracker on the diplomat's car was working. They knew exactly where the vehicle was at all times, didn't have to be right up behind him, and could happily deploy their team in the knowledge that Ivan Pushkin didn't know he'd been followed around the United Kingdom for the last three weeks. Oh yes, he's used his anti and counter-surveillance skills to the best of his advantage, but it hadn't occurred to him that his enemies had fitted a magnetic tracker to the underside of his car.

'Kilo Two Three, I think the boss will be pleased with this one. He's no diplomat on a trade mission.'

'Where is she?'

'In the Ops Centre, on the ticker. This is just another problem for her. She's going to love us when she reads the report.'

'Alpha Six, radio silence guys unless we have a problem. Subject now joining the motorway heading for London. Make ground. We must not presume he's making directly for the embassy. Make ground and keep it tight please, Alpha Six out.'

Ivan's fingers rattled on the rim of a steering wheel in time with music beating from the radio. Oblivious to his followers Ivan sped home having convinced himself he was infallible.

Back in Newcastle, the train arrived on time and disgorged its passengers into the thriving metropolis. Janice and Ricky met up with a surveillance team from Newcastle Central. In a seamless operation aided by encrypted radios and good mobility, they followed the two suspects who had delivered a holdall to Dina.

It was all over within an hour. The subjects were housed in the west end of the city and identified as two Asian brothers who were business partners. Enquiries revealed they bought and sold leather jackets for a living working out of a small retail unit close to the city centre.

A check of police intelligence records disclosed they were also known to Counter Terrorist Command. Both men were flagged because of their extremist views but neither was on a watch list or wanted for any kind of offence. They were known for expressing anti-western statements and pro-Islamic State comments in protest marches but they were merely exercising their right to free speech.

Janice and Ricky tidied up the paperwork, made good their thanks, and caught the next train back to Carlisle.

As their train pulled away from the platform a gentleman sitting opposite Janice unfolded his newspaper, shook it, and began to read the inside pages.

Janice could not help but notice the headlines on the front page...

'Argentinian battleship approaches Falkland Isles...'

Defence Secretary accuses Argentinian President of 'sabre rattling'...

*

Chapter Twelve

~

The Police Station,
Carlisle
Threat Level One - Critical

Boyd was on the phone to Sandra Peel.

'Yes, it is nice to spend some time with Meg and the children, Sandy. It's like working from home again.'

'What have you been doing with the family – anything exciting?'

'Just enjoying quality time. Anthea tells me you've worked out that Declan O'Malley is living in the Carlisle area under the name Declan Lynch. Is that right?'

Boyd listened, took a mouthful of coffee and edged onto the corner of a desk before continuing, 'Yes, that address was demolished some time ago. I know where you mean.'

Again Boyd took heed, nodded as if the superintendent were in the room with him, and stated, 'No, I'll support your theory. I like it. Declan O'Malley could quite easily be living under the name Declan Lynch when you explain it like that. If he is here in the city then he must be self-sufficient because there's no trace of him claiming benefits of any kind. I suggest we need to circulate his last known photograph and make enquires amongst the Irish community; unless you can think of anything else, Sandy?'

Listening patiently, Boyd explained, 'The local superintendent here has assigned half a dozen detectives to supplement Team Alpha so we're beginning to get a grip on things here.'

Eventually ending the call, Boyd turned to his colleagues and said, 'Okay, we need to wear out some shoe leather to find this Declan. But we also need to decide whether Dina Al-Hakim is a real threat to national security or not. What else do we know about her?'

There was a low murmur amounting to negativity from the gathering before Anthea reported, 'Nothing of any note, but as she came to our notice because of a possible threat to the royals I decided to dig into the archives and study some previous royal visits.'

'Thinking outside the box again, inspector?' suggested Boyd.

'Of course,' replied Anthea. 'It's what I do best. Actually, to be honest, Bannerman suggested we took a tour through some recent videos of royal events. It seemed to make sense as some of us are going to be on protection duties soon. I have to say it was like going back to school but I learned a lot about what goes on inside the mind of a protector.'

'Good, I'm pleased to hear it, Anthea because I've got you down for riding with the top lady,' smiled Boyd. 'That okay?'

'Of course,' laughed Anthea. 'Look, take a seat and watch this video Bannerman and I put together. We can pick out the strong areas of personal protection but Bannerman will also point out the weak areas.'

The group settled down as Bannerman activated a television set and ran a video before announcing, 'When Anthea told me you were interested in Dina I asked myself the question did Dina Al-Hakim go to any other royal visits?'

Anthea nodded and commandeered the remote control.

'And if so,' explained Bannerman, 'Was Dina a threat to the royals then? I'm trying to establish if she's a threat or not. Anyways, take a look at this.'

As the video ran on they reviewed press photographs and media videos. Pausing here and there as if it were a lesson at school, they picked out times when protection was close on the subjects and other times when protection might have been too far away. It was an imprecise relationship between the protector and the protected but Bannerman strived to make it a better science whenever he could.

Anthea paused the video and Bannerman explained, 'Here we have your Dina outside the Crown and Mitre in Carlisle at the last royal visit. Tell me what she's doing?'

Boyd studied the footage for a few moments and replied, 'Oh yes, that's the lady.'

Peering closer Terry offered, 'Tell me what she's doing. Am I missing something?'

'Look at her face and body language, Terry. Now what do you see?' advised Bannerman.

Squinting his eyes, Terry suddenly nodded his understanding and replied, 'Yes, she's watching and looking but not actually smiling, laughing or cheering.'

'Fascinating,' observed Boyd.

'And I thought it was just riding in the front of a fancy car,' remarked a local detective.

Boyd chuckled and said, 'I did too until Inspector Bannerman told me how wrong I was.'

'It's as if she has no interest in proceedings,' remarked Terry studying the screen. 'The others are clapping or flag waving. All she has is a rucksack.'

'A theoretical weak point,' explained Bannerman. 'Although how one would ever pass a law prohibiting people from carrying bags in such places is beyond me. That will never happen but from my point of view I have to teach the mental agility needed to afford excellent protection.'

The group nodded politely and Bannerman continued, 'So I'll raise Dina's ethnicity, her religious grouping at a Christian monarch's event, and the fact that when you study the subject in slow time like we are now, you find someone who is checking out the system rather than enjoying the event. Of course, someone might suggest my analysis is based on a racist reaction or religious bigotry but the truth of the matter is all terrorism, espionage, conflict and war is based historically on either religion or the sovereignty of lands, or a mix of the two.'

'You mean she's an enemy on reconnaissance,' queried Terry.

'Potentially,' remarked Anthea.

'Looks that way to me,' revealed Bannerman.

'And me too,' commented Boyd. 'Run it on, Anthea, I'm presuming she doesn't break into the national anthem or 'Donald where's your trousers' anywhere on route?'

'No, she doesn't,' replied Anthea activating the video again. 'But some do and you can also hear the strains of 'Rule Britannia' if you listen carefully.'

'Woa!' shouted Boyd. 'Stop right there!'

'What's the matter, Guvnor,' queried Anthea. 'It's just Dina and the crowd.'

'Go back! Go back,' implored Boyd. 'The man in the anorak!'

Anthea rewound the video, stopped it, and announced, 'I don't believe it. That's Declan O'Malley walking towards her. Can you see him? He's next to the clown in the union flag suit.'

'It certainly is,' replied Boyd. 'Terry, pass me Declan's photo and tell me what you think. Is that the wanted Irishman or not?'

Terry glanced at Declan's photo, compared it with the image on the screen, and returned it to Boyd saying, 'That's him No doubt in my mind.'

'It's a remarkable photograph,' stated Bannerman. 'If I'm picking you up correctly, I'm looking at two terrorists from two completely different organisations standing next to a fan who is completely obsessed with the royal family.'

'Precisely,' murmured Boyd thinking things through. 'And neither of them with a flag or a smile or their face, run it on, Anthea. Are they together?'

The video ran on and confirmed there was no evidence to suggest the two were connected, but the royal follower in the union jack flag was everywhere.

'Who's the man in the red, white and blue union flag suit?' enquired Boyd.

'Beats me,' came the reply.

'Pity,' responded Boyd. 'He might have spoken to either of them off camera or he might even know where they live.'

'I doubt it,' came a reply.

More coffee arrived when the phone rang and Boyd spoke to Commander Maxwell.

'Sir,' commenced Boyd.

'Any progress with your surveillance, William?' enquired the commander.

'I'll be sending you a full report within the hour, sir,' reported Boyd. 'But the bottom line is Dina received a holdall at the railway station off two brothers from Newcastle who are mildly known to us. More importantly we have video coverage of Dina Al-Hakim at the last royal visit. She appears to be carrying out a reconnaissance and is carrying her usual rucksack. I'm going to upgrade her because I believe we need to be all over her in the coming days, if not hours.'

'Agreed, I'll make arrangements regarding her phone and mail. How does that sound?' suggested Commander Maxwell. 'I'll send Team Charlie to bolster the enquiry.'

'That's good, sir,' delivered Boyd. 'Because we've got Declan O'Malley and Dina Al-Hakim on the same video shot at the last royal visit. Nothing to suggest they are working together but if you want to know where threat level one is then I'd suggest it's right here.'

'On the contrary,' replied the commander. 'Antonia rang. Her surveillance team have been following a Russian diplomat for the last three weeks.'

'Why?' asked Boyd. 'Pressure on the Russians because they keep flying into our airspace?'

'No, because he's a known member of the GRU and Antonia put him under the microscope as a matter of routine. He, too, is on reconnaissance having collated a lot of details about government ministers. Antonia also has technical intelligence on the subject. I'm putting you on stand-by because details of the intelligence case are being put together for the Foreign Secretary and the Defence Intelligence Committee.'

'Meaning?'

'Meaning we mount a long term operation on the subject and gather more intelligence on all his contacts in the UK or the government decide to withdraw his diplomatic immunity and he's deported as a spy. It's not my decision, Boyd.'

'I know that, sir. It just couldn't have come at a worse time. Everyone and everything is coming out of the woodwork at us.'

'I have made my thoughts clear to the powers that be, Boyd. You should also know that my liaison office in GCHQ reports more electronic traffic with regards to this man from Tikrit that is causing a stir. He appears to be very important to the extremists and the Home Secretary has instructed the Duke to re-evaluate our response to the subject. The man from Tikrit may turn out to be our main threat.'

'I'll put him in the 'to do' file along with the rest, sir,' responded Boyd.

'By the way, Boyd,' remarked Commander Maxwell. 'Pressure of work is such that you have twenty four hours to find me Declan O'Malley.'

'No problem, commander, no problem at all,' chuckled Boyd. 'I'm sure we'll find him in the car park downstairs. If not I'll hire a magician from yellow pages and work some magic for you.'

'Your best, Boyd, that's all I ask,' suggested Commander Maxwell ending the call.

Turning to his colleagues, Boyd announced, 'We've got twenty four hours to wrap Carlisle up. The commander is upgrading Dina. She's now a category two suspect subject to increased surveillance. Team Charlie is travelling to support us and we need to find Declan. Terry, can you take over back at the rental overlooking Dina's. I'd like you to plot Team Charlie around the area and you know it best. Once they've settled in and have the lay of the land leave them with it. I'll give them a ring and let them know what's happening.'

'Will do, Guvnor,' replied Terry Anwhari.

'And do you know what,' stated Boyd. 'We're going to start at the beginning?'

'Meaning?' queried Bannerman.

'At the Crown and Mitre hotel where he was last officially sighted,' delivered Boyd. 'Come on, let's burn some shoe leather.'

'I'll come with you,' replied Bannerman. 'I need to brief the search teams for the visit and I think a touch of fresh air might do us all good.'

The day wore on with a flurry of activity, phone calls, enquiries and investigation. Boyd, Bannerman and Anthea escaped the office and made for the city centre where Bannerman put his search team to work securing the royal route.

Boyd stood by the bandstand in the city centre seemingly lost in his own world.

'What are you thinking, Guvnor?' asked Anthea.

'Trying to superimpose the video onto the streets,' suggested Boyd, 'Leads me to think the royal car was there. Dina was here. Declan was there, and a police motor bike was just there.'

Boyd pointed to the spot and Bannerman replied, 'That's close enough for me.'

'Okay, let's fan out and check the nearest shops. Speak to the managers and shop assistants. Have any of them seen the man in our photograph – Declan O'Malley?'

'I'll take the dress shop,' smiled Anthea. 'It would be wrong not to. Maybe I'll find a new trouser suit to wear if I'm lucky.'

Bannerman elected the Crown and Mitre where his search team were deployed whilst Boyd sauntered down the lane towards the nearest pub.

Seating himself at the bar, Boyd's attention was immediately drawn to a group of noisy bikers downing alcoholic shots like they were going out of fashion. He ignored the group, asked to see the licensee, and ordered a pasty and a pint of beer for refreshment. Then he busied himself reading a magazine as he waited for the licensee. According to the sign on the door, noted Boyd, one Matt Hobbs should be in attendance. It was his pub.

Music levels increased when one of the bikers fuelled a juke box with more money and began to do a ridiculous drunken dance in one corner of the bar.

Saxophone and jazz were fine, thought Boyd but heavy metal at an ear-shattering decibel level were quite another. Quietly annoyed, he took a bite from his pasty before savouring his ale.

'Matt Hobbs,' announced the man before him suddenly. 'I'm the licensee. What can I do for you?'

Before Boyd could speak an almighty roar of laughter emanated from the other side of the bar when one of the bikers stumbled over a table and splashed his drink everywhere.

'Ignore them,' advised Matt. 'They'll be gone soon.'

But one of the gang didn't like being soaked with beer and promptly lashed out at this mate. Within seconds Matt Hobbs moved from behind the bar and approached the bikers saying, 'Okay, lads settle down. There's no need for any of that.'

Drunk, unable to speak coherently and wobbly on his feet, a middle-aged man dressed in oily jeans and a well-worn leather jacket stepped forward and threw a wild punch at Matt. The licensee ducked and held up both hands saying, 'Okay, that's enough. I don't want any trouble but it's time to go. Come on guys.'

Taking another mouthful of beer, Boyd then finished his pie, sighed unforgivingly, and turned casually to watch proceedings.

Polite and as understating as he could be, Matt couldn't burst the cloud of alcohol that had impaired the other's mind.

There was another wild swing which connected with a wall. This was followed by a kick that missed a body but hit a chair.

Matt merely shook his head but his reward was a mouthful of abuse that turned the air blue.

Taking hold of the drunk, Matt began to escort him from the premises but then a huge biker appeared and stood between the licensee and the door.

'Put my dad down or your dead meat,' threatened the biker. Standing over six feet tall, covered in tattoos, adorned with earrings, and the usual clothing of a biker gang's leader, the younger giant stood firm and scowled, 'I won't tell you again. Put him down.'

'Your dad?' queried Matt. 'Seriously?'

The thug stepped forward with anger in his eyes and his fists clenched.

Matt shouted to the bar staff, 'Police! Ring for the police!'

Boyd swivelled on his stool and engaged his wireless radioing, 'This is Boyd. There's trouble at the Kings Arms. Bannerman, can you come and help me sort it out.'

Both Matt and members of the biker gang glanced at Boyd who slid from his stool and said, 'Yes, I am the police. Now just take a deep breath everyone and settle down.'

The biker gang numbered about a dozen. They were mostly in their late twenties or mid-thirties and between them had made a major contribution to the pub's takings that day.

'Just one of you,' snarled the leader.

'Don't be silly,' replied Boyd. 'There's hundreds of us if you want to take the world on. Just settle down, get your things together, and leave quietly. That's all I ask.'

Father had different ideas and slurred, 'Leave my son alone.'

'No-one is touching your son,' said Matt. 'Now will you all just go?'

There was a roar when father suddenly erupted with anger and slammed his fist into Matt's stomach. Simultaneously, the son threw a haymaker of a punch which connected with Boyd's face.

Rolling backwards into the bar, Boyd saw stars for a moment but was conscious enough to see the gang rush towards Matt Hobbs.

Moments later, Matt tumbled to the ground under a barrage of drunken violent blows with Boyd wading in pulling the animals from the licensee and pushing people aside.

The front door swung open when Bannerman casually strode in.

'Oh yes,' he radioed, unbuttoning his suit jacket. 'Better send a couple of vans.' Then he dodged a thug trying to punch him and replied with an excruciating jab to the biker's ribs. 'And send an ambulance please,' radioed Bannerman.

All hell broke loose with people rolling about on the floor, tables and chairs overturning, and female customers screaming for all they were worth.

Bannerman strode into the pack, took hold of father and son, and promptly smashed their heads together as if they were a couple of rag dolls. A tooth, or two, flew through the air and landed at Boyd's feet.

'Yours?' joked Boyd.

Scowling, Bannerman hurled the two objects into a corner as he went about subduing the remainder of the gang. His pure height and build sent shivers down the spine as he punched anyone who raised a fist to threaten him and took to the ground those who refused to behave themselves.

Sirens in the background signalled the impending arrival of a couple of vans but, at this point, father and son were back on their feet. Son – the biker leader – snatched a bottle from the bar and began swinging it wildly about at the same time that Anthea entered the premises.

Initially shocked, Detective Inspector Anthea Adams immediately withdrew an extendable baton from her shoulder bag. She was about to use it when she changed her mind, paused as she studied its form, and then calmly put it back in her bag.

The drunken biker leader singled Bannerman out and approached him with the neck of the bottle broken on the edge of the bar.

Stepping sideways, Anthea raised her right knee to her chest and then stamped it down hard on the leader's toe. He screamed in horror but Anthea then spun round, moved her body weight onto the right leg, and promptly delivered a tremendous kick to his thigh. Screaming in horror and virtually legless, the leather clad leader fell to the ground like a pack of cards.

His father bent over his screaming son as uniformed police spilled into the bar and began to make arrests.

But Anthea was a sight to behold as she stepped back, picked another target, and slammed a foot into another thigh before twirling and thundering her elbow into yet another thug's stomach.

'One… Two… Three… Finished yet?' remarked Bannerman. 'And here was I enjoying myself until you came along. Best party I've been to in years. New moves, Anthea?'

'Portuguese Pilates,' snapped Anthea grabbing the drunken father and declaring, 'Men! I leave you and Boyd alone for five minutes and look what happens.'

Helping Matt to his feet Boyd propped him onto a seat and asked, 'Are you alright, Mister Hobbs?'

Rubbing his chin and feeling his stomach, Matt replied, 'I am now. That was close. It's a good thing you were here.'

Pouring a glass of water from a jug on the bar, Boyd handed it to Matt saying, 'You were doing fine at one stage. I thought it was going to settle down but the evil drink had done its work. Do you need a doctor at all?'

'No,' replied Matt, 'But he does,' pointing to the leader of the bikers.

It didn't take long to restore order and remove the troublesome violent crew. Boyd replenished his own drink, took a large mouthful, and arranged drinks and refreshment for Bannerman and Anthea before confronting Matt Hobbs.

'Sorry to trouble you, Mister Hobbs, but as you may have guessed we are detectives and we're looking for this man.' Boyd produced a photograph from an inside pocket and showed it to Matt. 'Have you seen him before today?'

Hobbs glanced at the photograph and discounted it immediately with, 'No!'

The three detectives exchanged looks before Boyd persisted with, 'Please use your eyes to look at it properly, sir. It's a simple question but I'd prefer an honest answer.'

Reluctantly, Matt Hobbs looked at the photo again before asking, 'What's he wanted for?'

'A chat,' replied Boyd. 'You obviously know him, Mister Hobbs. What's the problem?'

'You're not from round here. What are you?' queried Hobbs. 'Terrorist Branch or Murder Squad?'

'There's a difference?' asked Boyd.

Hobbs didn't reply.

'He's a wanted terrorist,' delivered Boyd. 'But you can keep that under your hat for your new found friends can't you, Mister Hobbs?'

'Yeah, thanks by the way,' offered Hobbs before begrudgingly repeating, 'Yeah, thanks for your help.'

'We don't just help at pub fights,' smoothed Anthea. 'And we wouldn't be asking these questions if we didn't think you could help.'

Hobbs took another drink of water and blurted, 'Declan Lynch! He's a regular!'

A look of relief crept across Boyd's face but he queried, 'How regular?'

'Weekly,' replied Hobbs. 'He should be in tomorrow if I'm not mistaken; tomorrow lunch time.'

'Alone or with others?' asked Boyd.

'Alone,' delivered Matt Hobbs. 'He takes a Guinness and a whisky, uses the phone, sits by the window, and then leaves. He's a quiet man – seldom has a proper conversation – but he never causes a problem other than that grating Irish accent of his.'

'Phone?' questioned Boyd. 'Mobile phone?'

'Landline,' remarked Hobbs. 'That one over there.'

Boyd followed the pointed finger of Matt Hobbs to a wall phone.

Anthea approached the phone and took its number as Boyd persisted, 'And Declan uses the phone regularly?'

'Of course, nothing wrong with that is there, Mister Boyd?'

'No,' answered Boyd. 'Not at all. But I think you need some additional staff tomorrow lunch time.'

By close of play, Anthea had investigated the number attributed to the public house wall phone and had uncovered a list of calls made from the pub to Seamus Logan in Ireland. Later that night, Team Charlie arrived and headed to relieve Terry Anwhari at the observations point close to Dina's flat. By then Boyd had renewed his plans and diverted Team Charlie.

'Terry,' explained Boyd on the phone. 'Hold your position there overnight. I'll send a local to work with you but if there's a movement through the night I want you on Dina's tail. Understood?'

'I thought Team Charlie was taking over here?' replied Terry.

'I need them fresh for tomorrow, Terry,' disclosed Boyd. 'I hope you understand but we have a chance to get Declan tomorrow and I'm using them for that operation. I want good men in the right place at the right time that's why I need you on Dina. Someone who knows why she is important; and someone flexible like you.'

'Okay,' replied Terry. 'Send your man as soon as possible, Guvnor, I need to snatch some shuteye.'

'Will do,' agreed Boyd ending the conversation.

Boyd held a dawn briefing and issued firearms and ammunition to his surveillance officers.

Morning broke and tiptoed towards lunch time with Matt Hobbs in his apartment above the bar and a couple of new staff in place in the main bar. Team Charlie was on site with a female detective sergeant playing barmaid and a male detective constable cleaning glasses and wiping a bar top with a clean cloth. Outside, on the streets of the city, the remainder of Teams Alpha and Charlie were strung out like a daisy chain surrounding the pub waiting for Declan to arrive.

'Why are we going to follow the man?' asked Bannerman. 'Why don't we just take him when he arrives?'

'Because I'm greedy,' smiled Boyd. 'And I like a good party.'

'That reminds me,' suggested Bannerman. 'How's your head this morning?'

'Slight headache last night and a bruise on the cheek this morning,' revealed Boyd. 'Truth is I want to know where Declan is living and who with. That's why we've got a big team out today.'

'I'll catch you later, Boyd,' explained Bannerman. I'm too big a hulk to play surveillance officer. I'll be in the Civic Centre helping to monitor the CCTV system.'

'Good luck,' offered Boyd.

The two shook hands and the operation commenced.

Boredom and silence took over for quite a while before Anthea's voice penetrated the airwaves with, 'Target spotted. He's wearing a green anorak in English Street towards the Town Hall. He's alone and striding out quite fast. Stand by.'

'We're on,' snapped Boyd eagerly radioing, 'All received, you have control.'

'I have control,' radioed Anthea from her vantage point. 'Target is in the pedestrian area approaching the House of Fraser and the junction with Saint Cuthbert's Lane on his nearside.'

Dozens of eyes poured over maps as Anthea spoke.

The city centre was small when compared with where these people normally worked. But the experienced amongst them had the city centre map firmly imprinted in their brain.

Bannerman stepped forward in the CCTV control room, studied the screens, and quietly asked, 'Where are they?'

'Screen four,' came the reply.

Taking a seat, Bannerman replied, 'Thank you. Now I'd ask you to keep up with the gentleman in the green anorak. Please don't lose him.'

A hand moved a control stick; a camera twitched slightly, and a voice replied, 'We won't. I'm a retired cop from your mob. I don't why you want him but if you're on him so am I.'

'Good man,' replied Bannerman studying the screens.

Declan Lynch knew the city well by now. He'd adopted a quiet lifestyle and hadn't sought a high profile preferring to spend most of his time reading in his flat, and planning the attack that lay ahead. He checked the time on the Town Hall clock and decided that his time undercover living a lie had earned him the right to a well-deserved pint of Guinness and wee Jameson chaser. If nothing else, it reminded him a little of home. It was the only time he'd ever left the flat other than for the necessities of reconnaissance and planning. He took in a lungful of fresh air, broke into a satisfying grin, and headed for the King's Arms.

'Coming to you now,' radioed Anthea. She paused and then continued, 'All units, he's in the pub.'

'Got him,' whispered a barmaid behind the bar. The she beamed a huge smile and said, 'And what can I be getting this lovely smiling man this morning?'

Unzipping his anorak slightly, Declan replied, 'A Guinness and a Jameson if you please.'

'Right away,' beamed the barmaid as a barman wiped the bar top and said, 'Can I get you anything else, sir?'

'No,' replied Declan. 'No, where's the usual man – the licensee?'

207

'Too much to drink last night, sir,' replied the barmaid placing drinks on the bar. 'He's just having a nap. He'll be down later, I'm sure.'

'You're new here,' Declan pointed out. 'I haven't seen you before.'

'Well, Tom and I usually work the back bar,' replied the sergeant as she nodded towards her colleague. 'So it's a nice change to work in the lounge.' She leaned across the bar and whispered to Declan, 'You meet a better class of people but don't tell anyone I said that.'

Contact made and verified the sergeant took Declan's money and ran it through the till. Then she backed away giving Declan plenty of space and leaving him with a satisfied smile on his face.

Declan helped himself to a newspaper lying on the bar and glanced at the headlines. The main story dealt with a NATO naval exercise in the Baltic which seemed to be clashing with a Russian exercise close by. Disinterested in the article, Declan turned to the sports page. Then, turning, he made for a table near the window as the airwaves updated the team outside.

From the counter, a new barman lit a cigarette and managed to point the covert camera inside it towards the man they knew was Declan O'Malley.

Fifteen minutes elapsed before Declan approached the wall phone and made a call. The barman lit another cigarette.

Half an hour later, Declan set aside empty glasses and emerged from the bar into the broad daylight carrying his newspaper. He retraced his steps and soon had the Town Hall behind him, along with Janice Burns radioing, 'I have him back along English Street towards the traffic lights. Stand by!'

Declan was relatively happy as he strolled through the heart of Carlisle's shopping centre. He knew nothing of his brother, other than he was in London and he didn't expect to meet him until later in the week. Pausing in the middle of the pedestrian area, Declan turned to look behind.

Head down, Janice walked straight past and strolled into a card shop as Ricky French stopped at a newspaper kiosk to buy the local paper.

Unfolding his newspaper once more, Declan scanned the headlines. This rag, thought Declan, shaking his head, is full of crazy items about Russian warships playing war games in the Baltic and daily incursions into British airspace by Russian bombers. Not a thing about my sphere of interests. Smiling, Declan placed his newspaper in the waste paper bin where he stood before continuing his journey.

'He's on the move again,' radioed Anthea.

Back in the pub the glasses used by Declan had been seized by the barmaid and secured for fingerprinting. It was always good to scientifically prove that the subject you were following was indeed the right person. Meanwhile, the detective constable was on his mobile telephone asking, 'Did you get that? Who did the target call?'

Declan strolled through the city centre glancing in shops and occasionally stopping to study the contents. The followers blended naturally into surroundings and accompanied him on his journey south towards the railway station.

Here, he paused, checked the time on the railway station clock and pressed onwards slightly downhill into Botchergate. Yet it was here that Ricky French had control when he radioed, 'Target is stepping it out now. He's increased his speed. Keep up everyone.'

Turning left, against the traffic flow, Declan hugged the collar of his anorak closer to his neck and strode into Aglionby Street. Here the traffic was less; there were fewer pedestrians, and the commercial heart of the city gave way to larger townhouses many of which were now divided into flats and apartments. The area was a rabbit warren of streets, lanes, and pathways that criss-crossed and dominated this particular residential area.

Declan suddenly spun right into a narrow lane and entered the side door of an end-terraced house.

'Number nine,' radioed Ricky as he strolled by. 'I confirm the subject entered the side door of number nine.'

'I'm taking the rear,' radioed an operative.

As Declan went to ground in his house, the airwaves were cluttered with team members gradually encircling the house in order to cover any movements.

Boyd had picked up Anthea and was driving in the area. He pulled into a vacant car space and answered his mobile.

Nodding, Boyd engaged Anthea and said, 'It's the team at the pub.' Boyd listened and then said, 'Thanks for that. I'll pass it on.' Turning to Anthea Boyd stated, 'The technical boys tell us Declan rang a mobile number in this satellite catchment area.'

'Interesting,' replied Anthea. 'I wonder who?'

'All units,' radioed Boyd. 'Stand by! Who has control?'

'Och me,' radioed Janice. 'Stand by! A blue Vauxhall had just pulled up at the front of the house.' Janice held her positon and said, 'Target is out of the house and into the rear nearside passenger seat. There are now four – repeat four – in the vehicle. I cannae see the number from here. Anyone?'

'Mine,' replied Ricky before he radioed the registration number of the Vauxhall.

Within moments the area was clear; the car gone, the subject in the rear of a car heading north with surveillance officers on foot trying to locate their partners and the potential for a total loss pretty high.

'I have control,' radioed Anthea suddenly as the Vauxhall drove past their position.

Boyd fired the engine and said, 'My guess is the mobile Declan rang is in the Vauxhall. They've picked him up by appointment. Game on, let's go.'

Following at a respectable distance Anthea began a running commentary on the target vehicle as the team gathered together and began to catch up to the convoy.

Ten minutes later, the city was behind them with Ricky French in control and Janice following on as the team stretched out along a country road on the outskirts of Carlisle.

'No deviation,' radioed Ricky. 'East towards Newcastle.'

'Coming through,' replied a surveillance motor cyclist from the rear of the convoy. 'Solo One is coming through.'

'Martin Duffy,' remarked Boyd to Anthea. 'He transferred from the Special Escort Group to the Special Crime Unit surveillance team. Now that's what I call a change.'

'Too true,' agreed Anthea.

The Vauxhall took a right, abandoned the main road, and headed into a network of country roads with no-one in the driver's rear view mirror.

'Solo One has control,' radioed Martin Duffy, the motor cyclist.

With narrow country bends every few hundred yards Duffy hung back from the rear of the Vauxhall and glimpsed over the hedgerows to keep an eye on his target. 'Solo One has control with bend to bend cover at five hundred yards,' he radioed. 'Hang back team.'

'Need air support,' muttered Boyd. 'We can't expect one motor cyclist to keep in touch on all these narrow lanes. We might as well advertise on the radio what we're doing.'

'Keep your fingers crossed, Guvnor,' offered Anthea. 'They've either turned off to check to see if they're been followed, or they're going to somewhere special.'

'Probably,' replied Boyd.

'And there's enough of us here to eat the job,' suggested Anthea.

'Provided we don't lose them,' replied Boyd.

In the Vauxhall, Declan O'Malley sat in the back seat next to Seamus Logan with the Teacher in the front passenger seat and Callum Finnerty driving.

'All clear, Callum?' asked Seamus.

Callum stole a glance in the rear view mirrors and replied, 'Sure it is, Seamus. We're clean.'

'Okay, let's go for it,' declared Seamus.

'Just keep on this road, Callum,' advised Declan. 'Take a left at the crossroads ahead.'

Turning to Declan, Seamus enquired, 'How long?'

'Five minutes, that's all,' replied Declan.

Seamus nodded and took in the surrounding countryside as their Vauxhall headed deeper into a rural environment and a surveillance tram struggled to keep up with them without being seen.

Seamus pushed the throttle and watched the needle on the speedometer climb before he braked suddenly for a corner

'Target is left, left, left at the crossroads,' radioed Duffy. 'Narrow lanes ahead, disperse. I say again disperse at the crossroads.'

Once the Vauxhall had turned left Martin Duffy continue to follow from a safe distance and studied a computerised mapping unit mounted to his handlebars.

At the crossroads the surveillance team dispersed. Drilled in the procedure, one in three travelled straight on, one in three turned right, and one in three took a left on the same route as the target vehicle.

Solo One was on his own. Success or failure was down to a man on a motor bike.

The follow continued with Martin Duffy constantly on the edge of losing sight of the target vehicle whilst the rest of the team studied their maps to plot routes through the narrow lanes to catch and converge on the target in due course. Those who considered they might be losing touch merely turned round and raced to catch up to the convoy.

Meanwhile, Callum checked the mirror again. It was clear but he still floored the accelerator and took top gear as he powered the vehicle through the narrow lanes.

'Take it easy,' suggested the Teacher. 'We're safe. There's no need to try and kill us.'

'Okay,' chuckled Callum easing back.

As the Vauxhall journeyed on Declan leaned forward and instructed Callum, 'Next left and mind as you go because it's a sharp one.'

Nodding, Callum braked hard and changed down a gear as a junction came into view.

'Hang back,' radioed Duffy as he changed down a gear and decelerated. 'Hang back. The target is slow moving; the roads are narrowing. Giving space, hang back team.'

'He's on his own,' observed Boyd.

'He's the only one with an eyeball on the target,' confirmed Anthea.

The unit's surveillance team slowed to a crawl as the roads narrowed to the width of a standard family car.

'If we meet a tractor on this road,' remarked Boyd. 'We will be well and truly in the shit.'

Ahead, out of sight, the Vauxhall took an abrupt left and headed downhill. At the bottom of the hill lay a humpback bridge which crossed over a stream. Prior to the bridge, Callum braked and steered the car onto a grassy patch next to the road. He snatched the handbrake and brought the vehicle to a standstill.

'They took a sharp left,' radioed Solo One. 'Stand by!'

Travelling slowly, moments later, Martin Duffy glanced to his left and saw the Vauxhall parked on the grass near a bridge with four men standing at the rear of the car.

'Solo One - I'm going through. All Units STOP! STOP! STOP! Stand by for message.'

As Martin Duffy carried straight on at the junction, Boyd hit the brakes and pulled into the side of the road whilst the rest of the team obeyed control and brought their vehicles to a standstill.

Duffy travelled on for a short distance before stopping his vehicle and updating the team.

Boyd listened, thought for a moment, and then said to Anthea, 'They're up to something in the middle of nowhere and I'll bet they're not fishing.'

'Agreed,' replied Anthea. 'But we need to get closer.'

Releasing a monocle from a leather case Martin Duffy employed it to good use before radioing, 'Target is about one hundred yards from my location. I'm backed into a wooded area with an eyeball on the target. The four men are now stood at the rear of the vehicle… They're at the boot… Solo One over!'

Nodding, Boyd radioed, 'This is Boss Car. Janice and Ricky with Anthea and me on foot. Armed covert approach! Solo One hold your present position and report developments. Team Charlie hold west. Wait for my call.'

Quietly unlocking the car, Boyd and Anthea stepped from their vehicle and crept cautiously along the hedgerow. Simultaneously, Ricky followed suit with Janice firstly delving in the car boot before joining her colleagues. Stealthily, the four detectives split up, climbed over gates, and made their way downhill by way of the neighbouring fields.

'No change,' radioed Duffy.

'All units,' radioed Boyd softly, 'I have control. No speech! Wait One!'

Callum Finnerty and the Teacher stood at the rear of the Vauxhall when Seamus and Declan removed shovels from the boot, donned Wellingtons, and made their way from the car towards the humpback bridge. At the bridge they paused, looked back towards Callum and the Teacher, and waited.

The Teacher lit a cigarette and allowed a circle of blue smoke to escape into the atmosphere. Then he looked left and right, saw the coast was clear, and leaned back against the car boot saying, 'All clear. Be as quick as you can, won't you?'

Disappearing beneath the bridge, Seamus and Declan began digging at the side of the stream.

'Solo One sees two targets disappearing beneath a humpback bridge which crosses a stream,' radioed Duffy. 'Two targets remain at the rear of the vehicle. Solo One out.'

Belly down, Ricky French dropped into a ditch by the side of the road and slithered towards the Vauxhall. Moving faster in the adjoining field, Janice hunched down and circumnavigated the lookouts until she was on their opposite side. Meanwhile, Boyd and Anthea had made the bank of the stream and paused for breath.

'No speech,' whispered Boyd on his radio. 'One click for in position; Two for wait... Janice?'

Janice clicked her radio transmitter switch twice before flattening onto the ground and then wading into the stream. She raised herself in the water and felt the current dragging at her ankles and swirling around her waist.

'Ricky?'

Likewise, there was a two click transmission from Ricky as he parted the grass with his hands and studied the lay of the land. Mud clung to his clothing and a frog croaked before hopping from side of the ditch to the other.

'What can you see?' asked Boyd of Anthea.

'Two men digging at the side of the riverbank,' reported Anthea. 'Worms for fishing?'

'We need to get closer,' whispered Boyd. Then he whispered into his radio, 'Moving closer, wait one.'

A mile away a car engine ticked over; an accelerator throbbed quietly, and an apple and flask of coffee suddenly found favour as the remainder of the team waited for instructions.

Squatting down again, Boyd radioed, 'Covert foot hold! Mobile units take closer order and hold.'

Beneath the bridge, a spade struck metal and was cast aside as eager hands reached down, grabbed hold of a securing rope, and hauled an iron trunk to the surface.

Boyd whispered on the radio, 'All units, we have an iron trunk dug from the ground. Stand by... Janice?'

Two clicks were transmitted.

'Roger?'

Two more clicks on the airwaves as the detectives used every ounce of stealth to creep closer to their target.

'Solo One reports no change. Two targets below the bridge and two still with the Vauxhall.'

'Team Charlie is a thirty second response away,' radioed one of the team from a mobile. 'In position.'

Anthea said to Boyd, 'Guns, Guvnor! They're pulling guns from that box.'

Beneath the bridge the stream flowed by oblivious to rifles and ammunition being hauled from the trunk.

Seamus handed a short stock rifle to Declan and said, 'This will do nicely. Short, clean, and ready to go. Ammunition?'

Handing a cardboard ammo box over Declan disclosed, 'Plenty, but take a pistol too.'

Seamus accepted a pistol, weighed it in his hands, and said, 'Anything else?'

'Dynamite!' replied Declan stretching into the box.

'That's enough,' radioed Boyd softly. 'The two targets beneath the bridge are armed. One rifle and one pistol but they are guarding a box from which those weapons came. All units exercise caution. Watch your backgrounds and arcs of fire. We are positioned for a blue on blue otherwise. Anthea and I are in position... Janice?'

Now twelve yards from two men beneath the bridge Janice depressed her transmitter switch once.

'Roger?'

One click reached Boyd's ears.

'Anthea,' whispered Boyd on the radio. 'Take the man smoking at the back of the car. One click acknowledgment please.'

Anthea clicked once.

'Ricky, take his mate.'

Ricky replied with one click.

'Janice, we have the two in the stream,' radioed Boyd.

One click from Anthea confirmed they were all in position.

'Solo One,' radioed Boyd quietly. 'Come! All units come…'

Martin Duffy stowed his monocle and kick-started his bike; half a dozen set of wheels rumbled towards the scene, and Boyd switched the safety catch of his handgun.

Taking a deep breath, Boyd radioed, 'STRIKE! STRIKE! STRIKE!' and then stood up and began running towards the bridge with his handgun reaching out ahead of him.

Ricky French emerged from a muddy ditch like an apocalyptic zombie, allowed the wet stinking mud to drip from his clothing, and shouted, 'Freeze! Armed police!'

Simultaneously, Anthea took two gigantic strides along the river bank and then jumped onto firmer land screaming, 'Freeze! Armed police!'

Beneath the bridge Declan turned to see Janice emerging from the stream onto the bank with a shotgun held at waist high shouting, 'Armed police! Freeze! Hands! Show me your hands!'

A siren on a motor cycle sounded and roared round the corner towards the bridge as Martin Duffy arrived, slung his bike on its side, and withdrew a Heckler and Koch MP5 machine pistol from a boot holster. Half a dozen saloon cars then skidded round the same corner and headed for the bridge.

The Teacher looked both ways, headed for the driver's door of the Vauxhall, and drew a gun from his waistband.

'Drop it,' shouted Anthea.

The Teacher pulled the trigger and fired wildly towards Ricky French who dived to the ground and fired two successive shots into the Teacher's upper body.

The Teacher fell to the ground as Anthea closed with Callum Finnerty shouting, 'Hands! Hands! Show me your hands!'

Seamus looked both ways and saw Boyd rushing towards him from one side and Janice from another. He hoisted the rifle to his shoulder and shouted, 'Back away!'

Declan turned to face Janice and held a stick of dynamite high in the air.

'Nah!' returned Boyd. 'It's over. Weapons down and hands high. Come on!'

A stack of cars arrived squealing and fighting for space as surveillance officers spilled from the vehicles with weapons drawn. The air filled with men and women shouting orders at the four suspects.

Janice walked calmly towards Declan and then squatted down on one knee with her shotgun pointed towards him.

'Back off,' shouted Declan holding the dynamite high. 'Back off or I'll blow us all up.'

'Aye,' replied Janice. 'But you've no detonator in the dynamite and it's no lit so what you gonna do, bonny lad?'

Declan glanced at the dynamite, looked down for a handgun, and then turned towards Janice.

'Aye, I'm right,' bellowed the feisty Scot. 'Now just stand yersel perfectly still. One twitch from your arse and I'll blow your nuts off. Understand?'

Frozen in fear, Declan had no time to reply.

Boyd snatched the dynamite from Declan's hand and pushed Seamus into the wall of the bridge as a posse of detectives closed in and took the men to the ground.

As the prisoners were taken away, Boyd opened the trunk and said, 'What have we got here?'

Moving in, Anthea replied, 'Looks like guns, ammunition and explosives, Guvnor. We've just won the lottery.'

'And we'd better get a forensic team here,' advised Boyd. 'There might be fingerprints all over this little lot.'

'Better still,' replied Anthea. 'I think we have Declan, Seamus Logan, and two others.'

'Makes you stop and ask yourself what else is buried in Cumbria's countryside?' suggested Boyd.

'I don't suppose we'll ever really know,' replied Anthea.

'I wonder if one of them is the Teacher?' asked Boyd. 'Isn't that what Toni's source said – Find Seamus and you'll find the Teacher and his gang – Something like that?'

'We'll work on it,' suggested Anthea. 'But I'm not sure about the chap Ricky shot.'

Glancing across the scene, Boyd and Anthea saw Ricky French lying beside the body of the Teacher. Turning towards them both, Ricky signalled with his hands and whispered, 'He didn't make it.'

*

Chapter Thirteen

~

The Operations Centre
MI5
Threat Level One - Critical

A bright red London bus drew to a halt at the traffic lights close to Thames House in Millbank, London. On a pavement nearby a street vendor held a copy of the Evening Standard in one hand and offered it for sale to passers-by. A dark cloud burst over the city and an unexpected shower soaked its citizens below as the vendor took yet another coin in exchange for the 'news'.

The newsagent's billboard read...

'Police smash Irish Terrorist Assassination Plot'

The newspaper was selling like hotcakes but a few hundred yards away in the headquarters of the Security Service the celebrations following those reported arrests were yesterday's history.

Today was another day, and an ever-developing threat to the nation's security had been identified.

'Great work yesterday,' announced Antonia Harston-Browne. 'I am so delighted for you all, Billy. That was a major coup as far as my service is concerned. You took out the top table in one awesome display of policing.'

'More luck than judgement,' replied Boyd. 'We went looking for Declan thanks to Sandy's tip and we got really lucky. But let me remind you, Toni, that you personally penetrated that dangerous little group years ago. If it hadn't been for you we wouldn't even have known who was who or what was what. The billboards outside are shouting about a police operation but there's an untold story and we all know it.'

'Just a pity my source Donal wasn't alive to enjoy the fruits of his labour,' remarked Antonia sadly. 'Still, four top men, a dozen rifles, sixteen handguns, and twenty five sticks of dynamite have been recovered from that trunk. It's amazing.'

'Not what you'd normally expect,' suggested Sandra Peel.

'Not at all,' agreed Anthea. 'But the Guvnor must have won the lottery because I can't remember the last time we got so lucky.'

'Absolutely,' intervened Commander Maxwell. 'An excellent operation but let's not dwell on it. I have recommended Janice, Ricky, Anthea and Boyd for a Commissioner's Police Bravery Award. I've also recommended Martin Duffy for a commendation relevant to his duties. The commissioner is dancing happily in his office and I understand the Home Secretary raised a smile.'

'Only a smile?' queried Boyd.

The commander chuckled wistfully and replied, 'According to the Home Secretary she's smiling because Antonia and Sandra have concentrated their efforts on that extremely expensive ticker system the government financed some years ago. It's the main way we analyse and prioritise I'm told.'

'And sanitise?' suggested Boyd.

Commander Maxwell continued, 'Possibly, that depends on what's on our plate. Suffice to say that the Home Secretary is somewhat worried. I'm going to hand you over to Antonia who has all the details.'

Antonia stepped forward. Her red hair swung loosely across her shoulders whilst that trouser suit clung closely to her body. That said the lady's beauty did little to hide perspiration flowing from her forehead.

'Threat level one in specific detail,' eulogised Antonia. 'Sandy and I think the primary threat may currently come from an Islamic State fighter from Iraq. We believe he is either on his way to this country or is already here.'

'A lone wolf, Toni, or does he have back up from the organisation?' questioned Boyd.

'We don't know actually,' offered Antonia. 'For what it's worth I'd go with the notion that it's a mix of both. There has to be others involved who are helping him to travel from the Middle East to the west.'

'What do you mean by the west?' asked Anthea. 'America?'

'Predominantly Europe but possibly America,' replied Antonia. 'We can't rule anything out and – if I'm honest – my remit is to concentrate on the UK.'

'His name, Toni?' queried Boyd. 'We need to start a search.'

'True name not verified but I'll come to that in a moment,' replied Antonia. 'Currently, you know him as the man from Tikrit.'

'Oh, not again,' complained Boyd shaking his head. 'It's an interesting snippet but the truth is we get tips every week about people leaving the UK to join terrorists in the Middle East. And probably as many tip offs telling us someone is coming back to blow us all up. Surely this has no substance unless you've been to a butcher and put some meat on the bones.'

'We have his first name as Salman,' replied Antonia. 'But there's more and what I'm going to tell you must stay in this room forever. Do you understand?'

'Doesn't it always and do we really need to know?' asked Boyd inquisitively.

'I believe you do need to know,' replied Antonia, 'Because we're going to be working together to find him.'

'Okay, we're listening,' stated Boyd. 'Just give it to us straight.'

'Sandy and I came across some old information on Ticker that a large number of Chinese Muslims from the northern province of Xinjiang in China left their homes and joined Islamic State. I'm talking hundreds, possibly thousands.'

'You're joking,' suggested Anthea. 'That's surely not possible?'

'Unfortunately it is and we're not joking,' replied Sandy. 'This happened a few months ago but the military are starting to feel the impact of extra numbers in the enemy ranks now.'

'Interesting,' remarked Boyd, 'And worrying at the same time.'

'But now we have his name,' replied Antonia. 'And this is where it gets complicated for me.'

'Really,' replied Boyd. 'What's the problem, Toni?'

'Our service has an informal relationship with Israeli Intelligence. We also have informal contacts with some of their operatives that are known to us.'

'Mossad?' queried Boyd.

Antonia nodded in agreement and responded with, 'The man from Tikrit is not an Arab. He's not even from the Middle East. In exchange for intelligence relevant to active anti-Jewish individuals known to western intelligence agencies Mossad has given us his name. It's not quite cricket as we know it because I can guess what Mossad will do with the list of names we gave them. It also means we have to let the Americans in on some of our operations.'

Boyd exchanged glances with Anthea and Commander Maxwell before replying, 'Speaking for myself, that's surely a matter for British Intelligence and Her Majesty's Government. How you conduct the preservation of national security at the global level is not my brief, Toni. I'm just a copper chasing terrorists. Personally I'd swop a piece of toast for a scone if it had butter and strawberry jam on it. I just need a starter for ten – a name?'

Antonia strolled to a window, thought for a moment, turned and said, 'The man from Tikrit is Mostafa Humayl.'

'Well that's something to go on,' replied Boyd.

'Mostafa means the chosen one,' explained Antonia. 'Humayl means a companion of the prophet. We're not even sure that's his real name but that's what Mossad have given us as part of the exchange. From where we sit Mostafa is obviously the chosen one and being a companion of the prophet at the moment doesn't lead me to believe he's going to pitch up at Speaker's Corner in Hyde Park and start preaching the Quran to all and sundry. No, to put it bluntly, GCHQ traffic is zeroing in on him but there's little doubt the leaders of Islamic State sent him.'

'What else can you tell us about him,' asked Anthea.

'He's a Uighur Separatist,' revealed Antonia.

'What the hell is a Uighur Separatist?' asked Boyd.

'It means he's from Xinjiang. It's a predominantly Muslim Chinese region that borders with Afghanistan and others in the North West province of China.'

'So this is the Salman that we've heard about?' asked Commander Maxwell seeking confirmation. 'I've read quite a bit about the man from Tikrit but have wondered whether there was any substance to the titbits flying around cyberspace.'

'Yes, commander, Salman – if Mossad is correct – is Mostafa Humayl,' explained Antonia.

'At least it's a start, Guvnor,' murmured Anthea.

'Yes, but I'd like you to tell us how Mossad got his name, Antonia,' remarked Commander Maxwell. 'I'd like to know how strong the information is.'

'Wouldn't we all?' responded Antonia.

'That remark doesn't fill me with confidence,' suggested the commander.

'Okay, I understand,' responded Antonia. 'Let me explain it to you like this. The UK is not the only nation in Europe that is aware of its own people leaving the country to go and fight in places like Syria, Iraq, and elsewhere. Even Canada and America can point to a large number of their residents who have travelled to join the extremists. Our problem is that jihad is right on the doorstep of Europe. Every European country has extremists from their own country fighting for Islamic State, Al Qaeda, and its various offshoots.'

'Yes, we're aware of that,' suggested Commander Maxwell, 'Allies of the Salafi Movement. Where are you taking us?'

'To Israel, commander, and to knowledge that over forty Arab Israelis left Israel some time ago and are fighting for Islamic State in Syria and Iraq.'

'Hence Mossad,' nodded Boyd slowly, 'A finger in every pie and a spy in every organisation throughout the world.'

'Probably,' admitted Antonia, 'And a Mossad source known to us only as Fathom.'

'You know about their sources?' enquired Boyd surprised.

'They're not the only spy company operating in the field,' suggested Antonia. 'We have our ways too, and we take prisoners to interrogate as you know.'

'Pleased to hear it,' remarked Anthea. 'Let me guess, one of the Arab Israelis is Fathom?'

'Not confirmed by our sources inside Mossad,' replied Antonia. 'But I'd say that was pretty damn close, Anthea. The point is Mossad agents penetrate Arab organisations in order to provide the State of Israel with intelligence.

'Are we sure about his name?' asked Boyd

His name is 'Mostafa and he's from the city of Kashgar,' disclosed Antonia. 'As far as Kashgar is concerned, the Chinese government openly admit to the presence of a triple evil. They define it as a mix of religious extremism, separatism and terrorism. Violence there is fuelled by repression against a religious and ethnic minority in the shape of China's Muslim Uighurs.'

'I do recall reading something about this some time ago,' declared Boyd. 'Something about lots of Chinese Muslims defecting to Islamic State, is this what you are talking about?'

'Correct,' smiled Antonia. 'Uighur culture leans more towards Central Asia than China. Consequently their culture is closer to Islam than any other religion. Ethnically they are Turkic Muslims and make up about forty five percent of the region's population. Uighurs argue they have been economically marginalised and fear their traditional culture is being eroded.'

'Sounds familiar,' replied Anthea. 'But I've never heard of Kashgar.'

'It's the last stop on the road before Pakistan and closer to Baghdad than it is to Beijing,' explained Antonia. 'Xinjiang is home to ten million Uighur Muslims but the point is China doesn't trust their loyalty. China worries about whether they are Chinese first or Muslim first.'

'Is it that important given the size of China?' asked Boyd.

'To the Chinese it is,' remarked Antonia. 'The Chinese Communist Party sees Xinjiang as an integral part of the People's Republic of China. It is determined to hold onto Xinjiang and expects a sacred trust from its Chinese patriots.'

'Fancy talk, but what does that mean in practical terms?' asked Boyd.

'The government have banned people from praying in a mosque and no one under the age of eighteen is allowed to enter a mosque,' explained Antonia.

'I have sympathy with that course of action,' revealed Boyd. 'It just might prevent radicalisation to some degree although how you would ever police that in any country is beyond me.'

'Is it right to prevent the population from a right to religion?' countered Antonia. 'Who are we to say whether people should or should not believe in religion and accept it as a part of their daily life? We can't be judge and jury despite the beliefs we may all hold.'

There was an undisturbed silence as Boyd and his companions considered Antonia's words. It was only broken when Anthea asked, 'If we forget the politics and religion for a moment how do these terrorists work?'

'Sandra?' invited Antonia.

Sandra Peel stepped forward and divulged, 'Recent incidents have involved a vehicle ploughing into a crowd and multiple attackers with knives and homemade explosives. Over two hundred people were killed in a matter of weeks but it's believed about half of them were carrying suicide bombs. You must also realise that police over there are armed. Most of the attackers were shot dead by police.'

'Really!' muttered Anthea making notes rapidly, 'Just what we don't need on our doorstep.'

Sandra explained, 'The Chinese government says these people are being poisoned by militant Islam; propaganda flooding across the border from Pakistan and Afghanistan on DVDs, mobile phones and internet. As part of a twelve month long counter-terrorism campaign the Chinese police held they managed to confiscate thousands of videos inciting terrorism. They've also blocked online materials teaching terrorist techniques.'

'And where are we locally with this?' questioned Boyd.

'GCHQ intercepted material from various locations suggesting the man from Tikrit is on route to take out a UK leader, presumably the prime minister or the monarch, your guess is as good as mine. In view of Mossad's intelligence, the Duke reckons we should tighten the net around the monarch and those most likely to be targets.'

'Any description?' queried Boyd. 'A photograph even?'

'He's Chinese – as discussed - and that's all Mossad told us. Apparently they don't have anything else.'

'We can alert all air and sea ports,' suggested Anthea. 'But if he's travelling on a false passport it's going to be almost impossible to trace him unless we turn over every Chinese visitor that enters the country.'

'Do we know where this man was last located?' queried Boyd. 'Please don't tell me it was China.'

'No, not China,' responded Antonia, 'We believe he is in France but personally I think we have a very sophisticated target to confront.'

'Anything else we need to know but can't talk about?' asked Boyd. 'It's an interesting profile but there's nothing there that's going to take us to him without a lot of good luck and good judgement.'

'Well, we have the man from Tikrit on one hand and a Russian spy on the other,' revealed Antonia. 'Oh yes, while you've been chasing the Irish and neglecting everything else I've had my eyes on a Russian diplomat.'

'We did have our hands full,' suggested Anthea.

'Of course you did,' smiled Antonia. 'The reality is there's no such thing as a quiet day at the office when the Russians start spying on the ground,' suggested Antonia with a twisted smile. 'I need to get a hold of that enquiry very soon. I'll need your help when we move in, Boyd.'

'Of course,' replied the detective.

'Meanwhile,' continued Antonia. 'I'd consider it a big help of you can make a start on tracing Mostafa as soon as possible. GCHQ tell me electronic traffic relevant to Mostafa recently centred on Paris. I've already spoken to my counterpart in French Intelligence. They have a number of addresses they are looking into but I personally have my doubts that he's still in France.'

'Paris?' offered Boyd. 'If that's the case then the man from Tikrit is only a couple of hours away – either by road, rail or air.'

'Time to put the shutters up before it's too late,' explained Commander Maxwell. 'Thank you Sandra and Antonia, now it's up to us to get on with it.'

'Paris?' queried Anthea who walked to a wall map and traced a finger across the city. 'Whereabouts exactly?'

'Goussainville,' remarked Antonia. 'Near the airport.'

In the United States of America the equivalent threat level system to that which is operational in the United Kingdom is known as DEFCON. In France the national security alert system is known as *'Plan Vigipirate'*. The plan was created in 1978 by President Valéry Giscard d'Estain, and is defined by five levels of threat. Each level is represented by five colours: white, yellow, orange, red, and scarlet.

Thanks to the man from Tikrit, the French authorities had declared *'Vigipirate Scarlet'* – the equivalent of Threat Level One.

The last time the alert level had been so high was when it was raised in the Picardy region the day after the Charlie Hebdo shooting in Paris.

Notification of a risk of major attacks had been received and analysed. The European Ticker Intelligence system suggested an attack on a leader in the west was imminent. There was cause to suspect attacks might lead to major devastation and a severe catastrophe had to be averted. Measures highly disruptive to public life had been authorised.

The Parisian, Francois Dubois, was leader of the region's DGSI: The General Directorate for Internal Security - *Direction générale de la sécurité intérieure*. It was the equivalent of Britain's Security Service, M15.

In this area of France, Francois was responsible for counter terrorism and counter espionage. Whenever his duties took him to the French capital he often worked with *Police Nationale*, formerly called the '*Sûreté*' who were responsible for policing in the big cities. It wasn't lost on a French government who considered that the successful removal of the threat known as 'the man from Tikrit' would cement relationships with the United Kingdom, other European countries, and the United States of America. As well as peace and democracy, there was much political capital to be made with the outcome of a successful counter terrorist operation.

Francois and his colleagues set up a temporary incident room in a nearby school and worked through the night analysing electronic traffic following a call from GCHQ. They put together an operation to take into custody a known band of Islamic extremists and supporters. The group was known to DGSI due to historic family traces to Northern Algeria and the Algerian War of Independence. Three males were of interest to Francois at the address recently put under surveillance. They were Sunni Muslims from the predominant Maliki School of jurisprudence which had been founded in the eighth century by Malik bin Anas. This particular school of Islamic faith took Sharia law from the Quran and the words and saying of the Prophet Muhammad to order their life and the lives of others. Francois knew that not all Muslims were violent or extremist but he was interested in this trio when he learnt of mobile phone traces between the Tikrit area and the group in Goussainville. Yet he was also aware of two unknown females who had been spotted inside the house. They were a mystery to Francois and his colleagues.

The threat was real enough as far as French eyes could see. They'd suffered their fair share of terrorism in recent years and were more than capable of hitting back above their weight. Recent intelligence raised the probability that the man from Tikrit –Mostafa Humayl – was hiding in Goussainville, but the proximity of access to a nearby airport was not lost on Francois as they surrounded both the airport and a residential area where Mostafa was thought to be.

During the night nearby households were evacuated but the reality existed that the immediate area was almost void of residents. Nevertheless, the mood in France was such that liberty was threatened once more. They would take no chances with extremists Francois knew were capable of killing at the drop of a hat.

The area was in lock down. Charles De Gaulle airport was on scarlet alert with armed police at every junction and armoured cars on the airport apron. Now was the time to prevent an atrocity and hit back for 'liberty'.

It was time.

A three bedroomed terraced house in the older part of Goussainville was the target of the operation – or to be precise the three men and two women who lived inside the run down premises and were believed to be sheltering Mostafa Humayl.

From the point of view of the police, the house was an excellent place to watch and surround since it had both front and rear doors opening onto the highway. Furthermore, the road was fairly narrow and had seen better days. Pot holes and rubble seemed to litter the highway in the immediate austere vicinity. There were more abandoned empty properties in this part of town than people cared to mention. It was testament to the high-rise development of a more modern Goussainville half a mile away. Here, the town was prospering, contemporary in architectural design, and vibrant in its economy.

Yet those who sought to shelter Mostafa knew and thought different. They'd been asked to cover him for a 'stop-over' before he caught a flight to who knows where. The base at Goussainville was a safe house as far as they were concerned. It was situated close to the airport, not known to the authorities, and represented no more than a temporary short stay bolt hole for those who needed protection.

Stubbing out a cigarette beneath his boot Zavier listened to his radio and waited for an order from Francois Dubois's office. The middle-aged policeman tightened his helmet and cradled a rifle happily in his arm whilst a handgun relaxed in a leather holster. A veteran to such proceedings, Zavier drummed his fingers patiently on the bonnet of his Peugeot patrol car. Used to waiting and watching at events such as this, Zavier had all the time in the world. And he wasn't alone. Over one hundred officers were in position covering the front and rear of the target house. No-one would escape today.

Yet, time-served or not, police the world over all experienced that cold empty feeling in the stomach just before the action began. You could train for it, experience it, do it over and over again – but when the time came the adrenalin flowed; the skin went cold as it stretched across the trigger guard, and sweat still managed to trickle into the corner of your eyes. After a certain

231

length of time boredom could quickly develop and dull the senses. It was vital to stay alert at all times.

The sound of a police helicopter approaching alerted Zavier and he felt for his pistol, switched the safety catch off, and then thrust the rifle butt into his shoulder. He took aim. The first shot would penetrate the ground floor window and deliver CS gas into the room.

Designated officers surrounding the building would simultaneously fill the building with CS gas and hope to end the incident as soon as possible.

Inside the terraced house, the male occupants ate a meal downstairs whilst the females upstairs packed and prepared to leave the building.

Outside, Francois studied his map and asked, 'Anything from the airport?'

'No trace of anyone by the name of Mostafa Humayl on any flight list,' replied an assistant.

'Very well,' replied Francois. 'And security and passport control – any images of a lone Chinese male boarding a UK bound flight?'

'Not in the last forty eight hours, sir.'

Meandering through the temporary incident room set in the village school, Francois nodded his head and replied, 'Good! Our man looks as if he is here.'

Smiling, Francois looked at a map of the target area, and then studied images on a screen sent by the police helicopter.

'Proceed!' instructed Francois.

Inside the target house Hussein heard the helicopter above. He made for the window, looked skyward, and then scanned the street outside before announcing, 'They're here. Later than expected but they're here now.'

'What kept them?' asked Bashar.

'I suspect they've been there all night,' remarked Saleem. 'It's time, my friends. Mohammad will watch over us but Allah has his arms open for us. He has given us all the hours we need to prepare ourselves.'

'The women?' enquired Bashar.

'They must go now,' instructed Saleem. 'They have served us well but it now it is time for them to leave so that we might carry on the fight. Get them, Bashar.'

Scurrying upstairs for a few minutes Bashar shortly returned saying, 'They will not go, Saleem. They want to stay with us and fight the infidels.'

'It is not possible,' declared Saleem. 'Get them downstairs and chase them outside with their bags. They have served their purpose. Tell them Allah is on our side and will lead them to paradise in a future life.'

'If we let them go, Saleem,' advised Bashar, 'They will be made to talk about our group and our warriors elsewhere in France and Algeria.'

'I will deal with that problem,' stated Saleem. 'Now, please, get rid of them, Bashar. I do not want such women spoiling my plans by getting in the way. I have much to do.'

In the street outside a radio call signalled Zavier to proceed as planned but then a white flag appeared at the front window of the target house. Zavier and his colleagues faltered, held their fire, and wondered what was going on.

The front door opened and a white flag was waved once more.

The wireless network was alive with the latest developments. Francois stepped forward and ordered the attack to be suspended until further notice.

Surely not, he thought. Surrender?

An officer engaged the target house with a loudhailer and watched as two suitcases were thrown from the front door onto the pavement immediately outside the house. Then he heard screaming from within and lowered his loudhailer.

Lowering his rifle a tad, Zavier sought his pistol. A feeling of euphoria swept over him when he decided they were surrendering without a fight. Why could he hear screaming? Has there been an argument of some kind, he wondered.

Another suitcase hit the tarmac and then a muffled indistinguishable voice sounded out from the house.

It sounded like a woman's voice, thought Zavier.

No-one replied causing Francois to grab the radio and ask the helicopter pilot what he could see.

'Nothing,' came the reply. 'No movement at the rear.'

'Where are the males?' queried Francois.

A veiled woman wearing Islamic dress appeared on the doorstep. She held her hands high and took a tentative step onto the pavement. Moments later, another lady wearing Islamic dress appeared at the doorway.

She might have been her sister, thought Zavier watching from the cover of his vehicle. But what's going on, he asked himself.

The two women were now on the street with their hands held high jabbering in a language no-one present seemed to understand. Then the women turned, took hold of their cases, and dragged them towards Zavier and waiting police lines. The older woman waved a white flag whilst dragging her case awkwardly behind her. Yet she was crying.

Tears are rolling down her cheeks, thought Zavier. She's crying like a baby. They both are, he decided.

'Not the suitcase,' radioed Francois. 'Take the women into custody but tell them to leave the suitcases on the street well away from police lines. They may be bombs. You never know. Search the women before interrogating them. I want to know everything they know.'

Francois's message had the effect of galvanising the police. Zavier's mind engaged top gear once more. He understood the word 'bomb' and immediately gripped the rifle tight into his shoulder, took aim, and shouted in French, 'Stand still!'

To his surprise, the women rooted to the ground with their hands reaching into the sky and tears pouring down their cheeks.

'Walk forward and leave your suitcases where they are,' ordered Zavier suddenly aware that he had taken control of the danger zone.

The females did as they were told and walked forward.

'Slowly,' bellowed Zavier. His voice penetrated the atmosphere and brought control and order to proceedings.

Watching their progress Zavier shuffled his weight onto the other foot and so shifted his position behind his patrol car.

'Stop!' he shouted. 'Turn round!'

The women turned to face the house they had just left moments ago and were suddenly met with a long burst of gunfire from an open window on the upper floor of the terraced house.

The older woman spiralled grotesquely with her hands in the air before falling to the ground. Her colleague slammed backwards into the tarmac when dozens of bullets tore into them. They died where they fell in a gathering pool of blood.'

'*Allahu Akbar!*' screamed Saleem at the top of his voice.

'It is what Mostafa wanted,' remarked Bashra who stepped in behind Saleem and let off another stream of gunfire towards police lines.

'And what Mostafa decrees Allah allows,' said Hussein joining in the slaughter.

With two females dead on the ground and a hail of bullets coming his way, Zavier threw himself flat on the floor and rolled to the rear of his car.

Saleem smashed out the upper floor window with the butt of his rifle and loosed off round after round at police lines. Then, uninterrupted, he aimed skywards and began shooting at the police helicopter.

The pilot veered to the left, downwards, and at high speed into a dive dodging bullets all the way.

Seconds later, police returned fire and peppered the house with a massive salvo of bullets.

Saleem retreated indoors and into the depths of the house.

Meanwhile, Hussein and Bashar threw everything into the firefight at the front of the house. Shooting indiscriminately, they aimed to left and right selecting anything that moved as a target. Steadfast, determined, Hussein continued to fire when Bashar ran out of ammunition and paused to reload. Nodding, Bashar fired repeatedly from the window whilst Hussein reloaded. It was pure hell with the smell of cordite filling the room like a silent unseen dust that bit into the back of the throat and watered the eyes.

At the rear, Saleem appeared at the window, took aim with a rocket launcher, and promptly destroyed two police patrol cars parked next to each other.

Two officers fell, badly injured.

Saleem reloaded and fired his deadly evil again before disappearing into the house once more.

From his control room Francois ordered, 'Full salvo and covering fire. Close with the subjects.'

Shaking his head in disbelief, Zavier glanced along the police line, left and right, and then nodded. He held high three fingers and began a count down. When the last finger closed down Zavier led the line, stood up behind cover, and fired round after round into the building in front of him.

As Bashar moved forward to give return fire, a bullet caught him in the shoulder and he fell back badly wounded.

Hussein ignored his wounded comrade and began lopping hand grenades towards the police ranks growling, *'Allahu Akbar!'*

Hussein laughed as he continued to shoot towards police lines.

From the depths of the house, Saleem shouted, 'Join me, my friends. Join me! We were told to expect a paramilitary response from the French police and our friends were right. But now it is time to turn the tables! Allah has called upon us. Come!'

A bizarre hush ripped through the house when the wounded Bashar and Hussein shouldered their weapons and joined Saleem.

Zavier lowered his rifle, took cover, reloaded, and then realised the shooting from the house had stopped.

'Anyone have a visual on the occupants?' he radioed.

There was no reply and he asked again but only to be told that there appeared to be some kind of ceasefire.

The loudhailer was brought into use again but attempts at two-way communication fell short when no reply was received.

'GAS… GAS… GAS,' shouted Zavier and then put the first CS gas cartridge through an upper window before deploying a second through the lower ground window.

'Follow up with flash bangs,' ordered Francois.

Dedicated officers armed with stun grenades complied. The house soon filled up with a mist of disabling CS gas and an explosion of noise designed to stun, incapacitate, and render the targets incapable of any activity.

'Now!' radioed Zavier.

The police lines moved forward with Zavier rushing to the front door as fast his legs would carry him. Slamming himself against the sandstone building he paused for breath and inched forward with his back hard against the wall. Poking his handgun forward he bent low and took aim at the entrance to the house waiting for the first of the trio to leave. Expecting them to be incapable of much movement and hardly likely to resist, Zavier felt good. His pulse raced and adrenalin inside rushed through his bloodstream energising him. Yet he knew it would soon be over once the prisoners had been taken into custody. Smiling to himself he decided he'd done well. He was so close that he would take a prisoner and, with a bit of luck and some good interrogation, much would be learnt from these terrorists.

Other officers nearby gradually closed with Zavier and prepared to reap the rewards of a successful operation.

It was then that Zavier realised the bodies of two women dress in Islamic garb lay only a matter of yards from him. His stomach churned when he glanced at the disfigured corpse ripped apart by lethal gunfire.

Zavier felt almost apologetic towards the women. It was as if he shouldn't be there and neither should they. What was it all for?

In a cellar of the target premises a slow burning fuse wire finally reached its destination and triggered an explosion.

The bomb detonated precisely on time and blew a hole in the cellar roof as it devastated the building. Within seconds, a mass of masonry dislodged, flew outwards into the street, crumpled as the walls collapsed and the roof came tumbling down. A fireball rushed in burning and destroying with its evil tongues of flame lashing out and scorching everything in its path.

Zavier felt the force of the bomb on his back when the sandstone wall exploded outwards pushing him into the roadway. Then the roof came down and a massive conglomeration of ageing timber and old sandstone crashed down on those below.

Zavier was killed instantly.

At the end of the row of terraced houses, Saleem led Hussein and Bashar through the loft spaces into the end terrace house. Head down, ducking the timbers that supported the roof, Saleem explained to Hussein and Bashar how pleased Ibrahim Hasan al Din would be.

'We made a good choice of base, my friends. Most of these buildings are close to dereliction or earmarked for destruction.'

The sound of the structure crashing to the ground behind them rang through their ears. A glance over a shoulder revealed dust gathering in a cloud that might follow them to their destiny.

They knew the bomb had killed and maimed those close enough to feel the wrath of the Algerian terrorists. Yet they felt no remorse.

'Our job is done,' confirmed Saleem. 'Salman is long gone in the front of a delivery van bound for Calais and a ferry to Dover. But we must follow his orders to the letter lest the power of his wrath catch up with us. We have succeeded in slowing down the police chase to give Salman more time. My friends, we've even tied up French intelligence and got even in the process.'

'Good!' replied Bashar. 'Salman said the French police would adopt a paramilitary style to attack us. The man from Tikrit thinks well for we have used the enemy's strength to our own advantage. Deliberately, we have drawn the spider into the web.'

Saleem did not know how many bodies lay on the tarmac outside when he opened the loft cover and dropped through the space with his colleagues following him.

Leading Bashar and Hussein downstairs, Saleem adjusted his jacket, slammed another magazine into his weapon and shouted, 'For Salman, for Mohammad, for Allah!'

'For Tikrit and Algeria,' roared Hussein.

Firing wildly from the hip the trio rushed out of the rear door of the end terrace house towards the police lines only yards away. Then, suddenly standing still, Saleem threw away his weapon. Feverishly, he pulled the rip cord on his suicide jacket and blew himself to smithereens along with Hussein and Bashar who simultaneously followed suit.

Body parts, nuts, bolts, glass and nails, flew through the atmosphere impacting on people, vehicles and buildings.

Terror in Goussainville was a war zone. It was as if hell had arrived in the suburbs of Paris where evil and horror ruled the day in unspeakable terms.

Smoke and flames from the incident climbed into the sky when Francois Dubois glanced through the school window. He rushed to the scene. His jaw dropped and his heart missed a beat when he witnessed the scene of death and mutilation that greeted him. With patrol vehicles wrecked and a building on fire, Francois meandered through the carnage counting the bodies that lay scattered around. Over a dozen police lay dead or dying in the immediate area of the multiple explosions and the sound of ambulance sirens and fire appliances suddenly erupted and threw his world into total disarray.

Making for a quiet corner Francois stopped and vomited the contents of his stomach onto the floor. They were no closer to catching the man from Tikrit. Salman, or whatever his name was, had disappeared leaving a trail of unspeakable evil behind him.

An assistant reached out with a mobile phone handing it to Francois saying, 'Monsieur Dubois, it is the President of France. He wants to know if we have the man from Tikrit in custody.'

Reluctantly, Francois Dubois accepted the phone and held it to his ear. He was about to speak when his brain deactivated and he decided no, not now. No!

Francois cut the connection, handed the phone back to his assistant, and walked back towards the school.

Chapter Fourteen
~

Reading,
Royal Berkshire.
Threat Level One - Critical

Close to the M25 motorway and the hub of the nation's motorway system, a village near the ancient town of Reading was home to the Foreign Secretary. Today the area was also the scene of a joint surveillance operation comprising of officers of the Security Service and the Special Crime Unit. The operational leader was the red headed Intelligence officer Antonia Harston-Browne who was talking on a mobile phone to Boyd.

'Billy,' she began. 'The subject is approaching the Foreign Secretary's home. There's no protection on site at the moment.'

'Why ever not?' queried Boyd. 'The minister oversees The Secret intelligence Service. What's going on? Has someone made a cock-up?'

'No! There's no protection because his home hasn't been built yet,' replied Antonia. 'And that's why Ivan Pushkin is here. The house is still under construction.'

'How would Ivan know this was the Foreign Secretary's new house?' asked Boyd.

'My team has been following our Russian friend for a few weeks now, Billy. We know he's clocked the Defence Secretary in Whitehall thanks to the CCTV system and we've had him taking photographs of the Defence Secretary's home in Epsom.'

'Anything else on his card?' asked Boyd.

'He's also been seen watching the Foreign Secretary's official residence in London. We know Ivan recently placed the Foreign Secretary under surveillance and followed him and his wife one day when he had no official functions to attend.'

'You mean Ivan followed our man from Carlton House Terrace?' suggested Boyd.

'Yes, in St. James's, Westminster,' confirmed Antonia. 'Of course it's common knowledge that's the official residence of the Foreign Secretary but it's not widely known that the minister is overseeing the construction of his new home out here. He's kept it well and truly under wraps. Personally, I think it may be his retirement home but then that's just a guess. Anyway, my team have followed Ivan following the Foreign Secretary and his wife out here to take a look at the progress of the building.'

'Who knows about his new pad?' asked Boyd.

'Us, the Prime Minister, and probably one or two of his close friends and family, he hasn't actually told the world about it for obvious reasons.'

'I see,' responded Boyd. 'When will it be finished?'

'The structure is up. They're on with the inside and very soon it will be properly secured and made watertight. That's scheduled for next week, I believe. So you can see why it's a great opportunity for a Russian spy.'

'Are you thinking what I'm thinking?' asked Boyd.

'Probably,' replied Antonia. 'I'm expecting him to take more than a passing interest in the house this time, Billy. Ivan doesn't know we're here and I don't want to burn any of my surveillance team. When necessary I'd like you to move your police team to the front and take over should the need arise.'

'Will do,' promised Boyd. 'We're at the back of the surveillance unit at the moment. Keep us posted.'

The call ended with Antonia pulling her team closer together as they meandered through the leafy lanes of Royal Berkshire towards the new build.

Standing in pleasant English countryside the building plot covered two acres and ran from a highway at the front to a stream at the rear. The stream provided a natural border before giving way to a panorama of green and lush meadows that complimented the nearby capital's green belt. Structurally, the building enjoyed walls, three floors, a roof, and interior corridors and room divisions. Plastering and tiling had commenced and would take some time due to the size of the house. Laying floors and finishing off the electricity supply to all the rooms would precede carpeting where required. Even the three bathrooms were clearly present and some of the plumbing was in advanced stages. But it was Sunday, and today the plot was devoid of tradesmen who knew only that it was being built for a London agency on behalf of some bigwig businessman in London.

Ivan checked his mirrors again. He decided no-one was following him and pulled into the side of the road close to the Foreign Secretary's new house.

Composed for a few moments, Ivan sat back in the driver's seat, watched his mirrors, and waited.

Two miles away a voice ran out across the airwaves with, 'Kilo Two Three, target is stationary one hundred yards from the house. No movement.'

'Alpha Six, noted, Alpha Three, Four and Five drive through in two minute intervals.'

'Boss car, confirm target is still in the vehicle.'

'Alpha Three, stand by.'

Ivan felt comfortable and relaxed. He had no knowledge of a tracker fitted to the underside of his vehicle and was blissfully unaware of a wireless signal the tracker device emitted to the MI5 team.

Checking the tracker image on her dashboard again, Antonia noted Ivan's vehicle was still stationary. Punching her mobile, she rang Boyd.

Close to the Foreign Secretary's house, Ivan Pushkin was busy.

Snap! Another photographic image surrendered to Ivan's camera but then he heard a motorbike and calmly lowered the camera as the bike drove past.

The motor cyclist ignored Ivan and his vehicle, didn't look at the two acre building plot, and stopped at the T junction.

'Alpha Three with reverse eyeball; the subject is still in his vehicle observing the house. I'm moving through.'

Alpha Three snatched first gear and turned left into the traffic flow with a powerful and deliberately carefree roar from the throttle.

A few minutes later a Skoda taxi drove through with one driver and two passengers in the rear seat. When the taxi reached the junction it turned right and the driver radioed, 'Alpha Four, no change. Subject still watching the house.'

'Noted,' replied Antonia. 'Alpha Five, hang back.'

'Will do, Alpha Five out.'

Antonia returned to her phone call with Boyd.

In a meadow at the rear of the Foreign Secretary's new house, Boyd and Terry Anwhari clambered uphill to a grassy knoll overlooking the house. Dressed in green camouflage combat gear and armed with high powered binoculars, the two detectives eventually flopped to the ground and then crawled on their bellies to the top of the rise.

'What do you see?' asked Boyd.

'Just the house, wait one,' replied Terry focusing his binoculars. 'And you, anything?'

Lifting his head slightly, Boyd re-focused his binoculars and said, 'I'm looking for the car but I can't see it.'

In the car, Ivan glanced in his mirrors again and satisfied himself he was alone. Carefully, he opened the driver's door and took in a breath of fresh air before casually walking round the vehicle and checking out the roadway. At the rear of his car, Ivan dropped onto both knees and began checking the underside of his vehicle. Moments later, he moved along both sides and the front often sliding his hand underneath the bodywork looking for any kind of device that may betray his position.

Eventually, Ivan stood up and returned to the driver's door where he reached across to the dashboard and removed a belt bag and a small cardboard box. He secured the belt bag around his waist, unfastened the cardboard box, and placed the contents into his pocket. Ivan made his way to the other side of the road just as an ice-cream van came into view.

The ice-cream van drove right past but at the junction the driver radioed, 'Alpha Five, subject is out of the car and making for the house. Do you have him?'

'Yes, Yes!' radioed Boyd looking through his binoculars. 'Thanks to you, we have the area covered.'

'Now I know why we use ice-cream vans,' muttered Terry. 'You can see them a mile off. I have the man and his vehicle now.'

'And from the top of a hill,' chuckled Boyd. 'What you got now, Terry?'

Checking his line of vison Terry replied, 'He's crossing the road and making for the house, Guvnor.'

'Come on, Terry,' replied Boyd. 'We can get much closer than this.'

Together the two detectives crawled through the grass before using the natural undulations in the land to break into a hunched run.

Making good time, but constantly checking left and right, Ivan entered the driveway and stepped out towards the deserted building.

Windows had been fitted to the ground floor and the outline of a tennis court and nearby swimming pool could be seen to the west of the building. They were both in the course of construction. But to all intents and purposes the house actually looked quite close to being completed. If there was work to be done it was virtually all interior work that was still outstanding.

Gingerly now, and quite composed, Ivan entered the open doorway and made for what would be the main lounge.

Boyd and Terry made the far side of the stream and engaged their binoculars once more.

'Got him yet?' asked Boyd.

'Nope,' replied Terry, 'But I reckon he's inside.'

'I'll take the west. You take the east side,' ordered Boyd wading through the narrow stream.

Inside the building Ivan Pushkin, trade diplomat and apparent friend to all American and European businesses, removed a long term listening device from his pocket and buried it in the fresh masonry of the newly built lounge wall. The device was no bigger than a matchbox and was as thin as a coin. He hid it behind a telephone socket then took a trowel and a small packet of powder from his belt bag and smoothed the plaster around the device until the new plaster blended with the older colour. It took time but it was Sunday and Ivan didn't expect to be disturbed. He did, however, expect that in the months ahead a signal would be emitted from a Russian satellite in geo-stationary orbit around the planet. The signal would locate the long term listening device, activate it, and his Mother Country would enjoy listening to the private and personal conversations of Britain's Foreign Secretary. No doubt the minister might discuss foreign policy with his beloved wife, his close friends, and his international guests who knew and respected him as a man of supreme political prowess.

This will help, thought Ivan as he edged his trowel carefully and delicately across the plaster. When he had finished he took a pin and pushed through the damp plaster until he struck the device. It was lying less than a quarter of an inch beneath the surface of the wall.

Excellent, thought Ivan. Excellent, that will give it good ears. Using the trowel once more, Ivan began to cover the pinhole and tidy up his work. He needed a smooth finish that wouldn't be seen in the days ahead.

Outside, Boyd entered by a rear door, made his way to the hall, and crouched down behind a door listening. The emptiness of the house was like a canon in Boyd's mind. His breathing alone filled his brain and sounded so noisy. He heard scraping. Cocking his head, Boyd's ear began to trace the location of the noise.

Close by, Terry Anwhari nudged open a downstairs window and climbed through into one of the reception rooms. Once on the floor, he held his breath and listened. Silence filled his head and he began to make his way to the doorway.

Now crawling on his belly, Boyd reached an open doorway and held back. He heard someone breathing inside the adjacent room. There was a sudden clatter when someone in the next room dropped a tool of some kind and sent a shockwave through Boyd's nervous system.

Damn it, though Ivan picking up the trowel. Take your time you idiot, he thought. Then he returned to smoothing the trowel over the drying plaster once more.

Terry's lungs were on fire and his heartbeat was racing wildly still suffering from the shock of a trowel falling in an empty building. But the noise pulled him towards Ivan's room as his spine hugged the wall for comfort.

Boyd's fingers nudged a door open a smidgen. Now he could see through a narrow gap between the end of the door and the door jamb. Ducking down, Boyd's line of vision hovered above a brand new bronze hinge and settled on Ivan Pushkin.

The Russian was almost finished his task. Carefully, he opened his belt bag and scraped the residue plaster from the edges of the trowel into a plastic bag. Then he put both the plastic bag and trowel into his belt bag.

Seizing the moment, Terry Anwhari removed a tiny camera from the knee pocket of his combat trousers and pointed it at the front door which he now had in sight. It's an opportunity not to be missed, thought Terry. If our Russian friend is in the room next to me then when he leaves I might just catch a photograph of him.

Terry slid down onto his knees and manoeuvred behind a large cardboard box lying to the side of the room. He nudged it with his knee and realised it was quite heavy.

On the top of the box, in red ink, handwritten words read, *'FRAGILE – TILES'*. Smiling, Terry gently patted the box and thought, bathroom tiles – you are now my best friend

Placing his matchbox sized camera on the top of the cardboard box, Terry focused it on the front door, ran a thin electronic lead from the body of the camera to a switching mechanism in his hand, and promptly hid behind the box and waited.

Finished, Ivan Pushkin stood, checked the immediate area and turned round. He faced the wall where he'd placed his high grade long term listening device and studied the area where he'd placed his device. Damp, he thought, just a little damp but it will be dry within the hour.

Ivan removed a handkerchief from his pocket. Gradually, he took backward steps towards the door and bent down slightly. He used his handkerchief to gently brush any dust from the floor. As a result, he unsettled the dust and powder that was the signature of a new build. The dust gathered into the air and then settled gently on the wooden floor again. Ivan continued to quietly brush away the footprints which led to the wall and his device.

Oh for a camera, thought Boyd watching though his narrow aperture.

Terry stole half a second and peeped round the corner of the box when he heard a man's weight tread on a floorboard and cause the noise of a creak. Catching a brief site of Ivan, Terry pressed his camera switch and began to take a series of photographs of the suspect bent low brushing away the evidence, and dust, from the floor of the newly built Foreign Secretary's home as he walked backwards towards the front door.

Of course, thought Terry, I haven't a clue what the camera is taking. I just hope I angled it and focused it correctly.

It seemed like an age, Terry would later recount, but Ivan Pushkin eventually made the front door, turned round, and set off back towards his car – his mission accomplished.

Certain Ivan had vacated the premises, Boyd rushed to the front window and hugged the wall as he peeped through the window and watched the Russian fire the engine of his car and drive away.

'Terry, did you get anything?'

Hurriedly recapping his camera Terry smiled and said, 'Beautiful! But he didn't smile.'

Terry showed the images to Boyd who remarked, 'That proves he was here. But what the hell did he do down there?'

'Toni?' demanded Terry.

'Sorry, of course,' replied Boyd engaging his radio. 'Boyd reporting - Target is back to his vehicle and driving away – same direction – we are static in the house investigating actions. Proceed without us.'

'Roger,' replied Antonia on the radio. 'We have the subject turning left, left, left at the junction. He's heading back towards the Reading area. All units form up and move out.'

As the radio filled with surveillance signals, Boyd turned the volume down and walked into the room which had recently been occupied by Ivan Pushkin. The faint traces of footprints in plaster dust could still be seen as the powder slowly settled on the wooden floor. Boyd followed the clues to a damp patch on the wall. Removing a penknife from his pocket, Boyd unearthed a tiny listening device and showed it to Terry saying, 'Got him!'

'Excuse my ignorance, Guvnor, but what is it?'

'I don't know for sure,' replied Boyd. 'But I'd like to think Toni's mob will confirm this is a long term satellite activated listening device. Put it this way, what else do you think it might be?'

'A battery for a mobile phone?' suggested Terry, his eyebrows racing upwards aiding a cheeky look.

'Well, you never know do you,' remarked Boyd. 'Come on, Toni has the surveillance under control. We need to get this back to the technical unit.'

Hours of driving round the M25 and into inner London eventually led Antonia and her surveillance unit to the Federation of the Russian Embassy in the west end of London – Kensington Palace Gardens to be precise. Standing down her team for the night, Antonia congratulated them all on what had been an exceedingly long follow. She returned to her office, logged onto her computer, made a short report of the day's events to her supervisors and then checked her emails. Ringing Boyd, she arranged to meet him and Terry in the Green Man in Oxford Street.

Dressed in casual clothing, Boyd found a table, bought the drinks, and waited for the redhead to appear. Heads turned five minutes later when Antonia Harston-Browne entered carrying a leather briefcase.

'So this is where you discuss the cold war?' queried Terry.

'Only when we're thirsty,' smiled Antonia glancing over her shoulder. When she was more relaxed and sure of their privacy Antonia continued, 'Well done, Terry. I picked up the emails before I left. The tech guys confirm our mutual friend left a long stay listening device behind: one they've never seen before apparently. It certainly looks like Ivan intended to eavesdrop on conversations for a very long time. You scored twice for us, my friends. Now we know what kind of electronic device our friends currently prefer to use and how they initiate them. Cheers!'

'Cheers!' replied Terry.

'Where do we go from here?' asked Boyd.

'I rang Phillip,' explained Antonia. 'He's taking it further and discussing the matter with the Home Secretary.'

'And the options, Toni?' delved Boyd.

'We can arrest Ivan for spying or we can put the device back and feed the Russians false information for the next ten years,' revealed Antonia.

'Provided the Foreign Secretary and his family agree to that, I presume,' suggested Terry.

'I wouldn't want to live like that,' remarked Boyd.

'Well, that's the options,' delivered Antonia. 'We'll know soon enough. But what do you make of the legal aspect. I presume it is a spying offence Ivan has committed?'

'Espionage is illegal under the Official Secrets Acts of 1911 and 1920,' explained Boyd. 'We need to prove that Ivan intended to help an enemy and deliberately harm the security of the nation, which basically means the offence is committed if he's done something prejudicial to the safety or interests of the State. It also includes a preparatory act that would assist spying or aiding another to spy.'

'Such as planting a listening device in a government minister's home and placing government ministers under surveillance?' queried Antonia.

'Oh yes,' replied Boyd. 'Making sketches, plans, models, articles, or notes, or other documents which might be useful to an enemy covers the offence of espionage.'

'We've got him then,' suggested Antonia.

'Bang to rights,' offered Terry. 'He could get fourteen years imprisonment.

'And who knows what we'll find if we arrest him,' suggested Boyd.

'Good,' remarked Antonia. 'Yes, I'm pleased about that. I'm pretty sure that one day we'll find out he's a member of the GRU – *Glavnoje Razvedyvatel'noje Upravlenije* – the Main Intelligence

Directorate of the General Staff of the Armed Forces of the Russian Federation.'

'I couldn't even begin to say that,' chuckled Terry.

'It's a mouthful isn't it,' smiled Antonia.

'Your decision then, Toni?' asked Boyd. 'Or ours?'

Opening her briefcase, Antonia remarked, 'That will depend on the reply I receive. Here, take a look at the report I submitted to Phillip.'

Antonia slid a two page document and half a dozen photographs from her case and turned them for Terry and Boyd to read.

Moments later, Terry whistled in awe whilst Boyd said, 'Brilliant! You've obviously been on this guy for some time. What happens next?'

'I've asked for the job if the go ahead is given,' stated Antonia. 'If it does it will be a police case initially. And it will be yours.'

Nodding slowly, Boyd asked, 'When will we know?'

'When my mobile rings and you order me champagne,' replied Antonia with a cheeky smile.

'On my salary?' complained Boyd.

'Terry can contribute too,' countered Antonia swinging her hair across her shoulders as she spoke. 'One of you found the physical evidence whilst the other proved the subject was on site at the relevant time. We've got his movements for the last two months and most of them are not conducive to being a member of a trade delegation. By the way, he doesn't have diplomatic immunity.'

'Just as well,' remarked Boyd.

Another couple moved to a table close by and Boyd stood up and suggested, 'Anyone feeling lucky? I've a pound or two for a one arm bandit.'

The trio moved to the gambling machine where Boyd fed the mechanism with coins.

'We've removed the tracker from his car,' continued Antonia. 'He doesn't even know we've been on him. In his eyes it may be all down to the police mounting surveillance on an empty house owned by a government minister.'

'Until he gets wise,' suggested Terry.

'And your file of photographs at various sites obviously helps,' reminded Boyd.

'True!' replied Antonia, 'It's much better if the police can take the initial lead. I'd prefer it if my team of undercovers can be kept out of it as long as possible.'

'Of course,' replied Boyd swopping looks with Terry. 'I understand that completely.'

Antonia's phone rang. She answered it, listened, nodded, and replied, 'Thank you, sir. I'll expedite that in the manner agreed.' Then she closed her phone and smiled at the two detectives.

'Well?' enquired Boyd.

'We can put the device back and feed it false information for the next ten years or….'

'Or what?' enquired Boyd. 'Get to the point, Toni,' demanded Boyd.

'Champagne! Bollinger's please! You're going to arrest a spy.'

Boyd pulled the handle. Four cherries rolled to a standstill on a line and a jackpot cascaded into the winnings tray.

'Bollinger's?' queried Boyd. 'No problem! A case or a bottle, Toni?'

Later that night, Antonia entered a plush hotel in Kensington, ordered a glass of chilled white wine and waited in the lobby. Dressed immaculately, as usual, Antonia selected a seat directly opposite the lounge bar and waited. Browsing through a collection of magazines, Antonia began thumbing a well-known fashion title before casting her eyes on Ivan Pushkin. He was in his usual position sat nearest to the bar talking to two other men.

The revolving doors leapt into life when Sandra Peel, Billy Boyd and Terry Anwhari entered the hotel lobby with Janice Burns and Ricky French in tow.

Antonia ignored the invasion but glanced through the door window into the car park where two liveried police cars were just pulling up.

Marching into the bar, Boyd located Ivan Pushkin and introduced himself as he revealed his warrant card.

'Ivan Pushkin, I am Detective Chief Inspector Boyd from the Special Crime Unit in New Scotland Yard. I am arresting you…'

One of Pushkin's guests stood up and asked, 'What's going on? Who gave you the right to barge in here and behave like a little Hitler?'

'Sit down and shut up,' snapped Peel. 'We are the police. Do not interrupt.'

A whiff of alcohol stifled the air when another of Pushkin's guests interfered with, 'Don't you know who I am? You can't just wander round the city like the gestapo you know.'

The man began to get out of his chair when Peel placed a hand on his shoulder, pushed him back down, and replied, 'You're too young to remember the Gestapo, sir. Now do yourself a favour and shut up before I shut you up for the night. Understood?'

Terry rounded towards the man standing up and said, 'You heard the lady.'

With all three men seated, Boyd continued, 'Ivan Pushkin, I am arresting you on suspicion of espionage under the Official Secrets Act.'

Ivan's jaw dropped as Boyd rattled off the caution. Then the Russian glanced towards the hotel entrance. It was his only way out.

Janice Burns filled the void, opened her jacket to reveal the butt of a pistol, and said, 'Go on, Mister Pushkin. It's your choice but I'll drop you before you reach the lobby if I have to.'

Settling for a moment, Ivan said, 'Ahh, you English, you have no sense of humour.'

'I'm a Scot,' growled Janice. 'All ten fingers and thumbs on the table. NOW!'

Shocked, Ivan spread his hands out on the table and felt Terry snap the handcuffs on.

'Mister Boyd is it?' asked Ivan.

'Detective Chief Inspector Boyd,' replied the detective.

'My friends are correct,' stated Ivan nodding towards the other two men. 'Actually I don't know these people. They are just staying in the hotel.'

'Is that correct?' asked Boyd.

The two men nodded in agreement and looked sheepish.

'And I am innocent of all charges,' continued Pushkin. 'I am, Mister Boyd, a citizen of the Russian Federation. My government will hear of this.'

'You bet they will,' responded Boyd emptying an envelope onto the table. Half a dozen photographs scattered across the table and Boyd said, 'But a man convicted of espionage in this country is liable to fourteen years imprisonment. Which photo is your favourite, Mister Pushkin? I like the one of you in the Foreign Secretary's house.'

'Mister Boyd,' replied Pushkin. 'Fourteen years?'

'That's right,' delivered Boyd.

'Mister Boyd, I claim political asylum.'

'That won't get you anywhere,' said Boyd. 'It will only delay things. The outcome will not change.'

Ivan Pushkin's world collapsed in the bar of a five star hotel in Kensington. His brain worked overtime and his mind recalled the leafy lanes of England, its capitalist approach to the twenty-first century, its shops, culture, and standard of living. Then he thought of his beloved Russia.

Boyd captured Ivan's eyes, studied them, and merely gave him time.

Standing up with his hands handcuffed and stretched out before him, Ivan Pushkin declared, 'I am a spy, Mister Boyd. I am a member of the *Glavnoje Razvedyvatel'noje Upravlenije*. I wish to defect to the country of the United Kingdom and swear my allegiance to that country. I want you to take me to a member of the British Security Services, Mister Boyd.'

Smiling briefly, Boyd replied, 'All in good time, Mister Pushkin. You will come with us to your room where we will conduct a search.'

'I insist, Mister Boyd. I want to speak to a member of the British Government. I have things to tell them.'

Nodding in an almost dismissing manner, Boyd continued, 'All in good time, Mister Pushkin. A good tradesman needs to displays all his wares before he does the job. We will also recover your motor vehicle and take you to a secure police station where you and I will discuss the matter further.'

'It is agreed then?' suggested Ivan. 'I am defecting, no fourteen years?'

Boyd studied the man who was an enemy of the State: a man who had suddenly abandoned allegiance to his country so that he might trade his nation's secrets for a quiet and peaceful life in some sleepy corner of England's countryside. Ivan Pushkin would never feel the discomfort of a cell.

Boyd shook his head and said, 'Terry, Ricky, take him away.'

'I'll handle the media,' suggested Sandra. 'With Russian aeroplanes invading our airspace and some strange goings on in the Baltic, I think we might justifiably crow a little a bit over this one. Let's show the rest of the world that we know how to hit back and hit back hard.'

'We won't take our prize out until you're ready,' remarked Boyd.

'Agreed,' replied Sandra lifting her mobile. 'I'll get on it right away. I'll ring you when I have all the major networks outside.'

Moments later, Antonia flipped over another page of her magazine as Terry Anwhari and Ricky French led Ivan Pushkin to his room. An arrest had been made. An admission was forthcoming. The searches for more incriminating evidence were underway. They would be fruitful.

Antonia Harston-Browne set aside her magazine, smoothed away her skirt, and walked from the hotel. There was a slight skip in her step when she stepped into the roadway and hailed a taxi.

A short time later - on the other side of London - Sir Phillip Nesbitt, Knight Commander of the British Empire and Director General of the Security Services, punched the digits on his mobile phone and waited for an answer from a colleague in GCHQ.

'Roberta, there's something you should know,' said Phillip.

Listening to his colleague for a moment, Phillip switched on a television set in the lounge. It defaulted to the news channel where a broadcaster was reporting events in Goussainville, France. The report revealed that a shoot-out with Islamic extremists had led to the deaths of seven police officers and widespread destruction when the gang of terrorists had blown themselves up.

'I'm watching it now,' replied Sir Phillip.

News ribbon then threaded slowly across the bottom of the screen…

Breaking News… Police hold Russian defector in London hotel…

'Yes, I know, Roberta,' replied Phillip. 'But let me tell you something you don't know.'

As Phillip told Roberta his confidential news, a listening device recorded the conversation. Then, suddenly, the battery inside the device died.

In Carlisle, northern England, a steam iron pressed a red, white and blue suit and then smoothed away a union flag tie. A brand new white shirt was presented to the ironing board, tenderly arranged, and then pressed to satisfaction. A tin of black polish was found along with a duster and a pair of black leather shoes. A smudge of polish covered the shoes initially but then the duster went to work and gradually buffed a bright smile on the leather toe.

Francis Littleton was making ready for a royal visit. It was his birthday soon and he wanted to share it with his best friends.

Out in the Baltic Sea, the Russian Fleet gradually encircled the commander of a royal navy vessel. The commander felt even more intimidated when a pair of Russian bear bombers entered his radar screen. Moments later, the aeroplanes overflew the two naval fleets on their way into the North Sea.

From the ship's bridge, the naval commander opened a frequency and radioed the Admiralty.

Whilst the Cold War was heating up the world was at peace – of a sort – but it was still Threat Level One.

*

Chapter Fifteen

~

That night,
Conwy, North Wales
Threat Level One – Critical

The long journey from his home in Epping Forest, on the edge of London, did little to dilute Sir Phillip Nesbitt's enthusiasm for what lay ahead.

Those that knew Phillip well would testify to his tenacity when chasing down a specific matter of importance to him. Others would tell you that he was a 'Jack of all Trades' and 'Master of None'. He was a fairly quiet and reserved individual despite being considered by some as occasionally arrogant or standoffish. The truth of the matter lay in his upbringing.

Phillip's parents were doctors when they were alive and had both been senior partners in a General Practitioner's surgery on the edge of Bournemouth. Upon their passing, they'd left a sizeable estate for their only to son to inherit. The size of the estate was such that Phillip would never actually have to work for a living in the future. But Phillip never intended to be a loafer and it wasn't the only thing he would remember his parents for. They'd provided a loving and caring environment for the youngster to find his feet and soon recognised the power of his memory. He had an uncanny ability to remember the slightest detail and took pleasure, as a youth, in learning the contents of the surgery's pharmacy products off by heart. He recited them 'parrot fashion'. It was a game he played with his parents, and he always won. Sadly, he relinquished such knowledge when the speed of development in the pharmaceutical industry reached such a rate that it became impossible to keep up with new products.

Being a wealthy doctor's child had its problems both at school and in his teens. He found it difficult to mix with children of a similar age who were from totally different backgrounds.

Grammar School preceded Cambridge University where he majored in Politics and Economics whilst flirting with courses and lectures relevant to Social Sciences and Overseas Development.

With degrees under his arm Phillip answered an advertisement in a national newspaper and began a lengthy application and recruitment program into the Security Service. Quietly proud of his achievements, Phillip would remind only his very closest friends that he had started on the factory floor – and worked his way to the top of the tree. He'd enjoyed a long career in the Service and specialised in both Irish and International Terrorism before rapid promotions followed in the realms of protective security and organisational administration. It was here that he gained a Knighthood and took the reins as head of the intelligence community.

Surprisingly, to some degree, Phillip was not the most popular man in the service. He'd deliberately chosen his friends carefully determined to do the best he could in his chosen profession. Charting his own career brought with it some accolades and eventually it was generally accepted amongst the rank and file that Phillip Nesbitt fitted the seat of Director General well.

Phillip's problem tonight was twofold. He knew he was falling in love with the slightly younger Antonia Harston-Browne, and he'd told her again that he was visiting friends in the north. He wondered if she suspected anything. His other problem was that he was on a mission that he could only really talk to himself about.

Slightly overweight, of medium height, light brown hair and brown eyes, Phillip was fairly nondescript in appearance, and dressed deliberately to cement that persona. Yet this quiet and reserved gentleman had an air of confidence that had the potential to beguile the unwary and unprepared.

Enjoying the beauty of the North Wales coast road, Phillip steered his car into the county of Conwy and took a left into the hills towards Snowdonia and the Welsh peaks. Eventually, he reached the castle and parked at the front of the building beside two large cannons that stood guard at the entrance.

Expected, and on time, Phillip was greeted by a footman who escorted him into the Great Hall where he was asked to take a seat and kindly wait a short while.

Doing as he was bid, Phillip occupied an old-fashioned straight back armchair and studied his surroundings. Row upon row of portraits peered down from the walls around him. It was as if the paintings were scrutinising his very presence, deciding whether they liked him or not, and considering his future. Two identical chandeliers occupied the ornate ceiling space. Circular in design, a cantilever structure of crystals twinkled upwards and gave light to the otherwise dark room. Here and there, along an opposing wall, a range of suits of armour lined up. Some carried axes and medieval weapons. Others merely stood at attention and filled the space provided with a melancholy air of a history long gone.

'The Duke will see you now,' announced the footman in his red and black livery. 'Follow me, sir.'

Phillip rose and followed his escort. Yet to his surprise he was taken into a side room where he was greeted by another attendant who shook hands with him and said, 'Thank you for accepting the invitation, sir.'

'Thank you for inviting me to your function. I'm looking forward to the evening.'

'And your inauguration?'

'Of course,' replied Phillip.

A large wooden door creaked opened and the Duke of MonkChester entered with a huge smile creeping across his face and his arm outstretched. Dressed in full military uniform and wearing a sword at this side the duke was a sight to behold.

'Welcome, Sir Phillip! Welcome to my humble abode.'

'A pleasure to meet you again, your Grace,' smiled Phillip shaking hands. 'A pleasure indeed!'

'I believe you have questions before the ceremony, Sir Phillip.'

'Confirmation actually, your Grace,' replied Phillip.

'Such as?' queried the duke.

'Some things are not always mentioned at length and I want to be sure that I have not been misled or misinterpreted.'

'Of course, I fully understand,' delivered the duke. His arms gestured wide and then closed to relax his hands by his side.

'How can I help?' he ventured.

'This isn't political in any way?' asked Phillip. 'Of that I must be sure, your Grace.'

'Everything is political, my friend,' answered the duke. 'But we are not members of, or affiliated to, any political party in either this or any other country. As you know, we are an establishment of specific individuals committed to the protection and sustainability of the monarchy. Membership to our order is by recruitment followed by invitation.'

Phillip studied the duke and bore into his eyes searching for a tell-tale flutter that might betray the truth of his words.

'A right wing group intending to overthrow the government perhaps, your Grace?' ventured Sir Phillip.

Continuing, The Duke of MonkChester braced himself and replied, 'I confirm to you, Sir Phillip that our Order is one which counts in its membership international currency controllers; arms exporters, army, navy, and air force personnel, special forces, medical and surgical personnel, senior police officers, internet providers, telecom owners, electronic hackers, and infrastructure providers. Such people have been carefully selected, recruited and invited to our Order which seeks to preserve the democratic way of life we have lived for many years. Individually, we may not all meet your requirements of neutrality but as a network, we can be formidable when we need to be. Once we were an idea in my master's mind but now we are a reality sworn to uphold our institutions in face of the evil that besets our nation from so many different sources.'

'And your master, your Grace?' enquired Sir Phillip. 'Who is your master?'

'I address my master as your Highness,' replied the duke. 'And surely you need know no more?'

Nodding quietly, Phillip stepped away from the duke and strolled casually along the wall of the Great Hall studying the portraits of the ancient past. History peered down upon him from the solid walls of aristocracy – each portrait a biography in itself.

At the end of the hall Phillip looked up and eyed an elegant and beautiful painting of the monarch.

'You came to find a traitor, didn't you?' demanded the duke.

'What did I find?' enquired Phillip.

'Your invitation awaits,' reminded the duke with a sly grin.

Turning, Phillip paused for a moment or two, smiled, walked towards the man in uniform and said, 'Then I accept, your Grace.'

'Wonderful, my friend! Wonderful,' declared the duke. 'The Order needs men like you Sir Phillip for it is people like you that give it strength and wisdom. Come! Come and dine with us. It is time for your inauguration.'

The duke spun on his heel and led Sir Phillip into a large dining room. A huge round table was covered with fine lace and decked with silver utensils and crystal glasses fit for a king. It was a sight that Phillip had never before witnessed.

When Phillip entered, he was escorted around the table by the duke to see more than a dozen well-known figures who stood to greet him.

Walking slowly behind the duke Phillip nodded to those he knew. The gathering was all the duke said it would be: an establishment of powerful men and women from multiple professions, trades, and organisations who underpinned the nation's culture and infrastructure.

The duke led Phillip to a position in front of a large painting of the monarch where he knelt by a statue of Saint George.

Withdrawing his sword, the duke approached Phillip. The room went quiet and then the duke declared loudly, 'Sir Phillip Nesbitt, Knight Commander of the Most Excellent Order of the British Empire, with my master's sword I dub thee Sir Phillip, Lord Protector of the United Kingdom and her Commonwealth, Defender of the Realm, and Member of the Order of Loyal Guardians to the Monarchy.'

The duke duly dubbed Sir Phillip who rose and embraced the duke. His Grace then escorted Sir Phillip to the table and offered him a seat.

There was a ripple of applause when Phillip sat. It began as a slow hand clap and gradually grew and grew in strength before it became thunderous applause

In Sir Phillip's house at Epping Forest, Detective Chief Inspector Boyd was dressed all in black as he removed one listening device from a television set and replaced it with another.

Got you, my friend, thought Boyd. I don't know what you're up to Sir Phillip but this little baby will probably spill the beans and tell me all we need to know.

Boyd pocketed the device he had just removed from Phillip's television, and carefully vacated the premises without further ado.

The tide swept quietly into Colwyn Bay and washed the sand for the second time that day. The Thames twinkled in the night bathed in the capital's lamp standards – row upon row – outside Thames House and Vauxhall.

In a room in MI5 Headquarters a list of Russians suspected of various infringements of espionage law in the UK was being drawn up.

Out in the Baltic Sea, the ocean swelled reaching towards more Russian aircraft 'exercising' close to a NATO naval exercise. Higher tensions between Russia and NATO were evident as the signal traffic between the Royal Navy and the Admiralty increased dramatically.

At the Embassy of the Russian Federation in Kensington a computerised communications device chattered out a long list of British dignitaries who were no longer welcome in Russia. A separate document detailed aerial movements that day in respect of Russian aircraft engaged in an air force exercise over the Baltic and North Sea.

Wide awake, Ivan Pushkin stared at his cell wall in a London police station and watched two lazy spiders climbing towards the ceiling. Ivan wondered what would become of him.

Deep underground in a bunker in Kent sweat poured down a forehead as tired fingers rattled across a keyboard in a bid to deflect an incoming cyberattack from a hostile enemy. The firewall protecting the computer system was under threat as three more operators entered, took seats, and logged in to be the latest edition to the cyberwar unit.

One computer closed down and a screen went blank when a virus destroyed a motherboard and a voice shouted, 'They're winning.'

*

Chapter Sixteen

~

Shanklin Operations Centre
The Isle of Wight
Threat Level One – Critical

A hail of bricks and stones flew through the air when the first group of anarchists tried to breach police lines and board a ferry bound for the Isle of Wight.

Superintendent Cheryl Mintoff's voice ordered, 'Hold the line.'

A police dog yapped and was joined by another on a longer leash as the handlers sought to drive the antagonists back. Moments later the bricks and stones were aimed at the dogs and the handlers withdrew their canine friends and retreated to the rear of the police lines.

'Hold the line! Hold the line!' bellowed Superintendent Mintoff.

There was another charge against the thin blue line of helmeted police officers. Shoving, pushing, and shoulder charging the line, a larger group of more organised anarchists tried to break through. It was to no avail, but police reinforcements bolstered the line and filled in behind the first rank in riot gear. Helmets were exchanged for sturdy headgear, flame-proof coveralls, gauntlets, and riot gear.

The event commander shouted again, 'Hold the line!'

Retreating momentarily, the antagonists reformed and pushed again. Everyone knew they would never make the Isle of Wight. It was never going to happen.

Sandra Peel was in charge in the Operations Room in Shanklin. Or to be precise, she was in charge of countering the threat from anarchists dedicated to disrupting the G8 conference. And she was winning. They'd searched and secured the conference venue, cordoned off a dedicated accommodation area in a country hotel where all the delegates were staying, and then surrounded the area with a ring of steel.

Politics and who liked who, why, and what for, were no part of Sandy's remit. Such matters were meaningless. Her assignment was to secure the G8 conference by reference to duly received intelligence. Of course, the Ticker system had been put to good use. She and Anthea had been glued to the computer screen in recent times and social media too. As a result Sandra had arranged for all the ferries to be checked, searched, and scrutinised. Scores of would-be demonstrators were turned back to the mainland. And with a look at the map and help from the Royal Navy Intelligence Section, a convoy of small boats had been prevented from crossing the Solent to the Isle of Wight. They too failed and turned tail in the face of a repulse from the Marine police. Sandra's team had even monitored the telephone system and dealt with half a dozen so-called bomb hoaxes. And they'd all been hoaxes. So many had tried to disrupt proceedings but the island was a fortress and Sandra Peel was waving the flag from the Castle Keep – or at least it felt that way to her and the two gentlemen who had been invited to watch her every move.

But outside on the streets of Portsmouth, Plymouth and Southampton, things were different. Irritation at not being able to enter the Isle of Wight by land, sea or air had turned to cold anger and fuming rage and the anarchists were determined to have their say – and their day.

Dressed in their usual black attire and black headbands, they charged again. They were shoulder to shoulder and head to head with the police. Then the ranks broke and a fist stuck out towards a policeman.

'Hold the line!' shouted in a muffled worried context by the superintendent seemed to have little effect.

A placard bearing the words *'No more Austerity'* crashed down on police ranks and then prodded into police lines. Suddenly

267

the antagonists were winning and pushing the police back towards the ferry landings

'Hold the line!'

Watching video coverage from the Shanklin Operations Centre, Detective Superintendent Sandra Peel checked her monitors covering the conference facility and hotel accommodation site. Everything was going according to plan. She had no problems. Her brief was secure. Should I or should I not, she pondered. Sandra studied the video coverage again, saw the demonstrators gaining ground, and picked up the phone.

As she picked up the phone she ran her fingers across the various venues on a map that signified her remit – Shanklin, Newport, Ventnor, Plymouth, Portsmouth, Southampton, the ferry terminals, the Solent.

The phone was answered and she explained her instructions.

Twenty minutes later the bloodied sweating anarchists were engaged in hand to hand combat in some parts of the line where police numbers needed bolstering. That was when the horses arrived. Sandra had redeployed her mounted unit from the country hotel to the front line. Trained and ready for action, an inspector led the unit and lowered his lance as he approached the police line. Simultaneously, a dozen mounted officers followed suit. At the end of each lance a wooden pommel protruded from the lance as a round shield.

Except the inspector did not use the pommel as a shield and ordered, 'Break the line! Break the line! Break the line!'

Police lines split and a line of mounted horses cantered through with their riders holding their lances in the low horizontal position.

Seconds later the first demonstrator felt the force of a wooden pommel firm in his chest. The lance thrust him backwards with tremendous force and the anarchists broke ranks and retreated.

Riding together the mounted police broke through allowing the police line to close behind them.

'Hold the line!' rent the air.

A lance pushed a youth to the ground and held him until two officers took him into custody. Then another row of lances pommelled a line of charging anarchists, destroyed their impetus, and sent them scattering for cover as the demonstrators lost ground and the police regrouped.

And then it rained. Rain! Any policeman present would testify that the best law enforcer in a public order situation was rain! And boy, did it rain. It lashed down.

The demonstration might have taken months of preparation and discussion but a cloud break over the ferry terminal put paid to things in five minutes.

Soaked to the skin and wet through, the anarchists began splashing each other in the puddles. They jumped in the puddles, sprayed the water with their hands, and splashed each other like kids on a beach holiday.

To all intents and purposes, the demonstration was over. The horses held their ground. The police held the line, and in the Operations Centre in Shanklin Sandra turned her attention to covering the conference entrance.

By nightfall, the event had taken place without problem. On the streets of the mainland there were a few bruises, one or two cuts and scrapes, but it had been a draw – according to one anarchist. Well, maybe, but the G8 conference had run its course without and intrusion. It was – all secure.

Standing next to Sandra Peel, Boyd and Bannerman studied the superintendent and took note of how she managed multiple video screens at the same time.

She really is as sharp as a razor, thought Boyd. She's got everything going on in her head. It's as if she is on the ground with the troops guiding them, advising them, providing the tools to win and hold the line. Sandra Peel is a leader sitting quietly in the background, decided Boyd.

Later that day, Boyd spent time on his phone putting together a mobile command centre for his first big royal event. He checked the venues, studied his maps, realigned CCTV coverage for the days in question, and made a list of his primary surveillance targets.

Then he took a call from Commander Maxwell.

'William, was your day on the Isle of Wight with Inspector Bannerman and Superintendent Peel useful?'

'Definitely, sir,' replied Boyd. 'I've learnt a lot about how to simultaneously police large events across multiple areas.'

'Good, because we're at breaking point and you need to secure operations with what you've got.'

'Things at Carlisle are somewhat static at the moment, commander,' reported Boyd. 'The latest surveillance reports from Team Charlie reveal no movement from the suspect, Dina, just a lot of praying and video making.'

'I don't like the sound of the video making,' replied Commander Maxwell. 'Her last post?'

'Could be, sir, we don't; really know at this stage, but she's praying a hell of a lot.'

'Can you free up any resources, William?'

'No, but I could make do with half a team to search and secure and begin the operation earlier than planned, sir,' suggested Boyd.

'Not going to happen, William,' instructed Commander Maxwell. 'The cupboard is bare and I have no more tools or advice to give you all. You'll have to make do with what you've got at the moment.'

'Very well, sir,' replied Boyd.

'Goussainville,' mentioned the commander.

'Yes, my heart goes out to them, sir,' reported Boyd. 'I can't imagine how it was.'

'But you must, Boyd, you must imagine how it was and how you would have handled it,' advised Commander Maxwell. 'There's a time and place to be sorry about things and time and place to recognise what might happen and get it right first time round. I know it's not easy, William, but remember Goussainville.'

'Very well, sir,' replied Boyd, 'Very well.'

At a railway station in London Mostafa Humayl - also known as Salman, and the Man from Tikrit – boarded the Leeds train and quietly shuffled through the carriages before finding a seat overlooking the platform. Taking his time, he scanned the platform area to reassure himself that he was not being followed. Relieved, he stowed his hand luggage in an overhead compartment and settled into the upholstery.

Unfolding a newspaper, Mostafa lifted it into a reading position and closed his eyes. He had no intention of reading the news, doing the crossword, checking his horoscope, or scrutinising the latest advertisements. It was a body signal as far as he was concerned and it said to others in the carriage, 'Do not disturb.'

Mostafa shook his newspaper, turned a page, and allowed his neck to drop slightly when the train took its first lurch forward on a long journey to Leeds and the county of West Yorkshire. All being well Mostafa would sleep for a while before taking light refreshment in the buffet car and preparing himself for departure.

But his mind was not yet relaxed. He had something else to do. Searching for his smartphone, Mostafa logged into a social media site, scrolled through the posts, and read the latest comments from Dina Al-Hakim. He chuckled and then moved on to a mail order site. Opening his fraudulent account he scrolled through the data to find details about his shipment. It was there and all was well. My mail order bride chuckled Mostafa. She is really quite beautiful.

If all went according to plan, he would meet an Imam – a leader of the Sunni Muslim community – near Leeds railway station, collect his mail order package, and travel north to Cumbria. He shook his head, switched off the phone, and yawned.

Mostafa was bored when he set his head against the window and watched the railway station flicker by as the train gathered speed.

Mostafa Humayl's assignment was in its final stages.

Chapter Seventeen

~

The Operations Centre
MI5, London.
Threat Level One – Critical

Boyd and Antonia were in cahoots.

With an adequate supply of coffee, pencils, notepads and tape recorders, they spent part of the morning downloading the listening device recovered from Sir Phillip's house.

Now they listened to the product intently and took notes accordingly.

'Who is Roberta on the tape?' asked Boyd.

'One of the senior analysts at GCHQ,' replied Antonia. 'She's actually Deputy Director at GCHQ.'

'Second in command?' suggested Boyd.

'Only in the military context, Billy,' replied Antonia. 'If it's question time who is this duke that Phillip seems to ring quite regularly?'

'The phone number is listed to the Duke of MonkChester,' reported Boyd. 'I checked it out as soon as it came into the frame. Phillip's other calls are to the office, his counterpart in MI6, and the rest are as you might expect – you, hairdressers, oil company for his heating, local restaurants at weekends, one or two close friends – but nothing out of place other than calls to this duke chap.'

'MonkChester?' exclaimed Antonia. 'Now something seems to rattle in my mind about that name.'

'It's a village on the Cheshire-Welsh border,' delivered Boyd. 'The individual is an extremely wealthy gentleman who is indeed a full blown duke. He's distantly related to the monarchy but essentially his family made their way trading in both the currency and commoditics markct.'

'Inherited wealth?' suggested Antonia.

'Yes, but some useful market savvy as well,' responded Boyd.

'So he's a big city trader. Is that what you mean?' asked Antonia.

'When he needs to be,' responded Boyd. 'Whilst the duke comes from wealthy stock he seems to have an uncanny ability to keep a low public profile. Did you know he's also a Knight of the Realm?'

'What?' exclaimed Antonia.

'Yes, his real name in Who's Who is given as Sir Edward James Monk Chester, K.B.E. That famous British tomb has dedicated the sum total of two lines to him. Edward James Monk Chester received a Knighthood for military services and has estates in Cheshire and Wales. That said, I've checked through some media news sites on the internet but there's no trace of him at all. He doesn't even attend any of the royal events or mix with the local county set. The Times newspaper doesn't refer to his movements in the royal announcements and you'd be forgiven for thinking that he might not be alive. The Duke of MonkChester has either got a very good rubber which he uses to erase his past or he's an odd ball we should know more about. What a strange situation. I've even checked a list of Lord Lieutenants and do you know what – he's not even mentioned, not even as a present or past Deputy Lord Lieutenant or High Sherriff. I find that quite strange given his relationship to the monarchy, his wealth, traces to nobility, and his title. One would have expected such a person to be chairman of the Cheshire Agricultural Show or the Welsh Leek Society.'

'Leeks?' queried Antonia with a wry smile.

'Yes, leeks – well you know what I mean, Toni. A man of wealth and power living in a castle would be just the kind of person you would expect to be a prime mover in community affairs. And he doesn't seem to be. I'm surprised you don't know him, Toni, particularly with all your contacts in the Establishment.'

'Perhaps we've met. I can't remember,' confessed Antonia. 'The name certainly rings a bell. I recall reading something in the Economist recently – or was it Forbes? If memory serves me well the article suggested he was in the top one hundred wealthiest men in Europe, but not much more. It's the name you see – MonkChester! I remember the name not the man.'

'He's a lucky man by the sound of it, Toni,' offered Boyd. 'Bags of money!'

'Yes, money,' remarked Antonia. 'It worries me that Phillip is cosying up to such a rich man.'

'Phillip doesn't need the cash,' remarked Boyd. 'I understand he is very well off himself.'

'Yes, but Phillip's neither a millionaire nor a billionaire like the Duke of MonkChester,' said Antonia. 'What do you make of these calls and the tape, Billy?'

'I'll keep an open mind for the moment,' replied Boyd.

'It worries me that this mysterious duke is lining up Phillip in order to either bribe or blackmail him,' suggested Antonia. 'Phillip occupies one of the most important jobs in the country so he's an obvious target, don't you think?'

'Agreed,' remarked Boyd. 'But does he know he's being lined up and, if so, by who?'

There was a knock on the door but the incoming personnel didn't wait for an answer. Roberta marched in followed by Sir Phillip Nesbitt.

'The tapes,' declared Roberta angrily. 'What are you doing with those tapes?'

'What tapes?' replied Boyd lying badly. He was shocked at the sudden appearance of the very people he had monitored on his listening device. For a moment Boyd was speechless.

'Those tapes,' growled Phillip reaching the table. 'Oh, I know what you're up to, Boyd so don't try to hide it.' Phillip clenched his fist around the listening device and scowled, 'This!'

'And we'd like to know what you're up to?' suggested Boyd eventually standing to confront the invaders.

'Nothing you need to know about,' replied Roberta.

'You mean it's need to know and I don't need to know,' remarked Boyd. 'Now that seems to be a phrase used by people like you who just don't want to answer any questions. Am I right?'

'We can soon remove you from New Scotland Yard if we have to,' suggested Roberta.

'Really,' chuckled Boyd impishly. 'And I thought we were on the same side. Do you think that's going to shut me up and turn me into an obedient little puppy dog?'

'You don't need to know about this, Boyd,' interrupted Phillip. 'I'll take this, your notes and the tape, and we'll mention no more of this.'

'Phillip,' implored Antonia. 'I thought we had something special between us. At least that's what you told me recently. Now you're treating me as if I'm totally irrelevant. I want to know why you've been visiting God knows how many castles in recent months. Or is there another woman – or even another man? I'm entitled to know for God's sake. What's going on, Phillip?'

Phillip swept Boyd's listening device and paraphernalia into a waste bin and replied, 'That's private between us and has nothing to do with this.'

'Oh, no it isn't,' snapped Antonia. 'The chief inspector isn't the only one with contacts, a very loud voice, and a muzzle that will never fit.'

'Threats now is it?' growled Phillip.

'By the way,' suggested Boyd. 'You can keep the contents of the litter bin, Sir Phillip. I copied everything and secured it before I began deciphering the product.'

Stunned for a second Phillip glanced at Roberta who offered no response.

'Yes, I really did,' confirmed Boyd. 'Now are you going to let Toni and me in on your little secret or we going public?'

The conversation paused for a moment before Boyd added, 'I can speak with Commander Maxwell or I'll just phone the Home Secretary. I have her number as you know. The business card! You were present at the meeting when she gave me it. She's expecting an update regarding royalty protection soon and she'll appreciate a call from the horse's mouth. How do you want to play this?'

Phillip lodged the litter bin and contents on the edge of the table, looked directly into Roberta's eyes, and said, 'I have to tell them, Roberta. I think they should know?'

Studying her colleague for a moment, Roberta replied, 'I told you it was the wrong thing to do when you started. You should have put someone else on it.'

'Maybe, maybe not,' suggested Phillip.

'It's decision time,' said Boyd flashing a business card in front of their eyes.

'I'm waiting, Phillip,' delivered Antonia. 'Who is she?'

'The Queen!' replied Phillip, 'Or the King! It all depends on who's on the throne at the time.'

Boyd and Antonia swopped puzzled looks before Antonia suggested, 'Are you mad? In fact, I'll say that again. Are you both mad?'

'No, it's just the way it is,' murmured Roberta. 'Tell them the whole story, Phillip.'

Nodding in agreement, Phillip explained, 'It all began about twelve months ago.'

'That long,' snapped Antonia

'It's not what you think,' replied Phillip. 'Roberta's unit at GCHQ began picking up a lot of electronic traffic from the Welsh border. Eventually they tied it down to a village called MonkChester.'

'Where the duke lives?' suggested Boyd.

'Precisely,' admitted Phillip. 'When we found out who was making all the calls we ran a covert operation and…'

'You mean an eavesdropping operation,' suggested Antonia. 'You began recording, deciphering and analysing what was being said.'

'Put that way, yes,' replied Phillip. 'Given the duke's connection with the monarchy, his wealth and power base, we decided to deny the operation to everyone in GCHQ and MI5 Headquarters I made myself case officer although you'll never find a file on the subject we're talking about because there isn't one. Only Roberta and I know about the story.'

'Which is?' persuaded an intrigued Boyd.

'We thought the monarchy might be at risk from a right wing coup led by the Duke of MonkChester.'

Boyd's jaw dropped and Antonia's eyelids shot up.

'What?' demanded Boyd, 'I don't understand?'

'It came to our attention that the duke was pulling together some pretty powerful people. He invited them to a security conference of some kind. Unfortunately we were late on the scene and we missed the first meeting. That said, we picked up enough to work out that some of the nation's top people were on board and the duke was at the helm.'

'By chance,' interrupted Boyd, 'Does the Duke of MonkChester have a historic claim to the throne of England that is a major grievance to him?'

Roberta exhaled deeply and Phillip replied, 'That's exactly what we thought at first.'

'So, tell me the Duke of MonkChester's oldest male ancestor was Edward the First's illegitimate son,' demanded Boyd. And he's traced his ancestry all the way back and is convinced he should be the King of England. Go on, we want to know.'

'No, not quite,' answered Phillip. 'Quite the reverse in fact! We set off thinking we'd penetrated the preparation of a right wing coup. The pair of us realised the duke had recruited Julian to the cause.'

'You mean Sir Julian Spencer K.B.E., Head of the Secret Intelligence Service – MI6?' enquired Antonia.

'Yes! Yes, of course,' confirmed Phillip. 'We learnt that Julian went to school with the duke. They were both at Marlborough College together. That was the connection between the two.'

'Struth!' remarked Boyd. 'You'll be telling us next the two of them were in the same Freemason's Lodge and have been lifelong buddies?'

'Actually,' declared Roberta. 'That's true.'

'Why didn't you just ring Sir Julian and ask him what was going on?' enquired Antonia.

'Because by then we'd discovered the duke was also in touch with some very powerful people. He was in the process of recruiting media owners, economists, political strategists, military leaders, internet network providers, bankers, people like that. It didn't take long to work out that the duke was in the course of assembling key people able to carry out a bloodless coup.'

'Bloodless?' questioned Boyd.

'Yes, if you control the military, the police, the intelligence community and the infrastructure providers, then you're not really going to get much of a rebellion when you dispose of the current government or monarchy, are you?'

'I'm not sure,' explained Boyd. 'It's not something I've ever really thought about. It wasn't mentioned in my basic police training package!'

'Well,' smiled Phillip, 'If our duke activated his planned coup and had arranged the media to glorify and orchestrate the coup then it would certainly nullify a lot of the problems that might come from Joe Public. Most people like to follow, chief inspector, very few like to lead other than by mouthing off opinion which they are unable to either prove conclusively or action professionally.'

Thinking for a moment, Boyd nodded and added, 'I'm listening. You're ranting. Go on.'

'Given the involvement of Julian and other powerful individuals, Roberta and I decided to keep it to ourselves. I made my interest known to the duke at a private dinner that I engineered my way into via my commodities broker.'

'What did you discover?' asked Antonia.

'That if the country is ever threatened by the possibility of a takeover by an Islamic Republic or any other terrorist organisation, or an enemy State, then plans are being made for the top secret removal of the monarch - whoever that might be – the Royal Family, and those so decreed as vital to the sustainability of the United Kingdom. And it's being masterminded by the Duke of MonkChester and the people he has recruited. They would be taken to a place of safety where a fight back might take place utilising the resources of the power base I have spoken of. It's as simple as that.'

'And you believe that, do you?' asked Boyd.

'I didn't until I joined,' replied Phillip.

'I would have thought we had plans like that in any event,' suggested Boyd. 'Isn't it the case that plans are in being to remove the reigning monarch from London in the event of an invasion?'

'But not to fight back and sustain the nation in the way I have described,' replied Phillip.

'Of all the threats that face our country,' suggested Boyd. 'You seldom expect an in-house coup from the left, right or centre of the political landscape. Well, not in the United Kingdom at any rate.'

'The duke did,' replied Phillip. 'And now I consider it my duty to monitor the duke's organisation in case it is ever taken over by a group of political activists' intent on using it for their own devices.'

'And presumably you'd be there if anything happened to the duke – His health deteriorates for example?'

'Precisely, chief inspector,' confirmed Phillip.

'Why didn't you put an undercover operative in?' asked Antonia, 'Or one of our agents?'

'Such a person wouldn't have lasted two minutes under Sir Julian's scrutiny. It had to be the real McCoy or no-one else,' replied Phillip. 'The point is Roberta and I made an assessment at the time. We thought it might have been an ultra-right-wing political organisation hell bent on destroying democracy as we know it. As it is it's an organisation dedicated to the democratic system we have today.'

'It sounds medieval in some ways,' remarked Boyd.

'Just what I was thinking,' suggested Antonia. 'All we need now is Knights in shining armour riding over the duke's drawbridge instead of arriving at a castle in big flash cars wearing smart suits and waistcoats.'

'Rather than be a threat to our country it is a potential saviour to the heart and soul of the nation,' remarked Roberta.

'Agreed,' replied Phillip.

The four members of the intelligence community exchanged looks and were lost in their own private thoughts for a moment.

'What are you going to do about this now that you know about it?' asked Roberta with a wry smile crossing her cheeks. 'You're officially on the 'need to know list' I suspect.'

'Nothing, I planted the bug,' admitted Boyd.

'I was never there,' suggested Antonia.

'I acted illegally,' declared Boyd. 'We might have the right story from you both now but we broke the law to get there.'

Phillip nodded and replied, 'Sometimes a person's idea of what is legal and what is not legal is complicated. Legality is not always conducive to the continued 'sustainability' of our sovereign nation.'

'I know,' replied Boyd. 'The law is an ass in some cases. I learnt that a long time ago.'

Smiling, Phillip announced, 'I never found a listening device.'

'I don't recall planting one,' suggested Boyd.

'And if you did the only aggrieved party would be me?' suggested Phillip, 'Unless we involved the State.'

'Correct!' admitted Boyd.

'It's between us then.'

'Yes!'

'A useful exercise?' suggested Phillip.

The ice suddenly broke.

Antonia smiled and said, 'An eccentric wealthy duke and a couple of crazy medievally minded intelligence officers who aren't sure what to do because of all the complex problems so obviously apparent! I'll buy into this because it's so bizarre that it just has to be right. The coup that was never a coup! I just hope no-one ever asks me to write this one up.'

A worried face cracked. A cheek wrinkled. A smile broke and then there were handshakes.

'Just one thing,' asked Boyd.

'Go on,' suggested Phillip.

'The duke, would he be anything to do with Cornelius Duke: the chief intelligence analyst, by any chance?'

Phillip glanced at Roberta who replied, 'Whatever gave you that idea, chief inspector?'

'Oh nothing, just the name,' replied Boyd, 'And an uncanny similarity in predicting the future perhaps.'

'I think not,' suggested Roberta.

'Funny that,' offered Boyd. 'Everyone in the intelligence community seems to know the duke – Cornelius Duke -but I've never actually met anyone who has met the man.'

'Well,' replied Phillip. 'The duke's team is rather good at what they do. Everyone speaks very highly of them.'

'My point exactly,' offered Boyd. 'Everyone speaks very highly of the duke and his team without knowing who they are. Are you on the duke's team, Roberta?'

'Mister Boyd,' enquired Phillip. 'Are you seriously suggesting one of Europe's most wealthiest and titled men is a mere analyst in GCHQ?'

'You words, not mine,' replied Boyd. 'Maybe Cornelius Duke is a jut a pseudonym. Maybe Cornelius Duke doesn't actually exist at all, which is the truth?'

'You are the only person who has ever asked that question,' remarked Phillip.

'The duke - Is it true?' repeated Boyd.

Sir Phillip paused for a moment and reflected on the issue before replying, 'What's in a name, Mister Boyd?'

'Oh you'd be surprised,' replied Boyd. 'I often spend months just looking for the right name to latch onto.'

Phillip chuckled and then replied, 'Sometimes those we need to protect go unseen and unknown, chief inspector. There are those who might turn a blind eye or issue false propaganda so that such a task might be accomplished.'

Mulling Phillip's words over, Boyd studied the Director General's eyes, returned a wry smile, and replied, 'Thank you, my eyesight is much clearer now, sir.'

'Port?' suggested Phillip.

'No thanks,' replied Antonia

'Yes, please,' admitted Roberta.

'If you'll excuse me I must travel north,' revealed Boyd. 'I have a royal visit to secure. But I'll tell you something now, Sir Phillip.'

'What's that?'

'If things go wrong I know exactly who to ring now.'

The door closed behind Boyd as he left the office.

Sir Phillip Nesbitt turned to Antonia and said, 'Antonia - Where on earth did you find him?'

*

Chapter Eighteen
~

The Channel Tunnel
That day
Threat Level One

A uniformed security officer flagged down the tourist coach and waved the driver into a slipway as it emerged slowly from the Eurotunnel into the morning sunlight.

When the coach pulled up, the driver switched off the engine and set the handbrake before speaking to the officer.

'Just a routine check, driver,' explained the officer. 'Any problems on board?'

'No, none at all,' replied the driver.

'Did you search the coach before leaving Calais?'

'Yes,' admitted the driver. 'It's the same passengers that have been with me since we left Paris.'

'And you're sure of that?'

'Of course,' replied the driver.

'Then you won't mind if we carry out a search of the vehicle and the cargo area?' enquired the officer.

'I expected it,' replied the driver. 'It's quite the norm these days with so many illegal immigrants getting into the country. Go ahead!'

One officer entered the coach and began his journey down the aisle occasionally stopping to ask for the production of a passport. Another officer stepped onto the bottom steps and guarded the door whilst two others began a search of the cargo area.

All was in order until the security officer neared the rear of the coach and spotted a gentleman of Arab extraction.

'Your passport please, sir,' said the officer.

The subject seemed worried and a little nervous as he rummaged in a travel bag for his documents.

'Problem?' enquired the officer.

'I seem to have lost it,' came the reply. 'I was sure I packed it in Paris but I can't seem to find it.'

'In that case, can you step this way, sir?' required the officer politely. 'It will be better to search your travel bag outside with the other luggage you have stowed in the cargo area.'

'This is all I have,' pointed out the Arab gentleman indicating a medium-sized leather travel bag similar to a common or garden sports bag.

'And your name, sir?' questioned the officer.

'Salman… Salman Mostafa,' replied the Arab.

Moments later the coach had been released and the Arab traveller from Paris sat in an interview room nearby waiting for police to arrive.

Dressed in a neat suit, clean shaven, of olive complexion and handsome in his looks, Salman sat uncomfortably as police and immigration officers poured over his travel bag and belongings whilst firing dozens of questions at him.

'Where do live?'

'Paris!'

'Whereabouts?'

'In the northern part of Paris just outside Goussainville?'

'Do you have an address?'

'Not yet, when I return from the UK I'll be moving into the centre of Paris to live.'

'With a girlfriend perhaps, or your parents?'

'No, on my own, why do you ask such a stupid question?'

'Because I want you to convince me that you are who you say you are and that you live in Paris at an address that I can verify.'

'Allah preserve me, I cannot do such a thing at the moment.'

'Where is your passport?'

'I've lost it. I'm sorry.'

'Goussainville, you say. Have you ever been to Tikrit?'

'Syria? Yes, my parents were born there. Why?'

The questions continued as they tried to penetrate Salman's lifestyle, his address, and his identity.

Later, still unsure of the Arab traveller, one of the police officers said, 'I think you are Salman Mostafa and I'm detaining you under the Terrorism legislation. You're not only an illegal immigrant, you're a wanted terrorist.'

'No,' declared Salman. 'No, you've got the wrong man.'

*

Chapter Nineteen
~

Carlisle, Cumbria
The Royal Visit
Threat Level One - Critical

'How's it going?' enquired Boyd entering the operations room set aside for the royal visit.

'We're flat out,' replied Anthea. 'The team have been hard at work but we're no closer than we were a month ago.'

'Tell me what you've done so far?' asked Boyd.

Bannerman handed over a sheet of paper containing a list of actions undertaken. As Boyd read the document he asked, 'Anything else that's not on here?'

'On the presumption that the man from Tikrit has used either the name Salman or Mostafa we've checked every credit card company in western Europe and extracted everyone with such a name who has been granted a card in the last six months?'

'And?'

'There was three hundred and twenty two and we've discounted them all,' explained Bannerman.

'What about cards taken out in Chinese names?

'Thousands, we'll never get through them in the time remaining.'

'Hire cars?' queried Boyd.

'Same story,' suggested Bannerman.

'Anything from the profile people?'

'Our problem is pretty obvious, Guvnor,' explained Anthea. 'We're looking for a male aged between twenty two and thirty eight who is probably a lean mean fighting machine. He has a Chinese appearance and will undoubtedly be a Muslim. Having originated from the North West province of China he probably has a love of open spaces and will prefer life in a rural environment rather than the city. He may or may not be a driver and it's likely that he'll live off the land using the hunter-killer syndrome. He'll make his way from A to B and back again using as few resources as possible and relying on as few people as possible.'

'A lone wolf?' suggested Boyd. 'Please don't cry wolf at me, the Home Secretary will have a fit if I declare we're looking for a lone wolf.'

'Sorry, Guvnor, but it's looked that way since the start,' offered Anthea. 'But he must have some sort of support mechanism in place.'

'Agreed,' replied Boyd.

'Are we monitoring the ticker system?'

'Twenty four seven!'

'Okay, get the kettle on and ask Sandra, Janice, Ricky and Terry to join me in the briefing room if you wouldn't mind.'

'There's another problem,' reported Bannerman.

'Such as?'

'You asked me to check with the palace to see if our royal visitor might cancel the visit due to unforeseen circumstances – such as a cold, toothache, or a virus of some kind.'

'So I did. And?' queried Boyd.

'Not a cat in hell's chance and don't ask the next question because they also refuse to change the route. The monarchy will not step aside because of a threat of whatever kind.'

'Damn it,' replied Boyd. Thinking for a second or two, he replied, 'Well bad news for us but good news in a way. I love it when such people stand up to be counted in their own quiet way.'

'They have indicated they are strong and won't bend to terrorism but it puts more pressure on us,' suggested Anthea.

'Pressure is what we eat and drink for breakfast, Anthea.'

The door opened and the first of many entered Boyd's briefing for the three day royal visit that was about to impact on the people of Cumbria.

Boyd spent the next hour explaining that this would be the first of many such operations. In future, they would match police and intelligence resources to an area to be visited by the monarchy and take whatever steps were needed to secure the visit and the individuals concerned. Much of their response would be graded by the degree of threat level known to the country at that time.

'This is my template,' he explained. 'If the threat level is high then our response must be high. If the threat level is high then we should be authorised to use extra-ordinary powers to secure all electronic transmissions from whatever source to investigate, and our staff numbers need to match the threat. Why am I short of manpower and fully trained personnel when the country is at threat level one?'

There was a murmur of agreement from around the room.

Boyd continued, 'We need to match our investigation and our response to the relevant threat level. Now I really appreciate all your hard work over recent weeks but the fact remains we are no nearer to locating the man from Tikrit than we were when we started. Yes, we've got his name but there's no trace of the name so if you come across Humpty Dumpty today be sure to check him out because we're looking for a needle in a haystack.'

'We're looking for a little fat man sat on a wall then?' suggested Ricky French.

A ripple of laughter ran through the room before Boyd chuckled and replied, 'All the king's horses and all the king's men won't be able to put Humpty back together again. Funny man! But you've cracked it because you're all good eggs.'

Moans of derision rattled Boyd's poor attempt at a joke which fell flat.

'Seriously though,' continued Boyd. 'You've ruled out dozens of security concerns and for that we are obliged. But today, it's back to basics. Eyes, ears and good old fashioned police work will see us through. You've had a chance to see the plans and read the brief. Now we're going to dissect it in full. Is everyone happy with their allotted tasks?'

There was no displeasure voiced and Boyd said, 'We could pray for rain because that usually works but I'm afraid the forecast is good. The brief is always going to be simple - To identify those who might pose a problem, to investigate, to define the threat and the origins of the threat, to define each individual who poses a threat, and to deal it with accordingly. In short, search, secure and protect.'

The briefing continued but by the end of the briefing, everyone present knew exactly what was expected of them and they filed out into the morning sunshine.

As the main group of officers left the room Superintendent Jack Beardsley approached Boyd and lazily said, 'As event commander I should thank you for a good security briefing, Chief Inspector Boyd.'

'Thank you, sir,' smiled Boyd.

'Except it wasn't,' replied Superintendent Beardsley. 'It was well and truly over the top. You made it sound as if we were at war.'

'We are, superintendent?' suggested Boyd, 'Against terrorism?'

'Really,' countered Beardsley. 'When will you people in your high flying office jobs stop listening to the politicians and their meaningless soundbites?'

'Office jobs! Never mind, I listen to the analysts,' replied Boyd. 'They tend to know what they're talking about.'

'Poppycock, Boyd – Completely over the top,' argued Superintendent Beardsley. 'Still, must go, I've got a visit to manage and then a report to do as to why we've no money left in the kitty for the rest of the quarter.'

'The budget?' asked Boyd.

'The budget,' replied Beardsley. 'Someone has to pay for this little lot and you guys would just spend it like it was going out of fashion.'

'What price security?' asked Boyd.

In the city, a group of VIPs eagerly donned their best dresses and smartest suits, checked their appearance in the mirror, brushed away the last smidgen of fluff, and made their way into town. It was their day as much as any others. They would be presented to the Royal Family.

Across the city, school teachers made ready the Union flags that their pupils might wave on the street that day. A Street cleaner swept the last piece of litter from the roadway and carefully brushed it into the shovel before depositing it in his bin. And a small team of council workers, led by Jim Beattie, gradually unloaded a wagon and pinned together a set of temporary pedestrian fences that defined a security area where the arrival of the monarch was expected. Once they'd finished Jim took his team deeper into the city centre to place even more security barriers.

Nearby, a liveried police van was parked and its occupants worked quietly searching the area. An officer pulled across a manhole cover before declaring the area safe, and securing the handle with a plastic handcuff.

It was early in the morning but Francis Littleton was showered and shaved and dressed in his Union Flag suit with all its finery and colour. Closing the door behind him he straightened his tie, smoothed his trousers, and walked towards his car. He fired the engine and drove into the city.

Vitally important, thought Francis, it's vitally important to get a good place on the street to see the monarch and the people taking part. And I know just where I'm going to stand – in front of the breakfast bar where I shall treat myself to a good old English fry-up.

It's going to be a memorable day, thought Francis as he checked to make sure his camera was loaded and he had spare film. Yes, a great day lies ahead. But it's my breakfast time soon.

Leaving the interchange of the M6 motorway, a dark blue hire car trundled into the early morning traffic heading down the

A69 and into the city of Carlisle. It was only a few hundred yards to the first significant traffic light controlled road junction and it was here the vehicle turned right and headed the towards a Tesco supermarket.

On arrival at the front of the premises, the hire car came to a standstill. There was a brief handshake between passenger and driver before Mostafa Humayl stepped from the nearside of the vehicle and headed into the supermarket's cafeteria.

Mostafa was dressed in dark training shoes, dark jeans, and a black blouson jacket that was zipped loosely half way up his chest. Clean shaven, handsome, and looking in the prime of health, as the hire car drove off, Mostafa stepped into the queue and eventually ordered a light breakfast before sitting at a table. He was only a matter of minutes from the heart of the city.

A short time later, two police vans arrived near the traffic lights. The officers alighted from the vehicles and stood on each side of the road monitoring traffic. Then they funnelled all the traffic into one lane and allowed it to proceed at walking pace. Every now and again a vehicle was flagged into the side and the occupants spoken to.

The brief was simple and had been top of the list for a few days now. They were looking for a male of Chinese appearance in his mid-twenties to late thirties. If such a person was identified he had to be stopped and checked out.

Vigilance was the order of the day.

Elsewhere, Dina Al-Hakim was also preparing for her morning. She'd risen early, undertaken the obligations of her religion, and was now in prayer. Quietly, reverently, she went about her business in the flat near the River Caldew in Carlisle.

Eventually, Dina changed clothes and dressed in camouflaged combat trousers, a grey top, a grey waistcoat, an anorak, and her favourite hijab: a dark grey headscarf that covered her hair and shoulders but not her face.

Tightening her trouser belt and zipping her anorak tight, Dina closed and locked the door behind her as she set off towards the city. Breakfast in town, she declared to herself. Yes, just this once I shall treat myself to a breakfast before the fun starts.

Moments later, a surveillance crew began plotting her every move as they followed on behind.

In Castle Street, Jim Beattie and his team of council workers had fixed the last of the pedestrian security barriers together and had withdrawn for the morning. Jim drove the low-sided wagon into Annetwell Street and parked up near the rear entrance to Tullie House Museum. Opening a flask of sweet tea and a packet of sandwiches, Jim offered his sandwiches to his colleagues as they began their break

Moments later a uniformed police officer tapped on the window and said, 'Sorry, lads, you'll have to move the wagon. There's no parking here today.'

'But we've just finished putting your barriers down for you,' protested Jim. 'Where do you want me to park - On Castle Street next to the regimental band?'

'Sorry,' replied the officer. 'My instructions are to keep this street free from parked cars. It's all to do with security, sir.'

'You mean car bombs and stuff,' moaned Jim.

'Something like that,' explained the policeman. 'Look, I can see it's a council van and I've seen you boys around the streets before. Do me a favour and pop it inside Tullie House for me.'

'Do you mean use the lane at the back here?' asked Jim.

'Yes please, you're off the road there.'

Agreeing, Jim said to his workers, 'Tell you what, boys, I'll park her up and finish my tea. Why don't you guys take some time off and wander round to the front and enjoy the show.'

All agreed and the policeman walked on intent on keeping the street clear as Jim Beattie bumped the wagon onto the pavement and through the rear gates of Tullie House. Laughing, his colleagues walked round the block towards the route of the royal visit. No more work until the royals were finished their tour.

Strolling along happily, it wasn't lost on the patrolling policeman that Annetwell Street ran parallel to Castle Street where the visit would take place. Only the Tullie House Museum divided the two streets. He'd been briefed to keep the streets clear. There would be no chance of a car bomb in the city today, not if he could help it.

Jim Beattie snatched the handbrake and tucked into another sandwich as he glanced down the lane towards Castle Street. The area was slowly filling up with people making ready for the regimental band, and the monarch's procession.

Gradually they came from far and wide – school children with their teachers and flags, ex-servicemen and their medals and berets, families with their toddlers and cameras, and Dina and Francis.

Suddenly, the city was alive and awake.

It was the first day of the royal visit.

Martin Duffy was happy. He'd been drafted into the Special Escort Group for the day and would ride the lead motor bike in the police convoy. Unlike the others in the motorcycle convoy, he would be armed and carry a machine pistol in a boot holster. Today of all days, he was pleased to be a detective yet he appreciated the irony. It wasn't that long ago that he was a dedicated motor cycle rider, but things had changed.

Smoothing a soft cloth across the windscreen and then his shiny exhausts, Martin finished off, stowed the cloth, and kick started his charge.

Looking across the police station traffic yard, Martin shouted, 'Okay, boys, let's go.'

Snapping first gear with his toe, Martin led the convoy out of the yard towards the city centre.

As Boyd, Bannerman and the mobile protection team crossed the yard towards their vehicles, Superintendent Beardsley's phone rang.

Simultaneously, Boyd's phone rang. He paused, answered his mobile and listened.

'Mister Boyd?'

'Yes, who is this?'

'This is the secretary to the Home Secretary's secretary. I've been asked to contact you by the Home Secretary about…'

'Who did you say you were?' queried an astonished Boyd.

'The secretary to the Home Secretary's secretary, I've been instructed by the Home Secretary to inform you that the man from Tikrit has been arrested and you must stand down your operation forthwith?'

'Has he really?' suggested Boyd. 'And his name is?'

'I'm not at liberty to inform you, Mister Boyd.'

'And I'm not at liberty to take calls from the secretary of a secretary. No disrespect, Miss, but if the Home Secretary wants to speak to me then tell her to ring me. I don't take orders from a third hand source.'

Boyd ended the call abruptly.

'Boyd!' snapped Superintendent Beardsley. 'I've got the chief on the phone wanting to speak to you. Your man has been arrested at the Eurotunnel attempting to enter the country.'

'Has he really?' offered Boyd.

Pondering the situation for a moment, Boyd then punched the numbers on his mobile phone, waited for a response, and said, 'Toni, is Sir Phillip with you? Can you put him on?'

Seconds later, Boyd declared, 'Thank you for taking my call, Phillip. Can you tell me the latest on the man from Tikrit? I've just been told he's been arrested at the Eurotunnel. I'm not convinced given the timescales. Is it fact or supposition? Can you confirm the latest for me?'

'Are you in the field, Boyd?' demanded Sir Phillip.

'Yes, I'm with Purple One.'

'I'll get back to you,' replied Phillip. Try Julian while I phone the office.'

Boyd nodded, ended the call, and then punched his mobile again. 'Sir Julian,' he declared. 'Detective Chief Inspector Boyd, I'm with Purple One. I really need to know now if the man from Tikrit has been arrested or not?'

'Two minutes!' replied Julian. 'I'm in the office at Vauxhall. I'll get back to you.'

Boyd's phone rang again.

'It's Phillip, the individual arrested at the Eurotunnel has nothing to do with the man from Tikrit. He has a similar name otherwise no connection.'

'Thank you,' replied Boyd who immediately ended the call and took an incoming from Sir Julian.

'Nothing to report, Boyd,' said Julian. 'The fugitive is still outstanding. Whoever told you this is mistaken.'

'I'm obliged for your time,' replied Boyd.

The phone rang again. This time Boyd recognised the phone number and opened the conversation with, 'Good morning, Home Secretary, and what can I do for you today?'

'You can listen for once in your life, chief inspector,' growled The Home Secretary. 'I've just informed the local chief constable that the man from Tikrit has been arrested. Very shortly I'll be speaking to Commander Maxwell to tell him the same as I'm telling you. I'm anxious to ensure you don't go over the top protecting the monarchy when there is absolutely no need to do so. I therefore require you to stand your operation down and let Her Majesty's protection team carry on as usual, and without your presence. My previous instructions to you are hereby rescinded. I wanted you to know immediately so that you could acknowledge compliance.'

'And save on manpower?'

'Of course, chief inspector, but the circumstances do not warrant your co-operation.'

'I'm afraid they do and I have to tell you that the operation has already started,' advised Boyd.

Superintendent Beardsley began flustering around Boyd trying to grab his attention.

Boyd turned his back and ignored Jack Beardsley.

'Then stop it now,' ordered the Home Secretary. 'It's an order!'

'Tell me again who's been arrested – his name please?'

'Salman Mostafa Muhammad!' replied the Home Secretary. 'He's from Goussainville near Paris.'

'Oh yes,' replied Boyd. 'Our unit is aware of that arrest from the ticker system but he's not our man. He's unarmed and merely has a similar name. He is an illegal immigrant from the Middle East but he's definitely not our man.'

'Of course he is,' countered the Home Secretary. 'The chief constable at the port has just told me.'

'Afraid not,' argued Boyd. 'And for your information I've just spoken to two Knights of the Realm – one who heads MI5 and the other MI6 - Our man is here. Your man was still in Paris after the Goussainville attack. Check the timescale yourself. He's a red herring that we have no interest in.'

'How do you know your man is here?'

'Because I feel it in my bones, that's why. We're looking for a real cool customer and today is the day.'

'You're wrong, Boyd,' contended the Home Secretary. 'And obviously stressed out, burnt out, and suffering from delusions of grandeur not compatible with an effective contribution to security. Since when did aching bones help a detective achieve their objective? I'll contact Commander Maxwell and instruct him to relieve you of your duties.'

'You do that then because I haven't got time for this and I'm not arguing with you. I'm doing what I'm paid to do.'

Boyd ended the call abruptly and turned to face Superintendent Beardsley who snarled, 'I told you so. I've got the chief on my 'phone and he's calling time on you. You've got to stand down the operation because the Home Secretary tells us the suspect is in custody down south.'

'Tell him I've just spoken to the Directors of MI5 and MI6. Tell the chief that the Home Secretary is wrong,' countered Boyd.

'You really want me to tell the chief constable that both he and the Home Secretary are wrong?' asked Jack, aghast at the prospect.

Closing his eyes for a second before taking a deep breath, Boyd replied, 'Forgive me, Jack, but I walked the same streets as you as a young copper many years ago. I shook the same door handles as you when we were trying up on nights. I probably arrested the same drunken idiots and two bit crooks that you did. We probably bit our first tooth on the same piece of tarmac. When I left this place I remember the chief then telling me that counter terrorism and national security had a minor role to play in the general scheme of policing. There were more important things to contend with, he argued. I jest you not! How wrong was he, Jack? Now I'm late and I'm in charge of security here. I've also got a national remit to respect and honour. Now stand aside or I'll walk right through you…. Sir.'

Detective Superintendent Sandra Peel shouldered up to Beardsley, smiled, and said, 'Jack, Chief Inspector Boyd has a lot on his mind right now. But take a tip from a fellow senior officer. He means it; he will walk all over you, and he is right. They've got the wrong man locked up down there. Now you tell your chief that because we've got a job to do. And while you're talking to the chief, tell him to ring the Home Secretary because the good lady who means so well – is wrong too. Try the facts….. Sir.'

Beardsley faltered, didn't quite know what to say, and began to speak.

He was abruptly cut off by Sandy when she ordered, 'Move out, Boyd! Let's go. We've got a job to do.'

There was a screech of tyres and a smell of car exhaust lingering in the traffic yard when Superintendent Beardsley peered at his phone, heard the chief's voice calling for him, and then gradually lifted it to his mouth.

'Chief constable,' voiced Beardsley, 'We've got a problem with this lot from London. Primarily, he used to be one of ours.' Jack Beardsley cringed at the reply and then said, 'Boyd, sir, Detective Chief Inspector Boyd, he seems to think he has a direct line to God.'

The royal train pulled into Carlisle railway station amidst a media scrum intent on capturing an image of royalty and the entourage. Held behind security barriers positioned a reasonable distance from the train, reporters panned their cameras whilst a plethora of flash lights cut through the atmosphere.

'Purple One is on site,' radioed Bannerman.

A royal foot touched a red carpet laid out as a welcome and a roar of approval rent the air. Dressed elegantly in a light blue two-piece suit and matching hat, she was a stunning reminder of Britain's enduring democratic system, and she was a marvellous ambassador to the country she served and reigned over.

Polite applause accompanied her walk as she approached a line of local VIP's who waited for introductions.

There was a bow and a curtsey, a smile, a nervous movement from one foot to another and then the lady was through the line, finished for the moment, and strolling towards the exit carrying a matching handbag towards the station master and a young girl.

The girl curtsied and presented a posy of flowers to the lady referred to by Bannerman as purple one. The lady smiled, shook hands, and then beamed a huge smile when the youngster stepped shyly back and hid behind the stationmaster.

She was moving on, taking her entourage of protection officers with her. There was a private secretary dressed in a morning coat and two ladies in waiting looking demure and elegant as they trailed behind their leader.

At the exit Bannerman radioed, 'Stand by, all units. We have an egress. Purple One is stage two!'

And into the morning sunlight she stepped to a tremendous bout of cheering and applause.

Bannerman opened the door of the royal car and Purple One paused, threw a wave or two, and was inside the car and waiting.

Martin Duffy checked behind, manoeuvred into position at the front of the convoy, and eyed Bannerman in the front passenger seat of the royal car.

Checking his passenger was seated securely, Bannerman nodded and said, 'Take it away.'

There was a purr from Martin's motor bike when he set off leading the convoy into Court Square before veering left into English Street, passing the Citadel, and heading for the traffic lights at the crossroads ahead.

Two police motor cycles overtook the royal car and positioned themselves at the traffic lights intending to stop traffic and secure the highway for royalty.

'Nice and easy does it,' murmured Boyd in the back-up car.

'Calm down, Guvnor,' suggested Anthea. 'Sandy spoke up for you. We all know you're right. Concentrate on the job not the argument you've just had'

Exhaling deeply, Boyd nodded and radioed, 'Boss Car, I have control…. The convoy is moving. It's a nearside pick-up for a nearside drop. Look sharp, look at the people not the car. Solo One, steady as she goes.'

'Solo One wilco,' responded Martin. 'Slow ahead the convoy, walking speed.'

'What does that mean?' asked Sandra.

'The subject under protection entered the rear nearside of the car from the kerbside and will get out of the rear nearside of the vehicle at the kerbside when it reaches its destination,' explained Boyd. 'Now everyone involved on the route knows where the subject is sitting.'

'I see,' replied Sandra. 'The subject? Let's not use her real name then.'

'No, I shan't,' replied Boyd. 'That's the protocol and that's what Bannerman expects. The subject is codename Purple One and that's it. He's not a man to get emotionally close to his subject. It's just a protection job to him.'

'I see,' replied Sandra. 'Strange man?' she queried.

'No, just a professional,' countered Boyd.

As the royal car travelled through a red traffic light into the pedestrian area of English Street, the convoy slowed at the behest of the monarch anxious to allow the citizens of Carlisle a glimpse of their royalty. She waved; they waved back their Union flags and cheered from behind a carefully placed thin line of security barriers that separated royalty from the people.

'At least there's no demonstration today,' said Anthea.

'Good!' acknowledged Boyd. 'We wouldn't want to upset the event commander would we?'

'I think he's upset enough already,' remarked Sandra.

Anthea smiled and Boyd radioed, 'Team Alpha to stand by. Team Charlie, where is your tango?'

'In a café in Castle Street opposite Tullie House, Guvnor,' came the reply.

'Keep her there if you have to,' ordered Boyd.

'Why not take her in now?' suggested Sandra.

'I think we've got enough problems with the local superintendent and the chief constable, Sandra. What are we going to arrest her for? Being a Muslim with a suspect package that she received a while ago, or meaningless chatter on the internet to who knows who?'

'Normally, that would do but I take your point because the locals here will go ape at the end of the day. You've upset the Home Secretary and probably most of the top landing at police headquarters, and it won't matter one iota about Sir Phillip and Sir Julian supporting you because they might as well be a million miles away when you stand on someone's toes. Taking in a suspect without hard evidence will be like giving them manna from heaven.'

'You're right. We should detain her but we're damned if we do and damned if we don't,' replied Boyd.

'You're worried about the politicians, aren't you?' asked Anthea.

Nodding, Boyd replied, 'You know me too well, Anthea. It's not just me. What happens to all of you if you follow me and we're wrong somewhere along the line?'

'Then we'll all be …. I don't know actually, Guvnor,' delivered Anthea. 'Let's cross that bridge when we come to it.'

Boyd chuckled, 'Okay, let's make a start.' Then he lifted the radio and said, 'All units from Boss Car, any suspicious movements anywhere on route, anything, anything at all?'

The radio remained silent and Boyd radioed, 'Team Alpha to stand by.'

A back up car behind Boyd pulled up and disgorged its passengers at precisely the same time as a regimental band burst into a rendition of 'D'ye ken John Peel'. The tune was immediately applauded since it was attributed to John Peel – an eighteenth century huntsman from Caldbeck in Cumbria – and it was appreciated in the county's capital. It was as if the band had specifically selected a piece loved by the locals to honour their beloved guest.

The convoy made its way into the pedestrian area of English Street as Bannerman's 'subject' waved at the crowds gathered to welcome royalty to the city.

Martin Duffy slipped the cutch and slowed to match the speed of the marching band on their journey to Carlisle Castle. They would lead the royal convoy marching along English Street, passing Carlisle's Town Hall, the cathedral, and Tullie House museum before crossing the dual carriageway and climbing the slight ascent into the heart of Carlisle's magnificent Norman castle. Here, a line of soldiers eagerly awaited their Colonel-in-Chief since they were ready to receive their medals for service to the country.

And then it happened. Team Alpha went into overdrive when they took up pre-determined positions beside the royal car to provide a thin blue line of security between royalty and the people. Sandra Peel headed the procession. She walked in front of the car but behind Martin's motor bike. Boyd adopted a position close to the rear nearside passenger door. Anthea took the offside door and the rest of the team encircled the unit providing a security bubble to the monarchy.

It wasn't the usual way the British police protected royalty but it wasn't the American or European way either. It was just a system, thought Boyd and Bannerman – an idea that might afford close protection whilst having the opportunity to study faces in the crowd. And they were all looking for Mostafa.

They were towards the junction with Bank Street with Sandra scanning the street and Boyd almost at the subject's shoulder as he walked beside the car. With one step in less than one second he could be closer to the lady. Yet he was far enough away to give an unencumbered view of the subject under protection. He was walking the line. They were all walking a line that allowed protection and security as well as a form of transparency for the people.

The convoy was through the junction with crowds cheering and a band playing. Flags waving, people clapping, cameras clicking, and no sign of Mostafa as they slowly padded across the pedestrian area towards the bandstand.

Jim Beattie was just about to drain the last drops of his flask when he saw a reflection in the wing mirror of his council wagon. He wound down the window and turned his head to see Mostafa approaching from the direction of Annetwell Street.

'What can I do for you?' asked Jim.

It was the last words he spoke.

Mostafa pulled open the driver's door and thrust the cold hard steel of his blade into Jim's side. Open-mouthed, Jim dropped his flask and fell towards Mostafa who bundled him back into the vehicle as he climbed in. Once inside the cab, Mostafa manhandled the corpse of Jim Beattie into the passenger seat.

Withdrawing his knife from Jim's body, Mostafa wiped it on the council worker's jeans, closed the driver's door, and settled himself into the driving seat.

Ibrahim, he thought. You promised me support to the very end but this is not the desert. This is not the barren wastes of Syria. It's a concrete jungle and the battle here is nothing like the war out there. Still, I have a weapon of a kind now. I shall use it well.

Less than two hundred yards away, in Castle Street, Francis Littleton sank the last remnants of his coffee, smartened his tie, and made for the café doorway.

'It's the band,' he rejoiced. 'She's coming in and the regimental band is leading the way.'

Excited, Francis brushed past Dina Al-Hakim on the way out, apologised, and then headed for his place at the security barrier.

'Excuse me! Excuse me!' he shouted barging his way into the crowd gathering at the barriers. 'I was here first.'

No-one argued with the city's number one fan when he began waving the Union flag as he looked down the street towards the oncoming procession.

The band broke into another tune. A trumpet blew, a trombone sounded, and a soldier beat a big bass drum as the drum major led the procession down Castle Street towards Tullie House Museum.

Dina checked her wristwatch, adjusted her hijab, and made ready to leave the café. Stepping towards the exit she framed herself in the doorway and studied the crowd standing on front of her. The throng was three deep, no more and no less, but it spread out along the pavement for the best part of half a mile. Standing, looking, Dina saw a sea of Union flags and row upon row of red, white and blue bunting flying from the lamp standards.

Behind her, in the depths of the café, surveillance officers from Team Charlie held their position. A quiet radio call alerted team members outside as they closed towards the lady.

Francis leaned across the barrier to get a better view but could only see the band. He relaxed, turned to speak to someone in the crowd, and realised he had left his camera in the café. It was then that he noticed Dina for the second time.

I know that woman, thought Francis. Was she at the last royal visit a few weeks ago, he wondered. No, he decided. She's different. It's not possible.

Francis Littleton stretched onto his tiptoes to get a better view of the slow moving procession.

Dina backed into the café once more, took a seat, and then began taking deep breaths.

Outside a surveillance officer radioed, 'Charlie Two has Tango One inside the café. No movements.'

Francis dived into the café, snatched his camera from a table, took another look at Dina, and returned to the excitement outside.

Boyd acknowledged the call with his throat microphone and continued to scan the crowd. There was a white man and a coloured man; a woman of oriental appearance and a woman with a dark ebony skin. Around him on the streets he could see thin and fat, and tall and tiny, but there was no sign of the man whose image was inscribed inside his brain.

At the rear of Tullie House Museum Mostafa turned the ignition key on the council van, heard the engine throb, and set off at a slow speed towards the entrance. Nodding, he confirmed that the lane ran at ninety degrees to the procession. As he followed the lane round, he saw two concrete bollards barring the way into the street. In front of the bollards, close to a line of security barriers, a mass of people flooded the footpath waiting for the procession to pass them.

Mostafa reached inside his clothing and removed the object of his mail order catalogue: a fully loaded semi-automatic machine pistol. Mostafa weighed the weapon in his hands, smiled bizarrely at the corpse sat beside him, and allowed the council wagon to drift slowly down a slight incline.

'Charlie Two, no change,' radioed the surveillance officer. 'Tango One held inside the café.'

'Roger,' replied Boyd acknowledging the call.

They were on their toes now. Adrenalin rushed through the bloodstream, a heartbeat thundered, a pulse pounded at the skin, sweat ran down a detective's neck. And still the drum beat, the trumpet sounded, and a trombone rent the air.

They were closer now. The sound of the bass drum pulverised the atmosphere as the music grew to a deafening crescendo and poor Francis Littleton covered his ears with his hands. Turning away from the music Francis peered into the café and glanced at Dina again.

What is it about her, he asked himself. It is the one I remember from the visit of the prince and princess. I'm sure it is.

The band was passing the café now and in the middle distance the royal car approached.

'She's coming,' shouted Francis fumbling for his camera. 'She's here now!'

It was almost a signal when Dina stood up suddenly inside the café and turned towards the door, mesmerised by the shouting, bombarded by the music.

Martin Duffy passed on the motor bike, and then Sandra followed close behind just ahead of the royal car with Boyd on one side and Anthea the other and Ricky French, Janice Burns and Terry Anwhari taking up wing positions as the entourage moved slowly down the highway.

Purple One waved. The crowd waved back and cheered for all they were worth.

This isn't normal, thought Francis. The detectives don't usually do this. A worried Francis lowered his hands, stopped waving, and said aloud, 'That's not right.'

Dina stepped forward. She was through the door and onto the pavement before Charlie Two realised.

Francis turned, glanced at Dina, and saw wires hanging from the bottom of her jacket. He pointed at Dina and shouted towards Anthea, 'Detective! She's wearing something under her anorak! It's a bomb!'

Sandra stopped in her tracks. Boyd glanced across the roof of the royal car. Anthea heard the voice of Francis Littleton, followed his pointed finger, and zeroed in on Dina Al-Hakim.

Stepping forward towards the barrier, Dina unzipped her grey anorak to reveal a suicide bomb jacket. The waistcoat was infested by hand grenades and sticks of dynamite carefully sewn into the jacket and held in place by a uniquely bizarre home-made line of wires and plastic tape. The wiring trailed away to a detonator device which Dina held in her hand.

Anthea vaulted over the barrier followed closely by Ricky French. Francis stood in awe. The rest of the crowd parted like the Red Sea. A woman screamed. The crowd panicked.

Inside the detectives' minds something registered. It was an amateurish gesture. It was a naïve attempt to copy the real thing. It was a fake! Or was it the real thing?

Dina pressed the detonator at the precise time Anthea clenched her fist around the detonator device and Charlie Two tackled her from behind.

The trio fell to the ground in an uncontrolled scrum before Dina broke free, got onto her knees, and was about to plunge the detonator again when Ricky French blasted two shots into the back of her neck from less than a foot.

Dina's head exploded in a horrible cloud of blood and mucus when the spinal cord shattered and a bullet ricocheted to penetrate and destroy the brain.

There was a twitch from Dina's lifeless body as it crashed headfirst to the ground with Anthea pulling wildly at the wiring and ripping Dina's bomb mechanism to shreds.

Screaming people competed with running panicking crowds on one side of the street.

Then there was a roar from a council wagon's engine when Mostafa slammed the accelerator hard to the floor and sped towards the bollards that barred his way.

The crowd turned, saw the council wagon racing towards them at high speed, parted into a mad cap scramble to escape, and watched in disbelief as Mostafa drove the vehicle right over the bollards into the front offside wing of the royal car.

Sandra spun round, fired from the hip and splintered the wagon's windscreen. Janice dropped to one knee and fired into the cabin whilst Boyd drew his weapon and pointed it at the wagon.

With his foot hard on the throttle, Mostafa pushed the royal car sideways as he fired from the window of the council van into the body if the car.

Inside the royal vehicle, Bannerman threw his body across the passenger divide and covered Purple One with his entire six feet plus of public defender.

'Drive!' he screamed. But the wagon had destroyed the royal car's ability to escape. The front nearside wing had crumpled and punctured a front tyre.

There was a wheeze from the monarch's chest when Bannerman squeezed down and tried to disappear into the upholstery.

'Don't,' cried a voice. 'You're killing me.'

'No, he's trying to!' shouted Bannerman. 'Make yourself a smaller target. Get down!'

Bannerman pushed Purple One deeper into the upholstery, ignored the complaints, and covered her body with his own.

Outside, Mostafa lowered the driver's window and pulled the trigger letting off salvo after salvo of deadly bullets at the royal car.

The dull impact tore into the royal car's metal but did not penetrate it.

Martin Duffy let the clutch out as the band in front of him ran for their lives leaving a big bass drum rolling down Castle Street and a trumpet or two abandoned in the gutter. Martin spun the motorbike round as the rear tyre burnt the tarmac and he snatched first gear to plough directly into Mostafa's wagon and bring it to a standstill.

Sandra Peel catapulted through the air and crashed into a pedestrian barrier when she took a shot from Mostafa.

Martin snatched a machine pistol from his boot holster and took out the wagon's windscreen with a hail of bullets.

Boyd sprinted towards the wagon, jumped onto the bonnet of the vehicle, and emptied his weapon into Mostafa Humayl's head and chest through the windscreen.

Mostafa looked up, tried to lift his gun, and then slunk back into the driver's seat when his life expired.

Bannerman opened the door of the royal car, helped Purple One from the rear, and bundled the subject into a back-up car which roared away in reverse to a place of safety.

The air smelled strongly of cordite. Blood flowed from Sandra's shoulder. Dina Al-Hakim twitched again but was no more.

Deep red blood swept the floor amidst the screams and panic of the city. Where moments before the sound of music, laughter and cheering had filled the air – now the atmosphere was only of evil giving way to an eerie silence that penetrated the core of life in Castle Street.

The regimental bass drum finally came to rest when it mounted a kerb, bumped into a lamp standard, and rolled onto its side with a gentle thud.

It was over, for now.

Chapter Twenty

~

Later
Threat Level One - Critical

Sandra Peel lay in a hospital bed in Carlisle watching the news on television. Under the influence of pain killers following surgery, and feeling very sore, she listened to brief snatches of the headlines…

'… *A terrorist attack on the Queen has been thwarted by counter terrorist officers following an armed shoot out on the streets of Carlisle. A palace spokesman announced that the Queen was unhurt and would be resuming her civic duties with immediate effect. Meanwhile, the city has been plunged into mourning following the brutal murder of Jim Beattie: a council worker who was killed by a terrorist during the attack. A married man, he lives three children behind. A police spokesman extended sincere sympathy to his family. A large turn-out is expected for his funeral…*

… A gang of youths have been arrested in London following an assault upon a local businessman protesting against their enforcement of Sharia law…

… A cache of stolen guns and ammunition has been recovered from the coastal area near the Solway Firth. A number of people are currently assisting police with their enquiries…

… A man who forgot his passport has been detained by the authorities at the Eurotunnel complex and is believed to be an illegal immigrant from the Middle East…

… Government officials refused to comment on an alleged cyberattack on a government website here in the United Kingdom…

… The NATO Naval exercise in the Baltic Sea has ended without further incident…

… A man identified as Ivan Pushkin appeared at Westminster Magistrates Court this morning accused of spying for the Russians. He was remanded in custody for seven days. No-one was available to comment on the case at the Russian Embassy in Kensington…

… A joint US/UK drone attack in Syria has reportedly killed Ibrahim Hasan al Din, one of the longest serving leaders of Islamic State…'

Sandra sighed, manipulated the remote control, and found a comedy channel. Quietly, she looked out of the window of the ward and checked the time. Later that night she would have her first visitors and they would be followed in quick time by the police investigators who would ask a hundred questions about recent events – before supplying a hundred different versions of what should have happened in a perfect world. I'll remind them about gallantry medals, she decided. A perfect world, she mused, wouldn't have firearms and we wouldn't be killing each other the way we do.

But how do I prevent the Dina al Hakims of the world embarking on their lone wolf adventures, she wondered. And how do we stop the likes of Mostafa from ever entering the country to inflict harm upon its people? Interesting, thought Sandra, one lone wolf and one with some organisational support, yet we were so very lucky – so very lucky in the work that we do.

And of the future, pondered Sandra as she channel hopped the television – Some we win, some we lose, and some we draw. Why? Because it's not a perfect world, that's why. But I'm going to be part of the future of that they can be sure.

Detective Superintendent Sandra 'Sandy' Peel switched off the television and carefully eased herself down to sleep.

A palace on the edge of the Cotswolds was the scene off Boyd and Antonia strolling along a gravel path admiring the magnificent historic edifice.

'Somewhere this week another soul will be inaugurated into Phillip's new found establishment,' remarked Antonia.

'Determined to prepare for an unsettled future, equipped, enabled, and dedicated to the preservation of the truly British way of life?' suggested Boyd.

'Hopefully,' replied Antonia. 'Hopefully!'

'At least we know it's not an extreme right wing political group planning to take over the country,' suggested Boyd.

'Not yet, Billy, not yet. But we are placed to monitor it if need be.'

Boyd's phone rang and he answered it.

'Billy?'

'Sandy, how are you?' asked Boyd

'Unable to sleep,' replied Sandra. 'I thought I'd ring you and let you know what's going on in my mind.'

'Go on,' offered Boyd. 'You should be trying to get some rest, you know that.'

'Yes,' replied Sandra, 'But why aren't you looking after Purple One?'

'We're all on garden leave pending the outcome of an internal enquiry, Sandy.'

'Of course, I forgot,' replied the superintendent. 'The use of firearms always calls for an enquiry. I think you'll be safe with this one.'

'One would hope so,' replied Boyd.

'I need to know something,' demanded Sandra.

'Such as?' responded Boyd.

'Were Dina and Mostafa working together?'

'Not that we're aware of at the present time,' replied Boyd. 'So far the evidence suggests they were working independently of each other. The only connection seems to be an internet chat room but there's no indication that the two of them ever met or even spoke to each other.'

'One lone wolf and one with a briefing and some support,' remarked Sandra.

'Looks that way,' confirmed Boyd.

'Anyway,' continued Sandra. 'I've decided not to pursue those assessment interviews that I insisted upon. We're far too busy and I really don't see the need to fill my tray with unnecessary paperwork.'

'Whatever you say, ma-am, you're the boss,' chuckled Boyd.

'Boss! But I don't play chess as well as you, Boyd,' stated Sandra.

'Chess?' queried Boyd.

'You do play chess, Billy?' persisted Sandra.

'No, Sandy, not me.'

'I thought you did.'

'I know some of the rules and how to get out of them,' explained Boyd. 'The game is all about pawns and castle, bishops and knights moving in and out of squares. It's far too complicated for me'

'That it?'

'What are you getting at, Sandra?' asked Boyd.

'These last few weeks have made me realise we're all just pawns in a great big game that someone else is playing. They just seem to move us around when they want too.'

'True, Sandy but you can upset the game if you try hard enough.'

'How?' queried Sandra.

'Lean backwards and roll with the attack and then hit back hard,' explained Boyd

'How much would you risk in the game, Boyd?'

'Nearly everything!'

Nearly everything?

'Yes,' replied Boyd. 'You can threaten my king but you will never take my queen.'

The call ended and Sandra drifted off to sleep whilst Antonia and Phillip enjoyed a tour through England's history.

Far away from Cumbria, out in the desert in a distant country that neither loved nor hated him, Jack Dooley wanted prisoners, and he was still hanging onto an umbilical cord as a helicopter crew scoured the ground below. Nothing appeared to have changed. Intelligence was still vital and a pre-requisite to victory. Often the means of obtaining useful intelligence was not only dangerous but often problematical, and controversial.

Jack would make another report that night and a different scenario would upload to the intelligence community. A whole new ball game would begin all over again.

The battlements stood tall and proud, testament to the men and women who had protected the surrounding countryside over the centuries. The castle keep dominated the flag, held sway over the local population, and boasted two flags flying from its flagpole: the Union Flag and the Flag of Saint George.

Three men walked along the battlements and paused to cast their eyes at the older flag of Saint George and the more recent Union Flag. They both flew unfettered from on high. One of the men withdrew a silver tankard, poured three tots of brandy, and handed them out.

Sir Edward James MonkChester smiled. Sir Julian Spencer nodded in agreement, and Sir Phillip Nesbitt – all Knight Commanders of the British Empire - raised his glass to announce, 'The flags fly well today, my friends, but what of tomorrow? Enough of tomorrow, my fellow knights, let us speak of today and our great nation. I give you - Regnum Defende'

A warm breeze billowed across the battlements as three Knights of England raised their glasses, turned to the flags that generations before had fought and died for, and together toasted, 'Regnum Defende.'

The End.... Nearly....

*

Regnum Defende

~ ~ ~

Sleep well my child,
Dream on your dream of peace.
Sleep well my child,
The secret war goes on.
Sleep well my love,
You need not worry now.
Sleep well my love,
Brave people venture forth this night.
Sleep well my friends,
Blue, green and khaki walk your streets.
Sleep well my friends,
The silent too, are there for you.
No words describe the secret war,
Fought by those within a corps.
Take heart and listen to this speech,
This battle to be won
is within our reach.
Yet seldom speak of what we do,
Such secrets, known only to a few.
But we will not shirk from the war ahead,
Whilst you slumber, silently, in your bed.
Sleep well my friends, one day the story will be told.
Sleep well my friends, soon you'll know of those so bold.
Sleep well my love, I will return when all is done.
Sleep well my love, my task accomplished in the morning sun.
Sleep well my child,
Dream not of strife and sorrow.
Sleep well my child,
I give you my tonight… for your tomorrow.

~

Extracted from a book of poetry entitled
'Sunset' by Paul Anthony

Author's Note / Historic References

~

1. Regnum Defende is a Latin term found at the bottom of a crest attributed to MI5. When translated it means 'Defend the Realm.' Often, it can be mispronounced to sound like 'Rectum Defende', which has an entirely different meaning…

~

2. The flags - It was known within the castle that the origins of the earlier flag of Great Britain dated back to 1606. James VI of Scotland had inherited the English and Irish thrones in 1603 as James I, thereby uniting the crowns of England, Scotland, and Ireland in a personal union, although the three kingdoms remained separate states. In 1606, a new flag to represent this regal union between England and Scotland was specified in a royal decree, according to which the flag of England (a red cross on a white background, known as St George's Cross), and the flag of Scotland (a white saltire on a blue background, known as the Saltire or St Andrew's Cross), would be joined together, forming the flag of England and Scotland for maritime purposes. King James also began to refer to a 'Kingdom of Great Britaine'. The present design of the Union Flag dates from a Royal proclamation following the union of Great Britain and Ireland in 1801. The flag combines aspects of three older national flags: the red cross of St George, the white saltire of St Andrew, and the red saltire of St Patrick to represent Ireland. It was also known that Henry II of England and Philip II of France agreed to go on a crusade and that Henry would use a white cross and Philip a red cross on their shields and uniforms. In 1188 the English king adopted the white cross and the French king the red one. It is not clear at what point the English exchanged the white cross for the red-on-white one. Tradition claims that Richard the Lionheart himself adopted both the flag and the patron saint from Genoa at some point during his crusade.

~

3. When addressing a member of the Royal Family one would be expected to use the term 'Your Highness'. When addressing a Duke, one would initially use the term, 'Your Grace,' before resorting to 'Sir.'

~

About Paul Anthony

~

Paul Anthony is a retired Cumbrian detective who has extensive policing connections throughout the United Kingdom and elsewhere. In the past he has been published by a Vanity House and a Traditional Publishing House but is currently an independent publisher with his own publishing imprint and editorial services business. Paul has written both television and film scripts either on his own, or with the award winning screenwriter Nick Gordon.

Paul Anthony is a pseudonym. Born in Southport, Lancashire, he is the son of a soldier whose family settled in Carlisle before he joined Cumbria police at the age of 19. As a detective, Paul served in Cumbria CID, the Regional Crime Squad in Manchester, the Special Branch, (Counter Terrorist Command) and other national agencies in the UK. He has an Honours Degree in Economics and Social Sciences, a Diploma in Management, and a Diploma in Office Management.

When not writing, he enjoys reading a wide range of works and playing guitar badly. He likes Pilates, kettlebells, athletics, keeping fit, dining out and dining in, travelling, and following politics, economics and social sciences. Married, he and his wife have three adult children and five grandchildren.

Paul is a former winner of the Independent Authors Network Featured Author Contest and was a Featured Author at the 'Books without Borders' Event in Yonkers, New York, 2012.

In earlier years he was a Featured Author at the Frankfurt Book Fair, Germany. This is his amazon page....

http://www.amazon.co.uk/Paul-Anthony/e/B001KDTZU2/

*

Definitely THE END

Printed in Great Britain
by Amazon